GALACTIC PIRATE BRIDES

VOLUME ONE

TAMSIN LEY

Twin Leaf Press

Paperback version
ISBN-13: 978-1-950027-27-9
Copyright © 2020 Twin Leaf Press
All Rights Reserved

Twin Leaf Press
PO Box 672255
Chugiak, AK 99567

RESCUED BY QAIYAAN

A FORBIDDEN LOVE ALIEN ROMANCE

CHAPTER ONE

"I recognize your ship, Captain Qaiyaan." The voice coming over the ship's comm deepened with menace. "You're interfering with a legal salvage operation."

The two ships rotating helplessly outside Qaiyaan's port screen told a different story than the human on the comm was telling; an eyeful of stars peeked through the blackened hole piercing the Syndicorp passenger ship's hull, while the second, unmarked vessel's short-range lasers glowed from recent use. "Seems you ought to be a bit more generous," Qaiyaan drawled. "What with needing our help and all. I'm gonna take first crack at the salvage, then we'll get you your part. You can have whatever we leave behind."

"I warn you, don't touch that ship!" blustered the voice on the other end.

Normally, Qaiyaan would wish the other pirate captain well and move on. Not today. His crew hadn't had a profitable job in half a denaidan year. This opportunity was too good to pass up. Besides, anyone who blew a hole in an unarmed passenger transport—Syndicorp or otherwise—left a sour taste in Qaiyaan's mouth. "I could simply wait here. My first mate estimated in half a day we'll have two ships in need of salvage. This is an awful deep part of space to find yourselves without a spare flux modulator."

"You fucking son-of-a-rakwiji-whore bastard! I have powerful friends, and I can make sure you never find safe harbor in this sector again!"

Qaiyaan crossed his arms and glared at the comm. "I'm the *only* friend you have in the galaxy at this moment, so I suggest you be polite."

Noatak, Qaiyaan's first mate, grinned at him from the navigator's seat, the copper sheen of his skin reflecting the multi-colored light from the control panels. The small cockpit, designed for humans, was barely big enough for the two denaidan males to breathe at the same time. "Want me to take us in for soft docking?"

Qaiyaan watched the human pirate ship complete another slow, helpless turn in the port monitor. "Take us in, but keep an eye out for anything suspicious. Could be a Syndicorp trap."

"Pretty elaborate for a setup." Noatak shook his head, the metal beads decorating his long hair and beard clicking softly.

"Chances of blowing both in-line flux modulators at once *and* not having a spare? Either he's stupid, or it's a setup."

"I say he's stupid." Noatak adjusted the controls to nose the *Hardship* toward the passenger wreckage.

Qaiyaan rose from the captain's chair. Shit happened, especially to ships running less-than-legal activities. He ought to know, having just forked out the proceeds from their latest heist to retrofit a new hull onto the *Hardship's* battle-damaged frame. The black market repairman'd all but asked Qaiyaan to bend over and spread his cheeks. Rotten, cheating bastard.

Turning to the door, he paused and looked over his shoulder at Noatak. "Just be careful. Even if it's not a trap, Syndicorp'll be looking for their missing ship, and I don't want to be caught with our dicks out."

After sealing the control room door, he slid down the ladder to the cargo bay, booted feet clanging against the catwalk grating as he landed. "Mekoryuk! Tovik! All hands on deck!"

Mekoryuk poked his clean-shaven face out of the med bay. He was the only crew member who chose not to wear the customary full beard the Denaida prided themselves on, citing a doctor's need for cleanliness or some such *anaq*. "What is it?"

"Salvage mission. Assume zero atmo. No time for suits. Syndicorp could be riding our ass any minute. Where's Tovik?"

"Where else?" Mek tilted his head toward the end of the hall.

Qaiyaan left the doctor and strode to where the hatch to the engine room stood open. As captain, he could appreciate the well-oiled hum of a ship's engines, but Tovik was a bit too much in love with moving parts. Squatting next to the hole, Qaiyaan yelled, "Tovik! On deck ready for void! And bring a spare in-line flux modulator! Now!"

Knowing his crewmen would comply without further prodding, he headed for the airlock. Through the portal, he watched Noatak guide the magnetic grappler into place. The captain of the human ship was probably apoplectic, watching his cash cow get raped by another ship. *Tough luck.* Qaiyaan'd be sure to leave the replacement flux modulator within reach, but not until the *Hardship* was ready to hightail it out of there.

The first mate finessed the grappler toward the other ship's open airlock, his voice crackling over the internal comm to the cargo bay. "You sure you don't want to take time to suit up?"

Mekoryuk arrived with a med-kit over his shoulder, and Qaiyaan shot him a grin as he answered. "No suits. These *qumli* need the practice."

Tovik pounded up, feet bare as usual, his scruffy beard and hair not quite the full mane of a mature denaidan male. Qaiyaan scowled at him, looking pointedly at his gleaming copper feet. The youngster said he had better control of his ionic abilities if his skin was bare, but one of these days he was going to lose a toe, or worse. At least the boy carried the spare flux modulator, as requested.

While Noatak secured the flexi-tube between the ships, Qaiyaan filled in the other crew members. "I'm not sure what we'll find over there, but it's not likely to be pretty. Grab everything not nailed down. We'll sort our inventories later."

Mek asked, "What about survivors?"

"There are no life signs aboard." Qaiyaan pointed to the modulator in Tovik's hands. "That'll stay with the human ship once we leave. Can you give it a slow push in their direction? I don't want it to reach them until we're long gone."

"You bet, Captain!" the young man nodded, likely already calculating trajectory and speed at which to push the thing.

"Stand fast for void!" Noatak's voice echoed through the cargo bay.

Qaiyaan barely had time to summon his ionic shell before the doors cracked open. A blast of air swept past, rattling the flexi-tube as it sucked into the other ship and out the gaping hole in its hull. The denaidan's ability to withstand vacuum had made them one of the most sought-after races for Syndicorp marine troopers before the catastrophe had ended their world. Now…

Now they were just pirates.

Concentrating on keeping his feet on the deck, Qaiyaan tapped his temple to activate his cochlear implant. A vestige of his days as a trooper, it came in handy in zero atmo when they couldn't bother with suits and the attached comms.

The three crewmen pushed themselves along the flexi-tube into the darkness of the other ship. Tovik, ever prepared, pulled a floodlight from his belt and slapped it to the inner wall of the passenger ship. The illumination exposed a passenger cabin surprisingly gutted of anything passenger-related. No nav-grav seats for humanoids, no methane tanks for garan'uks, not even any acceleration webbing for yanipa-nimayu. Instead, cargo containers of all shapes and sizes floated freely within the cabin, some cracked open and spilling their contents in haloes around them.

What the hell is this ship? Qaiyaan wondered. He'd been expecting the gruesome sight of space-bloated passengers. Not that he minded this alternative. He reached out and grabbed a floating package of hypodermic needles. *Medical supplies?*

He exchanged a glance with Tovik, who shrugged. Whatever this stuff was didn't matter; he'd much rather deal with salable goods than corpses.

Qaiyaan pushed toward the nearest container until he could get a hand on it and shoved the man-sized box toward the flexi-tube, relying on inertia to carry it most of the way. One after another, he moved containers, working until sweat coated his skin beneath his ionic shielding. Even in zero-G, it took effort to hold himself steady and force the heavy boxes into motion. At least twenty minutes passed before he grew light-headed. Using the ionic shell was much like a diver holding his breath, and he knew they'd soon have to come up for air. A tinny voice in his implant did the job for him. "We have incoming on long-range, Captain. Can't yet tell if it's Syndicorp, but they'll be in range for ID in eight minutes."

Anaq. They'd come looking faster than he'd expected. He raised his arm and caught the other men's attention, circling two index fingers overhead to tell them to wrap it up. The men dropped what they were doing and moved toward the exit.

As soon as the door sealed, blessed oxygen flooded into the bay, but it would be a few minutes before there was enough pressure to breathe. Still light-headed, Qaiyaan began helping secure the containers against the floor's mag-locks. He estimated they'd emptied at least half the salvage and was feeling quite pleased as Noatak began accelerating away from the derelict ship.

"Captain?" Mek called from behind a stack of containers.

At that same moment, Noatak's voice crackled through the bay's comm. "Confirmed Syndicorp ship closing in fast. We need to burn, ASAP."

"We need five minutes," Qaiyaan said, assessing the remaining cargo.

"Captain!" Mekoryuk called again. "We have a problem."

"What?" Qaiyaan leaned around the corner. Tovik and the medic stood over a cargo box, staring down at a portal in its surface. Blinking red light bounced off both their faces.

Tovik rubbed his hand vigorously across the small window. "Is that a girl?"

"You've got to be fucking kidding me." Qaiyaan slapped a mag clamp against the container he was securing and stood. "A cryo-pod? Who the hell picked that up?"

"You said grab everything," Tovik said. He looked up to meet Qaiyaan's gaze. "Can we keep her?"

Noatak came over the com again. "Captain, they're hailing us."

Qaiyaan scowled and thrust a finger at the cryo-pod. "She's not a *netorpok* puppy, Tovik. Just secure the damn thing so we can burn. We'll figure out what to do with it later."

"That's the problem," Mek said. "The cryo's failing. She won't survive a burn in this state."

"Fuuuck." Qaiyaan stomped over to the pod. He should have known things were going too easy. Looking at the face through the glass, his mouth grew suddenly dry. A young woman with long charcoal hair lay inside, a crescent of dark lashes against her high cheekbones. The blinking red light near her head illuminated her perfectly sculpted features, as if coating them with blood.

"Just vent it," Noatak spoke over the line. "Let Syndicorp pick it up."

Tovik grabbed the end as if claiming the pod as his own. "You can't do that. What if they miss her?"

Noatak answered, "Not our problem."

"You should see what she looks like…" Tovik continued.

Now wasn't the time to argue over crew shares of the spoils, but Qaiyaan felt a sudden desire to wrestle the pod away from his engineer and claim the contents for himself. He tamped down the feeling. If they didn't get moving immediately, Syndicorp troopers would shoot first and ask questions later.

Noatak's voice boomed over his thoughts. "*Anaq!* They just obliterated the human ship!"

Syndicorp is out for blood today. Clenching his jaw, Qaiyaan shoved Tovik aside and began pushing the box toward the airlock, averting his gaze from the breath-taking face inside. "If we vent her, they'll have to stop and pick her up, which'll give us more time to get away."

"But, Captain—" Tovik started.

"We're not murderers!" Mek shouted, moving to intercept the box.

The comm filled the bay again. "Captain, you're not going to like this." Noatak's voice had gone from excited panic to deadly quiet. Qaiyaan ceased pushing, turning to face the speaker as if he could read his first mate's face from here. Noatak only used that voice when something deadly was going on. "They took out the passenger ship, too. There's nothing left of either vessel but a haze of space dust."

The breath left Qaiyaan's body. Syndicorp'd destroyed their own ship? Why would they do that?

Mek moved close to the captain, his voice low. "Venting her is a death sentence."

Qaiyaan squeezed his eyes shut. Why could nothing ever be easy? This woman was probably some scrawny human female on an exorbitant corporate cryo-vacation or some such nonsense. But he couldn't just leave her, not to the mercy of space, and definitely not to a ship that was blowing up everything in its path. "How long do you need to wake her?"

"The waking cycle takes twenty minutes."

He leveled a glare at the medic. "I didn't ask how long it takes. I asked how long you need."

Mek shook his head. "I can pull her out now, but she'll take days to recuperate. And she'll still be too weak to strap in for burn."

"Days to recuperate will be better than minutes to end up as space dust. Pull her. We can link our ionic shells to protect her during burn."

Mek's right eye twitched. "We're exhausted from scavenging in zero atmo. I'm not sure we can withstand the strain."

"Do you have a better suggestion? If you do, make it now, because we're out of time."

"They'll be in range in thirty seconds, Captain," Noatak clipped out, his voice still deadly steady.

Mek's jaw bulged, but he nodded. "Fine. I think I've got enough stims to keep us up and running afterward. But let's not make a habit of it."

Popping the pod's seals, Qaiyaan knelt to lift the frigid human from the padded interior. She was naked, her nipples peaked from the cold. His hand slid beneath her nicely rounded bottom, every ionic sensor in his skin aware of the contact. He tried to remain focused on her face instead of the silky smooth curve of her hip cradled against his chest. Her eyes fluttered but didn't open.

Laying her on the deck, he stretched out beside her, grounding himself to the metal decking. Enveloping her in his power. Locking his body against hers.

Tovik sat cross-legged at her head, his bare feet tucked beneath him, and placed both his hands on her shoulders. But his gaze was on her upright nipples. Come to think of it, Qaiyaan's were, too, so he couldn't blame the young engineer. Mek spread out along her other side. An unfamiliar twinge made Qaiyaan want to shove them both away.

Hoping he hadn't just given all four of them a death sentence, Qaiyaan called out, "Engage full burn."

CHAPTER TWO

Lisa's entire body ached as if she'd been thrown down the stairs. Her muscles whimpered in pain, and she realized she was trembling. More than trembling. Freezing. *Frozen.*

Memories came back in a rush. *Hell, yeah, I survived!* Her gritty eyes flew open and her lungs sucked in an agonizing breath. Her brother, Doug, had reassured her Syndicorp wouldn't hurt her as long as they needed him. And he had a way of ensuring people needed him. Still, the corp could con even the most skilled grifter, as she well knew. If it hadn't been for Doug, she never would've agreed to be put into such a helpless situation. Stepping into that cryo-pod had been the largest act of faith in her twenty-six years of life.

Her frigid fingers tingled with renewing circulation and her eyelids fluttered as she tried to focus. Doug was supposed to be here to meet her. Her heart ached to see her twin again, to be sure the corp hadn't hurt him. Her nano-bots must still be inert from the time in cryo, or she'd have felt him immediately.

Above her, ceiling panels glowed with dingy light. She rolled her blurry gaze to the right. A wall of compartments stood a few feet away, the dull metal clean, but not what she'd come to expect over the course of a year as a Syndicorp test subject for nanite technology. These cabinets were part of a small ship's med bay; she'd seen her share of them over the years, mostly because her brother couldn't seem to keep himself out of bar fights.

So where was she, and why was she awake? Her journey was supposed to end at a new lab where Doug was undergoing super-secret test exercises. Something must've happened if she was out of stasis early. With effort, she rolled her gaze in the other direction. A steel counter ran along the far wall, a small sink embedded at one end and a computer station at the other. A broad-shouldered man sat there, three thick ropes of hair banded with metal hanging down his broad back.

Definitely not corporation.

"Nnnmm," she tried to catch his attention, but her tongue was as frozen as the rest of her.

The man looked over his shoulder, his concerned face reflecting the light as if he'd dusted with that fancy cosmetic powder the men on Enayshu Five always wore. He lacked enayshuan eye-ridges, but he was definitely alien. "You're awake. Excellent."

Spinning his chair to face her, he thrust one bronze-sheened hand toward her throat. This close, she was struck by how huge he was. She flinched, but he merely pressed his fingertips to her pulse. Manually checking her vitals? Shit, she *was* on a low-end ship. She felt like she was back in the underbelly of Whylon Station.

"What happened?" She couldn't wrap her tongue around the gravelly words, but the man seemed to understand her anyway.

"We're not entirely sure. We pulled you off a derelict ship."

"Derelict? I don't understand. Who are you?" Her voice sounded better, but still slurred.

"My name's Mekoryuk, but you can call me Mek. The captain wants to talk to you. I'll let him know you're awake."

She struggled to sit up, but her body only twitched like a dying fish. "I need to call my brother."

"You can barely form words. Stop trying to move." He pressed a solid hand against her collarbone, pinning her to the mattress. "I don't want you exerting yourself until your metabolism stabilizes."

"But I—"

Mek's hand pressed harder. "I'm going to get the captain now. If you fall out of bed, it's your own *usviiq* fault."

Lisa lay still, focusing on her breathing. The pressure of his hand eased, but he kept his gaze on her, as if reassuring himself she would do as instructed. When she didn't protest, he turned and left the small bay.

For a few minutes, she simply rested, listening to the beeping of monitors and the slight hum of the ship's engine. If there was one thing Syndicorp was good at, it was keeping hold of its property. Yet here she was on a strange, very non-corporate ship. Something had gone very wrong. She didn't care what Mek said about resting; she needed information.

Inside her head, her tiny robotic nanites were stirring. They swarmed and buzzed at her temple as if curious about the diode connecting her to the med-bay monitors. She was part of a test group for "cyber-sensitive" enhancements; a way to empower human brain waves to interface directly and intuitively with complex computer systems. The nanites sent and received data impulses using the host brain's synapses. Doug could hack into a nearby computer system with a mere thought. Lisa wasn't nearly that good and needed to be physically interfaced to hack into a system. Lucky for her, the diode provided just the corridor she needed. Hopefully, the medical computers were tied into the mainframe, and she could encode a call to Syndicorp. She squeezed her eyes closed, instructing the microscopic machines to investigate.

A voice interrupted her concentration. "How are you feeling?"

Her lids flew open to meet an electric-blue gaze. She'd thought Mek was handsome, broad-shouldered and roguish with his long, banded hair and clean-shaven face. This new fellow pushed the boundaries of rogue and headed straight to rugged, copper-skinned barbarian. His long hair flowed loosely around his shoulders, dark and wavy, offset by strands of silver that might be a metallic weave, or might be his own hair, she couldn't quite tell. Mostly because his eyes were so damned brilliant and captivating. Above those eyes, a silver loop pierced one dark brow.

Holy hell, were all the crewmen on this ship hot like this? The man's sensuous lips curved slightly upward, as if he was very used to smiling, although he wasn't at the moment. A well-trimmed mustache and beard tapered to two tidy braids under his chin. He'd just asked her a question, but her tongue felt too thick in her throat to respond.

Mek moved around from behind the barbarian at her bedside. "She may take a while to fully recover."

The second man raked her body with a gaze that left her tingling for his physical touch. She shuddered right down to her core, confused about this unusual reaction to a man—an alien. She'd been with plenty of guys—okay, a few guys—and not a single one had ever made her feel like this, in bed or out. Although she'd barely moved, perspiration prickled her skin as if she'd just climbed through the space station's high-grav service tunnels.

"I'm Captain Qaiyaan. Can you tell me your name?" The deep timbre of his voice sent thrilling little rockets along her skin.

"L-lisa. Lisa Moss." *Way to sound like an idiot.* She licked her lips, hoping her next words didn't come out like mud.

Qaiyaan's gaze followed the move, then flicked toward Mek, who began tapping at a polycom, probably searching the galactic web for her profile. *Good luck with that.* Her lips twisted into a smile. Syndicorp had made sure she and her brother disappeared when they'd joined the test group, wiping their slates clean of a handful of crimes and hiding the siblings from the black market Cartel that was seeking their heads.

"Lisa, we're trying to piece together what's going on. Why were you in a cryo-pod?"

Her smile dissolved. One wrong word and both she and her brother would lose everything, including the amnesty that kept them out of the Syndicorp prison mines and the Cartel's hands. She blurted out the first thing that came into her head. "Interstellar Myasthenic Carcinoma."

Shit. She must still be slow from her time in cryo. No one actually came down with IMC anymore. The cancer, caused by unshielded travel through dark nebula, was barely more than a horror story told by station rats consoling themselves for being stuck station-side.

Qaiyaan's eyes rounded a fraction, and he shot a glance at his medic, lips forming a thin line. Mek straightened to meet his gaze, his face equally stricken. "I didn't detect anything during my scans. Let me check again."

She scrambled to keep him from digging further and discovering the truth. She could do this. Had pulled cons a hundred times with her brother before the Syndicorp police had reeled them in, giving them a choice between the mines and the test program. Smiling weakly, she played her pity card. "That's okay, really. I'm on my way to a hospital for treatment."

Mek started pushing buttons on her monitors. "What stage are you at?"

A thread of panic threatened her composure. She had little experience with advanced medical treatments, nanites notwithstanding. Thinking of the microscopic robots roaming her body, she sent them to interfere with the doctor's sensor. Doug probably could've faked a reading for IMC, but she wasn't that skilled. Leaving her nanites to run amok, she focused her attention on the blue-eyed man standing next to her bed. "I—I need to let my brother know I'm okay."

Qaiyaan shook his head, avoiding her eyes. "I'm sorry. Our comm isn't set up for long-range boost. You'll have to wait until we get to a transfer station."

"How long will that be?" She fluttered her fingers, trying her damnedest to regain enough coordination to touch him. To her delight, he pulled a seat over and took her hand. His skin was warm and slightly rough as his thumb grazed the back of her fingers. She shivered right down to her nanites, a million little tingling sensors responding to his touch.

His thumb stilled, as if he sensed something, too, and he stared intensely into her eyes.

Barely infringing on her awareness, Mek's fingers probed the diode affixed to her temple. "Hold still. I'm going to swap out the sensor."

She shook her head. Her rapid heartbeat was sure to raise some alarms if he got the diode working again. "Don't bother. Something about my chemistry makes standard technology go haywire. I can't even wear a polycom without it fritzing out."

"Just let him try, okay?" Qaiyaan squeezed her hand gently.

Heart racing, she gave him her "brave-but-scared" smile and tried to think like a cancer patient. "I need to get to the hospital on Aleigh right away."

Mek stopped muttering under his breath and both men stared at her.

"You were going to the Syndicorp hospital?" Qaiyaan's brows drew together.

Her chest was tight, and she was sure Qaiyaan must be able to feel her trembling. Answering a question with a question was the best way to carry a grift, Doug always said. "Don't they have the best medical technology?"

Mek made a grunting noise and returned to making adjustments on his screen. She boosted her nanites to be sure they kept interfering. Qaiyaan shifted his gaze to her fingers, his strangely bronze thumb tracing a thin blue vein on the back of her hand. "You're quite a ways from Syndicorp space."

Oops. Part of the reason they'd put her into cryo for shipment was to keep her from hacking any systems and discovering where they were taking her. She'd just assumed they'd still be in Syndicorp space. "How far?"

"Fifteen or twenty parsecs, I'd say. And a long, long way from Aleigh."

Calling on skills she hadn't used in a year, Lisa drew her brows into worried lines. "They told me I was going to Aleigh." She'd always excelled at drawing out a target's empathy, playing their emotions to get what she needed. Right now she needed Qaiyaan to stop asking questions and give her access to a comm. "My brother must be crazy with worry. What do you think happened?"

"You have to watch your back with Syndicorp."

"Don't I know it." She laughed, then realized she was being too honest. Her doubts about Syndicorp were something she kept deeply buried, even from her brother, who was their star subject. She was fairly certain she hadn't been sent to the mines or handed over to the Whylon Cartel only because Syndicorp needed him. Her skills with the nanites were abysmal at best.

Qaiyaan's fingers tightened against her hand, and he rose. "Mek has some experience with cancer, so just relax and let him do his thing, okay?"

Her heart sank. Of course Mek would be some sort of cancer specialist. Why hadn't she claimed to be going to a rehab colony or something? "Please don't go to any trouble. I've already paid Syndicorp for the treatment. I just need to get to Aleigh."

Qaiyaan moved to the door, but stopped and looked over his shoulder at her. His blue eyes were wild sparks beneath his deep brow line. "Syndicorp's probably not your best option at this point. Give Mek a chance. I'll check back soon."

With that, he was gone, leaving the small med bay strangely empty without his presence. All Lisa could do was boost her nanites to fend off the doctor's repeated scans.

CHAPTER THREE

Qaiyaan shook his head as he stomped back to the control room. With effort, he could've forced himself to stay away from the med bay and the alluring patient within. But a woman with IMC? Cancer had been all but obliterated except for the rare kinds that took hold without symptoms until it was too late. Like the kind that had destroyed his entire race. Lisa's arrival was like the ever-sneaky *Ellam Cua* had connived to taunt him—his entire crew—with memories. Even Mekoryuk was obviously taken by the human female. She was so exquisitely vibrant, despite the lingering effects of the cryo. Despite the disease eating her bones. The perfectly sculpted curves of her body beneath the thin sheet had been difficult to ignore. And when he'd touched her hand... The almost electric jolt at the connection had almost made him wonder if she was denaidan, too.

But that wasn't possible.

Cancer had wiped every female from existence. *Syndicorp* had wiped them out. And now they were gunning for Lisa.

He hadn't had the willpower to ask her why they might be after her. Hell, they might not even be after Lisa. There could've been something on that ship the corp wanted to hide. Syndicorp wasn't above ancillary damage—they'd proven that on Denaida-Daru. No need to upset her

"

while she recovered. After he'd arranged for her medical attention, he'd explain how Syndicorp had destroyed her ship.

Sitting heavily in the captain's chair, he began scrolling through the star charts to line up the nearest non-Syndicorp hospitals. The galactic corporation had spread in influence and power since the destruction of his homeworld fifteen years ago. Few in the galaxy even remembered the name of Denaida-Daru, a backwater ag-planet with an indigenous population too empathically sensitive to join the rush-and-bustle of the galactic market. Denaidan women, in particular, could not withstand the proximity of other species' unfiltered emotions and desires, making it impossible to leave the planet; they were also the only females who could tame the intense sexual connection of a denaidan male, a fact Qaiyaan was more aware of than usual with the charcoal-haired beauty lying in his med bay.

Jaw aching, Qaiyaan dismissed a nearby hospital as having close ties with Syndicorp and pulled up the board members of a second facility to review their names. So many companies these days were mere subsidiaries of the Syndicorp conglomerate. He kept a sharp eye on the movements of Syndicorp's CEOs and holding companies, exploiting whatever opportunities he could. The few denaidan men who'd been off-planet during their world's destruction had formed a loose brotherhood of pirates, determined to make Syndicorp pay for their crime. The annihilation of his species couldn't be undone, but he'd make Syndicorp pay in whatever ways he could.

"Captain." The control room speaker popped with Tovik's voice, difficult to hear over the hum of the ship's engines in the background. "You there?"

"Go ahead." Qaiyaan continuing cross-referencing photos and names with his list of Syndicorp supporters, glad of the recovery stim Mek had provided after the grueling burn. Without it, he'd be laid out on his bunk right now.

"Have you found a buyer for these supplies yet? The climate control for the lower cargo bay is taking more power than I anticipated."

Qaiyaan looked up from the computer and scowled at the gauges on the control room wall. He'd forgotten about the salvaged supplies completely. Over half the inventory had turned out to be medicine, stored in cryogenic cases that were failing just like Lisa's. Keeping the fragile compounds viable until they secured a buyer had required some hack engineering on Tovik's part, and the fuel-cell gauges were flickering toward empty. Qaiyaan reassessed the star chart he'd been searching for hospitals. "How far can we get?"

"Three parsecs at full burn. Perhaps as far as the Bolisare system, but no more than that." Tovik didn't hedge his bets. What he said was the honest truth, no sugar-coating, no buffer for mistakes. "We've had to divert a lot of energy to the shields during the last three burns. That repairman on finofan must've skimped on some of the hull platings."

The repairman *had* skimped, but it was all Qaiyaan had been able to afford. His crew didn't know how fragile this bucket-of-bolts really was—or at least they pretended not to know. He did a quick run-down of the hospital facilities within a three-parsec sphere. Here at the edge of un-classified space, there wasn't much to be had. There was a garan'uk medical facility six and a half parsecs in, but even if the methane breathers offered services for humanoids, they were known Syndicorp allies, and Qaiyaan was a wanted man.

He widened the search. There was a saluqan healing temple on Oruq Nine, four parsecs beyond Bolisare in another un-classified sector. If they stopped and unloaded on Bolisare, they could fuel up and get Lisa to Oruq Nine in a week or so. Did she have that long? Not that he had much in the way of options for her. Mek was a genius in his own right, but the *Hardship* lacked medical equipment, let alone medicine for humans.

Adjusting the ship's heading, he said, "We'll head to Bolisare. I'll work on finding a buyer."

"Aye-aye, Captain." The hum of the engine room silenced as Tovik ended communication.

The *Hardship's* last visit to Bolisare hadn't been an exemplary experience. Noatak'd relapsed on recovery stims and gotten into a brawl with a prominent Cartel businessman. The crew'd been forced to break him out of prison. Luckily, Qaiyaan's contact on the planet was also on the alternate side of the local law. He wouldn't offer a high price for the salvaged medicine, but at this point, unloading it for cheap was better than having to jettison worthless cargo.

Feeling guilty about lying to Lisa about their comm system, Qaiyaan accessed the long-range channel for the planet's black market and sent an encoded message. The communication would take at least twenty hours to reach his contact and another twenty for a return message. By then, they'd be almost halfway there. Setting the navigation controls to auto, he headed to the lower cargo bay where they kept the workout equipment. His nerves were jangling from the recovery stims, and he needed to focus his ionic energy if he was going to have a clear head for bargaining.

He also needed to keep himself from hovering over the luscious human in his med bay.

Lisa pivoted to sit on the edge of the cot and wrapped the sheet around her, her body still naked from the cryo-pod. Mek had finally left the med bay, muttering about someone named Tovik who might have a fix for his malfunctioning sensors. He was dead-set on getting a reading of her cancer, and she felt bad for putting him through so much work for nothing. But she couldn't risk exposing the Syndicorp technology. For all she knew, these men were pirates and would sell her off to the highest bidder once they found out what she carried. Her ship's demise couldn't have been a mistake. Someone was after her, and she needed to let Doug know where she was. The only way to do that was through Syndicorp.

Planting her feet on the floor, she wobbled upright. Her feet left the ground unexpectedly, and she threw out both arms to keep her balance. *Whoa.* The ship's gravity was barely enough to hold her feet to the deck. The sheet came loose and slithered down around her hips before she caught it and secured it around her breasts again. This was going to be interesting. She moved carefully toward the door. While interfering with the doctor's scans, she'd determined that the med bay computer was only attached to the internal systems, and she'd need to find one connected to the external comm to get a message out. Her head hurt from controlling her nanites to block the doctor's probes, but she'd need to use them again in short order.

Cautiously sliding the door open, she peered into the half-lit corridor. The stark wall panels were similar to a half-dozen cargo ships she'd been on. *Damn.* Some part of her'd been hoping for one of those junker ships with exposed conduit running along the walls of every corridor. Should've known better than that, based on the orderly way Mek ran his medical bay. She had to find an access panel so she could physically hack in. Or find an actual comm unit. That would be way easier. Doug could've hacked in from anywhere on the ship, the lucky bastard. He also could've accessed the ship's blueprints and known exactly where to go.

Thinking of her brother made her chest tight. If someone was after her, they could also be after Doug. He was Syndicorp's star pupil, and much more valuable than she was. She prayed he was safe and waiting for her at the corp lab—wherever that was.

She stepped into the hall, listening for approaching crewmen. To her right, the passage ended at a closed airlock embedded in the floor. A door across from her stood open, revealing a lavatory with a shower head in the ceiling. Left, the hallway extended maybe fifty or sixty feet toward an open bay. Closed doors to either side likely led to crew quarters. Her nanites thrummed in the soles of her feet, telling her that engineering was down the airlock to her right. At the far end of the dim hall, on the wall near the catwalk, she spotted what looked like a conduit panel. *Jackpot!*

Her bare feet slid along the metal deck, her footing unsure in the low gravity. She reached the panel and pried the metal cover loose, her fingertips stinging from the effort. Inside, cables and wires entwined each other like a nest of snakes. Tracing her fingertips along several wires, she searched for a familiar interface, skin heating and temples throbbing with effort. Damn, why did a ship need to have so many separate systems?

From behind the nearby closed door, a man's voice cut through her concentration. "She said she paid Syndicorp for medical treatment, so she has to be on the galactic net somewhere."

"Well, she isn't. Not under the name Lisa Moss, anyway."

Lisa paused her search. It hadn't occurred to her that *not* having a presence on the galactic net might be just as incriminating as her real files. Syndicorp had removed every trace of her and Doug to prevent the black market Cartel on Whylon Station from tracking them down and exacting revenge. Looking back, she should've suggested arranging an "accident" to make it appear she and Doug had died rather than disappeared.

"Cryogenic containment isn't cheap," one voice continued. "She's got money to afford that, plus whatever she's paying Syndicorp. She probably told us a fake name to protect herself."

"Think her family will ransom her?"

"We don't know if she's Syndicorp yet. We don't target non-corp citizens."

"I'm just saying, our hull's got to be repaired—for real this time—and this latest heist isn't enough to pay for it. Especially if the meds go sour before we get there."

Heist? Queasiness roiled at the bottom of her stomach. So these men *were* pirates. They must've attacked her ship. But if they knew about her nanites, they hadn't revealed it.

"Let me take the money to the kwirn tables and—"

"*Usviilnguq!* Last time we had to haul ass out of Bolisare so fast, I didn't get my kiss goodbye."

"The house was cheating! And your limp *ucuk* isn't my problem, Tovik."

Suddenly, the door in front of her flew open, and she was looking at the broad chest of another monster of a man. Five long braids hung from his chin like tentacles, gathered at the bottom with a metal band. Her gaze followed them upward to meet a scowling bronze face.

She clutched at the sheet around her torso, stuttering out her backup excuse for wandering around. "Uh, where's the restroom?"

His gaze flicked to the open conduit panel. "Not in there."

"Sorry about that. I lost my balance, and the cover fell off when I leaned against it. So clumsy." Batting her lashes, she giggled and tried to affect an innocent smile. "Don't you guys believe in gravity?"

He grasped her left biceps with a hand that felt as hard as metal. Even his knuckles gleamed like bronze ball-bearings. "I don't like eavesdroppers."

A younger man appeared in the open door, his beard a bit scruffy around the edges. "She's awake?"

"I'm not eavesdropping," she rasped out. Her racing heart was making her dizzy. "I didn't even know you were there until you opened the door."

The hand around her arm tightened. "Liar. Your pulse is going supernova."

The younger man put his hands on his hips but didn't intervene. "Take it easy, Noatak. She's our guest."

Lisa yanked her arm out of the bigger man's grip. "I want to talk to Qaiyaan."

His upper lip curled into a sneer. "Oh, you're going to talk, all right." He targeted the younger man with a glower. "Tovik, check the panel. Make sure nothing's compromised."

Once again he clasped her arm, nearly yanking her off her feet in the low gravity. He dragged her the rest of the way down the hall and onto a catwalk over a large, mostly empty cargo bay. Below, a shirtless Qaiyaan was performing a slow series of moves that looked almost like tai chi. Only his feet weren't on the floor; he stood on the wall as if gravity had lost all meaning. His gleaming copper muscles bunched and flexed in ways that made Lisa's insides quiver.

"Captain!" the man beside her shouted.

"What is it now, Noatak?" Qaiyaan jerked to a halt. He turned his head and his electric blue gaze met hers.

As if gravity had suddenly returned, he belly-flopped against the decking.

CHAPTER FOUR

Swearing loudly, Qaiyaan scrambled upright, elbows throbbing from the impact. What was the woman doing out of bed? And in his cargo bay? The thin sheet hugging her curves exposed far too much skin for a ship full of nothing but men. *And Noatak has his hands all over her.* "Dammit, Noatak, what are you doing?"

Noatak merely quirked an eyebrow. "You think I dragged her out of bed?"

"I was looking for a bathroom." Lisa struggled against Noatak's grasp.

The first mate rounded on her, and Qaiyaan was half-way to the ladder without thinking. Noatak wasn't known for keeping his temper. But the big man only spoke with deadly calm. "She had the conduit panel open. And I'm pretty sure she overheard Tovik and me talking."

Qaiyaan's primary heart sank. *Shit.* Knowing Tovik, they'd been talking about Lisa—whether ransoming her or ravaging her, neither would be good. He pulled himself onto the catwalk, his gaze hard on his first mate. "No matter what she may have overheard, she now thinks the worst of us with you dragging her through the corridors in a bed sheet. Why don't you go check our heading? I'll take her from here."

Noatak's nostrils flared, one bronze cheek twitching. "Fine," he said through gritted teeth. "Yell if you need me."

"I think I can handle a girl in a bed sheet, thank you." Qaiyaan shot Lisa a conciliatory smile. Perhaps he could play everything down. Get her back to bed...

Her face remained hard.

Qaiyaan took a deep breath and gestured down the corridor. "Why don't we see about getting you some clothing?"

Gripping the sheet over the enticing swell of her breasts, she turned and shuffled ahead of him. His gaze was drawn to the two pert mounds of her ass cheeks. Damn flimsy sheet. Why was he so turned on by her? He'd had female passengers on board before and never felt a twinge of temptation. Denaida men could never consummate with non-Denaida. The prostitutes he and his men engaged were nothing more than accouterments to masturbation; three-dimensional pornography to be viewed, smelled, perhaps lightly touched or kissed, but never used for climax. The very act would put a non-denaidan into a coma.

Perhaps it'd been too long since he'd indulged in a release. Might she be willing to assist? His mouth nearly watered as he watched her move, imagining that sheet sliding from her curves in a sensual slither, his hands molding against the indentation of her waist. Those bare feet wrapped around his backside as he drove himself into her...

Shaking his head, he attempted to banish his rather obvious arousal. She'd suffered enough already under Noatak's brutish accusations. Not to mention she was terminally ill. How could he be so damned insensitive? He needed to keep his nether regions tamed. He walked slowly behind her, breathing deeply to re-center his thoughts. She trailed the lingering chemical scent of the cryo-pod, but underneath it, he detected a faint floral aroma that reminded him of denaidan lilacs. *Anaq. I definitely need some shore leave.*

At the end of the hall, Mekoryuk came bursting out of the med bay, his face dark with worry. He spotted them, and his shoulders relaxed. "Oh, thank *Ellam Cua* that she's all right. She shouldn't be out of bed!"

Qaiyaan shook his head at the medic and nudged Lisa toward his cabin. His palm itched against her bare skin. "She's fine. I'll have her back to you in a bit." He guided her into his quarters, suddenly wondering at the wisdom of being alone with her in his bedroom.

Lisa entered the small space and moved immediately to the far end of the room, turning to glare at him with her arms crossed and her chin down. "You're a pirate."

The accusation pierced him, though he wasn't sure why. All he'd wanted to do was drop her at the saluqan facility and leave her none the wiser about her rescuers. Be a knight in shining armor. Save a woman from her insidious disease, as he'd been helpless to do with his own people. Maybe it wasn't too late. He needed to verify what she actually knew versus what she merely suspected. Moving to his closet, he rifled through his few items of spare clothing. "How'd you come to a conclusion like that?"

"Don't bullshit me," she said. "You didn't just happen upon my ship floating derelict in space."

He chose his softest black tunic and a belt. His trousers would be far too long in the legs, but perhaps the shirt could serve as a dress. Turning, he held the pirelux silk up by both shoulders, assessing the length. "You're right. We intercepted a distress call."

Her full lips pursed in a scowl. "Right after you disabled my ship. Stop trying to double talk me. I've dealt with your kind before. I'll tell you right now, there's no one to pay a ransom for me, so you may as well drop me at the next space station."

There was a hardness lying just beneath her surface, a solidness he could sense in the beating of her heart, and he knew he was talking to a woman who'd been through some *anaq*. Something deeper was at stake here, something she wasn't telling him. Taking two steps forward, he offered her the shirt. "Wouldn't a pirate have jettisoned your cryo-pod the moment the Syndicorp trooper ship appeared, hoping they'd stop the chase to pick you up?"

A black scowl settled over her features, and she snatched the shirt from his hands. "Why didn't you?"

"They'd just blown your passenger ship to smithereens." He quirked an eyebrow at her and laid the belt on the desktop nearby. "I had a feeling they might do the same to you."

Her shiny dark hair had just poked through the neckline of the shirt. The scowl on her face slackened, and her creamy skin blanched bone-white. "Why would they do that?"

"That's what I was hoping you could tell me. Any reason Syndicorp might want you dead?" He sat on the edge of his bunk. While his eyes watched her body language, his ionic sense reached out to feel the nuances of her heartbeat, breathing, and skin temperature. He had nothing close to the empathic power of a female of his species, but he could still sense physical changes that might give a clue about another's hidden thoughts.

Lisa turned away from him, shoving her hands into the shirtsleeves. Her body was trembling, but her voice remained strong. "You're lying. "

"Why would I lie about that?"

"To get me to talk. To tell you my secrets, if I had any secrets." Her heartbeat spiked, telling him she likely did have secrets. The shirt hem fell almost to her knees over the top of the wrapped sheet. Still facing away from him, she picked up the belt he'd laid on the desk next to her and allowed the sheet to fall in a puddle around her ankles while she cinched her waist. Those long, sculpted legs poking from beneath the shirt's hem made him harden again.

He leaned forward with his elbows on his knees to hide his bulging crotch. "So Syndicorp *is* after you."

"I never said that. You attacked my ship and took me captive. But I'm telling you, no one will claim me." She began to roll up the too-long shirt sleeves as if she wore a man's clothing all the time.

Jealousy created a silent growl in the back of his throat as he thought of situations where she might wear another man's shirt. He took a deep breath to shove the feeling down. "And I'm telling you, we didn't attack your ship. We answered a distress call from the pirate who did. Then the Syndicorp troopers showed up and forced us to run. They destroyed everything we left behind."

Turning to him, she narrowed her eyes. "If you're not pirates, and you merely stopped to aid a ship in distress, how did my cryo-pod end up on your ship?"

"I never actually said we weren't pirates," he growled, tired of word games. He just wanted the truth out of her. He wanted her to understand that if Syndicorp was after her, he was on her side. Something she'd said in the med bay came back to him. "Why did you trust yourself to cryo if your chemistry interferes with electronics?"

A flush rose to her cheeks. "It... I'm... that's probably why it failed."

He rose and paced forward to stand over her. Even without his ionic sense, he knew she was lying. "What kind of cancer did you say you had?"

She licked her lips, her gaze sliding away, body breaking into a sweat.

"You don't have cancer." He didn't need her to corroborate his words. Beneath his palms, he felt the adrenaline flooding her system— the trembling muscles, the elevated heart rate, the shallow breathing. Even her nerve endings seemed to rise to the surface, to reach for him, telling him she was as aware of the closeness of their bodies as he was. Or perhaps that was just wishful thinking. He'd allowed himself to be manipulated by this woman. He'd made choices that endangered his ship and his crew because of her. Well, not anymore.

He clasped her shoulders and turned her to face him, her slate-gray eyes wide and fearful. Good. Let her fear him. Whatever it took to get the truth out of her. "That passenger ship you were on had been gutted and filled with cargo. Even the med bay's equipment was removed. Seems to me whoever put you on board didn't care if you lived or died. Considering Syndicorp destroyed its own ship, I'm thinking they may have even *wanted* you dead. If you want my help, it's time to tell me the truth."

CHAPTER FIVE

Lisa's heart threatened to beat its way out of her chest. Her secret was out. But with what Qaiyaan'd just revealed, she wasn't sure it mattered anymore. "S-Syndicorp did what?"

"They destroyed the pirate ship that attacked you. Then they moved to your ship, firing more than once. There's nothing left but space dust." His blue eyes looked into hers with an intense protectiveness she'd only ever felt from her brother. She was reminded of the time she was fourteen and had tried to con a drunken thug in a Whylon back-alley. Only it turned out he wasn't so drunk after all, and she'd found herself cornered and beaten until Doug arrived to chase the guy off. Her brother'd given her the same "what the hell did you think you were doing" look Qaiyaan was giving her now.

Still, she didn't want to believe Syndicorp might actually try to kill her. Her brother had promised she was safe as long as he was alive. "Maybe they hit my ship on accident while they were shooting at the pirate."

Qaiyaan shook his head.

She knew he wasn't lying; her nanites were reading him like lines of code. Her skin tightened into goosebumps. There was something very wrong with this story. And yet familiar. Cyber-sensitive participants who failed the program had their nanites neutralized, received a severance package, and were released. Yet they were mysteriously never heard from again. There'd been rumors the corp was neutralizing more than simply the nanites; they were eradicating any potential leaks in the program. Although Lisa seemed to fail more exercises than she passed, Doug insisted Syndicorp would never eject her from the program. They needed her as a bargaining chip for his participation.

But what if something happened to him? If the new tests they were giving him turned out to be fatal…

She grew light-headed, stumbling toward the bed before she collapsed. *No.* They were twins. She'd know if he died, she was sure of it. She couldn't imagine life without her brother at her side. But if Doug was dead, Syndicorp would see her as a liability. They'd ensure she was disintegrated to keep her nanites from falling into a competitor's hands. *He can't be dead!* She refused to believe such a thing.

Qaiyaan thrust out an arm to support her, lowering her to sit beside him. She gratefully leaned into his firm support, her nanites buzzing. "I need to find my brother."

"What does your brother have to do with any of this?"

She chewed her lip, contemplating how much to say. Qaiyaan was an admitted pirate, and if he knew about her nanites, what was to keep him from selling her out to the highest bidder? But she had to tell him something if she wanted his help, and the best grift was one with a whiff of truth. *Tell him about Doug's involvement. That should be enough.* Aware of his amber-and-cedar scent filling her senses, she began. "He's being held by Syndicorp as a test subject. It's top secret. *He's* top secret."

The arm behind her stiffened. "Test subject for what?"

Play the scared maiden. Swallowing, she twisted to look him fully in the eyes and let her voice tremble. "I'm not supposed to tell anyone."

"I'm no friend to Syndicorp." The menace in his voice would have been frightening if he'd directed it at her. "You have to offer me more if you want my help."

She took a deep breath. The idea of this burly copper alien acting as her protector was rather comforting. And if Doug was in trouble, she didn't have time to draw out the game. This close, she again noticed the satiny, burnished copper sheen of Qaiyaan's skin. He looked somewhat like one of the high-end cyborgs corporate bigwigs used as bodyguards. But his skin felt all-too alive where it touched hers, both a distraction and a draw. *Just offer another bite of truth, not the whole thing.* "Cyber-sensitivity. It's kind of like a psychic ability to hack into computers."

Qaiyaan made a surprised sound. "Psychic computer hacking. Interesting. How did he end up a test subject?"

"Doug was a hacker for the Cartel and knew a lot of backdoors." She didn't want to go into the whole backstory of how she'd fallen hard for a Cartel smuggler named Seloh, how he botched a job then tried to run. The cell leader made an example of him by torturing him to death, and she'd been unable to help. From that point on, she'd begged Doug to look for a way out. "Syndicorp offered us a deal."

"You turned on the Whylon Cartel? That's a good way to end up dead."

"I know. But it was that or the prison mines on Nunam-qa. The cyber-sensitivity testing was a sort of witness protection program."

A growl of disgust came from Qaiyaan's throat. "Slaves for the corp or dog meat for the Cartel. Either way, you lose."

She shivered, thinking of what awaited her at the hands of the Cartel's enforcers. Unlike Syndicorp, the Cartel wouldn't send assassins—they'd send torturers. "When the doctors wanted to move him to a new secret test facility, he refused to leave without me." She sucked in a shuddering breath, realizing how much she missed him. "He and I are twins. We've been through a lot together."

Qaiyaan still had his arm around her and gave her a gentle squeeze that made her eyes prick with tears. The deeply masculine strength of him was more comfort than she'd felt in a long time. Telling the truth to this man came far too easy. *Don't fall into trusting him just because he's gorgeous,* she reminded herself. *Seloh was gorgeous, too, and look where that got him.* Keeping men at a distance kept her heart safe. Her brother was the only man who could ever know the real her.

But she saw little harm in what she'd revealed to Qaiyaan so far. She continued, "The doctors at the facility did everything they could to get Doug to cooperate. Then I woke up one morning, and he was gone. The doctors told me he'd changed his mind." Her heart was pounding double time as she remembered those last few days without him. "He'd never leave without telling me. Never."

"You think they kidnapped him?"

"I *knew* they had. I tried to hack into the Syndicorp systems to find out where he'd gone—where they'd taken him—but they had firewalls within firewalls, most leading to dead ends." She half-laughed. "If the situation'd been reversed, Doug could've found a way of using his cyber-sensitivity."

"That still doesn't tell me how you ended up in a cryo-pod on a gutted passenger ship in the middle of unclassified space."

She licked her lips, remembering that awful moment when she'd been offered a chance to join her brother. "A corp rep called me and told me Doug was refusing to do any of the tests at the new facility until I joined him. I insisted on speaking to him, and they let me, but he couldn't say much. But he said they would transport me if I agreed to travel in cryo."

"Why in cryo?"

Her throat and chest felt tight, as if experiencing the helplessness of the freeze-chamber all over again. "If I was frozen, I couldn't access any travel logs or destinations. They want to keep the lab's location secret." In addition, the cryo had been to stabilize her nanites for space travel; not only did she suck at hacking, her nanites were what the doctors called "high strung" and didn't respond well to external stimulation, such as burn drives. But she couldn't tell Qaiyaan about her nanites. "Now I wonder if they ever meant for me to reach the lab at all. I'm worried about Doug, and I don't know how to find him."

Qaiyaan's handsome face twitched with disgust. "You can't trust Syndicorp."

"That's what I told Doug when we first joined the test program, but he said he'd do whatever it took to keep me safe." She shook her head. "He's always been overprotective."

"I would be, too." His voice was low and seductive. Attentive in a way that surprised her.

She was pouring her heart out to this man, this stranger she knew absolutely nothing about. Her gut instinct was screaming at her to confide in him—an unfamiliar sensation for a grifter who grew up on Whylon. She needed to deflect the conversation long enough to regain her balance, then she'd decide how much more to tell him. "Do you have any brothers or sisters?"

His eyes had been attentive and concerned until that moment. Now they turned stormy. Behind her, the muscles of his arm bulged with tension. "Not anymore."

"Oh." She hadn't expected that answer. The same instinct that told her to trust him now urged her to comfort him, and she wasn't exactly the nurturing type. She placed a hand on his knee. "I'm so sorry. What happened?"

He shook his head, his braided beard sweeping his chest. "Syndicorp killed them."

Her mouth grew dry. She might have more in common with this pirate than she'd imagined. Her parents had died at a young age, leaving her with little more than vague recollections of their presence. Now she only had Doug. And if he was dead…

Before she could ask another question, Qaiyaan continued. "Syndicorp destroyed my entire race, actually."

The way he said it, so matter-of-fact, suspended her worries about Doug. "Your entire race? How?"

Qaiyaan's eyes flashed like solar flares. "A genetically modified virus that was supposed to be harmless. It caused a chromosomal mutation much like cancer in denaidan females and spread like a plague across the planet. Every female died within months after Syndicorp began testing."

Lisa's stomach turned over. No wonder he'd been so intent on saving her. The illness was personal for him. She was usually immune to guilt, but right now, shame was making it hard to breathe. Her lie cheapened his loss. The deep, almost primal part of her urging her to tell this man everything threatened to blast right through her Cartel-hardened exterior. *Every girl needs a secret weapon*, she reminded herself, a mantra from her days in the station slums. Back then, it had been a knife in her boot or a magnetically charged hairpin for picking locks. Were nanites really so much different? She shook off the guilt. *Keep him talking about himself.* "Why would Syndicorp infect your planet?"

"Field testing a viral herbicide." Qaiyaan's eyes grew hard and hopeless as he stared at the wall past her shoulder. "When it became apparent that the virus had jumped species, Syndicorp sterilized the planet. Survivors and all."

If she'd thought the story was horrible before, now it was nearly unbelievable. Only planets with no sentient life were sterilized, most often prior to terraforming for colonization. "That's… inconceivable. Why wasn't it all over the news?"

Qaiyaan shrugged almost imperceptibly. "Syndicorp controls the media. They diverted attention to the civil war in the Pulati system and rerouted all the shipping lanes. That was fifteen years ago. The corp made sure no one remembers the name of Denaida-Daru."

Lisa was struck speechless. There'd always been rumors of that sort of thing, but no one ever believed it. Such an atrocity couldn't happen without repercussions, could it? Backlash. Revenge. She looked at Qaiyaan again with fresh eyes. "You're a pirate because you want revenge."

He turned his attention to her, the deadness in his eyes suddenly sharper than any knife. "I'm going to help get your brother out of Syndicorp's hands."

A wash of relief flooded Lisa's body, so intense it sapped her strength. She sagged against Qaiyaan's arm and took a deep breath. "Thank you."

His hand slid up her back, beneath her hair to her nape, his palm warm on her bare skin. Her heart skipped a beat. Maybe it was the endorphins rushing through her at his promise of help, but his lips looked imminently kissable. She felt like celebrating his promise of help. He was a partner, at least temporarily, both opposed to Syndicorp and wary of the Cartel, just like she was. She licked her lips, noting his gaze following the movement. *He wants you, too.*

Without thinking any further, she leaned forward for a kiss.

CHAPTER SIX

The shock of the human's lips contacting his own shorted out Qaiyaan's mind like a solar flare, sending fiery trails of lust through his veins. The hand he held behind her head, the one he'd placed there to sense her pulse for truthfulness, was instead inundated by her desire. His blood went from red-hot to molten, settling hard at his groin. His pants were immediately far too tight against his crotch, and he shifted, sending his body even closer to hers.

She wove her fingers into his hair, sending tingles along his scalp. Holy *Ellam Cua*, he hadn't believed it was possible for a non-denaidan to elicit a response like this, even if it was merely physical. He groaned against her lips. He shouldn't do this. Needed to pull away, now. Unlike his men, he'd never been comfortable engaging in foreplay with a woman, knowing he'd need to stop before consummation. But her kiss… Her kiss fed his soul like a long drink of water after a trek over the Favianese desert.

Her mouth moved against his with soft insistence, and he claimed her kiss, making it his own. Perhaps a few moments of bliss wouldn't hurt. Wrapping his free arm around her waist, he drew her closer, relishing her soft body. Every part of her felt like it was meant to be pressed against him. She smelled of denaidan lilacs and honey, warm and rich and completely edible.

Bending over her, he ravaged her mouth like a starving man, plunging his tongue into her to taste deeply. Before he knew it, she was lying back against his mattress, her breasts crushed against his chest, his hand knotted in her silky tresses. The contact of his skin against hers tingled with desire and his erection was an agony of pleasure against her hip. How would it feel to plunge himself, long and thick, into her folds? It had been fifteen years since his few bungling sexual encounters with denaidan women, but his body had not forgotten. His cock might not be able to experience that pleasure, but he could still touch her. Taste her. He could make her moan his name. What would she sound like when she came? A few intimate hours would serve him well in the lonely years to come.

Sliding a hand over the thin silk shirt, he cupped her breast, barely able to breathe from anticipation.

She, too, seemed as if she was starving. Her tongue matched his movements, flicking his teeth, stroking smoothly across his lips. Their shared breath settled deep into his chest, filling him with incredible warmth. His hand slid down her ribcage and molded itself to her waist, his thumb stroking her hip bone, highly conscious of her nakedness beneath the shirt's thin silk. More than he'd ever desired anything, he wanted to explore beneath the hem, discover her moist, hidden well, envelop himself within her heat.

As if in invitation, she arched, rolling her hips against him. He groaned again, knowing this fleeting indulgence was an illusion. He could never fully be with her. But the desire to grasp whatever he could before reality came crashing down overwhelmed him. He moved his hand back up to where a breast awaited him, nipple thrusting against the fabric. Cupping her soft flesh, he circled his thumb over the pebbled peak. The nipple grew even harder, and a whimper of pleasure escaped her. His cock jumped at the sound and his ionic senses reached toward her, seeking to envelop them in preparation for the most intimate act. The fuzzy sensation of her own resonance met him, spongy against his pressure. Inviting him to settle in. To find a home.

That sexual resonance was a deep well only another of his people should be able to touch. Holy *Ellam Cua*, she was going to make him lose control.

Breaking the kiss, he lifted his head to look down at her. Her ivory skin was nothing like a denaidan's lustrous copper, but it had a satin quality all its own. Her cheeks were flushed a delightful pink, the pupils of her slate-gray eyes wide and dark as she gazed upward at him. Stroking his jawline, she traced his beard with two delicate fingers to its very tip. The filaments there vibrated straight into his secondary heart. This wasn't normal. He wrapped a hand around her smaller one, stilling her caress so he could think straight. "You sure you're human?"

"Yes." Her breathy answer once again made his cock throb painfully. "What is your race called again?"

"Denaidan." He breathed deeply of her scent, wondering if the impossible lay here before him, both terrified and encouraged by what he was feeling. Could she be a mate? Testing the possibility might be deadly for her; during the moment of climax, a denaidan male emitted an ionic frequency which nature had designed to cause a female of his species to ovulate. A successful match was binding. Permanent. Undeniable. The alignment required between mates was an almost spiritual thing, a combination of effort by both parties to create an empathic connection which only death could break.

Unfortunately, the mating frequency destroyed a non-denaidan partner's synapses.

Because of that, any denaidan with any self respect denied himself the pleasure of women. Qaiyaan'd heard that men on other pirate crews didn't hold to such standards, but what a fellow captain allowed wasn't Qaiyaan's business. What remained of his people were no longer under any central governance, and each captain could choose to rule any way he chose. Qaiyaan's crew were honorable men, and that's all he cared about. He refused to endanger a female with his unbridled passion.

Lisa's fingers had resumed tickling his beard, and his eyes were about to roll back in his head. He couldn't. Wouldn't. Yet her sexual resonance brushed against him as surely as her breasts crushed against his chest. What if he was passing up the one non-denaidan in the galaxy who might, miraculously, be a match for him? Her lips trailed fiery kisses along his jaw, working upward until the tip of her tongue prodded the corner of his mouth. He groaned. There had to be a way to test his hope. If nothing else, a way to convince himself to stop. What if instead of physical consummation, which meant a loss of control, he only used his ionic power? He could throttle his frequency. Test her power to accept him. If she showed any stress at all, he'd pull out.

Taking a deep breath, he sent out a tentative pulse, releasing tendrils of power along the outer shell of her resonance. The kind he'd send a female to see if her vibrations might possibly match his. Lisa shuddered, her fingers clawing against his shoulders. Her hips rolled against him again, sending his cock into a spasm.

"God, that's good." She murmured against his lips.

He placed his mouth over hers, devouring her words. It *was* good. So incredibly good. Connecting his frequency with hers felt as natural as breathing again after a long stint in the void without a suit. Still kissing her, he opened his eyes, drinking in the long lashes feathering her cheeks, the slight arch of her brows, the tiny pulse of her veins beneath her eyelids. She brought one of her legs up and hooked it over his hip, drawing him closer to the heat between her thighs. He ground against her, imagining himself sheathed by her slippery folds. Plunging his tongue into her, he sent another ionic pulse.

Her eyes flew open in shock. She stared at him, brows drawn into a questioning line.

Then her eyes rolled back into her head, and her entire body went stiff as a board.

Lisa cracked her eyes open, lips tingling and swollen from the hot alien's kisses, feeling cold where his body had been. *Why had he stopped?* Overhead, the lights of the med bay threatened to burn through her eyes straight into her brain. Qaiyaan appeared in her view, his shaggy head blocking the painful light. Concern tightened his features. "You all right?"

Her nanites boiled with nasty intensity, and her head ached. Reaching a hand to her temple, she found Mek's diode back in place. She ripped it away, exhaling with relief as the pain reduced to a simmer. "What happened?"

Over Qaiyaan's shoulder, the young man with the scruffy beard— Tovik?—appeared, eyes bright with excitement. "She's awake?"

Qaiyaan frowned, ignoring the young man's question. The look in his eye was wary. "You had a seizure. Mek got his equipment working and was able to run some tests."

Uh oh. Her weak smile faltered. They'd discovered the nanites. She braced herself, wondering what came next. "What kind of tests?"

The copper-skinned doctor appeared next to Qaiyaan, elbowing the big captain out of the way. "Don't stress her. I'm not sure what sets the little buggers off." Mek lifted her eyelid and directed a bright light into her vision. She flinched and tried to twist away, but he pressed a cool palm to her forehead, holding her still. "Were you aware you're infected with nano-bots?"

She scrunched her face in discomfort, grateful when he released her eyelid. Keeping her eyes closed, she nodded. Never in her life had she regretted a grift as much as she did at this moment. These men weren't Cartel, they weren't Syndicorp, and even though Qaiyaan was an admitted pirate, his history made him more vigilante than villain. *Best face the truth right now, come what may.* "They're part of the Syndicorp medical testing I was telling Qaiyaan about. I was in cryo to keep them stable for space travel."

Qaiyaan's voice cut through the darkness behind her closed lids. "You said your *brother* was the test subject."

She slit one eye to look at him. "I told you we both were."

Qaiyaan crossed his arms, seeming to fill the small room with his presence. His concentration on her was an almost physical thing. "You most definitely did not."

"I said we were both at the test lab," she said weakly. Qaiyaan'd agreed to help her find her brother, and she repaid him with a lie. Waves of disappointment radiated off him, clawing at her to soothe him, to reassure him. This big alien was not one to be coddled, though. This man was the epitome of masculinity. Her sensitivity to his mood had to be some sort of girly hormonal response. Some biological drive she'd never experienced before.

From somewhere near the door, a gruff voice said, "She probably works for Syndicorp."

Blue eyes flashing with icy fire, Qaiyaan asked, "Are you working for the corp?"

Her ire rose. They may not have gotten off on the best foot, but she thought they'd had a pretty good conversation back in his room. And a fantastic kiss. She didn't just kiss anyone like that. She clenched her fists at her sides. "You think I want these things in my head? I'm a slave to Syndicorp. You said so yourself."

"She's a spy." Noatak's shaggy head appeared over Qaiyaan's shoulder. "What'd they pay you to infiltrate our ship? 'Cause I can tell you now, it's not worth it."

"Pay me?" Her voice rose an octave. "They tried to kill me!"

Mek elbowed the men aside, pointing at the door. "Out, all of you. I said don't get her stirred up."

"Hey, what'd I do?" the younger man complained.

The gruff man continued to glare at her without moving. "We need answers. What if she infected the ship with those bots from her head?"

Qaiyaan closed his eyes, his chest rising in a large breath. He pointed to the door. "Noatak, if you're worried, go run some diagnostics." He opened his lids and stared at the younger man. "Tovik, isn't there something you ought to be tinkering with in the engine room?"

Grumbling, both men disappeared.

"You too, Captain," Mek said.

The urge to reach out and grab Qaiyaan's hand overwhelmed her. For whatever reason, she wanted to keep him near. Did denaidans have a special power over women or something? She wished she knew more. Relief washed over her when his hand gripped hers, and she wondered if he felt the same need to touch her. He must since he'd reached out, right?

"I'm not leaving." Qaiyaan opened his eyes to meet Lisa's gaze. "I need you to tell me everything you can about these nanites. The truth. Were you attempting to infect my ship?"

CHAPTER SEVEN

Lisa fought to control her trembling lips. "The only reason I was trying to hack your ship was to contact my brother."

"So you *were* trying to hack it?" He seemed to grow several inches taller and drew back.

Lisa tightened her grip, refusing to let go. She yanked the towering captain toward her and sat up so she could glare at him more easily. "I'm carrying very secret, very expensive Syndicorp tech in my head, and my ship was just destroyed by pirates. Can you blame me for wanting to figure some shit out before blabbing the whole truth to you?"

Qaiyaan's lips thinned. "Syndicorp destroyed *your ship*. Every second you're on board my ship puts my crew in danger. Are there any other details you might want to tell me before we have troopers breathing down our necks?"

She sank back against the pillows. "I didn't ask to be brought ab—"

Mek interrupted their battle of wills by pressing a scanner to her temple. Pain arced outward from the point of contact, sending her flopping back against the pillow. She released Qaiyaan's hand, pressing both palms against her forehead and squeezing her eyes shut.

"What did you do to her?" Qaiyaan bent so close she could feel his breath on her skin. The sensation cooled her pain.

She opened her eyes to see Mek holding up the scanner in submission. "Her nanites aren't something I can read without equipment. She's going to need to withstand a little pain until I have more information."

After a moment, Qaiyaan straightened, making room for the doctor to continue his exam.

Mek lowered the scanner and squinted at Lisa as if trying to read her mind. "What were you doing when you lost consciousness?"

"Kissing your captain," Lisa groused, glaring at Qaiyaan.

Qaiyaan's copper skin flushed an adorable blue-green. Lisa wished he'd come close and kiss her again. The big man stared into her eyes as if he was thinking exactly the same thing. She licked her lips in anticipation. All she should be thinking about was getting well and finding her brother, and the topmost thing on her mind was making out? What was wrong with her?

The doctor cleared his throat. "I see. Well." He focused his attention on his captain as if his words weren't for Lisa at all. "I feel it's my responsibility to warn you that having sexual intercourse with captain Qaiyaan—with any denaidan—will kill you."

Qaiyaan made a choking noise. "I wouldn't! I didn't."

Kill me? Lisa frowned, examining Qaiyaan's broad shoulders and copper skin. The thrill of his massive erection prodding her hip and the pliable yet demanding way his lips had covered hers still coursed through her blood. She couldn't remember wanting a man that badly before, let alone an alien. "I don't understand."

"It has to do with ionic frequencies and brain waves. In the moment of climax, he would basically short-circuit your synapses." Mek's face was grim.

Lisa blinked, trying to understand. Sex with Qaiyaan would literally blow her mind? *Damn.* She wasn't sure if the tingling in her core was fear or curiosity. Probably both.

Mek returned to reading his scanner. "Qaiyaan, did you test her resonance, by chance?"

Qaiyaan's answer was husky. "I thought I had it under control."

Mek shifted to access his computer on the nearby counter. "Lisa, you said you were in cryo to keep your nanites stable. Did any of the Syndicorp doctors mention why?"

The headache his earlier scan had caused was rising again, and she could barely focus. Looking at Qaiyaan seemed to be the only thing grounding her. She wished he'd take her hand again. "Something about sensitivity to energy fluctuations during engine burn."

Mek twisted to look pointedly at his captain. "She's sensitive to ionic pulses."

"I get that. Believe me." Qaiyaan's brows were knit, but she no longer thought it was because of anger. He seemed… concerned? And he was fighting the urge to touch her again—she knew it. He pressed his palms against his rock-hard abs.

"But she survived." Mek raised his brows as if there was far more to his words than he was saying.

Qaiyaan's eyes widened. He looked at Lisa again, as if seeing her for the first time. "How?"

"I need to do more tests."

"Wait a second," Lisa raised a hand, not sure her throbbing head was letting her follow this conversation. "Survived what? We didn't have sex."

Qaiyaan wedged his body between her and the doctor. "I won't touch her again. Just keep that scanner away from her. It obviously hurts her."

"I need more data if I'm going to keep this from happening again. Her nanites are extremely unstable right now, but I don't believe they're the problem. I have a hunch it's something deeper, perhaps like an empathic migraine." Mek shifted to one side so he could see her around his captain's body. "Lisa, I believe I may be able to regulate your synapses. Do I have your permission to try?"

Syndicorp had said her nanites weren't stable, but even they hadn't known just how unbalanced she was; Doug had secretly reprogramed them a couple of times to get things under control. Even his expert hacking could only go so far. Her mind just didn't play well with the

Syndicorp technology. The thought of Mek's scanner touching her again made her want to cry. But the doctor spoke with such confidence, she wanted to believe him. Wanted to trust him. What if the problem wasn't with her nanites, but with her mind? Could Syndicorp have missed that possibility? She stretched and put a hand on Qaiyaan's hip, finding solace in the contact. "I want to try."

He turned back to look at her. "Are you sure?"

Biting her bottom lip, she nodded. She wasn't sure of anything, especially this strange connection to an alien captain. Needing Doug was awful enough. Attaching herself to Qaiyaan wasn't an option. Yet she required his help to find her brother. Whether or not Mek's tests fixed her, she needed time to think. "You should go."

Qaiyaan frowned and backed away. A moment later, he pivoted and left the room. Lisa took a deep breath and made a point of focusing on the doctor.

Mek watched him go, then lifted the diode from where she'd flung it aside and showed it to her. "I'm going to reattach this. Try to endure it as long as you can."

Lisa braced herself, just like she had during countless tests in the Syndicorp lab. "All right."

As the electric pain dug into her temple, she stared at the open doorway. She wasn't the kind of woman who needed a man in her life.

Qaiyaan paced the galley, eight steps one way, turn, eight steps back. Tovik perched on the edge of the counter, watching him. Noatak sat at the table, arms crossed. His scowl had become a permanent fixture. "Are you sure it's the bond you're feeling?"

"I'm not sure of anything," Qaiyaan said. "All I know is something happened when I tested her resonance, and now I can't seem to get her out of my head." The desire to be near Lisa, touch her even, threatened to block out all rational thinking. Even with her only down the hall in the med bay, he felt too far away. The disconcerting feeling inside him made him jittery, almost ill. He felt as if he'd been thrown into zero-G without his ionic shell. If this was the mate bond, he wasn't sure he wanted anything to do with it.

"But you didn't have sex with her?" Tovik asked bluntly. "Maybe you came a little bit in your pants."

Leveling a gaze at his young engineer, Qaiyaan ground out. "I think I'd remember if I had."

Noatak chuckled, rocking his chair onto its back legs.

Tovik flushed, looking at his knees while he drummed his fingertips on the counter to either side of where he sat. "Okay. Have you tried to communicate through the bond?"

Qaiyaan shook his head. Some denaidan couples were so well matched in frequency, they could speak to each other over long distances without the aid of a comm system. But he hadn't even thought of attempting to communicate. Testing Lisa's resonance instead of fucking her silly had been the most rational thing he'd been capable of.

Noatak let his chair legs thump back to the floor. "Initiating an empathic connection is the highest level of bonding, Tovik. Even most denaidan couples could never achieve that."

"But she survived his ionic test." Tovik frowned. "I bet it's her nanites."

Noatak placed his palms flat on the table and leaned forward. "Are you saying she might be hacking into his brain?"

Qaiyaan stopped pacing.

The young man swung his gaze from the ceiling to Qaiyaan's face. "Not hacking. But the nanites could act as an interface for your ionic resonance. Remember when we passed too close to that dark nebula, and I had to adjust the burn frequency on the engines because it was creating a sine wave that caused headaches? Her nanites are sensitive the same way. Sensitive to *us*."

"You mean sensitive to *Qaiyaan*," Noatak added. "I don't feel anything from her except trouble."

Tovik waggled his fingers like he did when he came up with an idea about upgrading the engine. "You know what this might mean? We might be able to create mates!"

Qaiyaan rolled his eyes. Surely such a thing wasn't possible? It sure as hell didn't sound ethical. "Spoken like a true engineer, Tovik."

Noatak remained rigid, his nostrils flared. "I don't like it. A bunch of micro machines in someone's head? It's unnatural."

Tovik scowled at Noatak. "At least you guys were old enough to experience a woman before the Termination. I'm going to be a virgin my whole life. Can we at least consider the idea?"

Qaiyaan balled his fists, every muscle in his body stiff. Considering the idea meant feeling hope, and that wasn't something he was comfortable with. All hope had been crushed by the destruction of his planet. Crushed by Syndicorp. "Even if she's capable of completing a mating, we can't trust her nanites. They're Syndicorp tech."

Noatak added, "She's probably a spy. Plus, she's wanted by the Whylon Cartel. Let's drop her on Bolisare, trade in these supplies, and burn out of there as fast as we can."

"If she bonds with Qaiyaan, we can trust her. *Ellam Cua* created the bond so we could always be sure of our mate's integrity." Tovik nodded sagely. At twenty-two, he was the youngest of the denaidan survivors, both on the *Hardship* and within the entire pirate fleet. The poor young man had almost no memories of his ancestral home, and only called upon their god when it suited him to do so.

"*Ellam Cua* isn't her god," Noatak inserted. "Let it go."

"But the captain said that's what this feels like."

"I have no idea what I'm feeling." Qaiyaan nearly growled in frustration. He glared at the door, imagining Mek alone with her in the med bay. Testing her. Touching her. Jealousy made his blood boil. Yet uncertainty turned him cold.

"She's not denaidan." Noatak slapped his hand on the table with a bang. "We don't know what might happen if he tries. What if the bond only works one way? What if Qaiyaan becomes her slave?"

If the room had been tense before, the air fairly crackled now. Qaiyaan thought back to that derelict ship. He'd originally thought it could be a trap. What if Lisa was a spy of sorts? Poisonous bait, offering the one bit of hope the denaidan pirates couldn't refuse? She didn't even have to know about it. Probably didn't. It would be just like Syndicorp to come up with that kind of plan. And they were reportedly growing weary of denaidan pirates nibbling at the edges of their galaxy.

Tovik's excited energy had settled, and his hands lay limp against his thighs. "I hadn't thought of that."

"Of course you hadn't," Noatak said. "Listen. I'm all for finding mates and whatever, but this girl came out of nowhere. We can't trust her or her Syndicorp nanites. We need to get rid of her ASAP."

CHAPTER EIGHT

Qaiyaan stared at the table's scarred surface. Noatak made sense. Sending Lisa on her way was probably the right thing to do. The smart thing. But the idea of parting from her caused an ache inside him. "Syndicorp blew up her ship. We should at least try to find out why."

Noatak started to argue, but Qaiyaan didn't hear him. His skin had begun to tingle and his chest burned. *She's coming.* Sure enough, Lisa's slight form appeared around the door jamb. She remained frustratingly just out of range of his touch, her gray eyes slightly narrowed.

Mek appeared in the hall behind her and gestured for her to enter the room.

Still watching Qaiyaan suspiciously, she moved to the table, careful to avoid touching anyone, and sat.

Qaiyaan raised a brow at Mek in question. "What's going on?"

"I gave her some recovery stim."

"You did what?" Qaiyaan balled his fists. The stim helped a denaidan recover more quickly after strenuous ionic exertion, but it was also highly addictive. Noatak had relapsed several times since his recovery, and Mek kept their supply under lock and key.

Lisa crossed her arms and took a shuddery breath. "I told him to."

"Why?"

Mek made some adjustments to his handheld's sensor. "I gave her the stimulant to alter her brain waves temporarily. I want to gather her responses to environmental input. Noatak, touch her hand."

Noatak did a double take and stepped back, while Qaiyaan stiffened, entire body tense with... jealousy? "Why does he need to touch her?"

"I'll touch her," Tovik held out a hand. But he kept a wary gaze on Qaiyaan.

Twisting in her chair to face him, Lisa stretched out her arm and brushed her fingertips against Tovik's. Qaiyaan's pulse thundered in his ears. He kept his focus off Lisa and instead bored his gaze into the doctor, who still looked down at his handheld.

"Huh," was all Mek said, then looked expectantly at Noatak.

Noatak crossed his arms tightly over his chest, his face hard. "For all I know, she's contagious, and now you're all infected. I'm not touching her."

"If we're infected, you are too. You already touched her when we caught her in the corridor," Tovik offered helpfully.

"Fine." Noatak dropped his arms to his sides. After a brief hesitation, he stretched one index finger toward Lisa, allowing her to press her fingertip against his in a strange sort of greeting. The first mate's lip curled and he pulled his hand away. "Satisfied?"

"Why are we doing this?" Qaiyaan grumbled, hating watching his crew manhandle her.

Lisa straightened her shoulders and met his gaze with an intensity that made him wonder if she possessed ionic powers of her own. "I refuse to let these things ruin my life. If I'm going to join your crew, I need to get them under control."

Join my crew? That was the last thing Qaiyaan expected to hear. A woman on board his ship? Permanently? *Anaq*, he wasn't used to being around women, let alone one as determined as Lisa. How could he keep his urges throttled if she was parading herself in front of him every day? "I, uh..."

Noatak moved shoulder-to-shoulder with him, creating a wall. "We don't need the likes of you getting in the way of our operations. Now go back to the med bay before we throw you in the brig."

"You have a brig?" Lisa's eyes widened.

Qaiyaan glared at his first mate. "No. We don't."

Mek waved his scanner at Qaiyaan. "Your turn to touch her."

A small thrill raced up Qaiyaan's spine, and through the air, he felt Lisa's matching shiver. Were they so in tune with so little effort? He didn't know how that could be, but it was a far better sensation than the vertigo he'd been experiencing in her presence earlier. Holding out his hand palm up, he allowed her to settle her small fingers over his in the lightest of touches. The thrill coiled into a knot deep in his belly. To his delight, a flush rose into her face.

Tapping a few filters on his screen, Mek looked up, his clean-shaven face alight with discovery. "Her brain waves show a remarkable similarity to denaidan empath response markers. If I can get my hands on some supplies on Bolisare, I believe I can stabilize her synapses."

Qaiyaan exhaled, long and slow. He'd been more worried about her than he'd admitted, even to himself. "That's great news."

"And just how are we supposed to pay for these supplies?" Noatak was glaring at Lisa. "Our payload is barely going to bring in enough to get us to the next spaceport."

Lisa cleared her throat. "Mek explained the situation, and I have a proposal. The Cartel has a contact moon side who launders money, provides supplies, all that sort of stuff. He can probably even get your hull fixed. He uses codes to charge the Cartel. "

"I thought the Cartel wants you dead?" Qaiyaan asked.

"They already think I am. I doubt they're actively looking."

Noatak approached the table opposite her and dragged out a chair to sit, his previously aggressive aura mellowed. "I take it you know the codewords?"

Qaiyaan, too, was torn between caution and the desire to fix his ship. "More important, are you sure your codewords are still good? You've been gone awhile. What happens if you give a bad one?"

"The Cartel is inherently lazy, and hardly ever changes them. No one dares misuse Cartel resources for fear of retribution." Her heartbeat fluttered through Qaiyaan's link. "But I won't take any chances. Get me close enough to one of their computers, and I can check they're still valid before we use them."

"With your nanites," Qaiyaan finished.

She nodded.

Tovik hopped off his perch on the counter and pulled out the chair next to Lisa, adoration in his eyes. *Great. She was turning half his crew into lovesick puppies.* Qaiyaan gave the boy a look and Tovik moved down one seat.

Tovik put his elbows on the table and leaned in. "I say we try."

Qaiyaan took the chair at the head of the table, directly to Lisa's right, where he could pick up her subtle lilac scent. "I'm not sure I like this plan. How are we supposed to get you close to a Cartel computer?"

She smiled. "It's been a while since I've worked a grift, but give me a sexy dress, and I think I can get close enough. Our contact runs the kwirn tables at the Solar Swan. I'll be just another girl looking for a man with money."

Noatak groaned and rolled his eyes. "We're not exactly welcome on that side of the planet."

Tovik snorted. "I'll say. I wonder if they still have your wanted poster posted at the spaceport?"

Glad for any diversion from thoughts of Lisa in a sexy dress, Qaiyaan let out an exasperated breath and glared at Noatak. "I knew I should've left your sorry hide to rot in that prison cell."

Lisa looked from one man to the other. "Well, I don't need any of you to go with me. Drop me off near the city and I'll check things out and report back."

A heartbeat of silence, then Noatak asked, "What's to keep you from turning us in for the bounty?"

She laughed. "I'm a wanted woman myself. How would I collect a bounty?" Taking a deep breath, she said, "But I'm not doing this out of the goodness of my heart. I need you to help me pull my brother out of Syndicorp's clutches. Then we can talk about my pay to join your crew. A couple of cyber-sensitives can be pretty useful in a heist."

Qaiyaan couldn't help the grin cracking his lips, and he was pleased to note the same grudging appreciation cross his first mate's face, as well. Tovik and Mek simply stared on with adoring eyes. She'd fit in well if she continued to hold her own against Noatak. Damn it all if he wasn't going to get off Bolisare with a reinforced hull, a belly full of fuel—and a woman at his side.

Beneath the pale blue light of Bolisare's second sun, Lisa lowered herself into the rickshaw, feeling Qaiyaan's hungry gaze on her exposed thigh before she drew her leg inside. To be fair, she'd let the supple fabric fall open along the side slit and perhaps allowed her leg to linger too long outside the carriage as she arranged her seating. But she liked his gaze on her. Liked the way he hovered nearby and seemed to anticipate her every need before she even realized she had the need herself. For instance; this dress. He'd somehow known her exact size and bought the lustrous gold garment while offloading the medical cargo to a buyer on one of Bolisare's moons. She pulled the sleek fabric inside the rickshaw and scooted over so he could slide in beside her.

"How'd you get hold of a dress like this so quickly?" she asked.

"I used the ship's 3-D printer." His gaze kept slipping toward her cleavage.

"You printed it?" She raised her brows. Many ships were equipped with manufacturing printers, pre-programmed with blueprints for ship parts and basic necessities. Cocktail dresses weren't usually on the list of plans, let alone garments of varying sizes. "Who designed it? It fits me perfectly."

He looked away, as if just realizing he'd been staring. "A captain has to be adept at everything."

That surprised her. "A pirate with a passion for clothing design?"

His copper skin flushed blue-green.

She laughed at his discomfort. She'd grown up among the diverse cultures on Whylon Station and had never found an alien attractive until now. This big copper-skinned alien delighted and confused her.

He was everything she'd ever defined as masculine; it wasn't fair that he was off limits.

Qaiyaan draped his arm over the back of the seat to make room for his massive frame on the bench beside her. He'd dressed in a sleeveless white tunic that made his copper arms look massive. Even the slightest brush of his skin against hers sent shivers of pleasure deep into her bones. Rational or not, she wanted Qaiyaan more than she'd ever wanted any man in her entire life, including that Cartel thug, Seloh. She'd survived Qaiyaan's ionic test, which according to Mek should have turned her into a vegetable. Didn't that somehow make her special? Her nanites were the source of so many problems—what if they were also the solution? If she was going to be part of his crew, she was going to have to find a way to get him out of her system.

CHAPTER NINE

Legs pumping furiously against the pedals, the six-legged yanipa-nimayu drove the rickshaw up the hill toward the Solar Swan, chattering Lisa's teeth in her head. They bumped and chattered over the uneven road; Bolisare wasn't an official part of Syndicorp, so the planet didn't receive the extensive transportation funding of classified worlds. The port was barely maintained by a hodgepodge of shippers and traders, both legit and not. The mishmash of aliens and humans, wealth and poverty, was almost as richly diverse as Whylon Station. The casino presided over the town in a garish display of flashing neon lights.

"So, what's this guy look like?" Qaiyaan asked as they passed a billboard that read *What happens on Bolisare, stays on Bolisare.*

"He's a posungi who goes by the name Nupnup. Supposed to hang out near the tables most of the day."

Qaiyaan made a noncommittal noise, but he pulsed with worry. "You ever talked to a posungi before?"

She knew what he was really asking. Posungi were an egg-laying species, but the males were known for their appreciation of sexual interludes with warm-blooded partners. She chuckled. "Once he thinks I'm a Cartel agent, he won't ask me to do anything outrageous."

The rickshaw made a sudden turn onto a side street, throwing her against Qaiyaan's ribs. He wrapped his arm around her shoulders, sending jolts of pleasure across her skin. "How are you supposed to identify yourself to him?" he asked.

"I'll ask if he knows a place to rent a cottage. He'll ask if I want blue or yellow. I'll answer turquoise, with three bedrooms and an ocean view."

Qaiyaan frowned. "That's it?"

She shrugged. "Never said it was complicated. The number of bedrooms lets him know which Cartel sect to charge his services to."

Shaking his head, Qaiyaan returned to watching the crowds as the rickshaw whipped past.

They arrived at the massive front archway of the Solar Swan, a concrete structure covered with huge electronic billboards instead of windows. The arch's open doors were purely ornamental, the hinges twined with thousands of multi-colored lights.

Qaiyaan disembarked, holding out a hand to help her rise from the seat. His dark trousers molded to his chiseled thighs, rippling with every flex of muscle. The toes of his gleaming, knee-high boots were coated with a layer of dust from Bolisare's filthy streets. His clean, well-cut frame was even more appealing because of the two braids spilling from his chin and the wild mop of hair loosely bunched into thick locks about his shoulders.

She took his hand, insides quaking at his touch. Standing, the top of her head didn't even reach his shoulder.

A passing woman's manicured brows raised in appreciation. "Nice bodyguard."

Lisa grinned and looped her arm through Qaiyaan's. Together, they sauntered inside, the windowless interior lit in a raucous display of colors from the many slot machines and other low-end gambling opportunities. She looked around for the kwirn tables. She'd never been to Bolisare. Luckily, Qaiyaan seemed to know exactly where to go, urging her past the buzzing, whirring, chiming machines to a hallway on the other side of the bar. He leaned close, his voice a tickle in her ear. "See him?"

She shook her head, mouth suddenly dry as a pair of gold-scaled rakwiji stalked past her, their dorsal spikes tipped black with what she hoped wasn't blood. Rakwiji were the Cartel's preferred bounty hunters, the most ruthless species in the galaxy, and always traveled in pairs. Torture was part of their mating system, the thrill of another being's pain a stimulus for the couple's sexual pleasure. Rumor had it that Seloh's death had resulted in a litter of three offspring for the Cartel's Whylon Station pair. She still couldn't view the aliens with any sort of forgiveness. Suppressing a shudder, she kept walking.

The hall opened up to a room peppered with downward funnels of light illuminating regularly spaced tables. Among the games, she spotted the usual assortment of cards and dice, two attahat wheels, and finally the kwirn tables with their stacked glass betting shelves and hexagonal playing pieces. She squinted into the dim spaces between the tables, searching for the orange tentacled face of a posungi. She found her quarry bending low beneath one of the lights to swipe a three-fingered hand over the betting shelves.

Nudging Qaiyaan, she thrust her chin in the posungi's direction, then pointed toward the bar. "Why don't you go get a drink? I'll signal if I need you."

Through the elastic connection that seemed to be growing stronger between them the more time they spent together, she felt a protective wash of energy. But to his credit, he didn't argue. "Be careful."

Lisa pushed her shoulders back and sashayed through the room, stopping at an attahat table to laugh at some inane joke, then pausing long enough at a hand of blackjack to pretend to make up her mind not to play. If she made a show of heading straight to the posungi's table, he'd be on his guard. As she approached, she surveyed Nupnup's short, thick torso for an indication of where he kept his polycom. Her pulse roared in her ears and her nanites were making her skin itch as she grasped at her strands of courage. She'd probably only have time for a brush of her hand to hack into his tech. One shot. And she sucked at speed-hacking.

She stopped at the opposite corner of the table and pretended to be interested in a human who was obviously losing. This part she could do; the slow, lazy grift that made a man—or a posungi—think whatever she suggested had been his idea. The human grinned at her and put an arm around her waist to pull her close. "Hey, baby. You here to be my good luck charm?"

The human stank of too much saluqan gin and his hand slid from her waist to the under-curve of her bottom too quickly. From across the crowded room, she felt Qaiyaan bristle. Damn. He wasn't helping here. Working hard to remain outwardly friendly, she leaned into the human, affecting a sultry voice. "You don't seem like the type of fellow who needs luck."

He drew himself straighter and looked around the table as if he'd just won the round. "Damn straight."

The players placed their bets and cycled through another complicated round of moving pieces from shelf to shelf. When Nupnup swept her human's piece off its shelf, she let out a disappointed hum and pulled away in exaggerated disdain.

"Don't worry, baby." The man tried to pull her close to his side again. "I got plenty of money. Why don't you come up to my room and I'll dig into my stash?"

She raised an eyebrow and shot a glance around the table in silent, communal derision of the loser. The other players, including two men and a finofan who'd painted his ear frills a garish yellow, chuckled at the human's expense. Turning up her nose, she extricated herself from the man's grip and sidled around the table toward the posungi. "You seem to know what you're doing. Why don't you tell me which one of these lovely men is the best player?"

His second set of eyes blinked out of sequence with the others, and his lower tentacles lifted in the equivalent of a shrug. "They are all inferior to a posungi."

She smiled at him and leaned in, stroking a hand along his arm. "I love a man who's confident in his game."

He emitted a raspberry of appreciation and let all four eyes rake her body from head to toe. "I enjoy a woman who knows how to play, as well."

The double entendre wasn't lost on her, and she giggled, pressing her body to his, searching for the electric signature of a polycom. She had to hold her revulsion in check as his three-fingered hand drummed excitedly against her hip. It didn't help that she also felt Qaiyaan's low boil of rage from across the room.

She sent her nanites in search of the nearby frequency of Nupnup's polycom, but there was a lot of low-level noise from other gadgets in the room. Syndicorp had made her and Doug practice homing in on a single electronic signature too many times to count, but she'd always found ignoring the other signatures difficult. Snuffling close to her ear, Nupnup made a joke. She laughed at it without actually hearing. *Dammit, where's his device?*

To her relief, he let her go long enough to lean over the table and set his pieces on the shelves. She concentrated harder, her nanites buzzing through her veins and making her muscles tremble. With a jolt, she located his polycom's frequency. The sudden flow of information made her legs weak, forcing her to lean heavily on the posungi. Not that he minded. His arm torqued around her, fingers digging into her ass cheek. His tentacles waggled close to her face, one making contact with her lower lip. Only years of practice at the grift kept her from shuddering in revulsion. Her nanites were collecting data as fast as they could, throwing it at her in an indecipherable wave. She needed a few moments to interpret.

Qaiyaan's resonant voice behind her made her stiffen. "There you are."

The posungi's roving fingers halted, and he stared over her shoulder. "You are looking for me?"

Lisa turned, pulse thundering. The pirate captain stood facing them, his stance wide and his arms crossed over his broad chest. The waves of emotion rolling off him mingled with the data stream from Nupnup's device, further confusing her. Mentally, she begged him to back off. She wasn't ready.

"I hear you can rent me a cottage," Qaiyaan said, staring down his nose at the much shorter alien.

Nupnup belched out a breath, fluttering his chin tentacles. "You need it immediately? I'm busy at the moment."

Qaiyaan nodded curtly, his gaze flicking over Lisa as if just noticing her for the first time.

With glee, she located the file with the encrypted Cartel information and fumbled with the code.

The posungi's grip on her slackened as he turned to face Qaiyaan, but didn't fully release. "You have a color preference? Blue? Red?"

Lisa's vision danced with an overlay of information, and she found the directive with the Cartel codewords. They hadn't changed. Relief flooded her. Looking at Qaiyaan, she nodded imperceptibly.

His chin lifted, gaze never leaving the orange-faced posungi. "It has to be turquoise. With an ocean view and three bedrooms."

Nupnup's arm dropped from her waist. He straightened. "Three bedrooms? Are you certain?"

A flicker of indecision only she could feel tickled the air, but Qaiyaan nodded firmly. "That's my requirement."

This time, Lisa caught a strong whiff of indecision from the posungi. She stepped back, unsure what to make of that. Had the physical contact with the tentacled alien made her start to bond with him now? She shuddered in disgust. No, she was just out of practice with grifting, and Qaiyaan had an abnormally powerful effect on her senses.

Nupnup's tentacles writhed. "If you are sure. Let us find a place we can discuss what you require."

Without a glance back at her, Nupnup moved off into the recesses of the Solar Swan, Qaiyaan trailing close behind. She knew better than to follow without an invitation. Besides, all this exercising of her nanites had given her an idea. She was a hacker; weren't her nanites simply little computers themselves? Doug had reprogrammed them a few times for her when the lab tests overwhelmed her. But what if she could do it herself? She could program a few to hack into the others, and perhaps re-write their code to protect her from Qaiyaan's resonance.

Then she and pirate-captain Qaiyaan could have a little fun on Bolisare after all.

CHAPTER TEN

Qaiyaan followed the posungi to a small room behind the bar, where the orange alien sat on a high-backed wing-chair that had seen better days. A small table beside him held a decanter and two glasses, but he didn't offer refreshment. A second, smaller version of his chair faced him; too small to be comfortable for Qaiyaan, so he remained standing. To the left, a large mirror dominated the wall, and when Qaiyaan sent an ionic pulse in that direction, he sensed someone watching from behind the one-way glass. He'd dealt with aliens like Nupnup before. Much of what transpired would be bluff and bravado. He'd expected no less.

Keeping his face passive, he waited as Nupnup reviewed the list Mek had put together. Finally, the tentacle-faced alien looked up. "You are requesting many specialty medical items. What do you need them for?"

"No questions asked." Qaiyaan reiterated what Lisa'd said about the contact.

Nupnup made a small, disappointed noise. "Your ship is quite antiquated and will require special considerations for repair. That may take some time."

Scowling, Qaiyaan crossed his arms and glowered down at the alien. "Are you calling my ship junk?"

Nupnup wriggled a tentacle in dismissal. "I would never call a captain's ship junk to his face."

Qaiyaan grit his teeth at the sideways insult. "How much time?"

"I can procure the medical items and send them over this afternoon. But I cannot estimate the hull repair until my man has looked at it." He ran one tentacle over his blubbery lips. "Tracking down the appropriate parts might take a solar week. Perhaps you would like to rent a room?"

Using his ionic senses, Qaiyaan assessed the alien's heartbeat, breathing, and skin temperature. He'd had limited dealings with posungi, and without a baseline, it was difficult to interpret Nupnup's integrity. He seemed calm enough. But Qaiyaan's black market dealings made him wary. *What other choice do you have?* "Just get me what I need and I'll be out of your hair, uh, tentacles."

The posungi's four eyes seemed to wink at him. "I'll send someone over to assess your ship's requirements."

"The sooner, the better." Qaiyaan spun and left the small room.

Back in the casino, he scanned the floor for Lisa. A garan'uk trundled past in its mechanized methane tank, blocking Qaiyaan's view. Dodging right, he headed toward a glint of what appeared to be gold fabric near the bar. He cleared the attahat wheel only to discover a rakwiji talking loudly to the bartender, sharp teeth reflecting the nearby neon lights. Lisa was nowhere in sight. *For Ellam Cua's sake, where'd she go?*

Earlier, as she'd moved across the room, he'd nearly busted out of his skin with jealousy, aware of every set of male eyes drawn to her swaying hips. She'd played the patrons like a pro, pausing with just enough of a smile near one table, then laughing at a stupid joke at another. Once she reached the posungi's table, he'd been relieved the ordeal was almost over. But then she'd latched onto that smarmy human for an entire round before moving to the target. By the time Nupnup had his tentacles all over her, Qaiyaan'd been at his wit's end. He knew he'd moved in too fast, but he couldn't take it anymore. He figured he could stall the guy long enough for her to get her reading, and he'd been right; she'd sent him the very clear and distinct body language to proceed.

Her cyber-sensitivity was going to make his crew a lot of money, plus, she probably knew the black market underground even better than he did. She'd be a valuable member of the crew—if he could keep himself from ripping her clothes off and finishing what she'd started back in his cabin. The hard-on he'd been fighting for the last two days had only grown more persistent as time passed. She had a keen wit, and a body any man would die for. Then she'd put on that dress…

You just need some time to get used to her. But he had a hard time believing anything about Lisa would ever become mundane or ignorable. While he searched the room, he tapped his cochlear implant. "Tovik, someone'll be arriving to evaluate the hull for repairs. Keep an eye on him."

"Aye-aye, Captain," the voice in his head replied. "How long you going to be?"

"Not sure. I'll let you know."

Moving down the hall toward the slot machines, his ionic senses grew desperate, yearning to call out to her. He hadn't thought to set up a rendezvous point in the event they were separated. A true mate-bond would come in very useful right now, enabling them to talk, no matter how far apart. Not that he had any hope of that, with her or with anyone.

He took a deep, calming breath and kept looking. Spotting the shimmer of gold fabric near the slot machines, he discovered Lisa flirting with two young finofans. He paused, watching her throw back her head and laugh, obviously fake. But the finofans were falling over themselves to touch her, their fluorescently painted ear fins fluttering with aroused excitement. One leaned in close to her to whisper something in her ear, and a heated surge of jealousy—a sensation he was becoming all too familiar with—flooded his limbs. Then he saw her fingertips dip into the male's pocket and extract a key. *What the hell's she doing?* The one thing he didn't need was a repeat jail-break like he'd had to do when Noatak'd fallen off the wagon with those recovery stims.

He marched over, towering above the young aliens, and glowered down at them. "This female's mine. Beat it."

The finofans cowered, ear fins flattening against their skulls, then scurried away without a sound. Lisa chuckled low in her throat. "Just in time," she said, taking his hand.

Before he could question her about the key, she was leading him to the elevator. Inside, he turned to her. "Want to tell me what you're up to?"

"Play along." Her gaze flicked to a high corner of the car, and she wrapped her arms around his neck. Over her head, he spotted the camera. Who was she concerned was watching? Before he could tell her no, her mouth was on his, her tongue pressing between his lips and lighting his blood on fire. Every atom of his being surged with desire, polarizing toward her. He'd been dreaming of this since his cabin, the flavor of her filling him, floral musk and sweet feminine skin.

Her soft body molded against his hard one, and a shudder ran through her. He was sure she felt it, too, this hunger and volatile urgency. This wasn't a performance for the camera. This was real, primal. He splayed his palm against her lower back, fingertips electrified against the skin exposed by her dress's scooped back. Her hands clawed into his shoulders as if hanging on for dear life.

Taking several measured breaths even as he tangled his tongue with hers, he reined in his urge to nudge her, tamping down his ionic power and walling it up. Instinct battered against those walls, weakening his resolve almost as quickly as he gathered it.

To his relief, the elevator chimed. Her lips swollen from the bruising kiss, she blinked glazed eyes. Her voice emerged a husky whisper. "Our floor, I think." She broke the embrace. "This way."

His skin ached in the void where her body had been, urging him to reach for her, to draw her close. He balled his hands into fists and followed her. This couldn't go any further. He knew that. But his ionic power roiled inside him like a class five hydrogen nebula.

They reached the room, and the door opened in a warm rush of air, temperatures fit for finofan comfort. He breathed deeply, the change a welcome distraction. Inside, the standard decorations included two double beds and a vid-screen view of a pink sunset over deep golden mountains. She gestured him inside, then secured the lock, turning to press her back against the door panel. "So? How'd it go?"

He moved to the bed and sank heavily onto the mattress. The kiss *had* been for the camera. He was relieved yet still clamoring for her touch. "I'm not sure I trust that Nupnup fellow."

"You shouldn't. He might not be Cartel, but he works for them." She moved toward the replicator console on the wall. "Tula cream cocktails on ice. Two."

Qaiyaan couldn't keep his gaze from her well-rounded curves or the long swath of leg peeking from the gown's slit every time she moved. He'd done far too good a job designing that dress. That's what came of years enduring "look-don't-touch," he supposed. "He's sending the medical stuff Mek needs for you. The hull repair may take a week."

Looking over her shoulder at him, she frowned. "A week? Mek thought you needed a simple patch or something. Is the damage that bad?"

"I try not to alarm my crew. But yeah," he answered truthfully. There was no reason to keep secrets from her. "We've been about to bust a seam for a while now."

"I guess that means we have some time to kill, then. Courtesy of my finofan friends." Grinning, Lisa retrieved the drinks and offered one to him.

He gratefully sipped the icy cocktail. The smooth, buttery flavor of tula fruit and cream washed over his tongue. She sipped hers, and he watched the lines of her throat tighten while she swallowed. Damn, this woman was the most alluring thing he'd ever seen. "What if they come back?"

"Don't worry." She set her drink on the bedside table and moved to stand between his knees. "Those fellows won't find a hook-up for hours with the lines they're using."

Her musky lilac scent flooded over him, and once again, his cock stirred. Even if he hadn't been able to sense her matching arousal through her resonance, it was obvious in the hardened nipples outlined by the thin fabric of her gown.

She ran a fingertip down his cheek and along his bearded jaw. "I want to try something."

His heartbeats sounded like full-thrust engines roaring in his ears. "We can't. You know we can't."

She tilted her head. "We kissed in the elevator and I'm okay."

He licked his lips, remembering. "I had my guard up."

"So did I."

That made him pause. "What do you mean?"

"I've been hacking my own nanites."

He blinked, confused. "You can do that?"

"That's what I want to test." She reached down and picked up his hand, placing his palm between her breasts over her fiercely pounding heart. "If I'm going to be a member of your crew, we have to learn to be around each other."

Exactly what he'd been thinking. And if she could fix her nanites… He took a deep breath of her delicious scent. If she joined his crew, he'd eventually find himself touching her. May as well test it now instead of once they were in deep space. "It could be deadly."

Her mouth twisted into a playful smile. "It could be fun. One kiss."

He groaned and closed his eyes. He was thinking of more than a kiss. He was thinking of sheathing himself inside her, feeling the quiver of her body around him. Was she sending this emotion? It didn't matter. If she was asking, he'd give whatever she wanted. Opening his eyes, he slid his palm from between her breasts to rest over her throat. Her pulse throbbed beneath his fingertips. "One kiss."

CHAPTER ELEVEN

Lisa's nanites jittered in anticipation, heightening her awareness of Qaiyaan's touch. Her *desire* for his touch. She wanted his hands all over her body. The danger involved only heightened her arousal. *Just remember to keep tabs on those nanites.* The kiss in the elevator had proved to her that her reprogramming was working; the nanites could match Qaiyaan's dangerous frequencies.

He rose to his feet, towering over her, the heat of his muscular chest a hairsbreadth away. Her nipples hardened at his nearness. When he bent his head to capture her mouth, the kiss stole her breath. Rockets of desire raced down her body and pooled between her thighs. If this was how close he could bring her to orgasm with a kiss, what would sex with him feel like?

She melted forward until her breasts made contact with his solid chest. His hand snaked around her backside to bring her toward him, his erection thick and insistent against her. The jolt to her nerves from the touch made her dizzy. *No passing out.* She bolstered her nanites, much the same way she'd done to resist the doctor's scans, and the dizziness subsided. Elation rushed through her. *You can do this.*

Raising a leg around Qaiyaan's hips, she shivered in anticipation as his cock pulsed and twitched against the thin fabric of her panties. His lips broke from hers only enough to murmur, "Okay?"

She nodded furiously and drew her other leg up, locking her ankles behind him.

He turned and dropped them both onto the bed, his weight above her a hot, pulsing mass of desire. She cupped his bearded face with both hands, her mouth as hungry as his, their tongues and lips tangling and dancing, each trying to devour the other. Her dress had been pushed almost to her waist, and his hand found her thigh, skimming up to cup her bottom. His rock-hard chest crushed against her aching breasts, and her panties were soaked where his erection pressed between her legs.

Broad palm massaging her hip, he worked his way up her side until he reached a breast. His breath caressed her cheek and throat as surely as his hand caressed the soft mound beneath her gown. Trailing kisses along her jaw, he sucked at her throat while massaging her aching breast, thumb circling her areola, teasing her into an aching peak. Then he dipped down and eased her free of the gown's low neckline, revealing her tender flesh to his tongue and the delightful tickle of his beard. She moaned, arching upward to meet him as he nipped and suckled her nipple. His other hand slipped between their bodies and cupped her sex, massaging her through her panties.

"Take them off," she begged.

He slipped his fingers beneath the fabric and stroked a finger along her slick cleft before plunging it inside. She cried out, bucking against him. He pulled out in a long, slow agony of pleasure. Raising her hips, she begged for more. Still sucking her nipple, he slammed into her again, his palm connecting with her clit. The electric jolt from the contact arced straight to her core.

Qaiyaan groaned and wriggled his thick finger deep inside her, grinding against her outer lips as she squirmed. His other hand hooked the neckline of her gown and the fragile garment parted down the front. Tongue tracing a searing path along her ribs, he lapped and sucked his way across her belly while his fingers continued a rhythm deep inside her. Then he tore her panties away and buried his face between her legs.

His mouth worked her swollen nub until hot flashes of pleasure ripped through her. His tongue, oh, his tongue! Her hands wound themselves into his mass of hair as he circled her clit, his fingers plunging inside her with a friction that was rapidly bringing her to the brink of climax. She bucked and arched against him, wanting more, wanting his cock. He kept teasing the sweet spot he'd found deep inside her with his finger. The pressure built fast and hot until her entire body trembled with desire.

"Yes, Qaiyaan!" she cried, her head thrashing back and forth.

He picked up speed, adding a third finger, stretching her in an agony of pleasure. Her pulse raced so frantically, she thought she might have a heart attack and die. Pressure deep in her belly swelled, hovered. His hand that had been toying with her breast moved down to push gently on her lower abdomen, increasing the pressure of his fingers inside her.

The added sensation sent her tumbling over the edge. She screamed, her pulsing epicenter shooting mind-numbing waves of pleasure outward to her head and toes and every part in between. Never in her life had she experienced anything so intense. Her nanites were like streams of fire in her blood, lighting up every nerve ending as if the very universe couldn't contain their power.

The orgasm went on and on, longer than any woman had a right to come. The tiniest part of her realized she was in trouble only a moment before the world began to spin. She reached for her nanites, knowing it was too late. A program crash had begun. *Not again!*

Qaiyaan loomed over her, his copper-skinned face lined with concern. "Lisa?"

Clinging to consciousness, she blinked up at him. Put her fingertips to his cheek. Then everything faded to black.

With Lisa light as a twig in his arms, Qaiyaan shoved through the crowded casino as if the building was on fire. Local medical assistance wasn't an option—Bolisare was all but a pirate planet, and word of her nanites would expand like a supernova. He'd called Mek, who'd told him to stay put, but there wasn't a moment to spare. Qaiyaan could get Lisa to the ship faster than the doctor could gather his equipment and flag down a rickshaw. What were those bastard Syndicorp nanites doing to her right now? He felt for her pulse again, reassured by its steady beat yet terrified about what was happening to her mind.

He'd been so proud of himself back in the room, remaining in full control, focusing only on her pleasure. But he should've known better than to believe Syndicorp tech might actually benefit him. He bared his teeth at a long-limbed rakwiji bouncer standing in the path ahead with her scales flared in aggression. She grimaced back, long teeth glinting in the multi-colored lights, then seemed to think better of a confrontation and scurried out of the way.

He burst from the dark casino onto the brightly lit sidewalk outside. Ignoring the outraged looks of other patrons, he shoved to the front of a line waiting for rickshaws and set Lisa in the back of the nearest one. When the human who'd been haggling price with the driver tried to argue, Qaiyaan shoved him out of the way. The human skittered backward and fell onto his backside, his companions shouting in outrage. Qaiyaan didn't give an *anaq*. As he climbed in next to Lisa, he shouted at the driver, "Spaceport. Now. I'll pay double if you can get us there in under fifteen."

The driver lunged against the pedals, pulling the vehicle away from the curb and into the line of traffic. Picking up speed, the rickshaw careened past an oncoming u-bus, taking the corner toward the space station at breakneck speed.

Qaiyaan tapped his cochlear implant. "I'm on my way."

Mek's voice entered his head. "I told you to stay put."

"I'm not standing by helpless while you get your limp *ucuk* in gear. Where can we meet?"

A sigh. "The cargo doors. Any improvement?"

Qaiyaan pulled Lisa's torn dress closed over her breasts, wishing he could see into her brain. "No."

"You're sure you didn't nudge her?"

His previous pride about keeping control tasted like ashes. Had he nudged her? He'd been so into her, so tranced by her amazing body, that he wasn't sure. He didn't think he had. He hadn't felt a need to. The connection was already there, already calling him, telling him what she liked, what she needed. A presence that was uniquely Lisa. And she'd never told him to stop. Never warned him she was losing control. Her orgasm had washed deliciously over him, a moment of shared pleasure like he'd never felt before. His cock had been ready. Then the intangible bond had snapped. Twanged with a resonance that still rang through his bloodstream. He provided Mek the only answer he could. "She wanted to experiment. To see how far we could go."

The silence over his implant expressed Mek's disapproval far better than his words. "What the fuck were you thinking?"

Guilt clogged Qaiyaan's throat. Instead of answering, he tapped his implant to silence it then shouted at the driver, "Can't you go any faster?"

His entire crew was waiting at the open cargo bay doors when the rickshaw skidded to a halt on the blistering-hot tarmac. Qaiyaan lifted Lisa from the seat and strode toward the ship. Behind him, the driver clambered after him, cursing loudly for his promised fare. Shouting at his first mate to pay the angry yanipa-nimayu, Qaiyaan headed for the med bay. Mek ran alongside, waving a portable scanner over Lisa's limp form.

Normally in an emergency situation, Qaiyaan would've sent a surge of ionic energy to his feet, allowing him to leap onto the second-level catwalk toward the med bay. But his terror of using any of his powers around the fragile woman in his arms sent him climbing the stairs three at a time.

In the med bay, he lay her gently on the exam table, pulling her gaping dress closed against his crewmen's gazes. When he felt Mek's hand on his arm, urging him away, he stiffened, instinct demanding he defend his woman. Then Mek's voice brought him back to reality. "I'm not sure what's causing her blackouts, but you're the common denominator. You need to leave."

Nausea rolled through him. He was the common denominator. Great *Ellam Cua*. What if he'd killed his only chance for a mate? He stepped backward, his attention glued to the woman on the table. To his *mate* on the table. Consummated or not, there was no denying that now. "She was trying to reprogram her own nanites. Trying to make us compatible."

Mek narrowed his eyes. "Was she successful?"

"Obviously not." Qaiyaan croaked out, his chest full of regret. Why had he ever allowed her to talk him into this?

Tovik moved between Qaiyaan and the exam table, his green eyes full of compassion. "Come on, Captain. I know where you hide the *akluilak* wine. Let the doctor do his thing."

Reluctantly, he followed his engineer to the galley.

CHAPTER TWELVE

Three shots of wine later, Qaiyaan felt no calmer. His soul felt like it'd been ripped in two. Tovik had been called away to talk to Nupnup's repairman, and Noatak now sat in the galley in silence, both feet propped on the neighboring chair, arms crossed over his chest. They both watched the door, waiting for Mek to make a report.

When the doctor arrived, he paused, face down-turned as he read his handheld. Qaiyaan wanted to strangle him for taking so long, yet was hesitant to interrupt the doctor's analysis. Noatak broke the silence. "Stop being an ass, Mek. If you're not ready to talk, go back to the med bay. The captain here's about to go into a rasvrid leviathan rage on our galley furniture."

Mek continued staring at his handheld. "Her brain waves are way off kilter, but it's different from last time. The nanites are reproducing and reprogramming at a rate I can't track. Her synapses can't keep up and I don't know how to stop it. She's so sensitive to energy frequencies, I can't get decent readings with my low-level sensors and I'm afraid anything more intense might make things worse. I've given her a test dose of a synaptic equalizer, but I'm not sure how human physiology will react." He lowered the device. "Can you tell me exactly what happened? Start at the very beginning, from the moment you left the spaceport."

Qaiyaan rose, scrubbing both hands over his face and up through his hair. He relayed every move they'd made, sanitizing their intimacy, yet making it clear they'd taken that step. "But I didn't nudge her, I swear. I went no further with her than any of us have with women during shore leave."

"I warned you that any intimacy could be too much for her." Mek's recriminating gaze barely touched Qaiyaan through his own quagmire of guilt.

"I know." Qaiyaan grabbed the wine and took a long swig directly from the bottle.

Tovik arrived, gaze sweeping from Mek to Qaiyaan. "The hull guy's almost done scanning the damaged panels. What'd I miss?"

Noatak kicked his feet off his makeshift footstool and reached for the bottle. "Mek just made the captain kiss and tell."

"Aw, man!"

"Shut up, you two," Mek warned.

Qaiyaan paced the small galley. The helplessness and rage he felt now were nearly as strong as what he'd felt upon hearing about the destruction of his planet and everyone he loved. "This is all my fault."

Mek once again consulted his handheld. "I wish I understood her nanite programming. It's made her more sensitive to a nudge than even perhaps a denaidan female would be."

Tovik sat next to Noatak. "Or she just doesn't know how to shut the sensitivity off. Isn't that why our women couldn't leave the planet? They couldn't shut out the other races' input?"

Qaiyaan planted both hands on the table. "If she can't shut them off, can we remove them? Purify her blood or whatever?"

Mek's brows drew together. "I'm afraid it's not that simple. They've become so enmeshed with her synapses, removing them may do more harm than good."

An image of Lisa's mind overrun with tiny fucking robots filled Qaiyaan's mind. Robots she could never shut down. "She's still sensing me, isn't she? That's the problem."

"Perhaps. But she should avoid using her nanites until we figure this out."

"*She's* sensing him? Or those Syndicorp nanites are?" Noatak asked. "What if she's transmitting all this straight back to Syndicorp spies? I say we stick her back in cryo."

Mek nodded thoughtfully.

Qaiyaan put his hands on his hips and faced his crew. "We're not sticking her in cryo."

"Don't be so hasty. The idea may have merit." Mek was scrolling his handheld, gaze darting over the information as if he couldn't read it all fast enough.

"She's not a threat to us, not like that," Qaiyaan insisted. "And she nearly died in cryo last time."

"It's not that we don't trust her—" Mek started.

"*I* don't trust her," Noatak said.

Mek frowned at the first mate. "You're not helping." He turned back to Qaiyaan. "Slowing her nanites might break the programming cascade and allow her mind time to regain control. Plus, we still haven't addressed the issue of her withstanding burn frequencies once we leave Bolisare. Cryo would stabilize her until we figure something out."

Qaiyaan took a deep breath, trying to remain rational. Much as he hated to admit it, Mek might be right. "So where do we get a cryopod?"

Tovik drummed his fingers on the table. "I made repairs to her old one. It should work even better now."

Noatak raised an eyebrow. "No offense, Tovik, but I'm not sure we should put her in one of your new and improved inventions."

Qaiyaan nodded. Tovik's most recent improvement to the *Hardship's* lavatory shower had used up half their water supply before they realized what was happening.

"Hey!" Tovik glowered at all three of his crewmen. "My upgrades have saved our asses more times than you can count."

"And I appreciate it when things work, Tovik. I really do. But this isn't the three of us going balls out to escape some heist. This is..."

Qaiyaan wasn't sure how to explain. "This is Lisa. I'll go back to Nupnup and ask for a pod."

An unfamiliar voice spoke from behind him. "Too late for that."

Qaiyaan spun, hands balled into fists. A human male wearing a repairman's jumpsuit blocked the doorway, aiming a fully charged pulse pistol straight between Qaiyaan's eyes.

Lisa felt Qaiyaan's turmoil, a tug that reached deep into her soul and pleaded with her to pull free. The maelstrom surrounding her refused to let her go or even give her a chance to find solid ground within her own mind. Around the edges, she was also aware of the crew scrambling for options. Sweet Tovik's adoring concern. Mek's analytical worry. Even Noatak's grudging and conflicted wish to help her, despite his reluctance to hope. None of these connections could pull her free.

Then her cyber-sensitive nanites picked up an encoded message. They snatched bits out of the turmoil, piecing the packets of information together. There was a stranger on the ship. A Cartel intruder.

And there were more on the way.

Adrenaline flooded her system, honing her focus. She had to warn the crew. The men who'd risked so much to save her were going to suffer and die. The Cartel would punish them for helping her. Torture them as much for fun as retribution. The memory of a rakwiji bounty hunter using its claw to trace a bloody Cartel tattoo over Seloh's chest slammed into her. She had to wake up. Now.

The nanites she'd reprogrammed continued to battle against those locked into Syndicorp protocols. Synapses in her brain fired at random, creating an ever-changing maze she couldn't escape. *You hacked the systems once. You can do it again.* She grabbed hold of one nanite. Just one. It took all the strength she had. But she gave it a single directive.

Wake me up.

The tiny computer burrowed its way through the electronic storm of her mind, dragging her behind like a kite. She bobbed to the surface of consciousness, sucking in a breath as if she'd been underwater. Her eyes flew open, blinded by the soft fluorescent lighting of the medical bay. She was alone in the room. After a couple of breaths to gather her strength, she attempted to sit, but her body refused to obey. *Come on, move!*

One finger at a time, one hand, one arm. She pushed herself upright. Using the nanite that'd brought her awake, she began reprogramming the others. But Syndicorp's programming was fighting back. Her forces were eroding. Instinct told her to shut everything down, initiate a reboot. But that would probably knock her out again, and she wasn't sure she'd ever wake up if that happened. All she could do was create a wall between her consciousness and her cyber-sensitivity to keep the Syndicorp faction at bay.

She swung her legs to the floor, her knees threatening to buckle. Her dress was held together across her chest with strips of medical tape, and an IV line trailed to her arm. She yanked the needle out and planted unsteady palms on the bed for support while she surveyed the med bay for a weapon. Anything to fend off the Cartel infiltrator. She had no idea how he was here, or if the crew even knew about him yet. All she knew was he was waiting for reinforcements. Her hand fell on a pair of scissors, the only remotely aggressive thing in the bay unless she intended to bash him with a scanner. Threading her fingers through the loops, she crept out of the medical bay.

Down the hall, she heard Qaiyaan's outraged voice. "Who the fuck are you?"

A stranger dressed in workman's coveralls had his back to her, bracing himself with one foot in and one foot outside the galley door.

"That's the hull repairman," Tovik said from inside the room.

The man gestured to someone inside. "Pick up the rope and tie your friend, there. You guys made a serious mistake trying to put one over on the Cartel."

Lisa ducked across the corridor into Qaiyaan's quarters and peeked around the doorframe. The galley was two doors down, only about fifteen steps away, but her legs felt weak as jelly. She caught her breath and fought to keep her nanites under control.

"There must be some sort of mistake," Qaiyaan said. "I want to talk to Nupnup."

"Oh, you'll be talking to Nupnup, all right. You can explain to him how you're charging services to a cell Syndicorp took out of commission six months ago."

Lisa's stomach dropped. Of course cell three had been destroyed. That cell had been the point of entry she and Doug had provided when they'd signed on with Syndicorp. How stupid could she be? The code words hadn't been changed because they were obsolete. Now Qaiyaan was in danger because of her mistake.

"Taken out? How the fuck did that happen?" Qaiyaan asked. "We've been in deep cover."

Good explanation, Lisa thought to herself and slid out of the room, creeping toward the stranger. *Keep him talking.*

Lisa?

Qaiyaan's voice in her head sent her to her knees. The scissors went clattering across the metal deck. Stars swam in her vision and she struggled to stay conscious, ordering the few nanites she controlled to subdue her misfiring synapses. She was barely aware of the sound of a struggle, of the zipping noise of a pulse gun, shouting and cursing. She had to help them, but her control of her body was sluggish, as if the nanites were trying to take over her motor skills now, too.

Feet pounded the decking nearby, and hands cradled both sides of her face. She blinked up into Qaiyaan's blue eyes.

"Lisa! Thank *Ellam Cua* you're alive!" he breathed.

Her nanites swarmed toward his touch as if yearning for the contact of his copper skin. But that meant the few she controlled weren't keeping her synapses in line, either. She jerked away, breath coming in painful gasps. "We have to lift off planet. Now."

"I'm all for getting off this hell-hole." Noatak had a knee planted firmly on the Cartel member's back, keeping the guy pinned against the deck. Waves of anger emanated from both men, smashing against her nanite-battered synapses and making her want to curl into a ball.

The stranger struggled, his gaze settling on Lisa. "Lisa Moss?" His eyes narrowed. "The Syndicorp spy. Gedan Jaru will pay big bucks for proof you're alive."

One of his brown eyes went opaque white, then dark again. *Shit.* He had a cybernetic camera. Did he have a transmission unit, too? She couldn't tell without using her nanites, but wasn't sure she could keep her synapses under control if she did. The little computers were going crazy, as if picking up every nearby emotion. The tumult in her head was making it hard to think. "He has a camera in his left eye."

Qaiyaan grabbed the stranger by the hair. "Someone get me a knife."

"What are you doing?" Mek asked.

"Removing his camera."

"He's probably already sent his intel." Mek held out a warning hand. "Cutting it out won't do any good."

"It'll make me feel better," Qaiyaan growled. The protective urges rolling off the big captain might've seemed sexy if Lisa hadn't been so overwhelmed with the emotions pressing in from all around her.

Noatak wrenched the stranger's arm backward at an awkward angle. "He mentioned Syndicorp spies. He could have useful info."

"*Anaq!*" Qaiyaan swore and released his hold.

The stranger bared his teeth, but kept his gaze on Lisa. "I have lots of intel. What's it worth to you?"

CHAPTER THIRTEEN

Lisa held her body stiff as stone, fighting off the oily waves of greed coming from the stranger. But she also sensed a wobble in his emotions. A hesitation that could only mean one thing.

The stranger was stalling, waiting for an opportunity to send the photo to Gedan.

She stared at him, her eyes burning as she realized what that meant. *He doesn't have a transmission unit.* She could delete the picture.

Rising, she wobbled over to the man, dropping to her knees beside him. "I'm going to hack into his camera and erase the picture."

Noatak grabbed both her wrists, stopping her before she made contact. "So you can wipe what he knows about you? I don't think so."

She glowered and jerked away. "I can't reprogram his brain, only his camera."

"How do we know that?"

Lisa balled her hands into fists until her nails cut into her palms, using the pain as a focus. "You don't. But if word gets out I'm alive, every Cartel contact in the galaxy will be after our blood."

Freed from Noatak's arm-wrenching, the stranger propped himself on his elbows, craning his neck to look behind him. "I have a proposition. How about we split the money? She's pretty. We can have some fun with her, then turn her in."

In an instant, Qaiyaan yanked the stranger out from under Noatak and slammed a fist against his cheekbone. With a satisfying crunch, the stranger rocked backward, colliding with the wall before sliding down it in a daze. Qaiyaan loomed over him like a pillar of rage. "How about you shut the fuck up?"

Grimacing, Noatak pointed at Lisa. "If the Cartel wants her this bad, maybe we should give her to them. Making a little cash sounds a hell of a lot better than adding to our list of enemies."

"You want some of this, too, Noatak?" Muscles coiled and hands balled into fists, Qaiyaan stepped toward his first mate.

But Lisa knew Noatak was partially right. The Cartel would never stop coming after her. Anyone associated with her was doomed. Qaiyaan deserved better. The crew of the *Hardship* deserved better. Taking a deep breath, she said, "If the Cartel finds out you helped me, you'll never be safe again. I won't let that happen. Leave me behind."

Qaiyaan scowled and clenched his hands at his sides. "We don't abandon crew members."

Tovik gestured down the hall with his pulse pistol. "We can't leave you. They'll find you for sure."

"I spent most of my life on Whylon Station hiding from one Cartel goon or another." She nodded toward the stranger. "Destroy the camera. And when you're done questioning him, it's probably best if he dies." She hated to think like the Cartel, but she saw no other way.

Pushing to her feet, she ran through potential contacts here on Bolisare. She'd have to start at ground zero, picking pockets and living on the street like she had on Whylon. Only on Whylon, she hadn't had a bounty on her head. Plus, she'd had Doug at her side. How was she going to find him without help? Her vision swam in and out of focus, and she directed all the energy she had into fortifying the walls her nanites had built. She had to stay upright long enough to get off the ship and find a place to hide. Then she'd think about finding Doug.

As if he could read her thoughts, Qaiyaan said, "I promised to find your brother."

She swallowed and took a step toward the cargo bay. "You already rescued me once. For that, I thank you. But I don't need your help."

Qaiyaan crossed his arms, widening his stance to block the narrow corridor. "I'm not leaving you."

All this arguing made it feel like she was standing on a two-g planet. Fierce protectiveness swelled off Qaiyaan in waves, burying Tovik and Mek's concern, and even consuming the stranger's oily greed. Only Noatak's distrust, filling the air around her like a windstorm, pounded against her with an equal force.

Lisa scowled at the first mate. "I'm leaving, Noatak, so stop bombarding me with your doubts. I can barely keep my brain from exploding from Qaiyaan's feelings as it is."

The tension in the room faltered. What could only be described as a curtain dropped between her and the chaos, muting the gale force without completely silencing it. The sudden break from emotional pressure was such a relief she wanted to cry.

Noatak squared himself to face her, his face blank. "You can sense my emotions?"

Lisa nodded.

"Can you sense mine?" Tovik asked.

She smiled weakly. "I think I'd be able to feel yours even without nanites."

"Try to talk to her, Qaiyaan!" the young man said.

Lisa closed her eyes against the renewed pressure of Tovik's excitement. "Tovik, can you scale it back, please?"

"Sorry." The flickering emotion dropped.

Noatak curled his upper lip, but Lisa could sense the hope behind his disgust. "How can a human sense us? She only has one heart."

Uncertainty hung like a cloud around Qaiyaan. "I thought I heard her talking in my head earlier."

Lisa met his gaze, her heartbeat fluttering as she remembered the touch of his mind. "You heard me? I thought I heard you, too. That's what made me trip in the hallway."

Mek scratched his stubbled jaw. "The nanites might be creating a synaptic flow without the aid of a secondary heart. I'd like to try some medication and see if she stabilizes."

"In case you've forgotten, the Cartel will be here any moment." Noatak jammed a knee into the stranger's kidneys and began tying his hands behind his back. "We don't have time for science experiments."

Startled back to the moment, Lisa regarded the stranger and licked her lips. "I still think you'd be safer without me."

"If you think we're letting you go now, you're crazy," Tovik grinned at her. "What I wouldn't give for a woman I could link with."

"Tovik, hush." Turning to Lisa, Qaiyaan sighed. His electric blue eyes sought hers. "Please let Mek do those tests. He may be the only doc in the galaxy who knows how to help you. And us."

She swayed from the tangible power emanating from the captain's powerful frame. She wanted to accept. To stay and make him hers. But if the Cartel caught them, it would be Seloh all over again. She couldn't bear to see Qaiyaan tortured to death like that.

Qaiyaan stepped close and lowered his head until his breath caressed her skin. "I need you to stay with me. Please?"

She raised her eyes to his, biting her lip. If anyone could hold their own against the Cartel, Qaiyaan could. And she needed him. Not just to find Doug, or fix her nanites. She needed his strength. His presence by her side. Taking a deep breath, she nodded. "All right."

Qaiyaan watched Lisa depart to the med bay, her gaze lingering on his until she disappeared around the corner, then turned his attention back to the stranger. "Sure would be handy to have a brig right now, wouldn't it?"

"We should just push him out the back during liftoff." Noatak tightened the rope holding the man's wrists behind his back. "No telling what other cybernetic gizmos he's got on him that might sabotage us."

"We could stick him in the cryo-pod," Tovik said.

"Not a bad idea." Qaiyaan grabbed the stranger by the collar and hoisted him to his feet.

"You were just saying the cryo-pod wasn't working!" the man choked out, struggling feebly against Qaiyaan's grip.

"Would you rather be pushed out the airlock?" Qaiyaan started pushing him toward the cargo bay. "Noatak, get us airborne. Tovik, with me."

After stuffing the struggling and cursing man into the pod and slamming the lid closed, Qaiyaan watched Tovik fiddle with the controls. The man's muffled shouts could be heard through the pod's thick lid, his breath clouding the small window. The light inside alternated from amber to red and back again. Qaiyaan asked, "You sure you don't need Mek?"

"Nah, I got the basics." The light settled on amber, then flashed green. Tovik stood, brushing his hands together in satisfaction. "See?"

"All right." A surge of extra gravity set the deck thrumming. *Liftoff.* So much for getting the *Hardship's* outer plating fixed before they had to endure another burn. *Ellam Cua, let it hold together.* He and his men could withstand the void if the ship popped a seam, but he had a new crew member to consider. What were they going to do with her when it was time to burn? They still hadn't resolved her nanites' sensitivity to burn frequencies.

Tovik headed for the engine room, while Qaiyaan took the catwalk stairs two at a time. He reached the small control room in time to see the pale blue lower atmosphere transition to violet and then black outside the view screen. Mek stood hunched next to Noatak, who leaned over the dashboard from the nav seat. Lisa sat buckled in the captain's chair, her eyes squeezed closed. Someone had given her a loose shirt to wear over the bodice of her dress, but a long, sexy slice of leg still peeked from the side slit.

Noatak's fingers darted over the command surface, guiding the ship to avoid incoming traffic. "Air control isn't happy with us right now."

Qaiyaan couldn't read the screens from his position at the door, and there were already too many bodies in the cramped space. "How long until we clear the buffer?"

"Sixteen or seventeen minutes, assuming I can avoid any orbiting Cartel." Noatak tapped an adjustment into his controls as a spiny garan'uk pleasure vehicle slid past the view screen. "You have a destination in mind?"

"Any place but here."

"If we find my brother," Lisa's voice could barely be heard over the engines. "He can reprogram my nanites."

Qaiyaan put a hand on the door frame to steady himself as the ship rocked under Noatak's guidance. "Let's tackle one thing at a time, okay? We need to clear air control."

The deck shuddered, and Noatak made another adjustment to his controls. "We've got a tail."

"*Anaq*," Qaiyaan swore. A tail already? He squinted at the viewscreen, unable to tell friend from foe among the scattered couriers and cargo vessels coming and going from the surface. But Noatak had done this often enough; Qaiyaan trusted he was right. "Can we slingshot off the atmosphere, straight to burn?"

"Lisa can't take the stress unshielded," Mek said.

Qaiyaan leveled him with a gaze. "I'm fully aware of that. We'll have to stabilize her like we did last time."

Mek said, "You can't—"

"Don't lecture me about over-using recovery stims," Qaiyaan interrupted, acutely aware of Noatak's addiction to the drug. Everyone generally tread carefully around the subject with him. "We don't have time to argue. We can do this."

"*We* probably can." Mek pointed between himself and Tovik. "*You* can't. You send her into a coma when you touch her."

Air suddenly refused to enter Qaiyaan's lungs. How could he have forgotten that? *Because you don't want it to be true.* He met Lisa's gaze. Her eyes had the same glazed look he remembered his sister having after her empathic suppression classes. "Can the two of you stabilize her?"

Mek glanced at Tovik and shook his head. "Not alone."

Qaiyaan swallowed and faced Noatak, who remained facing the controls. His friend had been with him long before the planet's destruction and was as close to Qaiyaan as a brother. They'd enlisted together and served on the same task force with the troopers. They'd grieved together at the loss of their world. And Qaiyaan had been at Noatak's side every moment his friend had struggled to overcome his stim addiction. But he needed to help Lisa. *They* needed to help Lisa. She held the key to their future, Noatak's included.

Before Qaiyaan could even form the words to ask, though, Noatak swiveled in his seat. "Take the helm. And watch your six for that tail."

"*Iluq*, are you sure?" If Qaiyaan'd ever felt guilt in his life, it was nothing compared to this moment.

Noatak's voice remained calm and quiet. "We don't leave crew behind."

Chest tight, Qaiyaan spared a final glance at Lisa as he slid into the nav seat. He wasn't nearly as good a pilot as Noatak, but he'd get them out of here.

From the door, Mek said, "Give a shout when you're ready to burn."

"Keep her safe," Qaiyaan called back. But Mek and Lisa were already down the corridor. He felt their departure like a void.

CHAPTER FOURTEEN

Qaiyaan banked the *Hardship* starboard as he cleared Bolisare's atmosphere. They'd been strafed by at least one laser blast during their escape, adding to the hull's numerous scars, but he'd lost their tail by weaving between the thick stream of traffic coming in and out of the station. Luckily, the Cartel didn't appear to have a ship waiting in orbit, and Qaiyaan skimmed the planet's gravitational pull while picking up speed. He planned to slingshot off the nearby moon—a highly illegal move in most populated systems— but this was Bolisare, not some Syndicorp-governed speed bump. He intended to use every advantage to get them as far away as possible.

He programmed the burn drive to aim for the Milicon quadrant, a parsec away from Aleigh. His constant tracking of Syndicorp CEOs and shipping activity gave him the gut feeling that the lab Lisa was looking for might be at that particular edge of Syndicorp space. While the burn drive pulled at every molecule of his being, he gripped the arms of the nav chair and stared at the holocube Noatak kept on the dashboard, the image of his parents a constant reminder of what Syndicorp had destroyed. A constant reminder of their mission as pirates. Stealing Lisa's brother from Syndicorp's clutches was going to be satisfying on so many levels.

The burn itself only took a handful of seconds, but it always felt like the event lasted hours. When the galaxy finally realigned itself, Qaiyaan checked his sensors for nearby ships. Unless a ship had been in his immediate wake and prepped for burn, he couldn't have been followed. But he hadn't lived this long by not being careful. Scanners showed nothing but empty space. Good. He needed to check on Lisa and the rest of his crew. Lifting himself on unsteady legs, he stumbled out of the control room airlock and down the stairs to the med bay.

Lisa was sitting up on the medical table, forehead pressed against her bent knees. Qaiyaan took a deep breath of relief. "Thank *Ellam Cua* you're all right."

She let out a shaky gasp in response, as if unable to summon anything more.

He wanted—needed—to pull her against him, to feel her heartbeat against his. To reassure himself she was indeed alive and whole. But touching her would definitely not accomplish that. A bone-deep sorrow filled him, knowing that his deepest desire might forever remain out of his reach. Instead, he knelt next to Tovik, who was slumped on the floor against the medical bay cot. Mek and Noatak were similarly sprawled around the bed. They must've all stood around her for the burn, holding her and then collapsing with exhaustion afterward.

Qaiyaan reached out to find Tovik's pulse. Alive but unconscious. He rose and checked the other two, then stepped over the doctor's body, opening the cabinet where they kept the recovery stims. Priming the stim gun with a dose, he administered it to Mek.

The doctor stiffened, eyelids flying open, pupils constricted to pinpricks. He sat up unsteadily, his voice thick and languid, but coherent. "The others?"

"I wanted you up and running first." Qaiyaan primed the stim gun with a second dose.

Mek nodded. "Noatak wants to recover on his own. I'll see to him. You handle Tovik."

A lump filled Qaiyaan's throat, and he moved to the young man. Much like Mek, Tovik awakened with a start, eyes wild. But he also had a grin on his face. "Whoa." He twisted and pulled himself upright to peer at Lisa over the edge of her bed. "Wild ride, but we did it."

Lisa looked out of the corner of her eye at the young man, a tiny smile tweaking the corner of her mouth.

Tovik's enthusiasm was infectious as always, but Qaiyaan's thoughts remained heavy. Mek was arranging a limp Noatak on the second med cot. The energy required to hold one's self through burn was bearable. Using it to hold another person steady was exponentially more exhausting. Noatak would take days to bounce back without the aid of stims.

Adjusting the gown around her legs, Lisa swung her legs over the edge of the bed, her attention also on the doctor's activity. "Will Noatak be all right?"

Mek's lips remained tight.

An inkling of fear settled in Qaiyaan's hearts. "Will he?" He searched for Noatak's ionic signature. His first mate's hearts beat slowly, nearly undetectable, but steady. "Thank *Ellam Cua*."

The doctor turned to gather supplies from the cupboards. His hands were shaking, full of erratic, stim-induced energy. "Give him some time."

Lisa stood, her bare feet making no sound on the floor, and moved to Noatak's side. The fingers of one hand fluttered over her mouth. "This is because of me. God, what if he dies?" She looked up at Qaiyaan. "You shouldn't have let him do this."

Noatak's voice creaked from the cot. "I'm not dead."

An exclamation of surprise escaped Lisa, and she leaned down to press her cheek to Noatak's.

Tovik, still sitting on the floor, let out what could only be called a giggle, his fingers waggling in response to whatever stim-inspired ideas were swimming through his head. "Noatak's too bad-tempered to die."

Qaiyaan turned to shove the stim gun back into its cabinet. He longed for Lisa's touch, her cheek against his. The sensation of her voice in his head earlier could only mean one thing—she was his mate. Their resonances aligned. Yet despite the connection, despite his conviction that she was the one, he'd never be able to touch her. Never be able to truly make her his own.

The overhead lights flickered as if in response to his thoughts, and the hull groaned. *Anaq, what else can go wrong?* Qaiyaan spun and stepped over Tovik toward the door. "I should check our system. No telling what that guy in our cryo-pod did to the ship before this all started."

Noatak pushed Lisa away and tried to sit up. "I'll help."

Mek placed one palm flat against the prone man's chest. "Don't try to move. I need to check your secondary heart."

"What's wrong with his heart?" Qaiyaan paused halfway across the small bay.

The doctor and Noatak exchanged a glance. "It's nothing, captain," Noatak said. "Just let the doc do his job. You concentrate on finding this mystical, magical brother who can fix Lisa's nanites. I can't hold her steady every time we engage the burn drive."

Lisa snuck in one last flutter of her fingertips over Noatak's brow. "Thank you again."

He scowled and rolled his eyes, which was about as much of a "you're welcome" as Noatak ever gave anyone.

Noatak grunted, ignoring the doctor's orders, and sat up. His copper skin seemed abnormally dark, its satiny gleam dulled by a greenish cast. "I can get started looking for that secret lab. Where'd you eject us, Captain?"

"Milicon sector. Captain Kashatok's been working the shipping lanes here since the Termination. He might know something."

Mek let his scanner fall to his side and glared at Qaiyaan. "You're going to trust that drunken excuse for a denaidan?"

"He knows the sector," Qaiyaan insisted, ignoring the nausea riding low in his belly. Kashatok ran one of the seedier crews among the denaidan pirates, but he was also the only actual Cartel member among the fleet and a source of valuable intel.

"I can hack into the darkweb," Lisa said. "I'm sure I still have contacts who—"

"No." Noatak and Mek said simultaneously.

Tovik dragged himself onto the mattress like a nerelian ice slug. "You can access the dark web?" His words were slurred. "Can you track down the schematic for a pynergic quark converter there?"

"We have more pressing concerns, Tovik." Qaiyaan tried to glare, but concern for his engineer weighed heavily on his already guilty-as-hell conscience. Two stim doses this close together could cause serious damage.

Mek sighed and plodded over with a scanner. "I'd better sedate him. Hold still, Tovik."

Qaiyaan turned to Lisa. "The darkweb's too dangerous. We have to assume your contacts have been compromised." The lights browned out and flickered back up again, accompanied by a throaty vibration through the deck plating.

"I should check the hull." Noatak attempted to rise but ended up flopping back down on the cot.

"I told you to stay put," Mek said, leaning heavily on the edge of Tovik's cot.

"You should rest, too." Lisa pushed the chair from the nearby computer toward him.

"A doctor's job is never done." Yet Mek's big frame collapsed onto the chair, bending forward to rest his head on the edge of the mattress next to Tovik.

Qaiyaan took a deep breath. Between Tovik and Noatak, Mek had his hands full. Yet the hull needed checking, which meant someone had to go outside. A diagnostic needed to be run to make sure the electrical system wasn't going to short-out life-support. He had a prisoner in the cargo bay who should be looked in on. Everything fell on Qaiyaan's shoulders.

"You have an extra crew member now." Lisa moved to within arm's length, sexy as hell in that loose shirt over her gold, form-fitting dress, her charcoal hair in an alluring disarray.

"You know how to run a ship diagnostic?"

She raised an eyebrow and tapped her temple. "I'm pretty sure we can figure it out."

Mek sat up woozily. "The synaptic equalizer I gave her could wear off unexpectedly. She should avoid using her nanites. Let me do it."

Lisa crossed her arms. "I can run auto-checks without using my nanites. You need to stay here." She moved to the door before anyone could deny her. "Besides, I know computer systems far better than I understand alien physiology."

Qaiyaan couldn't help checking out her perfectly rounded ass until she disappeared around the corner. If it took him the rest of his life, he'd look for a way to be together, starting with finding her brother. He snapped out of his lustful thoughts and dodged through the doorway after her. "Seal the airlock behind you. I've got to void the ship so I can work on the hull. I'll be sealing off the cargo bay, but I'd prefer you behind double airlocks. I'll let you know when it's safe again."

"Be careful, okay? I'm not talented enough to make this ship chase you if you go floating off into space."

He chuckled and reached for her, intending to give her a kiss, then caught himself. They exchanged an awkward glance, then turned their separate ways.

CHAPTER FIFTEEN

Lisa sealed the airlock and settled into the captain's chair, pulling up the ship's diagnostics. The injection Mek'd given her just before burn had eased the chaos in her head. She knew the nanites were still warring, but her synapses no longer fired in response to the attacks. The doctor had explained how it all worked; something about human synapses being promiscuous and hooking up in new ways? The biology was way over her head, so she'd just nodded and been grateful for the relief, however temporary he warned her it could be.

On the dashboard, she slid aside a holocube displaying the 3D image of a much younger Noatak wearing an innocent smile sitting next to a man and a woman. His parents? She'd have to take a closer look later. Right now, she needed to figure out this ship's systems. The control panel lit up with several segments of data at her touch. During her time in the corp lab, she'd practiced hacking ship systems, but it had never been intuitive for her. She could recognize basic sequences without the aid of her nanites, so she looked for the code controlling life-support.

Every vessel's interface was slightly different, and after setting life-support's auto-diagnostic, she noted the ship had an internal camera system. After a few minutes of fumbling, she engaged the one in the cargo bay. An image came on-screen just in time to show Qaiyaan venting the bay door, the barest hint of a shimmer around his body. He'd explained that he could endure the vacuum of space for ten or twenty minutes—even longer if he didn't exert himself. She bit her lip, sure he was about to be sucked out of reach. But his feet remained locked to the floor, his long hair and beard pulled outward in the escaping air.

As if sensing her watching him, he looked over his shoulder at the camera and nodded once. His cochlear implant would allow her to speak to him through the comm, but he couldn't respond in the vacuum. His flowing hair relaxed into a billowing halo at the same moment her stomach fell out from under her; the gravity system had dropped. *Whoa.* He hadn't mentioned losing gravity. Her ass lifted off the captain's seat, and she put a hand up to keep from bumping her head on the ceiling.

Luckily, the control room was small, and she grappled for the safety straps on the chair. The ship shuddered while the big bay doors cranked the rest of the way open. Qaiyaan took a few slow steps down the cargo ramp. His broad shoulders cut angular lines across the velvet blackness of space beyond. As if he wore a full vacuum-worker's suit, he walked around the edge and disappeared.

She checked the scrolling diagnostics again. Several blinking red lines indicated issues, but they'd already been flagged at some point by the crew and obviously pushed aside until later. She was looking for something new. One of the panels chirped at her, and she scanned the surface of the dash for the source. The proximity sensor. Probably Qaiyaan walking around on the ship. She returned to the diagnostic. The ship shuddered, rocking her in her seat harness. Frowning, she looked at the cargo bay camera again and gasped. The dull, black patina of a Cartel courier ship sat parked in the bay.

"Qaiyaan!" She scrambled toward the comm. "There's a Cartel ship in our cargo bay!" Where had it come from? Had they seen him?

The small black ship's doors winged open, disgorging two rakwiji in vacuum helms, packing military-grade pulse pistols. Their hard, scaly hides allowed their bodies to withstand vacuum without a suit. Bile rose in her throat. "Two rakwiji with pistols."

She didn't even know if Qaiyaan could hear her. What if he hadn't seen them and came back to a trap? She had to do something. She looked around for a vacuum suit, but the control room was empty.

Qaiyaan's voice filled her head, solid as if he was standing right next to her. *Stay put. I'm coming.*

Her breath choked off at the sensation of him in her mind. Her nanites shot woozy sparks across her vision. Was Mek's shot wearing off?

One of the bounty hunters clumped to the bay door controls, magnetic grav-boots slowing his movements. It carried a disk the size of a man's footprint. At the control panel, it slapped the disk over the keyboard.

The doors began to close.

Her vision swelled and shrank in time to her thundering heartbeat. She keyed the comm again. "Hurry, Qaiyaan! The doors!"

Fingers flying over the controls, she tried to override whatever the invaders had done. Error messages popped up across every screen. ACCESS DENIED. They'd placed some kind of lock on it, probably that big disk. The doors sealed shut with a thump she could feel through the deck. Terror settled like a rock in her stomach. How long could Qaiyaan stay out there? "I can't override them!"

Warn the others. His voice floated into her mind again.

She engaged the comm to the med bay. "Mek, Noatak, Tovik, wake up!"

No response.

She pulled up a second screen with a view to the med bay. All three men lay sound asleep, strapped to the medical cots to keep them in place without gravity. Again, she keyed the comm. "We're being boarded! Wake up!"

The men didn't budge. She called Qaiyaan again. "I can't wake them up."

He didn't respond, either.

She scanned the comm diagnostics. The comm wasn't transmitting.

She'd been locked out. She couldn't warn the crew or Qaiyaan. She was all alone and rakwiji were on board. Her heart threatened to break through her ribcage. *Qaiyaan!*

Stop panicking. His mental voice was calm. Reassuring.

She took a deep breath, looking around as if he might appear next to her. *You can hear me?*

Yes. Now tell me what's happening.

Her nanites hummed at the edge of wakefulness, but she tamped them down. She wasn't sure how she was talking to Qaiyaan without them, but she knew in her gut she couldn't give them control. *They have the ship systems completely locked down; communications, navigation, even life support.*

There's another access portal near the thrusters. His thoughts sounded strained. *Can you open it?*

I'll try. Eager for a solution, she read through lines of code, looking for a way around the block the rakwiji had put on the systems. If only Doug were here. A block like this would be nothing more than an inconvenience for him, even before he'd received the nanites.

Full gravity returned with a jarring rush, pressing her into the seat cushions and slamming her arms against the control panel. She checked on the men in the med bay again, but they still hadn't budged. They must be even more exhausted than they'd let on. Either that or Mek'd given them something to help them rest. She wished she had sight of Qaiyaan, but she could no longer access the other cameras.

She continued trying to hack into the portal in engineering. Panic was making her brain jumpy. How would Doug look at this code? Maybe if she thought like him, she could find a way in.

The rakwiji crouched in feral positions, conversing next to their ship, their helms still in place. Although they'd engaged gravity, they'd elected not to reestablish atmosphere. They probably thought they had the crew at a disadvantage. The larger one pointed to a nearby cargo box, a sharp-toothed grin visible inside its face-plate. A familiar, blinking green light illuminated the viewport on what had been her cryo-pod.

The smaller rakwiji moved toward it, its mate scuttling close behind. The two exchanged leering gazes, and then the first rakwiji extended a necrotic claw, tracing the viewport. With slow, almost sensuous movements, it tapped a command into the pod's control panel. The second rakwiji rocked back and forth, scales rippling with excitement as the light in the pod flashed red.

The lid popped open, and Lisa could imagine the hiss of escaping air as the Cartel guy half-fell from the box. He rolled onto his side, looking up at his rescuers with a horrible grimace. His face turned purple and his eyes bulged. One pleading hand extended toward them, but the rakwiji only stepped back and watched, toothy grins gleaming through their faceplates. Lisa couldn't look away, reminded of Seloh's torturous death at rakwiji hands. Is this what would happen to Qaiyaan when he could no longer keep up his shield? She wanted to vomit.

Jabbing at the control panels, Lisa tried to force the internal comm system to work. Tried to think like her brother. But her clumsy hacking attempts only covered her screens in error messages. She had to warn the crew. Make them get up. Get ready for battle. But they were all but helpless in the med bay.

With the Cartel man dead, the rakwiji headed for the catwalk, side-by-side like the prey animals they were.

Qaiyaan, they just killed their own man. Silence roared in her ears. *Qaiyaan?*

I'm working on it. Qaiyaan's frustration pounded at her. His need to breathe couldn't be masked. He was running out of air.

She pictured his face, his beautiful copper skin darkening, his features disfiguring. Adrenaline had her hands trembling as her fingertips pounded the control panel with every hacker command she knew.

ACCESS DENIED.

Qaiyaan's voice reached her, faint along the mental connection. *I want you to know that I love you, Lisa.*

Every muscle in her body tingled. This was not how she wanted to hear his feelings. *Don't give up.*

She stared at the error boxes plastered across her screens. Her skills weren't good enough, not without help. There was only one thing to do. Squeezing her eyes shut, she placed her palms flat against the dashboard and gathered her nanites. Qaiyaan would die if she didn't get him inside. She needed to override the lockouts, to at least give him and the others a chance.

Packets of cyber-information threatened to knock her flat against the nav chair.

Don't. Qaiyaan's voice held command, even though she could sense he was failing. *I'll figure something out.*

There's no time. Savoring the last brush of his mind across hers, she said, *I love you, Qaiyaan.*

And dove into the ship's system.

CHAPTER SIXTEEN

Qaiyaan stared at the blackened streak across the *Hardship's* hull, his oxygen-deprived brain turning the laser damage into a monstrous grin under the beam of his headlamp. *Lisa?* She was no longer answering his thoughts. His heart beat too rapidly in his ears, burning precious oxygen at a rate he couldn't afford. *Anaq, Lisa, answer me!*

He grimaced at the damage and pounded a fist against the plating. His body lifted away, free-floating toward open space. Clamping his fingers around the edge of the nearby landing fin, he dragged himself back toward the ship. Maintaining his ionic connection was becoming more difficult.

Maybe you should just let go. If Lisa was gone, what did he have to live for, anyway? His crew was comatose, at the mercy of Cartel bounty hunters who would probably chop up the *Hardship* for salvage—right after they chopped up the crew.

No. That was the oxygen deprivation talking. He'd die before he gave up.

Hand-over-hand, he pulled himself between the landing fins and paused at the sealed access door into engineering. The entry panel was dark and unresponsive. *Anaq.* He'd hoped Lisa would be successful.

That some miracle might give him a fighting chance. Instead, the woman he loved was in trouble. *Lisa, wake up!*

He couldn't feel her in his mind like he had before. He panned the light of his headlamp along the hull again, as if the dull metal surface might provide more options. His lungs burned with a desire for air. The Cartel ship must've pulled into the *Hardship's* wake mere moments before the burn and somehow hidden here in a blind spot between the fins during his initial scans. Sneaky Cartel bastards.

The comm webbing embedded across the hull was broken by laser fire in a couple of places. Tovik had connected an external booster to the comm array to act as an independent backup if they took too much damage. The chance of someone being within signal range was slim to none, but at the very least, Qaiyaan wanted to leave a message. A legacy. The other denaidans out there deserved to know how close he'd been to finding a mate. Mek's medical notes had to be worth something.

Edging along the ship's exterior, he reached the comm junction and had to pause to calm his breathing. The dire cold of space was leaching through his shield and sinking into his bones, making it hard to move. His fingers were stiff, but he managed to open the junction box. Inside, Tovik's booster keypad was affixed to the side wall. The micro-screen blazed to life at Qaiyaan's touch. Using the frequency the denaidan fleet used to alert each other of Syndicorp activity, he entered the ship's coordinates then encoded the message:

Under attack by Cartel. Medical breakthrough on board.

The message was so inadequate. He laughed, and the expulsion of air caused his oxygen shield to slip. Icy vacuum nipped at his skin before he re-established control. Fuck it, he thought, and typed in:

If you ever hope to have sex again, send help.

That ought to get the fleet's attention. Putting the broadcast on repeat, he headed back toward the access door to engineering. The message would continue to play until the booster's battery pack ran out. Maybe someone in this sector would stumble across it. Someday. After he and Lisa were long gone.

Ahead of him, the door's keypad looked like it was glowing. His vision swam, stars pressing in around the edges of consciousness. His ribcage felt as if bands were tightening around his torso, keeping him from taking a full breath. Staying connected to the ship took every bit of his concentration. He reached the access door, every muscle quivering with cold and exhaustion.

The keypad was live.

Lisa steeled herself and hacked at the blocking codes like she was wielding a machete. Each blow sent her reeling backward into darkness. Pulling herself out of the depths to renew her attack grew more and more difficult. She'd never been as good as Doug. Never would be, with or without the nanites. She wished for her brother, wished to know he was okay. Or at least tell him goodbye. *Doug, I'm sorry. I wanted to find you.*

Little Sis, is that you? The words froze her in place. They couldn't be real. Could they?

Doug?

Lisa? Are you here? Unlike Qaiyaan's rich, reverberant tones, this voice had a tinny quality, but it was Doug.

Thank God you're alive! she projected, her nanites thrumming like live wires. *Where are you?*

Syndicorp told me you were dead. His uncertainty reminded her of their years in the slums, each day a question of survival.

It's okay, Doug. Lisa reached through the connection for her twin, seeking to ground herself, to ground them both. The physical contact might not be there, but the mental one felt just as real. *The corp didn't kill me, but the Cartel is hot on my tail. We're under attack by bounty hunters, and I can't remove the block on this ship's systems. My nanites aren't strong enough. Can you help fix them like you used to?*

Cartel? How did they find you?

Doug, there's no time to go into that. I need your help right now!

We're communicating faster than you realize. Doug's presence fluttered through her mind, as if turning the pages of a book. *The mind can process thousands of gigabytes per second, and memories are just data, after all. Your ship must be acting like an antenna between our nanites.* In nanoseconds, he knew everything; Syndicorp's betrayal, Mek's work on her synapses, her newfound telepathy, and her growing love for a copper-skinned alien. In return, she sensed a series of bright lights and examination tables, advanced implants, escape attempts, and a heartbreaking sense of loss from her brother.

Doug, what have they done to you? This was her twin, the person she'd shared everything with since before birth. Yet he was somehow different. Something was really wrong.

Soon your body won't be your own anymore, Doug responded, heartbreak in his voice. *The nanites will take over. You'll be more machine than human. They're nearing critical system deployment already.*

Shock loosed her grip on him. *What are you saying?*

You need to get rid of them. The sooner the better. They're changing you, and once they engage their core protocols, you won't be able to live without them. Syndicorp will own you. As they do me.

No! Tell me where you are! Once we rescue you, we can come up with a plan to use our nanites against the corp.

His presence slipped from her grasp like mist. *It's too dangerous. Don't look for me. Stay far away.*

Stop being overprotective. Qaiyaan and his crew have promised to help me. As soon as I wake up and get rid of these bounty hunters, we're coming to find you. She stretched out and grabbed hold of him, this time refusing to let go. *Have you tried to reprogram your own nanites? I've done it a little with mine, and you're way better at this stuff than I am.*

You think too much of me. His wry smile transferred through their connection as if she was looking at his face. *Unfortunately, I can't reprogram their core function. I've tried. The machines will conquer the biological part of you in the end. The only option is to get rid of them.*

Dread chilled her to the bones. *How am I supposed to get rid of them?*

They are sensitive to certain ionic frequencies. With the right kind of electromagnetic pulse, they become inert. Of all things, it felt like Doug gave her a wicked grin. *I believe your denaidan friend may be able to help you with that.*

What are you talking about? Lisa's adrenaline was making her thoughts jumpy. *I can't even wake up right now, let alone find Qaiyaan, regain control of the ship, or defeat the rakwiji on board.*

I can't help you with the rakwiji, but I can reset your nanites for now and help you with the ship. With that, Doug grabbed hold of her nanites and twisted their programming at the same time he shattered the ship's lockouts. As she reeled from the backlash of power, his presence receded into the abyss. *Love you, Little Sis.*

aiyaan slapped the airlock button, barely waiting for the door to open before squeezing himself inside. Lisa had done it. This could only mean she was alive. *Lisa, you did it! I'm in!*

No answer. Was she unconscious? Mek had said it was dangerous for her to use her nanites. Possibly even deadly. He had to get to her, quickly.

Inside the airlock, the interior seal stood ajar. The bounty hunters had re-engaged gravity, but not life support, which probably meant they were suited up. Wouldn't they be surprised to discover the crew could resist vacuum? *Most of the crew.* The denaidan ability to endure space wouldn't help Lisa if the bounty hunters forced open the door. He had to get life support up and running.

Depressing the button to close both doors, he slipped between the gleaming, angular machinery that filled Tovik's domain. The engineering control panel was near the ladder up to the main level. Where were the bounty hunters at this moment? It was too much to hope they'd come straight to engineering. They'd head for the control room, and Lisa'd said they carried pistols.

He looked around for a weapon, anything that might improve his chances against armed invaders. Next to the burn drive, Tovik's messy tool cabinet hung open, spanners and spare parts strewn across the decking. A battered pulse pistol lay among the scattered items.

Qaiyaan snatched it up and tucked it into his waistband. These bounty hunters were going to regret boarding his ship. He re-initiated life support, knowing the hiss of air through the ducts would take away the element of surprise.

Pistol ready, he poked his head from the trap door. The corridor was empty. From the direction of the med bay, a grunt of pain broke through the thin air. He pulled himself clear of the hatch and launched himself toward the open door. Inside, broken medical equipment littered the floor. Two rakwiji, their scales rippling with excitement, held Mek trapped in one corner. He stood bracing himself against the cabinet with both arms, his shirt slashed and darkened with turquoise blood. Tovik and Noatak both lay unconscious on their beds.

The smaller rakwiji slashed out with a knife, adding to the cuts on Mek's chest. Mek flinched, but had nowhere to go. The larger bounty hunter, who held a pulse pistol aimed at the doctor's head, removed its helmet, revealing a flared crest of scales as it lifted its muzzle toward the hissing life support duct.

"Hey!" Qaiyaan shouted, taking aim at the larger rakwiji and pulling the trigger.

Nothing happened.

Both rakwiji bared gleaming razor teeth and the big one swiveled its gun toward Qaiyaan.

Qaiyaan pulled the useless trigger again, then flung the weapon at his attackers before ducking back into the corridor. Plasma from the rakwiji's weapon impacted the corridor wall behind him, sending visible ripples of heat through the air. The smaller bounty hunter burst around the corner on the heels of the blast, still armed with the curved knife.

Typical rakwiji. They got off on playing with their prey. Qaiyaan obliged by stepping forward and ramming an ionically-powered fist into his attacker's scaled solar plexus. The surge of power through his already tired system threatened to buckle his knees, and his knuckles flared in pain against the creature's hard thorax. But the pressure sent the rakwiji flying halfway down the hall.

The bigger creature burst through the door and slammed into Qaiyaan, crashing him to the deck. Its cloyingly sweet yet sulfurous breath made Qaiyaan's eyes water.

Bringing up a knee, Qaiyaan wedged it between their bodies, using his ionic power to hurl this attacker off. He rolled toward the med bay, reaching for the bounty hunter's pulse pistol where it had fallen to the floor.

The big rakwiji lunged again, burying a necrotic claw into Qaiyaan's calf. Leg flaring in agony, Qaiyaan twisted, snarling at his attacker. Yanking its claw free, the bounty hunter opened its toothy mouth, its words a throaty growl. "I will peel that shiny copper skin from your body before you die."

Venom pulsed a fiery trail up Qaiyaan's leg. He had only minutes until it reached his heart. He had to kill his attacker now, before it finished him and moved on to his crew and Lisa. Both hearts pounding furiously, he grabbed a scalpel from the scattered implements on the floor. He jackknifed toward his attacker, slashing the blade at its throat.

The scalpel skittered ineffectually across the rakwiji's scaled hide.

The rakwiji laughed, tongue lolling between its spear-tipped grin. It opened its mouth wider and lunged as if to tear out Qaiyaan's throat.

Qaiyaan thrust the scalpel forward again, aiming for the creature's mouth. Humid breath encircled his hand and wrist, razor-sharp teeth grazing his skin. The rakwiji stiffened, trying to halt, but there was too much momentum behind its attack. With every ounce of ionic power he had left, Qaiyaan drove the blade upward through the rakwiji's palette and into its brain.

The beast collapsed, teeth digging into Qaiyaan's arm as it fell. From the doorway, the smaller rakwiji made a horrific screech as a pulse pistol blast cut the air above Qaiyaan's head. The creature turned and fled.

Twisting to free himself from the death throes of the big rakwiji, Qaiyaan spotted Mek holding both pulse pistols in trembling hands. The doctor set the weapons aside and turned to fumble in his medical supply cabinet.

Qaiyaan tried to rise to his feet, but the poison was taking hold of his muscle control. The skin showing through the tear in his pants was no longer copper, but a gnarled and lumpy web of black as the poison leached into his bloodstream. He flopped awkwardly against the deck. "I need to get to Lisa."

"We need to reverse the poison or you'll be dead within minutes. *Ellam Cua*, I know I have a vial of antidote here somewhere. Aha!" Mek turned, holding an inoculation gun and a handful of vials. "Hold on, captain. This'll take a minute to work."

Qaiyaan's tongue had grown too thick to speak. While Mek cut away his pants, Qaiyaan stared at the door where the alien had disappeared. *Lisa, can you hear me? It's coming for you!*

CHAPTER SEVENTEEN

Lisa opened her eyes, her head pounding. The control panel still scrolled its diagnostics, all systems green. He'd done it! Thank God! *Doug, are you still there?* No response. *Qaiyaan, can you hear me?* She received a garbled blast of pain instead of words. *Qaiyaan!*

Leaning forward to look at the camera images, she clutched the arms of the chair. A huge rakwiji had a claw buried in Qaiyaan's leg. "No!"

She lurched upright, but the chair's gravity restraints held her down. Fumbling with the buckles, she followed the struggle on the monitor. *Qaiyaan!* She wriggled loose and started for the door, then paused. A weapon. She needed a weapon. She scoured the small control room. How could these men call themselves pirates when they didn't even keep weapons in here?

Her gaze lit upon the small holocube of Noatak's family. It wouldn't be much of a threat as a missile, but the dozens of small beams it used to form the holo-image could be focused to create a low-level torch. *Better than nothing.* Muttering a quick apology to Noatak, she grabbed the cube and cracked open the casing. Weapon in hand, she cycled open the airlock door.

A rakwiji stood in the corridor clutching a curved knife.

It growled, spittle flying from its teeth and head crest flaring. Lisa swung her makeshift laser toward its face, squeezing the power cell. Her aim was off. The modified beam danced ineffectually across the rakwiji's shoulder.

A wide row of pointed teeth slowly appeared on its face. "The little human tries to poke me with a pin light? Do you think I am a Xeimir worm, afraid of the sun?"

Lisa's heart hammered. The rakwiji was so close, she could smell its sulfurous breath. The lasers might not be able to pierce its scaled hide, but that didn't mean her weapon was worthless. Taking aim again, she slashed the light across the bridge of the creature's muzzle, pointing it directly into its eyes.

The rakwiji dropped the knife, roaring and pressing both hands over its face. Unfortunately, it also remained blocking the doorway.

Praying the blindness lasted, Lisa crouched to retrieve the knife from beneath its feet.

The rakwiji slashed the air where she'd stood only moments before.

Blade in hand, Lisa squirmed backward, keeping the navigator seat between her and the yowling rakwiji. The blade would be useless against its scales, but it still felt better to be holding a weapon.

"You will be my final trophy." The rakwiji's eyes wept tears, and the entire room stank from its breath. "My mate and I will rut over your pain throughout eternity."

Lisa searched for a way out, but the rakwiji's bulk left no room to slip past. Sooner or later, its claws would find her. She shrank against the control panel, palm slick around the knife handle. The rakwiji took another shuffling step forward, still cursing, its legs wide as it sought her out.

Her gaze fell on the one place a rakwiji didn't have scales—its crotch. Dropping to her hands and knees, Lisa squeezed under the edge of the navigator's chair. She only had one chance. Once she let the creature know where she was, it would bury its claws into her. Pulling back her arm, she coiled every ounce of her strength.

The rakwiji stepped forward.

She drove the weapon into its genitals.

The knife sank to the hilt, sending hot blood pouring over Lisa's fingers. The rakwiji's expletives cut off mid-insult.

Yanking the knife free, Lisa somersaulted forward. She reached the door and chanced a look over her shoulder.

The bounty hunter was on its knees, clawed hands between its legs. A geyser of blood pulsed from between its fingers. "*Rrhuk'ni,* carry me into the afterlife, where I may rut in the blood of my enemies for all eternity."

Lisa curled her lips in disgust. "Have fun trying to enjoy your afterlife without any junk, you asshole."

She then fled toward the medical bay.

Qaiyaan opened his eyes, surrounded by the familiar walls of his cabin, to find Lisa gazing down at him.

Her cool hand brushed the hair from his forehead. "You're awake."

She was touching him. Lying next to him on his bunk, propped on one elbow, her body pressed along his. Which could only mean one thing; they were both dead, and this was *Ellam Cua's* final gift. He reached out to stroke her satin cheek. "I'm sorry."

"For what?"

"For letting us die. But I'm glad *Ellam Cua* has placed us together."

Lisa smiled and leaned forward to brush her lips against his. "We're not dead, silly."

Qaiyaan wrapped his hand around the back of her neck and drew her toward him again, craving her musky lilac scent. Her lips felt pliable and oh, so real. "I'm touching you," he murmured against her softness. "So we're either dead or this is a dream."

Her tongue flickered between his lips, teasing him. For long moments, he was lost in the coaxing warmth of her mouth, the intimacy of her pillowy breasts against his side. His cock throbbed in response, but his leg still tingled from the rakwiji's venom. He wished the fatigue hadn't followed him into death. The afterlife was supposed to be free of pain and worry. Plus, there were several very naughty things he wanted to do to her. He traced his fingers along her shoulder blade, following the curve around her side and under her arm to cup her heavy breast. The nipple hardened beneath her shirt.

She moaned and slid one hand down his chest to rest upon his erection, and he realized he wore only his briefs. *Convenient.* He pumped his hips upward and groaned, the pressure of someone else's hand a sensation he'd not felt in over fifteen years.

Her fingers slipped inside his briefs and wrapped hotly around his shaft. "I dare say you are very much alive."

With a surge of motion, he flipped her onto her back so he could take over the lovemaking.

She sucked in a breath, her brows raised. He paused, realizing how rough he'd been. How *real*. This wasn't a dream. He twisted to look at his injured leg. The poison had left a dark spiderweb of broken capillaries up and down its surface, but whatever antidote Mek'd given him must've worked, because other than the residual ache, he felt fine. Alive. And very, very horny.

He returned his gaze to Lisa's, both hearts threatening to pour their way out of his chest. "How're we touching?"

"I found Doug." She grabbed his beard with both fists, her eyes dark with desire. "Don't stop what you're doing."

His thoughts spun, unable to keep up as he lowered himself to her mouth. Hope and lust surged through him. "He fixed your nanites?"

"Not exactly. He says I need to destroy them." She brought one leg up around his hip, then the other, squeezing with her heels until his cock ground against her. "He seems to think this might do it."

Despite the throbbing desire in his cock, Qaiyaan paused. "Whoa, slow down. Might?" He pushed up onto both hands to look down at her. "I thought you needed your nanites for us to be together."

"What I need is your cock inside me. Right now."

Her words alone were nearly enough to make him come. "*Ellam Cua*, woman! I need to know I won't kill you before we go any farther."

She sighed and eased the pressure of her heels. "Let me try this. It's faster."

Inside his head, a flurry of information appeared, as if she was reading him a book on fast forward. He experienced her joy and her sorrow while speaking to Doug, and understood the mystery of her nanites in ways he'd never imagined possible. She once again tugged his beard, trying to draw him toward her. "I have to destroy my nanites before they destroy me. And the only way to get rid of them is with an ionic pulse." Her lips twisted into a sassy smile. "Doug suggested yours."

He lowered himself to within kissing range. "Mine specifically?"

She pressed tiny kisses to his throat beneath the line of his beard, working her way toward his ear. "Yours."

Qaiyaan groaned. His cock was so hard, it was painful. Years of self-control warred inside him. "Are you sure you want to? What if…"

"Mek's standing by. And yes. I want to feel you inside me." Her breathy voice against his ear sent a shiver to his toes.

Turning his head, he captured her lips in a kiss. The sweet pressure of her tongue in his mouth was pure bliss. Slowly, savoring every moment, he kissed her, cupping her cheek with one hand. His other hand sought a breast, teasing the nipple into a rigid peak. The intimacy of her body close to his was something he'd never thought possible, but even stronger was the soft and gentle pressure of her thoughts brushing against his. Her lust for him rivaled his. He reached for the latch on her waistband, wanting to feel her. To sink his fingers into her dusky curls. To feel her slick opening part for him.

She wriggled, lifting her hips to help him shimmy her legs free of her clothing. Her hands roamed his torso, as desperate for him as he was for her. Her gasping breaths fanned his desire.

Pants removed, he pulled back, looking down at her body. He'd never seen anything more beautiful. Charcoal depths of her eyes filled with lust, she let her legs fall open to expose her soft, wet entrance and held her hands toward him, seeking to draw him near.

He swallowed, offering one last attempt at control. "I won't be able to stop if we go any further."

She scooted her bottom closer to him, spreading her thighs even wider, and lifted herself so her backside rested against his thighs. "Shut up and fuck me."

Groaning, he dragged her hips toward him until the head of his cock grazed her slitted heat. The slick folds caressed his length with delicious, slippery promise. She quivered, fingertips digging into his forearms as she wrapped her legs around his hips.

Qaiyaan shuddered, the head of his cock glistening with pre-come. If he wasn't careful, he might fulfill Tovik's prediction and finish before he'd even started. He ground his teeth, holding back while she wriggled, part of him still resisting this ultimate commitment. Then she reached down, grabbing his shaft and settling the head against the center of her opening. Without conscious thought, his hips surged forward.

Her heat enveloped him in sheer bliss.

"*Ellam Cua,*" he breathed, eyes rolling back in his head. His hands dug into her hips, holding her steady. "Don't move."

"I can't help it!" She threw her head back, heels digging hard into his backside, driving him deeper than he thought possible. Her core pulsed around him, on the edge of orgasm. She whimpered and licked her lips, her pink tongue an invitation. He fell forward to kiss her again. Tangling his tongue with hers, he thrust forward, crushing her body beneath his. She accepted every thrust, pumping her legs in time to his rhythm. Deeper, harder, faster.

A moan rose from her lips, a sound that resonated in his chest as if she were the one with ionic power rather than the other way around. Her voice grew higher, and he moved faster, knowing she was almost at her peak. The base of his spine tingled with electric desire, balls tightening with the need for release. *No, not yet, hold on a little longer...*

She grabbed his beard, her back arching. "Qaiyaan!" Her pussy convulsed around him, and her entire body quaked with her release.

His balls exploded, his vision bursting into a million stars...

When he came to his senses, he lay on top of her, panting. Horrified, he pulled back, clumsy-drunk from his orgasm. He never remembered coming so hard in his life. He searched her face. Cheeks flushed and eyes closed, she had a slight smile on her lips. Sending out a small ionic nudge, he detected her heartbeat, steady and quick. Her body was alive, then, but what about her mind?

He spoke her name in a reverent hush. "Lisa?"

She turned her head slightly without opening her eyes. "Mmm?"

He let out his breath in a whoosh and lowered himself until his forehead touched hers. This was a miracle he'd never expected. A gift he didn't deserve. "You survived."

"Did I? I'm not so sure." She wrapped both arms around his chest and dug her heels into his backside. "I think we need to try again."

"Your nanites?"

Only a momentary pause, then her luscious mouth spread into a grin. "Gone."

Qaiyaan tilted his head to meet her lips, his heart soaring. His cock had fifteen years of celibacy to make up for.

CHAPTER EIGHTEEN

Lisa sat in the galley, trying to pay attention to the crew's conversation about the Cartel ship now sitting in their hold, but even with Qaiyaan seated at the opposite side of the table, she couldn't keep from touching him. She slid one bare foot up the inside of his leg until his hand caught it near his crotch.

His face remained impassive, but he pressed the ball of her foot against his bulging erection while he spoke. "How much can we get for that ship? We need the credits to fix our hull." His gaze met hers, lust simmering beneath the surface. "We have precious cargo aboard."

Lisa felt every eye in the galley fall on her. She flushed, still uncomfortable with their awe over her and Qaiyaan's mating. "You guys need to stop doing that. I'm just another member of the crew."

"A loud member." Noatak smirked at her. "Especially at night."

The heat in her cheeks intensified, and she tried to draw her foot back, but Qaiyaan held firm, massaging her arch with one thumb. His cheek twitched with mirth. The bastard was enjoying her embarrassment. She muttered under her breath. "Damned thin-walled ship."

Tovik nodded, his copper face flushed with iridescent blue-green.

"Noatak, I'd be happy to put up a hammock for you in engineering. The engines help buffer the… noise."

Now Lisa's face felt like it was about to burst into flames. She'd never been prudish about her sex life, but she'd also never had a group of men so focused on it. These guys needed mates of their own. She turned to Mek. "How are the nanites doing?"

The mood in the room sobered. The physical changes the nanites had made to her body allowed her to be with Qaiyaan, but now her nanites were gone. She was no longer a source for additional samples. With only a few remaining vials in existence from her previous tests, the doctor worried there wasn't enough to continue his testing, let alone enough to create new, compatible mates.

Mek shook his head, his gaze sliding away from hers. "I've been unsuccessful in culturing more of them. They need a host."

Tovik leaned forward. "So we go find some hosts."

Noatak thrust a restraining palm toward the younger man. "Slow down, Tovik. You don't want to end up bonded to just any random woman."

"There could also be side effects to the nanites themselves." Mek scratched at one stubbled cheek. "I just don't know enough, and we have a limited supply for testing."

Lisa sat up straighter, this time successfully pulling her foot free of Qaiyaan's grasp. "Doug has nanites." The only thing that had remotely intruded on her new infatuation with Qaiyaan was the knowledge that her brother was still alive and imprisoned by Syndicorp. Her throat constricted as she imagined what new, horrific tests they might be doing on him now. But if Mek needed more nanites, freeing Doug would serve a double purpose. "When we free him, we'll have all the samples you need."

"I thought he didn't tell you where he was?" Noatak said.

"I can still hack into the darkweb, even without my nanites. That's where I'll pick up a trail to the Syndicorp lab. I just know it. I only need access to a boosted console."

"I can boost our array pretty easily," Tovik offered. "I already stripped a bunch of the comm webbing off the Cartel ship."

Qaiyaan sat up straighter, his eyes narrowing dangerously. "You did what?"

Tovik drew his shoulders up to his ears and grimaced. "And I might have accidentally fried the control hydraulics when I tried to incorporate the secondary stage burners into our forward drive."

Noatak dropped his chin and shook his head. "At least you didn't blow the *Hardship's* systems." Sighing, he stood. "Well, let's get Lisa set up on a console."

"Cool your jets, everyone." Qaiyaan rose. "The darkweb is a sketchy place. I don't want to put Lisa in any more danger. You know how important she is to me."

Noatak turned. "She's important to us all, *iluq*. But she's the only one with a plan at the moment."

"I'll contact Kashatok and see what he can find out," Qaiyaan insisted.

"He's a *qumli* with no honor," Noatak insisted. "We can't rely on him to help us."

"He'll be on board once he knows what's at stake," Qaiyaan said, but the rest of the crew continued to look doubtful.

Lisa stood and moved around the table to wrap her arms around Qaiyaan's waist. "I want to work on this, too. All I need to do is access a console and type queries into the keypad. No nanites involved. I'll be fine."

He enveloped her in his amber-scented embrace, shaking his head. "We can't go anywhere until we get our hull fixed."

"You're just making excuses." Lisa tilted her head to look up into his face. "There's no reason I can't start looking into the darkweb while you do the hull repairs."

"Last time I went outside to look at the hull, we almost all died."

"So you're just going to never look at it again? That's no solution."

Tovik threw both hands into the air. "Listen! That's what I'm trying to tell you guys. The hull's all good."

"How?" Qaiyaan asked.

"I sort of borrowed most of the plating off that Cartel ship."

The other three men groaned in unison. Noatak slumped against the doorjamb. "Is there anything left of that ship to sell?"

"The hull needed fixing." Tovik shrugged and looked sideways at Lisa with a wink. "And I needed to go outside for some peace and quiet."

Lisa grinned back at him, pressing her cheek against Qaiyaan's solid chest. Tovik was feeling more like a little brother by the moment. Doug was going to get a real kick out of him.

"There're some pretty good parts left to sell," Tovik continued, and began rattling off flux modulators and other unrecognizable components, ticking each item off on his fingers. "Although I want to save the fuel matrixes for a fixed acceleration project I've been working on."

Qaiyaan's voice was low and gruff, but Lisa could sense the amusement behind his words. "Tovik, one of these days we're going to have to start charging you for your little science experiments."

"My experiments have paid for themselves almost every time." Tovik crossed his arms and scowled. "I get no appreciation around here."

Lisa released Qaiyaan, sliding a hand down his arm to entwine her fingers with his. "Then I guess we'll start looking for Doug?"

Qaiyaan's fingers tightened around hers. "Fine. You check the darkweb. I'll reach out to Kashatok. Let's go kick some Syndicorp ass."

EPILOGUE

Captain Kashatok towed the thrashing posungi mechanic down the *Kinship's* corridor by the scruff of his neck, the metal walls echoing with the thud of his heavy boots. The orange tentacles around the mechanic's face fluttered, as if in search of an escape that didn't exist. A whimpering human female scurried a few steps behind them.

"Cap'n, please," the posungi begged, his voice quivering as much as his appendages. "It was... I was drunk, sir. She asked to—"

"Silence!" Kashatok's voice echoed off the steel bulkhead. Revulsion gurgled in his stomach, as potent as the acrid scent of burned circuitry lingering in the ship's corridors. But the circuits weren't the current reason for his fury. "There's only one rule on my ship," he ground out like he'd just been chewing on shrapnel. "One law that even the densest scum in the galaxy should be able to remember."

A shaggy head popped from a doorway in the corridor ahead: Alek, Kashatok's first mate. He blinked as if he'd been woken from sleep. "What's going on?"

"Rule breaker needs to be punished." Kashatok's lip curled as he pointed toward the female behind him. "Get her off my ship." He jerked the wriggling mechanic forward past his first mate, swallowing distastefully as a waft of *cirripi* weed filled his nostrils.

"*Uminaq*," Alek grumbled, falling into step behind his captain. "Can't we at least let him finish the repairs first? The *Kinship* isn't going to fix herself after that last skirmish with Syndicorp. Finding a new mechanic will delay our departure."

Halting, Kashatok speared the first mate with a narrow-eyed glare. "There are no second chances."

The woman cowered behind Alek, peering fearfully around his muscular, copper-skinned arm. "What are you going to do with him?"

Kashatok growled at her and tightened his grip on the posungi until the man yelped. The crew knew the rumors of Kashatok's past, of the darkness living within his soul. There was only one rule on his ship, but it was for a very good reason.

The woman ducked out of sight, and Alek raised his hands, palms out. "No second chances, I know."

The posungi resumed his begging, the slits of his pupils dilated with fear. "P-please, Cap'n," he blubbered, tentacles writhing uncontrollably. "It was a mistake. I promise I'll never slip up again."

Ignoring the pitiful pleading, Kashatok resumed his march down the corridor, the posungi stumbling behind him. At a branch in the hallway, he veered right toward the starboard airlock.

Behind him, Alek spluttered again. "Uh, Captain? Starboard side is for—"

"Disposals," Kashatok finished coldly, never slowing his stride. "I'm well aware, Alek."

"You can't seriously mean to jettison him. We're docked, so—"

"Punishment is spacelocking. He knew that when he signed up." He glanced behind him at the port hallway and caught sight of the female fleeing toward the exit. In the distance, the hums and clangs of the Whylon Space Station echoed through the *Kinship's* hull. The station had no real law other than captains like Kashatok, who each reigned supreme over their miniature kingdoms. It was a haven for the galaxy's scorned and forsaken. But Kashatok would've jettisoned the mechanic, regardless of where they were docked. "My ship. My rules."

"No," his captive gasped, "Please, no!" The stink of piss filled the air, and Kashatok's lip curled at the sight of a trail of orange urine soiling the hallway in their wake. The crew member on janitorial duty today would not be happy.

Alek sprinted forward and grabbed his free arm. "Sir, wait."

Fury exploded inside Kashatok's chest. It was bad enough the posungi had broken the ship's number one rule. Now his first mate was being insubordinate. Baring his teeth, Kashatok shoved Alek against the corridor wall, his forearm against the man's throat. He leaned in until his nose was nearly touching his first mate's. "I don't take kindly to having my orders questioned, much less repeatedly."

Alek's copper-skinned face looked ashen, but he held Kashatok's gaze without flinching. "Tossing crew into space while we're docked is bad for morale."

"I don't give a damn about fucking morale." Kashatok released him and readjusted his hold on the squirming posungi. "Tell the crew that if anyone objects, they can step forward and I'll gladly expedite their departure."

"Come on, now." Alek rubbed his throat beneath the veil of his thick beard. "The men have urges. We all do. Even you've been known to break a rule once in a while." A whisper of a smirk lifted the corner of the man's mouth.

A thought coiled in Kashatok's mind, venomous and unsettling. He looked down at the posungi, who was staring at Alek with beseeching eyes. Why was Alek defending this piece of shit? Had the first mate been aware the woman was on board? Fixing Alek with a stare that could freeze plasma, he asked, "Did you know?"

All signs of humor dropped from Alek's face. "I know better than to cross you."

The sideways answer only made Kashatok's blood boil hotter. He'd had a few confrontations with Alek before, but right now, the challenge to his leadership felt personal and raw. "Did. You. Know?"

Alek cleared his throat, a bead of sweat tracing a path into his beard. "I swear on my life, I didn't know about her." He stood straighter, as if preparing to salute. "I'll talk to the crew and make sure this doesn't happen again."

Good. Kashatok resumed his path toward the airlock. "See that it doesn't. Or next time it's on your head."

Lips set into a grim line, he opened the airlock and shoved the screaming posungi inside, sealing his fate with a press of the purge button. He watched through the porthole as his former mechanic's body jettisoned into the dark void. *No one defies my rules. Not on the Kinship. Not while I breathe.* After this, he dared any man to forget the consequences of breaking his rule.

RANSOMED BY KASHATOK

A STEAMY SCI FI ALIEN ROMANCE

CHAPTER ONE

Facing the cantina's dirty restroom mirror, Joy gripped a hunk of her curly brown hair in one hand and scissors in the other. Behind her, a wall-length screen flickered with an ad for inter-alien contraceptive products, haloing her with eerie green light.

Just do it, she thought. *Hair grows back, no big deal.* Except that her mother, a Syndicorp Communications CEO, already liked to goad her about her fashion sense, saying it was a good thing Joy was smart, because she'd never get by on her looks. Yet even being smart wasn't good enough, not unless Joy used it to climb the corporate ladder.

When Joy signed on as a reporter with RealTime News, her mother'd almost disowned her. How was she going to react when she found out Joy was doing an undercover exposé? *At least I'm not disguising myself as a prostitute.* Not that her producer at RealTime hadn't hinted at how sensational *that* would be. But Joy had tools other than her tits to secure this story. Being tall for a woman, she'd decided to go the complete opposite direction with her disguise. Her canvas cargo pants and mechanic shirt were boxy and genderless, and she'd even gone so far as to wrap her breasts to mask her curves.

She just needed the finishing touch.

Taking a deep breath, she squeezed the scissors. Her long tresses fell away with an oddly satisfying sensation. A lopsided reflection stared back at her with startled brown eyes. "No going back now," she muttered.

Her square jaw wasn't quite manly, but she was plain enough that with the right attitude, she could pass for a boy. And she'd already proven she had attitude doing a year of volunteer work for Syndicorp's planetary emergency services division in their fleet mechanic shop. Joy'd loved the hands-on problem-solving and the smell of hydraulic fluid and hot metal until Mother learned she wasn't handing out cookies and pulled her.

Satisfied with her hair, Joy pulled mascara out of her purse and dabbed it beneath her nails, rubbing it into her skin for good measure. No one trusted a mechanic with clean hands. When she was satisfied, she once again looked into the mirror, winking her left eye to engage her cybernetic camera. A recording of her reflection would make a decent, gritty opening scene for the exposé. One benefit of having a Communications CEO for a mother was that Joy had access to technology other newbie reporters would die for.

"I'm at the edge of unclassified space, looking for information about pirate activity. These ruthless men and women have been plaguing the shipping lanes since Syndicorp sent its first colonization envoys outside the Aleigh system." Joy spoke in a husky, conspiratorial tone, glancing over her shoulder at the restroom door. The chances of someone entering were slim to none with the hotel door grav-loc she'd placed against the door stop, but her pulse beat loudly in her ears even so. "Stay tuned as I go undercover into the swashbuckling world of black market trading and deep-space piracy—bleh."

Sighing, she stopped the camera. She sounded like a game show host. Everything about this broadcast had to be perfect. Serious. Anchor-worthy.

She tried again. "My informant just sent word there's a notorious pirate in this very bar. I'm going to try to join his crew. For the next few weeks, I'll be broadcasting the RealTime stories of these men."

The door rattled. Joy quickly cached the recordings on her polycom to edit later and removed the grav-loc, brushing past the annoyed saluqan woman outside. "Watch it. Door sticks," Joy mumbled and dove into the crowded cantina. She had a pirate captain to find.

Captain Kashatok pried Jhikik's tail from around the bottle of Kantarellian rum and poured himself another tall serving. On board ship, he often drank straight from the bottle. For the purpose of interviewing new crew members, he was attempting to look civilized. He had enough rough edges on his crew, and attracting yet another discipline problem was not in his plan today.

The little netorpok chittered at him in reprimand and climbed up his arm to sit on his shoulder, his lavender fur tickling Kashatok's ear. Jhikik had come into his possession as a pup, and, much like an actual child, liked to nag him about his vice. "Keep it down."

Too late. A woman who'd been perched on a stool at the bar was heading in his direction, her sizable cleavage jiggling above the low neckline of her tight blouse with every step. Happened every time. First, she'd fawn over the netorpok, then turn her attention to the broad-shouldered owner. Women loved a man with a pet. And Jhikik loved the attention.

"There's a reason I never leave the ship," Kashatok muttered, glowering at the woman. Female company was never on his agenda and never would be.

Thankfully, the oncoming woman took the hint and veered toward the restrooms. As the cantina's band started up a new set, Kashatok rose from his chair and scanned the dark interior of the cantina for his first mate's shaggy head. Aleknagik was supposed to be escorting prospective shuttle mechanics to the table for interviews. Across the dimly lit floor, cantina patrons parted like an outgoing tide around the tall, copper-skinned denaidan. *About time he found someone.* Settling back into his chair, Kashatok downed the rest of the rum in his glass. Aleknagik pulled up to the table and stopped.

Kashatok scanned the conspicuously empty space around to the big man. "Well?"

Aleknagik shook his head. "Word's gotten around about what happened to our last mechanic."

The muscle in Kashatok's jaw tightened. "And?"

"No one's exactly excited to be the next one tossed out the airlock."

"I have one hard rule. No women aboard my ship." Not only that, but what the mechanic had been doing to that poor female deserved retribution.

Sliding out a chair, Aleknagik sat heavily, the reek of cirripi weed wafting off him. He leaned forward, both elbows on the table. "Listen, I understand why you made that rule. But with those nanites Captain Qaiyaan's been talking about, we might be able to change that. Plus, your non-denaidan crew members might appreciate some leeway."

Kashatok gritted his teeth. The *Kinship*'s core crew of denaidans could not enjoy the pleasures of women, and Kashatok's rule had never made much of a difference to them. Until the nanites. Once again, Syndicorp had planted a seed of hope within the denaidans. No, not a seed. A spore. A *virus*. A Syndicorp engineered virus. And it was fucking with his ship. "My ship—my rules. If someone's not okay with that, they can get the fuck off."

His first mate frowned but kept silent, his eyes full of questions and distrust.

Grabbing the rum, Kashatok took a long pull of the burning liquid. There'd never be a woman for him, anyway, nanites or not. He couldn't be trusted, not after Aiyana… He took another swallow. His past was none of Aleknagik's business.

An olive-skinned human appeared just past Aleknagik's shoulder, wide brown eyes darting between the back of the first mate's head and Kashatok. The moment their eyes met, Kashatok felt a jolt, a desire to protect that was at odds with the hard-assed captain he tried to be. The kid reminded him of his own first insecure days off-planet, seeking jobs in seedy cantinas just like this one. The visitor moved up beside the first mate, both hands shoved deep in the front pockets of his baggy cargo pants. "You're looking for a shuttle mechanic?"

Aleknagik twisted in his seat, eyes nearly level with their visitor's. "You know one?"

The young man stretched a hand forward. "Name's Joey."

"You?" Aleknagik laughed.

Jhikik leaped from Kashatok's shoulder onto the tabletop. Kashatok snatched hold of the tip of the creature's tail, drawing him up short. Not everyone appreciated the creature's curiosity.

Turning to Kashatok, Aleknagik jerked a thumb toward Joey, eyes dancing with mirth. "What do you say, Captain? Think this *qumli* could hold his own among our crew?"

The kid was barely old enough to leave his mother's teat, let alone stand up to a rowdy crew. Kashatok sent out a tightly controlled ionic pulse. Alcohol dulled his sensitivity, but he could still assess the kid's heartbeat, breathing, and skin temperature. Joey was nervous, for sure. But his hands were dirty, and the look in his eye was hungry. Would it hurt to let him have his say? Kashatok pushed the rum bottle forward without accepting the handshake. "Have a seat."

Dropping his hand, Joey pulled out a chair and sat. He didn't touch the rum. They locked gazes, and Kashatok had to hand it to him—the kid didn't look away. "You don't seem old enough to be a mechanic."

Joey shrugged one shoulder. "Only been at it a year, but I'm a fast learner."

Kashatok retrieved the bottle and tilted back for a long swallow. May as well let the kid see the real him. "You familiar with the CrossX Spacer Elite?"

"Sure." Joey tilted his head and squinted his eyes in thought. "I helped with a thruster rebuild. And adjusted the flux coil on one of the newer models."

"Huh," said Aleknagik, nodding. "Where're you from?"

Joey scowled. "Why's that matter?"

Aleknagik dropped his bearded chin to glower back. Jhikik crept forward, eyes on the stranger.

"What?" Joey crossed his arms. "Pirates don't have pasts. Or they shouldn't."

Kashatok repressed a smile. This kid might just be capable of holding his own after all. He stroked his fingertips along Jhikik's long tail until the little creature spun and batted at his hand. "You heard about our last mechanic?"

The young man's left eye twitched. "Tell me."

"Space-locked." Kashatok paused a moment. Joey's heart beat so rapidly, Kashatok barely had to engage his ionic senses to feel it.

"By you?"

Kashatok nodded slowly, keeping eye contact. "There's only one unbreakable rule on the *Kinship*. You can't bring women on board. Think you can handle that?"

Joey took a long breath and let it out slowly. "That's all? Sounds easy. What's my cut?"

"Ha!" Aleknagik clapped the young man on the shoulder, rocking him forward. "I like him!"

Joey kept his gaze on the captain.

For some reason, Kashatok hadn't expected the mercenary question, probably because the kid had seemed more interested in the adventure than the money. "Probation gets you one share. Things work out after the first score or two, we'll talk more."

Nodding, Joey once again thrust out his hand. "Deal."

This time, Kashatok took it. The palm was softer than he'd expected, but maybe that was just a human thing. "We're parked in slip A21P. I'll be pulling out as soon as we're restocked, so I suggest you get your ass aboard sooner rather than later."

"Aye aye, captain."

Alek laughed again. "We don't say that, human."

Joey licked his lips, and Kashatok found the move oddly disturbing. "Sorry," said the kid. "I do call you captain though, right?"

"I don't care what you call me, as long as you do your job." Kashatok rose, grabbing the rum bottle and holding out an arm for Jhikik. The netorpok gave Joey a longing look, then skittered up to rest on Kashatok's shoulder.

As Kashatok turned to leave, Joey called out, "I'll keep your shuttle in top shape."

Kashatok kept moving. Behind him, he heard Alek giving advice. "Young man like you's got urges. Long as you take care of them offship, you'll be fine. Oh, and stay away from the captain's rum."

Stopping at the crowded bar, Kashatok ordered one last bottle to go.

CHAPTER TWO

J oy dodged a six-legged yanipa-nimayu bulling its way through the crowd and halted to allow an armed rakwiji to cross to a nearby cantina. Ahead, above the throng, a beat-up sign pointed toward slip A21P. A posungi reeking of cirripi weed brushed against her, facial tentacles waving, and she gripped her satchel tighter, wary of pickpockets. Her time volunteering with Syndicorp's emergency services division had exposed her to some rough men, but nothing like the throng pressing around her now. Hoping things improved once she was on board the ship, she kept her head up and strode forward with purpose. Sometimes just appearing to look like you knew what you were doing was enough to deter trouble.

She reached the docking corridor connecting the station to the ship, expecting a guard or someone to greet her. The entrance was wide open and vacant. Interesting. Kashatok was obviously very confident with his reputation. She'd done a few minutes of preliminary research before heading over and learned that he and his crew specialized in hijacking entire ships, scrapping them, and selling out the parts. As the new shuttle mechanic, she'd likely soon be doing the same. She'd hoped to get more background on the big, copper-skinned alien who was to be her captain—she'd never encountered a man like him before—but there were surprisingly few records on him.

Well, that would change with this exposé. Squeezing her left eye, she took a few still shots of the open entry. She could add some narrative later.

She stepped into the docking corridor, her heart hammering. The captain's rule about no women on board had almost made her change her mind. But after asking around in the cantina, she'd learned more about the crewman she was replacing. He'd brought a woman on board, and Kashatok'd set the woman free, ejecting only his offending crew member into space. The other woman probably hadn't known the rule, but Joy had been warned. What would happen if she was discovered? Would he space-lock her? Her stomach churned. Maybe she should turn around. It wasn't too late. No one had seen her.

A tug on her pant leg drew her attention from the dimly lit cargo bay ahead. Something scurried up the folds of her cargo pants, little claws digging through the fabric to prick her skin. She let out a squeak, stiffening as a set of dark eyes stopped within inches of hers, staring up from its hold on her chest.

The captain's pet.

She regained her balance and stared back, hardly daring to breathe. Just because it was adorable didn't mean it was friendly. The face had a row of small horns set between its eyes and its feathery-looking ears fluttered. Was it just allowed to run free? At least she didn't see any exposed teeth.

Nose wriggling, it sniffed her, flicking its long, furry tail back and forth. The flattened end curved up over its shoulder toward her, revealing octopus-like suction cups on the underside. She laughed nervously as the fuzzy tip stroked her jawline. She'd never been allowed to have a pet, but her friends had owned species of varying friendliness. Keeping her fingers curled inward in case the thing decided to bite, she ran her knuckles along its lavender-furred shoulder. "Hello, little fellow. What's your name?"

The creature made a little "jweek jweek" sound and closed its eyes.

She opened her hand and stroked the feather-soft fur. "Is your master aboard?"

In answer, it clambered the rest of the way up her chest and settled on her shoulder, long tail wrapping gently around her throat. It closed its eyes and settled down as if to sleep.

"Okay, then." Strangely fortified by the greeting, she continued into the cargo bay. A beat-up CrossX Spacer Elite sat to one side of a dimly lit, industrial-gray area. She breathed deeply, relieved she'd taken a few minutes to download Syndicorp's specs for the shuttle. Her accessibility to the galactic web after she was on board was uncertain, and she needed to look like she knew what she was doing. Against the far wall, two open airlocks provided her no guidance.

"There you are." A deep voice made her spin, and she collided with a broad chest smelling of sweet rum and ginger. Her gaze roamed upward from the silver-banded dark beard bisecting the captain's chest to his firm but sensuous mouth. She wasn't used to feeling so short. His hair, pulled into a top-knot, exposed silver earrings, and one strand had come loose to hang between his intense, obsidian eyes. Had he been waiting for her? An unfamiliar yet exciting thrill fluttered in the pit of her stomach.

"Come here, Jhikik." He plucked the little creature from her shoulder, taking no more notice of her than if she'd been a tree.

He was looking for his pet, not waiting for her. The strange feeling in her stomach subsided. She adjusted her satchel. "What kind of animal is that?"

He settled the creature on his own shoulder where it chittered loudly. "Netorpok."

"I've never heard of it."

"Endangered species." He adjusted its tail around his neck as if it was choking him. "Banned on most worlds."

"Oh." Joy tried to be nonchalant, but there could be another story here. Some exotic pets were banned because their intelligence made them more like slaves than pets. "Is he sentient?"

Kashatok shook his head and rubbed two knuckles along the

creature's forehead on either side of its horns. "Though sometimes I wonder."

His gaze shifted to her for the first time since she'd bumped into him. Her breath caught. She'd never been particularly attracted to bad boys, but this pirate's attention made her quiver low in her belly. "Um, where should I put my stuff?"

A muscle in the side of the captain's jaw twitched and his copper skin darkened with a slightly blue-green tinge. He took a long drink from the bottle in his other hand. "Bunk room's down that corridor behind you."

Bunk room? Joy's throat grew tight. Passing for a guy would become exponentially more difficult if she had to share quarters with a bunch of other men. What if they took communal showers or something? She hadn't thought this through very well. "I don't get my own quarters?"

"You could." The first mate's voice startled her from behind. She jumped, nearly stepping on Kashatok's toes. "A private room'll cost you your share, though." Aleknagik leaned against the corridor exit, arms crossed over his chest.

Relief flooded her. Little did they know she didn't need the money. In fact, she'd pay extra for a private room if it wouldn't blow her cover. But she was supposed to be a greedy pirate here, so she pretended to pause and consider. "My entire share?"

"Actually, two shares." Kashatok's voice at her back held a note of warning.

She swallowed, feeling trapped between the two men. "But I only get one share."

"Exactly." Kashatok glowered over the top of her head at his first mate. "Aleknagik shouldn't get your hopes up."

Aleknagik pushed himself off the wall and took a step closer. He was just as big and copper-skinned as the captain, although instead of keeping his hair pulled up into a queue, he'd braided it into several rows along his scalp, leaving the back portion as wildly unkempt as the vast beard covering his chest. "Syndicorp's breathing down our necks, captain. We don't have time to find a new mechanic."

Joy clutched her satchel tightly against her chest. They needed a mechanic, and that gave her leverage; a real pirate would probably ask for more at this moment. Calming her breathing so she could speak, she squeaked out, "I want three shares."

Kashatok lifted an eyebrow, and she swore she saw a smile lurking at the corner of his mouth. "Don't push your luck, kid." He took another long drink, then once again pierced her with his dark eyes. "One share, and you can sleep in a storeroom by yourself. Fair enough?"

Wondering what he'd look like if he really smiled, Joy nodded. She'd pushed enough to appear genuine, and she'd gotten what she really needed to make it to the next port without blowing her cover.

Kashatok spun without another word and strode down the nearest corridor, surprisingly steady for someone who'd just consumed almost half a bottle of rum.

"This way," Aleknagik said, walking toward the opposite corridor.

Joy jogged after him, glancing over her shoulder toward the corridor the captain had taken. Before she left this ship, she was going to get the captain to smile for the camera. He was going to make a fabulous centerpiece for her exposé.

Kashatok leaned back in his desk chair and stared out the view screen at the scatter of ships coming and going from the berths as the *Kinship* pulled away from the station. The sporadic burbling from the hydroponic garden in one corner of his sitting room did little to calm him. He pulled another bottle of Kantarellian rum from his desk drawer. He hated the exposure of the docks and itched to hit the burn drives. The empty coldness of space was preferable. If he didn't need to offload goods and pick up intel or let his men blow off steam, he'd be happy to never leave the confines of his ship.

He took a long drink to calm his anxiety, relishing the heat hitting his stomach. Another thing that made him edgy was that new shuttle mechanic. Something about the kid had Kashatok's mind going places it shouldn't—like the idea of him sharing a bunk with the other members of the crew. In lieu of female company, his two human crewmen were not above scratching each other's itches. As far as he knew, it was consensual, but who knew what might happen with the introduction of someone as young and fresh as Joey? A core part of him had been relieved to offer separate sleeping arrangements, even if some of the crew might grumble about preferential treatment.

Needing to stop dwelling on the new crew member, he dug in his pocket and retrieved the data chip his cartel contact had handed him on his way out of the cantina. While most denaidans were ex-troopers, he'd been with the cartel since long before Syndicorp had terminated Denaida-daru. The cartel hadn't cared that his people considered him a monster. That he'd left his world in shame. Only now, with his race all but extinct, had his denaidan brothers accepted him back into the fold.

Or perhaps they didn't remember.

Whatever the reason, it hardly mattered to Kashatok. For a fee, he shared his cartel information with the rest of the fleet, keeping the top-level intel for himself. The chip he held now was fresh off Syndicorp's servers, not even on the darkweb yet, and should hold information about some decent scores. Plugging the data chip into his desk monitor, he perused ship stats, gauged distances and travel times, and calculated the value of the posted manifests.

He crossed off passenger ships and colonist charters, preferring to target ships transporting commodities or bulk electronics, which were easier to cash out. One ship on the list looked promising, a K-class freighter routed between the mining strips within the Brandton asteroid belt. Problem was, it was at least three burn cycles away. He sighed. Denaidans could do the jump in a single burn, but his posungi gunner was extra sensitive to long burns and his two—now three— humans wouldn't respond much better. Plus, he wanted to break the new mechanic in slowly.

Sending the coordinates to the bridge, he glanced out the view screen at the thinning traffic. The ship would take another hour to clear the station's burn buffer. "Think our new crew member's settled in, Jhikik?"

Kashatok didn't usually fraternize with his crew, but events of late seemed to be pushing him to pay more attention. First, he'd caught his previous mechanic performing sadistic acts of pleasure with a woman in the ship's weapon locker—while they were in port, no less. Kashatok suspected some crew members had even known, but he couldn't prove it. The way some of them talked about females made him queasy. But as long as things didn't happen aboard his ship, it wasn't his responsibility; everything and everyone aboard this vessel was.

His mind returned to the crew's most recent addition. *Ellam Cua*, his fucking men better all be getting along.

Grabbing the rum in one hand, he held out the other. A little more attentiveness by the *Kinship's* captain was long overdue. "Come on, Jhik."

The netorpok scurried up his arm and settled on his shoulder.

Exiting his stuffy cabin, Kashatok headed toward the galley. The smell of broiled kemeg wafted down the hall, and Chignik's laughter echoed from the galley's open door. *Good.* He'd been correct assuming that's where they usually gathered. He hoped laughter meant everyone was getting along.

As he passed the door to engineering, Joey stepped out, almost colliding with him. "Oh!" The kid drew up short, blinking at him before attempting a smile. "Hi, Captain."

Jhikik chirped and scurried half-way down Kashatok's arm toward the new crewman, long tail twitching.

Hindered by the bottle in one hand, Kashatok snatched at the creature. His crew tolerated the netorpok, but the men could be less-than-gentle on the rare occasions Jhikik chose to interact with them— usually because he was running away with one of their socks.

Joey opened both hands to catch him, but Jhikik scurried over the kid's head, his tail forcing Joey to scrunch his eyes closed. "Always wanted a pet."

"He's more of a companion than a pet." Kashatok surprised himself with his own jovial candor. He was accustomed to protecting Jhikik from a disgruntled crewman and occasionally dodging a cantina female. Joey was neither, yet the netorpok seemed to like him. *Score one for the kid.* Kashatok's mouth twitched into a wry smile. "And he's usually far more loyal."

Joey laughed and pulled Jhikik's tail away from his mouth. "He's just curious."

Aren't we all? thought Kashatok. But one thing he'd learned during his years with the cartel was not to ask questions. Questions led to questions, and Kashatok had no desire to provide answers about himself. "Crew usually gathers in the galley between burns. You coming?"

Joey nodded emphatically. "Gassy went on ahead. Said he needed to soften the crew up before I got there for a game of cards." He chewed his bottom lip. "But I've got nothing to wager."

Distracted by the kid's bottom lip, Kashatok turned toward the galley. "Never admit that. A pirate must always bet more than he has."

"Got it." Joey hustled to keep up beside him. "I'm gonna use that line someday. So, what should I bet?"

Kashatok immediately thought of several bawdy suggestions and bit his tongue. Bad enough the kid would get it from the crew. He didn't need to be ribbed by his captain as well. "You seem fairly proficient with a spanner. How about I float you a loan, and you can do some maintenance on my hydroponic system? Know anything about those?"

The kid shrugged, loosening Jhikik's tail from its stranglehold around his neck. "I know pumps and thermostats. That's all hydroponics is."

"There you go then. I'll front you a few credits."

Joey grinned at him, and Kashatok suddenly needed a drink. Luckily, he still held the bottle in one hand. He took a couple of swallows and avoided looking at the kid until they reached the galley.

Inside, Gassy, the ship's grizzled denaidan engineer, sat at one end of the U-shaped table slapping down cards with Ekwok and Chignik. Chignik threw his cards down and leaned back in his chair, crossing his copper-skinned arms over his chest. "*Anaq,* you beat me every time, Gassy."

The engineer swept his gnarled copper hands out to gather the cards, tapping them into a pile. "Benefits of age and experience, my friend. Your deal, Ekwok."

Shaking his buff-colored mane of hair, Ekwok took the cards and glanced toward the door. When he spotted Kashatok, he half rose from his seat. "Captain? Something wrong?"

From the cushioned seats in the entertainment alcove, Aleknagik twisted to look over his shoulder. Manopup's orange-tentacled face rose above the back of another chair. "Captain?"

Skin heating, Kashatok moved forward and set his bottle at an open spot among the gamers. "Just thought I'd make sure the new crewman's fitting in. Deal me in."

The crew blinked at him for an uncomfortable heartbeat before settling warily back in their seats. He'd come to keep things settled. Hopefully his presence wouldn't rile them up instead.

Gassy looked past Kashatok toward Joey and tapped the tabletop next to him. "Saved you a seat, kid. Know how to play Ongaru Flip?"

Joey raised an eyebrow and sidled over. "Used to beat my supervisor all the time back on Tenben."

As the kid took a seat, a small part of Kashatok surged with jealousy at the easy camaraderie. *You shouldn't be surprised. These men work together.* He also shouldn't be a stranger on his own ship.

Ekwok dealt the cards, and Kashatok handed a few credits to Joey to start off. That got him some raised eyebrows, but no one said anything. After several rounds, Joey'd won eighty-two credits and Chignik's promise to take over Joey's next shift cleaning the bathrooms. Gassy tossed in his hand and rose. "This old man's out. Going to catch a few winks before we burn."

Jhikik bounded across the table as if chasing him away, sending cards fluttering to the floor in his wake.

"Little *tunrak*," Chignik swore. "Go find some socks to chew."

The netorpok chittered and disappeared into the hallway ahead of Gassy.

Ekwok shoved his cards to the center of the table. "Gotta go, too. It's my shift on the bridge. Good playing with you, Captain."

Kashatok scooped a few cards from the floor. He had to admit, this was more fun than pacing his cabin and watching Jhikik try to pull naujiar leaves through the hydroponic cage. "Chignik, Joey, you still in?"

Chignik shook his head. "One turn cleaning bathrooms is enough for me."

Joey remained seated. "I'll do one more round."

Suddenly nervous, Kashatok glanced at the entertainment alcove. "Aleknagik, Manopup, either of you in?"

No answer but a snore.

With only two players, the game became more difficult, and in the first two hands, Joey lost everything except Chignik's writ to clean the bathrooms.

Kashatok settled back. "Looks like you're out of currency. And captains are exempt from bathroom cleaning."

Joey chewed his bottom lip, a habit Kashatok was still trying hard not to notice. "We never actually talked about a price to fix your hydroponic system. What's it worth to you?"

Kashatok plopped his rum on the table, realizing he hadn't finished the bottle. "You like rum?"

"Ordinary rum?" Joey rolled his eyes. "For my extraordinary skill and effort?"

That made Kashatok laugh. "All right. How about I cover the first payment for your private bunk?"

"Now you're talking." Joey snatched up another card.

Smirking, Kashatok countered Joey's next flip.

Joey hit back with a double reverse and closed out his hand for a winning blow. "Ha! That means at the end of this job, I get two full shares!"

"Two?" Kashatok tossed the remainder of his hand on the table and crossed his arms. The kid was nothing if not tenacious. "I'm pretty sure we agreed to one."

Joey lifted his chin, crossing his own scrawny arms. "A private bunk is worth two, you said."

Kashatok held back a smile. Two shares certainly wouldn't break him, but he couldn't appear to give in too easily. "Tell you what, you fix my hydroponics, and I'll give you three shares at the end of this job. How's that sound?"

"Deal." Joey thrust out one hand.

Taking the kid's small palm in his, Kashatok grinned. Assuming Joey really could fix the hydroponic system, Kashatok'd gotten the better end of the deal. He wondered what else he might be able to get Joey to fix.

CHAPTER THREE

"Up and at 'em, kid."

Joy opened her eyes at the first mate's gruff voice, nausea rising in her throat. Two burn cycles in rapid succession were more than she was used to, and Gassy told her there would only be a short break between this one and the next. She pulled one arm free of the chair's compression cavity and rubbed her eyes. These seats weren't exactly the first class modules she was accustomed to. Her mother's private transport seldom traveled long distances, and the charters Joy'd used for longer journeys provided two or even three days between each burn to allow passengers time to recuperate.

Blinking to engage her camera, she glanced around at the rest of the crew. Of the ten other crewmen, seven of them were the same species as the captain—denaidan. She wondered why she'd never encountered their kind before. There had to be a story here. As soon as she had a private moment to access a comm, she planned to pull up some intel on denaidans. She pushed the chair's frequency modulators off her temples, recalling Kashatok leaping three meters into the air to a ledge no wider than her hand. Her female demographic would go gaga over that bit of footage.

Beside her, the single posungi crewman stumbled out of his chair, facial tentacles flushed more vibrantly orange than she remembered. The wiry human on his other side shoved a flexible container toward him. "Keep it off the floor this time, Manopup."

The posungi snatched the container and shoved his face into it just in time to wretch violently. Several crew members laughed, but Joy's stomach roiled as the putrid stench of vomit wafted her way.

"New-boy's looking a little peaked, too, Cooper. You got a bucket for him?" the second human commented, looking down his crooked nose at her. He was almost as tall as the copper-skinned crewmen, but his bald, tattooed head was a distinct contrast to the shaggy-haired aliens.

"I'm fine." She loosed the chair's restraints and pushed herself upright. She had to pee, but could hear the voices of other crewmen in the lavatory. Although she slept in the storeroom all by herself, she still had to share the other common rooms, and had needed to be very careful with her personal grooming over the last couple of days.

"Come on, kid," Gassy called from the doorway. "We need all systems optimized before the next burn."

Feeling a headache beginning, she turned off her camera and wobbled toward the door, leaving the gagging posungi and the two humans behind her.

In engineering, the air felt like a sauna. Gassy sent her into the twisted piping and thick conduits he called "the jungle" to manually adjust the burn drive's coolant system. Squeezed in among the valves and pipes, the air was even hotter and the hum of pumps and fans drowned out all other sounds. Sweat poured between her breasts, soaking the under-wrap that kept her chest flat. God, she felt like she was suffocating. What she wouldn't give for a shower right now. But she doubted she'd get enough privacy for a shower anytime in the near future.

At least the job was interesting, reminding her of her days with emergency services. She adjusted some valves, then ducked out to a nearby console to verify that the gauges matched the ship's computer readings. Everything was within tolerances. She shot a glance over her shoulder. Gassy was busy at the main engineering station and Moore'd just exited pushing a cart of supplies. Now was her chance for a quick bit of research without anyone looking over her shoulder.

Turning back to the console's comm interface, she typed a query about denaidans. Several suggested spellings popped up, plus a few personal profiles on people with the name Aiden, but no intel. *Strange.* She tried a different spelling. Deneyeden. Even fewer options. Den—eye-don. Nothing.

"Ahem." A throat cleared just behind her shoulder.

She spun, cheeks heating as she stared up into Gassy's bearded face. *You haven't done anything wrong—at least, not that he knows about,* she reminded herself. "Uh, whatcha need?"

"You won't find anything about denaidans on the galactic web."

Her throat felt tight. "Why's that?"

"Syndicorp controls the news services."

Mention of the media had her stomach doing flip flops and reminded her to start recording. "Why would Syndicorp want to keep your race a secret?"

The lines around his eyes hardened. "Because they destroyed our planet and everyone on it."

She sucked in a breath and half turned to the comm as if it might refute his story. "That can't be true. I'd've heard of something like that."

He snorted and turned toward the cargo bay. "You underestimate the corp'. And with most off-world denaidans being troopers, it made it easy to eliminate the few people who cared about the Termination. Those who escaped, well… There're only about a hundred of us left in the entire galaxy."

She followed him out of engineering, her mind swimming with so many questions, she wasn't sure what to ask first. Pausing to pan the camera over several crew members prepping weapons and gear for the upcoming hijacking, she asked, "You were a trooper?"

"Aye." He continued past the men toward the bay door.

Taking a long, slow perusal of Kashatok sitting on an empty cargo pod with a long pulse rifle across his knees, she was startled when Aleknagik thrust the butt ends of two pulse pistols in her direction. "What's your preference?"

Her stomach lurched into her throat, and she stared at the guns. Did a shuttle mechanic also take part in the fighting? Once again, she realized she hadn't fully thought this plan through. She didn't think she could shoot someone, even if her life depended on it. Yet refusing to take part would certainly raise questions. Extending one shaky hand toward the smaller weapon, she tried to keep her voice low and steady. "What're we shooting?"

From across the bay, Kashatok called out. "The kid's staying on board."

Thank goodness. She flicked her gaze toward the captain once again. His intent stare made her insides flutter. With one hand, he reached absently for the rum beside him, but Jhikik chose that moment to leap to the floor, long tail toppling the bottle. The crash of breaking glass filled the cargo bay.

Kashatok rose, his face cut into deep scowl lines. "I ought to use you for target practice."

Jhikik scurried up Joy's pant leg, settling on her shoulder. His soft tail wrapped loosely around her neck as he peered around her head at his master.

Aleknagik guffawed. "What do you know? The little monster likes the new boy. Just watch your socks, kid."

One of Kashatok's eyes twitched in irritation. "Jhikik, come here."

Joy nudged the creature, but instead of moving, it purred in her ear. Maybe she could at least take some of the heat off the poor little thing. "Uh, you want me to clean up for you, captain?"

That only made Kashatok scowl more. "I can do my own cleaning. Gassy needs you. Go."

Turning, she hurried to the docking platform where Gassy stood watching the events. He surveyed Jhikik, still perched on her shoulder. "I guess you can work with him hanging around. Odd, though." The old engineer met her eye. "He doesn't generally like other men."

Her breath caught. He'd said men, not people. Did he suspect she was female? Looking for a quick change of subject, she tried to resume their previous conversation, her gaze drifting back toward Kashatok. "Was the captain a trooper, too?"

Gassy turned to the console and began pulling up sensor data. "Nope. He left Denaida-daru to join the cartel. Still the only cartel member in the fleet."

"Huh. I thought all pirates were part of the cartel."

He shook his head. "Rest of the fleet traded with the cartel in the past, but there's been some bad blood between us and them lately." He handed her a calibration unit and pointed to the bay door. "Take this over there."

Joy complied, following his instructions with ease. Her mind was on her exposé, which was turning into a bigger story than she'd first imagined. Every time she asked one question, a dozen more popped up. And she was still baffled that she'd been unable to pull up anything on the denaidans, especially if some of them had been troopers. A small piece of her had begun to fear that at least some of what Gassy claimed about Syndicorp might be true.

If it was true, there had to be records somewhere. Her mother was the Communications CEO; perhaps she could provide some clues, assuming Joy could catch her with her guard down. *What will she think if I blow open a major Syndicorp cover-up?* Part of Joy was terrified at the thought. The other part was rubbing her hands in glee.

Kashatok woke at the sound of his alarm and reached for the rum, rinsing his mouth and swallowing before rising from his bed. He'd had to drink himself to sleep to clear the kid from his mind and hoped he didn't regret it during today's burn. Although he hadn't experienced a hangover in years, even he had limits. He rolled over, looking for Jhikik, who was usually in his face looking for breakfast. The little *tunrak* better not have started sleeping with the kid, too.

He found the netorpok chewing on a sock in the corner. "Really, Jhik? That's disgusting." Sighing, he retrieved the sock and tossed it into the recycle bin before opening the hydroponics cage and plucking a few naujiar leaves. "Here."

After checking the water and nutrient levels, he relocked the cage.

His little friend couldn't be trusted with the plants any more than he could be trusted with the crew's socks, and the small garden was the creature's primary source of food. He was a little worried at the number of dying branches he'd been trimming. Soon as they'd finished this job, he'd get Joey in here to look at the thing.

Returning to the desk, he keyed his desk comm. "Aleknagik, we ready for final burn?"

"Uh, you're going to need to come down here and talk to Gassy about that."

"Why?" Kashatok drew out the word. Gassy'd been growing a little forgetful of late, but he'd been with the ship so long, Kashatok hesitated to retire him.

"There's something going on with the docking tube." In the background, raised voices sounded like they were arguing.

Grumbling, Kashatok jerked away from the desk and stalked toward the door. "Come on, Jhik."

The netorpok stuffed the last leaf in his mouth and leaped onto Kashatok's outstretched arm for the brisk walk to engineering. Gassy's voice echoed down the corridor from the cargo bay, his gruff tone underscored by a dull roar. "There's a differential in the hydraulic pressure you have to take into consideration when you make your adjustments."

Continuing past engineering, Kashatok paused at the threshold of the cargo bay. A flat piece that looked suspiciously like a piece of the docking ramp hung suspended from the ceiling. Gassy's broad-shouldered figure loomed beside someone short and thin. Each wore a blocky face shield, and Gassy directed the blue flame of a welding torch along a portion of the ramp, sending out sparks. The smaller figure pointed and said something Kashatok couldn't make out over the roar.

Kashatok stomped into their field lof vision. "What in the name of *Ellam Cua* is going on here? We need to get off this station."

Gassy switched off the torch, throwing the cargo bay into sudden, echoing silence. He lifted his visor to reveal his craggy copper face and iron-gray beard. "Glad you're here, captain. Can you climb up there and steady the alignment spanner while I adjust this coupler lock?"

"Me?" Kashatok grit his teeth. Gassy had been trying his best for years to turn Kashatok into an engineer. "Why do you think I hired a mechanic? Is he not qualified?"

Gassy's face flushed blue-green. "Joey's the one who noticed the coupler was loose, so don't you be firing him. I'm the engineer. It's my responsibility." The lines in his face deepened into a scowl. "Just go back to your bottle. I'll comm you when we're done." Slamming his visor back down over his face, Gassy limped back to the coupler and resumed welding.

Feeling a little stung by Gassy's dismissal, Kashatok turned to the kid. Gassy'd been with him a long time. He was the only one who knew the real reason Kashatok'd joined the cartel. The one person the captain actually attempted to please.

"Can I talk to you a sec in private, captain?" Joey chewed one corner of his bottom lip, his brows drawn tightly together. There was a smudge of grease on one cheek, and Kashatok had to resist the urge to reach out and wipe it away.

What the hell is wrong with me? Regretting leaving his rum bottle behind on his desk, he waved a hand for Joey to follow. He stalked across the cargo bay, stopping on the other side of the escape pods. Joey had to jog to catch up, his curly dark hair bobbing in the dirty light. Kashatok put his hands on his hips and forced himself to frown. "Well?"

"Did you notice his foot?"

The question caught Kashatok off guard. He dropped his hands. "What about it?"

"He tried to walk up the wall as if he was wearing grav-boots. He fell pretty hard." Joey shook his head, a furrow between his brows. "He's claiming to have superpowers."

"He does. Usually." Kashatok stepped out from behind the pods so he could see his old engineer. "Is he okay?"

Joey blinked, looking confused. "I think so. But I'm afraid he's going to try it again."

Satisfied his old engineer was indeed all right, he turned back to Joey. "Gassy's getting on in years, which is why I hired a mechanic in the first place."

Joey looked away, face turning a luscious shade of pink. "I'd go up there, but the grav-boots don't fit me. Gassy tried to put them on, but they didn't fit him, either."

Kashatok licked his lips, wondering why he was noticing such minor details about this kid. Why he so badly wanted to make everything all right. It had to be his concern for Gassy bleeding over. Or maybe he'd reached an age where he needed to find a protégé. "We'll get you a pair of grav-boots at the next port." His elbow brushed Joey's arm on his way back toward the dangling ramp, tingling through his nerves clear into his chest. *Damn, I need a drink.* "I'll help Gassy out this time. We're going to miss our opportunity if we don't get going soon."

Joey nodded, scurrying beside Kashatok to keep up. "Yes, sir."

"But I want you to stick close to him and call me if he has trouble again."

"Yes, sir."

Gassy lifted his visor at their approach, one eyebrow raised. He pursed his lips and examined Joey a fraction longer than Kashatok liked.

Kashatok picked up the alignment spanner, feeling oddly defensive. "You can't expect the kid to do everything you can do."

"Never said I did," the old man replied.

"I'll get Joey some grav-boots at the next stop. But I can help you right now so we can get out of here before Syndicorp arrives."

"Sure." Gassy lowered his visor again. "Hop on up there and we'll get it done."

Joey picked up his own visor but didn't put it on, watching Kashatok instead. The kid's gaze made the captain want to hold his spine a little straighter. Kashatok summoned his ionic power and leaped to the top edge of the suspended ramp with one graceful bound. For a moment, he balanced on one foot along the narrow upper edge of metal, acutely aware of Joey's increased heart rate even at this distance.

The visor fell from the kid's fingers, and his brown eyes went wide. "You actually *do* have superpowers?"

"Ionic powers. I told you." Gassy tilted his head. "Stop showing off, captain, and hold that spanner steady."

Kashatok did as requested, and soon the coupler was back in place and the ramp reattached. When he returned to the bridge for liftoff, his steps felt lighter than they had in a very long time. Maybe he'd take the kid under his wing after all.

CHAPTER FOUR

For this final leg of the journey, Kashatok planned to come out almost on top of the freighter. The denaidan crewmen were using their ionic shields instead of nav-grav seats, standing battle-ready in front of the cargo bay door. Kashatok strapped a second sidearm to his belt, watching Chignik and Ekwok do the same. Normally, he'd man the bridge while his men handled boarding, but today he relished the diversion. What was it about the new crewman he found so distracting? His mutinous pet seemed infatuated, too, and was sitting on Joey's shoulder in the nav-grav seat right now. *Just wait until the kid grows some whiskers, then he'll be as distasteful as the rest of the crew.* Yet somehow Kashatok doubted that.

The familiar, slightly nauseating sensation of the ship exiting burn raced through his veins. Aleknagik's voice came over the comm. "Sensor range in sixty. Venting cargo bay now."

Kashatok took a final breath before strengthening his shield against the vacuum of space. Chignik's multiple braids whipped and coiled like live snakes in the hurricane of depressurization. The denaidan ability to withstand vacuum gave them a strong edge when it came to hijacking ships; no waiting to synchronize the ship's atmospheric shielding.

The deck shuddered, and Aleknagik's voice vibrated in his cochlear implant. "Captain, we're taking fire. Brace for evasive maneuvers."

Scowling, Kashatok bent his knees slightly. While it wasn't unusual for a freighter to carry light armament, his intel hadn't included information about heavier guns. The ship vibrated again and jerked left. After a few more maneuvers, a hard jolt told him they'd made contact. "Grapplers in place. Captain. They're refusing to evacuate the bay."

Kashatok grunted. The moment his men popped the door, the freighter's cargo bay would lose pressure. The sudden equalization wreaked havoc on living organisms, and he hated dealing with dead bodies. If he could've sighed, he would've. Well, they'd been fairly warned. Crossing the boarding tube, he popped the freighter door's control panel and shoved his palm against the wiring, sending an ionic pulse through the mechanism. Most ships were frightfully unprotected from ionic pulses. The door slid ajar, allowing a mist of air to blow by as the two cabins equalized. Catching Chignik's eye, Kashatok nodded the go-ahead.

His men surged across the boarding tube, weapons drawn.

Inside, the freighter's cargo bay was lined with stacks upon stacks of detention cells.

Kashatok's twin hearts sank. He'd hijacked a fucking prison ship? Painted lines on the floor delineated walkways between the cages and Syndicorp emblems glared from the walls and floor. To prevent breakouts, Syndicorp would run ships carrying convicts under false manifests, but there were usually tells; excess loading of supplies, cargo weights that didn't change between ports. This sector was a long way from Nunam-qa, however, so the possibility of a prison ship hadn't crossed Kashatok's mind. *Because your mind was preoccupied, you stupid shit.* Fuck, he needed a drink.

From behind the bars, humanoid faces stared back at him, arms groping and eyes bulging as their bodies reacted to the reduced pressure. He opened his mouth to order his men to find the controls for life support, but Chignik was already on it. There was a chance the prisoners would survive. Closing his eyes for a moment, Kashatok was tempted to offer up a prayer to *Ellam Cua*, although he'd stopped believing in any sort of deity long ago. Why hadn't the freighter's captain mentioned the bay was full of prisoners? Or had he told Aleknagik, who then chose not to mention it? Sometimes Kashatok and his first mate didn't see eye-to-eye.

The moment the cargo bay was at full pressure, he opened the interior airlock and strode down the hall toward the bridge. The other cargo holds likely held more people, but he'd leave his men to sort through them. He was going to find the captain and secure the prisoner list. If there were any cartel members on board, he might yet break even on this job. Ransoming a high-ranking cartel member might even make the hijacking worthwhile.

The empty corridors echoed with the wail of sirens. Ahead, a man stepped from a doorway, his pulse rifle aimed in Kashatok's direction. Kashatok threw the full force of his ionic shield in front of him and took the blast without slowing a step. Pulling his own pistol, he blasted the fellow right between the eyes and continued forward.

As expected, access to the bridge was locked. He blasted the interface and shoved his palm against the wiring. The door hissed and popped open a crack. Heat seared past his cheek as someone inside fired through the opening. Stepping to one side, he pulled the sliding door the rest of the way open. More pulse fire heated the air.

He waited until they paused to let their weapons cool, then hardened his shield and stepped into view. Two human males wearing bandoleers aimed weapons his way. A third had his back toward the door, his pale blue shirt darkened by sweat. Kashatok dodged, sweeping the closer gunman's feet out from under him. Then he dropped the one farther back with a single shot to the chest.

The third man grabbed a nearby pistol and spun to face him. Kashatok fired again. Sparks erupted from the console as the man dove to one side.

The nearby gunman regained his feet and lunged. Kashatok slammed an ionically charged fist into the man's face. The man's eyes rolled up in his head and he toppled backward over the captain's chair.

Spinning, Kashatok caught a searing blast across his shoulder from the man in the blue shirt, who dodged into the corridor. Ignoring the pain, Kashatok leaped for the door in time to see Chignik lay the man out with a point-blank shot to the chest. The man's body flew backward and landed spread-eagle on the floor. The scent of burned flesh filled the hallway.

Chignik hooked a thumb over his shoulder toward the cargo bay. "Captain, you're not going to like this."

"There's not a single thing I *do* like about this," Kashatok replied, pressing a hand against the burn on his shoulder. His fingers came away sticky with turquoise blood. "Ruined my lucky shirt."

"There's kids on board."

The words stopped Kashatok cold. His frustration at this being a prison ship transformed into revulsion. No one sent kids to Nunam-qa, not even the corp. Kids on board only meant one thing. "Slavers."

Chignik nodded. "Looks like it."

"*Uminaq!*" Kashatok looked at the splayed man with disgust. He wore combat pants tucked into the tops of his boots, but his blue shirt was definitely not military or even prison-issued. The pulse pistol lying a few feet away was also not standard-issue. Kashatok swore again.

Back on the freighter's bridge, the first gunman was dead, but the one he'd punched was still breathing. "Tie him up," Kashatok ordered. "Then release the slaves. I'll be on the *Kinship* trying to salvage some of this mess."

"Aye-aye, Captain."

Kashatok strode back through the cargo bay and across the boarding platform, trying not to think about the bottle of rum in his quarters. These slaves were going to need assistance, and his men weren't going to be happy there was no profit in this hijacking. He hoped at least one of the slaves could fly the damned freighter.

Joy joined the rest of the crew at the big U-shaped table in the galley, her camera taking in each face in turn. While she'd been relieved to be spared the fighting, she'd quickly realized it would be impossible to gather footage while Gassy had her adjusting valves in the jungle. She lingered her recording on Kashatok's wide-shouldered frame. One shoulder of his shirt was torn and stained dark turquoise down one arm, which she could only assume was his blood. This story was going to pack a wallop once she'd put it all together. She not only had pirates and gunfights, but slave traders. *All I need now is a love story to round things off,* she joked to herself. Not that there was much love to be felt in the room at the moment.

Across the table, Cooper dragged a hand over his bald head, his dark eyes nearly buried in his scowl. "How the fuck'd this happen?"

"Bad intel." Kashatok set his rum down and placed both palms on the table. "However, as your captain, I take full responsibility. Next job, I'll relinquish my shares to make up for it."

"After we stock up on rum." Gassy smirked and gave Joy a wink. He passed a second bottle of rum in her direction.

No one else chuckled, and the scowl on Kashatok's face made Joy think baiting him wasn't a good idea. She pretended to take a sip and passed the bottle on.

The other human, Moore, licked his lips. "They were probably destined for some sex planet. Enayshu Five pays top credits for kids."

Joy cringed. Slaves were bad enough. Child sex slaves? What the hell had she gotten into?

"How many slaves are there?" Manopup's upper tentacles writhed. "I know a man on Orlenny who may be able to unload a few of the males at the beryllium mines."

Kashatok bared his teeth. "We don't deal in slaves."

"You're not going to sell them?" Joy blurted. The black market still traded sentient life, especially outside of Syndicorp space, so she'd assumed that's what would happen.

"No live cargo." Kashatok spoke through gritted teeth.

Gassy laughed and pointed at Jhikik pacing the back of the captain's chair. "Not since that shipment of exotic pets ran amok."

Joy affected a scowl. While the little netorpok'd been a pleasant companion, she was concerned his affection would give her away. She'd already had to shoo the little creature off twice since sitting down at the galley table. "What'll happen to the slaves, then?"

"Not our problem," Aleknagik said.

Kashatok added, "Doc's over there now, sorting out the casualties."

Joy re-counted the crew, realizing one of the denaidans was missing. She hadn't exactly been formally introduced to them, and keeping track of the odd names had been difficult. The crew seemed polarized, with the denaidans turning to Gassy and the other men turning to Aleknagik. Like planets around a sun, they all maintained a respectful distance from their captain.

"Fucking waste of our medical supplies, you ask me," Cooper grumbled, with Moore nodding in agreement.

"I have some added bad news." Aleknagik waved away the rum as it came in his direction. "We took light damage from their guns during our approach. Long range sensors are down."

Leaning back in his chair, Kashatok sighed. "I also damaged the freighter's bridge with my pulse pistol during the fight. It'll need repairs. No sense rescuing them, only to let them sit here and rot in space."

Joy's assessment of the captain shifted once again. Sexy. Mysterious. And now, altruistic. *Like some kind of Robin Hood.* He was totally going to smash her female demographic. She zoomed her camera in on his face once more and panned down his chest to where his fingers toyed with Jhikik's tail. What would those fingertips feel like tracing across her skin? She shook her head to clear it. Yep, going to smash 'em.

Gassy grunted. "Joey can handle the freighter's bridge repairs while I go outside and have a look at our sensors."

"You sure, Gassy?" The denaidan with a buff-colored beard asked. "I could take a camera out for you."

Gassy scowled at him. "Don't be treating me like an invalid, Ekwok."

"Just trying to help." Ekwok held up both hands defensively and turned to a denaidan with elaborately braided beard and hair. "You find someone on board able to navigate?"

"A few seem capable. I'm more worried about them maintaining their systems until they come up with a safe place to go."

Cooper crossed his big arms and scowled around the table. "I can't believe we're just handing a perfectly good freighter over to a bunch of slaves."

Aleknagik sprawled back in his chair and cut a sideways look at the captain. "I wonder, as well."

Kashatok rose slowly, his presence suddenly filling the entire room. "You want to argue with me?" Edgy silence filled the galley. "As soon as they're on their way, I'll have a new job lined up." Joy's heart nearly leaped out of her body as he leaned toward her. "I want you to pull up any corp' information you can find on their system while you're over there fixing their bridge."

She cleared her throat, feeling light-headed under his smoldering gaze. "Syndicorp information? But they're not a corp' ship."

"Don't fool yourself, kid." Kashatok broke eye contact and swept his bottle to his lips for a long swallow. "Syndicorp turns a blind eye to its subsidiaries as long as they're turning a profit."

She'd eavesdropped on enough of her mother's conversations to know the corporation didn't always play aboveboard, but slavery? No way. Still, she didn't want Kashatok's anger directed her way. "Aye-aye, sir. I'll run a check."

Kashatok lowered one arm to allow Jhikik to scurry up his shoulder. "I don't want to spend a lot of time here, everyone, so get your jobs done and let's burn out of here. I'll be in my cabin."

Joy rose with the rest, declining another sip of the shared rum, and headed to the freighter with her tool kit. Anything she could do to stay off the captain's radar was fine by her.

She crossed the boarding tube, camera taking in everything as she entered the other ship's bay. After hearing the crew talk about the decompression, she'd tried to prepare herself for what lay ahead; the reality turned out much worse than she expected. Rows of corpses lay on the floor, and the stench of unwashed bodies clogged her throat.

How long had these people lived in these small cages? At the end of the huge bay, the tall, copper-skinned denaidan doctor was administering oxygen to one girl, while a man cradled a limp child nearby. A wailing woman knelt a few bodies over. Others walked among the rows, obviously searching for loved ones.

Joy steeled her spine and turned her focus toward the corridor to the bridge. Footage be damned; if she looked any more, she'd lose it. The air reeked of devastation and heartbreak. *Do not, under any circumstances, cry.* She marched with heavy footsteps, holding her breath as long as possible across the cargo bay.

Reaching the bridge, she found two men and a woman already had a damaged console pulled apart. The discolored panels and melted wiring lay scattered on the floor. She cringed. She wasn't completely familiar with the freighter's systems, and now she didn't even have a baseline for how it had looked put together to begin with. Sighing, she showed one of the ex-slaves how to reroute the main interface, then checked on the other systems.

After sending two ex-slaves off to readjust the life support, she plugged a data cube into the system and set up parameters to look for anything related to Syndicorp. The freighter had been destined for a stop in the rakwiji-controlled Onskzu system. She shuddered, imagining the horrible things planned for slaves owned by rakwiji. Another stop was scheduled at a Syndicorp aligned planet in the Pulati system. She double checked, frowning. The freighter had valid planetary access codes.

Fuck.

The captain was right. Someone inside Syndicorp must be running slaves. Mother was going to be pissed. On the other hand, this might be an even bigger story than an exposé on pirates. Joy settled in to download the slave ship's files. After she finished with these pirates, she was going to track down the Syndicorp slavers and blow the lid off their operation.

CHAPTER FIVE

Kashatok's men were discontent now, and rightfully so. Hell, he was pissed, too. This entire effort had been money and time down the drain. He swiped past cartel information that was already outdated because of his careless selection. Even a relatively wealthy fleet ship like his existed on a job-to-job basis, and what he didn't invest in fuel and supplies, he spent on rum. His men had nothing to spare, either. Between gambling and drinking, his denaidan crew always came back penniless, while the posungi and the humans understandably spent most of their time and money at a brothel.

Looking up from his review of manifests and shipping routes, he rubbed his lips. What would Joey choose to do once he was awarded a share?

Realizing he was daydreaming, he resumed his search for a new target. While he didn't mind ransoming an odd prisoner or two, selling innocents into slavery was a completely different level of piracy in Kashatok's view. He avoided passenger or colonist ships for a reason; he didn't want to offer his men the option of making money selling slaves. If he let that happen, they'd be raping and pillaging people's homesteads.

His desk interface flashed as the ship's warning lights went on.

"Captain," Aleknagik's voice came over the comm. "The freighter must've gotten off a distress call. We have troopers on short-range scanners. They'll be in range in less than five."

"*Uminaq.*" Kashatok shot to his feet, sending Jhikik scurrying away. "Disconnect and ready us for burn."

"Doc and the new kid are still on the freighter."

"Tell them to get their asses back on board."

"I already told the doc through his implant. But I can't reach the kid."

Kashatok swore again, striding to the door. The *Kinship* came first —his crew knew that—but he'd sent Joey to go fix the freighter. It was Kashatok's responsibility to make sure he made it back aboard. "Hold position until I tell you to break."

"Aye-aye."

Racing to the cargo hold, Kashatok covered the boarding platform in two bounding strides and headed for the freighter's bridge.

A scrawny slave blocked the corridor, eyes wide beneath his bushy brows. "Is something wrong?"

"Troopers." Kashatok shoved past him toward the bridge. "If you want to hang onto this ship, I suggest you get this ship operational and fly your asses out of here."

Aleknagik's voice vibrated in his cochlear implant. "We're taking fire, Captain."

"I'm on the freighter. Hold until my say so." He dashed the last few steps to the bridge.

Joey looked up at him from the freighter's comm seat. "Captain?"

"Come on." He held out a hand.

"Uh, okay." The kid licked his lips and looked around. "Let me gather my things."

"No time." He grabbed Joey's arm and all but dragged him past the gawking slaves. The ship shuddered and alarms wailed in protest.

He picked up his pace, but Joey's shorter legs were no match for his ionically-enhanced strides. Barely pausing his steps, he swept the kid up across his shoulders, wincing as his wounded arm took the weight, and ran for the boarding platform. Ahead, the airlock to the cargo door stood partway closed, a canister lodged between the panels. Air rushed past him toward the gap. *Great Ellam Cua, the boarding tube was compromised?*

The airlock behind him clanged shut.

Debris-filled air rushed around him, emptying from the nearby compartments. On instinct, he brought up his ionic shield, shutting out the impending vacuum. Joey's weight wriggled against his neck. He couldn't extend his shield over the kid in this position. Setting Joey down, Kashatok shouted over the roar of evacuating air. "Climb on my back and don't let go!"

Joey hunched against the insistent pull of the wind and mounted up without any further encouragement. Wrapping his legs around Kashatok's waist, he pressed his chest against Kashatok's back. The unmistakable sensation of breasts met Kashatok's shoulder blades. *What the hell?*

But there was no time to think on that now. The air would be gone in moments. Kashatok drew hard on his power, shrouding Joey along with himself. He couldn't maintain the extended shield for long, but the boarding platform was only a handful of strides away.

He shoved the blocked airlock open wide enough to allow him to pass. The cargo bay on the other side was already empty of anything and anyone not locked down. Through the gaping maw of the cargo hatch, he could see the *Kinship* drifting away. *Uminaq!*

Aided by the last of the escaping air, he bounded across the floor and leaped out the open hatch toward the boarding platform. Joey's cheek pressed hard against his shoulder, limbs like trembling bands of iron around Kashatok's hips and shoulders. On all sides, lifeless slaves spun in a slow-motion dance, following the slow wake of the *Kinship's* departure.

Framed in the light from the open boarding hatch, Aleknagik stood with one hand poised on the boarding tube control. The atmospheric retention shield flickered to life over the opening. The tube continued to retract. Kashatok strained forward, but even his ionic power could do nothing except hold back the vacuum. All he had was his momentum to catch the ship.

He reached the narrowing opening moments before the hatch shuddered to a close, pulling himself and Joey over the lip and into the cargo bay. Rolling across the deck, he circled both arms to protect Joey's head. He came to a stop poised on both elbows, looking down into very feminine, liquid brown eyes.

For the first time in over a decade, he thought of Aiyana. Remembered her dual, racing heartbeats in the final throes of passion. A giddy, anxious rhythm not unlike this woman's now.

He lurched to his feet, wrenching himself away from the bittersweet memory.

And from the desire to do it again.

Clinging to Kashatok's back through the empty weightlessness of space without a suit—and surviving—had been more than Joy could process. Now he leaned over her, breath caressing her face. She was paralyzed. Exhilarated.

Kashatok stared at her as if she'd slapped him, then rose to his feet without a word and faced his first mate. "You fucking pulled the boarding tube."

Joy rolled to her knees, heart racing with adrenaline. A hard jolt nearly flattened her against the deck.

Aleknagik held up both hands. "We're taking fire." The deck shuddered as if to prove his point. "I couldn't hold the door forever, not if we expect to raise our shields and hit burn before they blow us up. Besides, you made the jump."

The lights flickered, and alarms began to sound. The comm crackled. "Direct hit! Burn drive is offline!"

"Fuuuck!" Kashatok stumbled to the nearby console.

Joy's racing heart skidded to a panicked halt. No burn drive? And they were under attack? She struggled to her feet. Gassy would need her help.

Kashatok shouted into the comm. "Gassy, can you get us up and running?"

Silence.

Kashatok repeated, "Gassy, report."

Joy bent her knees, trying to remain upright on the shuddering deck, and aimed herself toward the door to engineering.

"Aleknagik, get your ass to the bridge and pilot us out of here," Kashatok ordered behind her. "I'll help Gassy."

The first mate darted past her without a hitch in his stride, apparently not walking on the same ship she was on. Then a huge hand all but lifted her by the scruff of her tunic. "You. To a nav-grav seat."

She kicked her legs, pedaling along helplessly. "But—"

"No buts. I don't know what your game is or why you're on my ship, but until we hit the next port, you're to stay in your quarters."

He knew. Holy hell, he knew she was a woman. Well, of course he would. Every inch of her had been locked against him during the jump back to the ship. There was no way he didn't notice her softness against his broad, hard back. Yet surely he wasn't going to relegate her to quarters now? "But Gassy may need my help."

He growled—actually growled—a low sound that carried up his arm and into her bones where he held the collar of her shirt. "This ship is no place for a woman."

Half-carrying, half dragging her, Kashatok propelled her toward the area behind the bridge with the nav-grav seats, the deck rocking and swaying beneath them. As they passed the open door to engineering, the scent of melted conduit and burning hair wafted out.

Kashatok released his hold on her tunic and took a step inside the doorway. "Gassy?!"

Steam and coolant misted from the room, but Joy spotted the engineer in the jungle, wedged between two mangled pipes. She pointed. "There!"

Ducking past Kashatok, she wove between the pipes and edged past an arc of scalding spray to reach the shutoff valves. Everything was coated in boiling coolant. She grabbed hold of the scalding metal and twisted, ignoring the heat against her palms. The spray slowed to a trickle.

Turning, she found Kashatok lowering the engineer's motionless body to the floor. "Gassy, can you hear me?"

The old man still breathed but remained unconscious. Ugly welts covered his skin, and part of his hair had been scalded away.

Joy backed toward the door. "I'll get the doc."

"No." Kashatok lifted the big engineer as if he weighed nothing. The ship jerked and shuddered. "Stay here and see what you can do to get us out of here. I'll take him to medical." His gaze cut into her like a welding laser. "When I get back, I expect some answers."

Part of her smirked, but now was not the time to gloat about him needing her skills. The ship shuddered with another impact. She was on a pirate ship, and they were under attack.

Swearing in every language she knew, she got to work on the diagnostics, only half aware that she'd forgotten to turn on her camera.

Kashatok lay Gassy on the exam table and held up a hand as his medic began to ask questions. "Just take care of him."

Doc pressed his copper-toned lips into a thin line and turned to search his cabinets.

Without time to dwell on the fate of one man, Kashatok dashed from the medical bay. The entire ship was about to be blown to bits. He burst onto the bridge, taking in the massive trooper frigate filling the rear view screen. "Update," he commanded.

"Our sensors are still offline," Aleknagik ground out from the pilot's seat, his shoulders rigid while he worked the controls. "Continuing evasive maneuvers."

Cooper called over his shoulder from munitions, "Starboard guns are down."

"Rear shields at half strength," Ekwok reported.

Bracing his legs as the deck rocked under another impact, Kashatok scanned the internal diagnostic over his starboard gunner's shoulder. The *Kinship* wasn't heavily armed to begin with, relying more on speed and surprise. He watched the shield rating tick down another notch.

He glanced back at the forward view screen. "How far are we from the mining belt?"

"Just under point-one parsec," Chignik said.

"Aleknagik, help Ekwok with shields." Kashatok moved to the co-pilot seat on Aleknagik's right. "I'll take the helm."

As he splayed his fingers over the controls, Kashatok gauged the cloud of rocky debris on the view screen. The system had been mined for generations, creating a belt of dust that smugglers used for rendezvous. He swung them toward the nearby spray of asteroids, taking in trajectories and clearances with an intuition built on years of piloting the *Kinship*. Even so, maneuvering without the use of sensors was going to push his limits.

"Captain, you certain that's wise at this speed?" Aleknagik's hands lingered over the pilot controls.

Kashatok wasn't sure, but he preferred random asteroid dust over the torpedoes that were targeting the *Kinship's* weak spots. With any luck, the asteroid particles would interfere with the frigate's targeting system. He bared his teeth and pushed the thrusters to maximum. "Direct all power to shields. If we can't run, we'll hide."

The view screen lit up from the impact of a small asteroid as Kashatok dodged an L-shaped chunk of rock twice the size of the *Kinship's* cargo bay. He spun the ship on its axis, slipping between a rotating trio of asteroids. The hull rattled and pinged with small impacts. Another torpedo slammed into them from behind.

"Shields at twenty percent, captain!" Ekwok cried out.

"Redirect power from life support if you have to!" Kashatok glanced at his aft view screen. "Just keep up those shields!"

The pursuing ship had slowed, too large to dodge between asteroids, and was now pacing the edge of the field. More rocks exploded into glittering mist in the *Kinship's* wake as the frigate continued firing. *Let them see through that*, Kashatok thought.

Coming up on a particularly large asteroid, Kashatok dropped the ship into a nosedive. The dark, pitted surface loomed in his view screen. He thought he heard someone groan just before he pulled up, leveling out along the uneven surface. The *Kinship* bucked and jerked.

He reigned in his throttle, coming to a full stop next to a jutting column of rock and ice. The ship slammed into the protrusion and rocks cascaded over the hull, bouncing and sailing into each other in a veil of floating debris.

He cut power to the thrusters and shouted into the comm, "Power down all systems!"

The bridge went silent. One by one, the consoles and lights flickered off, leaving only the dull yellow of a single emergency backup. For a few breathless moments, they all sat there staring through the limited angle on the view screen while the asteroid they rested upon rotated them into the frigate's line of sight.

Impacts still blossomed throughout the asteroid field, shattering rock and ice. A blast landed nearby on the asteroid's surface, but it was only one of many hitting the surrounding debris. The weapons fire shifted farther away, leaving behind jagged, gyrating hunks of rock. Their asteroid rotated them out of sight.

Back into sight.

The torpedo fire tapered to almost nothing.

After a few moments, Aleknagik spoke softly. "I think they lost us."

"Maintain full silence," Kashatok ordered. *Let them think we're part of the debris.*

No one dared breathe for long moments.

The frigate's fire ceased. For a while, it paced within range of their view screen. Finally, it moved back in the direction they'd come.

"Long-range scanners are still down," Chignik whispered, as if afraid the frigate might hear him.

Kashatok asked, "How long can we sit here without life support?"

"Humans got a couple of hours," Ekwok replied.

"All right." Kashatok rolled his shoulders, looking around at his men. "Cooper, Moore, hit your bunks. I don't want you using up any more oxygen than you need to. We'll sit here awhile and hope they don't come back. We need time to repair our burn drive, anyway." He took a deep breath. "Just so you all know, Gassy's been injured. It doesn't look good."

Ekwok and Chignik hung their heads. Cooper let out a string of curses.

"Aleknagik, you have the bridge." Kashatok headed for the door. "I'll be in engineering with… the kid." Damn, he had a female on board. Worse yet, he couldn't just confine her to quarters. Without Gassy, he needed her. How could this have happened? His gut churned. Women were not meant for this kind of stress. Hell, he wasn't meant for this kind of stress.

She put herself in this position, he thought.

But that didn't really make him feel any better.

CHAPTER SIX

Joy put all her weight against the wrench and pushed. The floor was still slippery with coolant, and her feet scrabbled for purchase. She couldn't determine what was wrong until she got the coolant flowing again, and she could barely see to work under engineering's single emergency light. And this bolt refused to budge. If she couldn't prove herself useful, she worried what Kashatok might do. But she was fairly certain she wouldn't be tossed out an airlock, at least. He'd surprised her with his weird, chivalric—or was it chauvinistic?—demand she go sit in a nav-grav seat. It felt like he was trying to protect her. A gentleman rogue. Maybe that's what she would title her exposé… If she could convince him to keep her on board.

She threw her weight forward again, swearing as her feet went out from under her.

Two powerful hands gripped her waist, holding her upright.

She stiffened, skin tingling. Turning slowly, the warm, masculine scent of sweet rum hit her senses. Kashatok stared down at her, face darkened by shadow. "Why are you on board my ship?"

She licked her lips, unable to speak or look away. What had she been thinking? He wasn't gentlemanly at all. He oozed danger.

He stepped closer, forcing her back against the tangle of pipes, stopping with the entire length of his body pressed against hers. "Do you have any idea what I could do to you... what my men could do to you if they find out?"

His breath fanned her face. Damn, he smelled great. Her heart threatened to burst from her chest. But she knew there was only one way to handle a bully. Lifting her chin, she said, "So don't tell them."

His nostrils flared and she could feel his muscles tense against her as if he was on the edge of restraint. He stared down into her face for a long moment. When he spoke, his deep voice felt strangely intimate in the silent engineering bay. "You don't know what you're asking."

She barely dared to breathe. He was close enough to kiss, and she wasn't sure whether she should be terrified or excited. Her nipples hardened against his chest. She steeled herself, trying to make her voice authoritative. "What I do know is you need the burn drive fixed. And Gassy's probably in no shape to do it."

Without warning, he stepped backward.

It was all she could do to stop herself from trailing after him like a lamprey on a shark. Here she was getting turned on while he was worried about his engineer. Softening her voice, she asked, "How is he?"

He shook his head, his dark eyes pinched. "Doc's doing what he can."

Her chest tightened. Gassy had been so good to her. Inviting her to cards. Standing up for her with the captain. What would she do without his mentoring? "Anything I can do?"

"Get the drive fixed," Kashatok said through clenched teeth.

"I'm trying." She gestured to the pipe behind her. "I can't get this bolt loose. The diagnostics won't work until I replace this valve."

Lifting one arm, he leaned past her, filling her vision with the mouth-watering copper skin above his neckline and the metal bands holding his beard. With one push, the bolt gave with a teeth-grinding squawk. His breath fanned her cheek. "This just proves my point."

Keeping a logical thought in her head was next to impossible with him so near. *He did that on purpose.* She clutched the baggy sides of her cargo pants to prevent her hands from wrapping around his middle and pulling him even closer. "What point?"

"Women don't belong on my ship."

Well, that ended that moment. She stood taller, temper rising. "That's not fair. You used your superpower, or whatever you call it. You wouldn't have expected Cooper to move a bolt like that."

His features remained hard.

"Fuck you, then. Fix it yourself. I'll go back to my bunk." She placed both hands against his chest and shoved. A shock like a static electric discharge tingled up her arms, but he didn't budge.

He stared down at her for a long moment. A vein on his forehead pulsed. "I can't."

She rolled her eyes. This guy was a tangle of contradictions, strength and vulnerability, sexiness and terrifying anger. She wasn't quite sure what to do with him. "So you do need me?"

His shoulders rose and fell with a breath. Finally, he backed up. "Can you just tell me what to do?"

She moved to the nearby console. "The main flux point's been blown. Start by replacing that valve."

"I meant tell me and then go to your bunk."

"No." She laughed and turned around, resting her bottom against the console. Like she was going to let him hide her away and take all the credit. "I won't know each step until we fix the previous one and run a new diagnostic."

He sighed. "Can you handle it alone?"

Her shoulders sagged. "I'm a shuttle mechanic, not a ship engineer. K-class vessels are complex. I'm going to need help from someone who knows this ship."

Covering his eyes with one hand, he squeezed his temples, then ran his fingers down his face and beard. "Fine. What do we do next?"

She was proud of herself for resisting a grin as she moved toward the cabinets where Gassy kept spare parts. She was going to work the captain like a dog.

And get a ton of footage while she was at it.

J oy removed the tertiary coil matrix and pulled aside all the conduits to the lateral thrusters before shimmying herself into the tight space in the bowels of the main drive. She stared at the fused electronics inside the frequency inverter. How was she supposed to fix that? She couldn't repair a frequency inverter. The part was a specialty instrument that required calibration both before and after installation. Without the frequency inverter, they had no burn drive, and without a burn drive, they had only thrusters to get them out of here.

So much for proving herself useful.

Holy hell, what was she going to do? She wriggled out of the narrow space, swearing at the baggy pocket of her cargo pants as it tore on a protruding bolt. What were they going to do? She could always call her mother. Yet after what Kashatok had just put them through to escape the troopers, she had a feeling that calling on Syndicorp for help would not only ruin her exposé, it would probably end with these men's executions. Kashatok might be a pirate, but he didn't deserve the death penalty.

The captain entered engineering as she emerged from the jungle carrying a heavy toolbox in one hand. He leaned forward and took the handle from her. Her heartbeat thrilled as his skin brushed hers. Since discovering she was a woman, he'd avoided getting within touching distance, which for some reason made stupid moments like this more exciting.

"What's wrong?" he asked.

Her face heated, and it took her a moment to remember her task at hand. "How far is the nearest space station?"

Kashatok's forehead drew into a frown. "Maybe half a parsec? Why?"

Jhikik took the opportunity to scramble down Kashatok's front, using his long beard as a rope, and reached for her. She accepted him without thinking, distracting herself by petting his soft fur. She wasn't a navigator, but she knew parsecs were usually measured by burn cycles. How long would it take to travel half a parsec using only thrusters? Probably a really long time.

She swallowed. Now that she couldn't fix the drive, would he relegate her to quarters? She didn't like the idea of being trapped in that storeroom for months while the ship limped back to civilization. She chewed her bottom lip, seeking any last-ditch alternatives. "Is Gassy awake yet?"

"Sort of. Doc says he's doing better." Worry still filled Kashatok's eyes.

Joy gulped. Poor Gassy. "Can I see him?"

Kashatok nodded, and in silence, they headed to the medical bay, Kashatok's long strides keeping him well ahead of her.

Gassy lay inside a shimmering sterility chamber on one bed, huge blisters covering most of his skin. Despite the guilt churning through her gut, she turned on her camera. Gritty footage brought ratings, and that's why she was here, right? She hung back as Kashatok approached his bedside and zoomed in on Kashatok's face.

"How're you doing, old man?" asked Kashatok.

The engineer cracked open one eye—literally cracked, the crusted blister making an audible sound as the lid lifted. His other eye remained swelled shut. "I'll snap out of this in no time." His voice sounded like rocks grating against each other. He caught sight of her and one corner of his blistered lips turned up in what might've been an attempt at a smile. "Hey, you. Got my baby up and running yet?"

Joy stepped forward and tried to smile encouragingly. "You don't happen to have a spare frequency inverter hidden away, do you? Or know how to fix one?"

His already horrific-looking face crumpled. The flashing lights tracking his vitals flickered red. "That part's beyond a ship engineer's skills."

Well, at least that made her feel a little less inadequate. But it still didn't solve the issue of being stuck on board this vessel for weeks, maybe months, while they languished in dead space.

"So now what?" Kashatok kept his gaze on the injured man.

Gassy fumbled for a tube of water next to him, taking a moment to pull it toward his lips. Joy yearned to help him, but wouldn't dare breach the sterility chamber. When he'd finished, he said, "Put out a distress call."

Kashatok squeezed his eyes shut. "It could take weeks for a distress call to reach someone in the fleet."

"Last I heard, the *Hardship* was running this quadrant. They may be close by." Gassy's one good eye glinted with something Joy couldn't quite decipher.

Kashatok's skin flushed blue-green, and Joy realized for the first time that denaidans blushed green. Kinda cute. Then Kashatok's upper lip broadened into a sneer. Not so cute. He looked at Joy, his gaze traveling from her face to her breasts, then he narrowed his eyes and turned back to his engineer. "What are you saying?"

Something inside Joy's gut twisted, and she glanced down at her chest, half expecting her boobs to be hanging out. Nope, still well covered by her baggy shirt.

Gassy answered, "C'mon, Kashatok. You must know. I figured it out right after the first burn when Jhikik wouldn't leave her side."

Joy's breath caught in her throat. Had he just said 'her?'

Gassy knew?

"U*minaq*." Kashatok fisted his hands at his sides, refusing to look at the female beside him. He'd been in her presence for a day and a half now, feasting his eyes on her every move and forcing himself to keep his distance. And here Gassy'd known all along? Kashatok'd never needed a drink more than he did right now. "And you didn't think to say anything?"

"So you could do what?" Gassy's voice creaked, and he reached for the tube of water again. "We were already headed to the job. And she's a damned good mechanic. I needed her help."

Kashatok flared his nostrils. If the old man hadn't been critically injured, Kashatok might've considered slugging him. "We burned past at least three inhabited worlds. It would've taken us no time to drop her off."

"She got you to come out of your damned cabin. First time I've played cards with you in years. It's good to see you paying attention to something besides rum." Gassy chuckled, which transformed into a horrible wet cough. "She's fitting in fine. Give her a chance."

Kashatok threw both hands up, chest blazing with anger. "A chance at what? A life of danger? A pirate ship's no place for a woman."

Gassy spoke softly. "With the nanites, we may not always be pirates."

Not be a pirate? The fire inside of Kashatok went out as if all the room's oxygen had been sucked away. He'd left his planet at sixteen, and was fast approaching the day he could say he'd spent more days on a ship than he had on land. If he wasn't a pirate, what else was there? Yet he couldn't stop his gaze from drifting to the dark-haired woman at the foot of Gassy's bed. He'd found her intriguing even before discovering she was female. How long had it been since he'd craved company of any sort? *Ellam Cua*, he wanted her as much as he'd ever wanted anyone or anything. And that only made him more dangerous. "You believe that corp' bullshit? Their technology is the reason denaidans need something like the nanites in the first place. Anyway, you know that can't help me."

The female's brows were drawn together. "What kind of nanites are you guys talking about?"

Gassy ignored her. "I know you believe you can't be around women, but I've always said your story has some holes. And consider this—she needs the nanites for her own safety. We can't risk anything happening to her. She's the only one who can get this ship up and running."

The female placed her hands on her hips. "*I* need them? Kashatok, what's he talking about?"

Kashatok refused to look at her, his eyes instead focusing on Gassy's brittle looking skin. "*You're* my engineer, old man."

Gassy lay back against the pillows. "I won't be returning to engineering anytime soon, and you know it. Go make that distress call.

Then I suggest you educate your new ship engineer about denaidan birds and bees. I'm going to take a short nap now."

Hearts thundering, Kashatok stood there a moment, staring down at the closest thing to a mentor—maybe even a father—he had. Gassy's assumptions about the female both grated on Kashatok and nurtured a seed of hope; the engineer really believed in the nanite's potential. Even for a man who'd caused his lover's death.

Shaking his head, Kashatok looked away. Gassy was wrong. Aiyana had died in Kashatok's arms. The female was not safe with him, and the nanites wouldn't change that. Yet he didn't trust that she was safe anywhere on this ship, either, not with the way the men joked about females. Impossible as it seemed, he'd have to keep her close and keep himself under control.

Reaching out, he grasped her arm, fingers easily encircling her biceps. "Until we reach port, you're not to be out of my sight."

"What? Why?" Her flesh trembled beneath his fingers, but she didn't try to pull away. "Are you going to tell me what's going on?"

He propelled her toward the door and into the corridor. The physical connection with her arm thrummed through his senses as if her very blood flowed into his veins. *Anaq,* he wanted rum. But there'd be no escape to the bottle for him, not as long as she was on his ship.

She hurried beside him, breathing hard. "Are you going to tell me what this is all about?"

He turned toward his cabin, praying they didn't run into anyone along the way. He never invited anyone into his cabin, and if the men saw Joey enter, they'd know something was up. *If they don't know already.* Gassy had known and not said a word.

The corridor remained blessedly empty. He pushed her inside ahead of him, closing the door behind them. Alone with her, he realized just how precarious the situation was. Every flutter of her heartbeat brushed his senses like a seductress's caress, and he couldn't seem to drag his gaze away from the kid's... the female's... Joey's?... mouth. "What's your real name?" he demanded.

"Joy." She lifted her chin defiantly. "I never lied to you."

His lip twitched, fighting an involuntary smile. *Cute.* Female or not, she was a little punk. "And why are you on my ship? I specifically told you I forbid females."

Through his heightened senses, he felt Joy's body temperature increase. He saw a light sweat break out on her brow. Jhikik, who'd been quietly nestled against the crook of her neck this entire time, perked up and jumped to the floor. Kashatok ignored his querying chirp, refusing to break his gaze.

The pink tip of her tongue moistened her lips before she bit down on her plump bottom lip. Finally, she breathed out, "Shouldn't you be making that distress call rather than worrying about me?"

Resisting the urge to dip his head and claim her mouth, he frowned more deeply. Unfortunately, she was right. He let out a slow breath. There wasn't time to get into a game of words with her, not while they were hanging on the edge of an asteroid with limited power and a busted burn drive. Pivoting, he marched to his desk comm and coded a distress call on several secure fleet channels. The sooner he could get the ship fixed, the sooner he could rid himself of this distracting female.

Once he'd finished, he looked up to find Joy bent in front of the open door to his hydroponic system. Her loose cargo pants had spread tight across her ass, revealing the roundness of her hips. He felt his cock stir, something that hadn't happened in a long time. *Ellam Cua*, bringing her to his cabin may have been a mistake. He forced his attention to the gleefully chittering netorpok swinging among the branches inside the cage. "I don't let him do that."

She looked over her shoulder, one hand still buried in the innards of the hydroponic control box. "Who?"

"Jhikik. He'll eat every leaf in sight if I let him."

She straightened to watch the netorpok drop from one limb, suspended only by his tail, only to swing onto another branch. "But he seems so happy."

He marched over, reaching past her into the cage door. Jhikik chittered and dodged, but Kashatok caught him by the scruff and dragged him out. The little *tunrak* sunk his tiny teeth into Kashatok's thumb before scurrying away indignantly. Kashatok couldn't blame him, but he couldn't let him have free rein, either. "You know better, Jhik."

Joy's breath brushed his arm. "Be gentle. He's just doing what netorpok do."

As if she knows what netorpok do. Over the subtle perfume of the naujiar flowers behind her, he picked up a scent like sun-warmed citrus coming off her skin. The heady mixture made his mouth water. He forced himself back a step. "Tell me why you're here."

She tilted her head, once again chewing her lip. Her pulse pattered with erratic indecision. Finally, she took a deep breath. "What if I told you I'm filming a documentary?"

It took him a moment to understand what she'd said. Then he laughed. "You're making a movie? Of us?"

"Not a movie. A documentary for RealTime News. I want to show viewers inside the swashbuckling world of black market trading and deep-space piracy—"

"Hold on. You're a reporter?" He hadn't seen that coming. RealTime News was known for sensationalistic reality reporting, but that could be a front. "How do I know you're not a corp' spy?"

She lifted her chin. "You don't. But I'm not."

It wasn't a lie. He could feel it in her heartbeat. In the steadiness of her eye contact.

She continued, "I plan on blowing open that Syndicorp slaving ring after I finish my pirate story."

He narrowed his eyes. "Fixing ships and making newsreels aren't exactly complimentary skill sets. Tell me how that happened."

"I'm not incompetent at either one, if that's what you're implying." Her slender throat rippled as she swallowed.

He took a step forward. She'd basically admitted she wasn't a mechanic. How could she take over Gassy's job? "If you aren't going to be able to handle the repairs, I may as well skip all this self-control bullshit."

She leaned back against the cage wall, her gaze remaining locked with his. Her racing pulse kept time with his own, and her eyes were dilated almost black. "I can fix the ship once I have the part."

He took another step, senses on fire. She smelled so delectably fine, the faint and familiar tang of mechanical grease overridden by warm citrus and naujiar perfume.

"But who needs self-control?" She licked those plump lips.

The move was too much. His mouth was against hers before he knew it. Joy's mouth met his, lips softly parted and ready. She arched her back so her breasts made contact with his chest.

Like awakening from a nightmare, his entire body seemed to recover consciousness. Her lips were like a first taste of a rare drug. The softness of her body against his like the warm kiss of the sun after winter.

She opened to him, melted against him, the tip of her tongue tracing his upper lip. He braced both elbows against the cage on either side of her, molding his body against hers.

Her hands slid around his sides, settling beneath his arms, sending rivers of desire coursing through his newly awakened bloodstream. She tasted as good as she smelled, and he delved into her mouth, snaking one hand to the back of her head to hold her. Her short hair felt like pirelux silk between his fingers.

He shifted, placing one leg between hers. She widened her stance to accommodate him, and the heat from her core radiating against his thigh made him groan. Cock throbbing with desire, he broke the kiss and trailed his mouth along her cheek to below her ear.

She exhaled his name, tilting her head back and wrapping her hands around his shoulder blades to pull him closer.

Her feminine scent was stronger here, enveloping him until only this moment existed. Only Joy existed.

"*Kinship*, this is the *Hardship*." A man's unfamiliar voice caused him to jerk away from her as if he'd been electrocuted. "We've received your distress signal. Please send coordinates to your location."

CHAPTER SEVEN

Joy reeled in the aftermath of Kashatok's kiss. Her lips tingled, and her skin craved his nearness and warmth. After telling him she was a reporter, the last thing she'd expected was a kiss, especially a kiss like *that*. Damn. She should've told him the truth a long time ago.

Across the room, the captain had his back to her, shoulders rigid as he brought up a holo image on his desk comm. A copper-skinned face appeared, hovering above the desktop with a shaggy mane of hair rivaling Ekwok's tawny mess and twin-braided beard. Did all denaidans look so barbarically hot?

Kashatok's fingers danced across the desktop controls. "Good to see you, Captain Qaiyaan. Relaying exact coordinates now. Keep an eye out for that trooper vessel."

Qaiyaan's beard swayed as he looked down, presumably at his screens. "Looks like we can reach you in a few hours. We don't have a frequency inverter for a K-class vessel on board, but I think we can figure out how to piggyback your ship to the nearest station for repairs."

The face of a gorgeous human woman with charcoal eyes and dark hair appeared over the other captain's shoulder and whispered something in his ear. Apparently banning women from ships wasn't a denaidan thing or a pirate thing. Did that mean it was personal?

Joy straightened her baggy shirt, watching the familiar way the woman laid her fingertips on the captain's shoulder as she spoke. A strange yearning broke open inside Joy's chest, forcing her to swallow, hard.

The man on the holo nodded, then turned back to the screen. "Captain Kashatok, we're still hoping you can track down information about a secret corp' test lab in this sector. Have you had a chance to look into it?"

Kashatok glanced over his shoulder at Joy. "Now's not a good time, Captain. I'll see what I can pull together before you get here."

"You understand how important this is?" Qaiyaan's eyes glittered with intensity. "That lab may hold the only key to our people's survival."

"I said it's not a good time." Kashatok killed the connection.

Joy frowned at Kashatok's back. "Was that a good idea? We kinda need him to help us."

"He'll come." He continued to stare at the spot the holo image had occupied.

She mulled over what she'd heard. The pirates were looking for a corporate test lab. Did it have anything to do with the destruction of their planet? Why was he being so secretive? *He must still believe you're a spy.* "I'm not recording, just so you know. I told you I'm not a spy. How can I convince you?"

He turned slowly, his gaze raking her from head to toe. Her own gaze flicked downward to the obvious bulge at his crotch, and her lower region tightened in response. The sudden return of sexual tension in the room made it difficult to breathe. She licked her lips, remembering the kiss. Hot guys rarely looked twice at her, but he was definitely looking. Maybe she did know a way to convince him...

"You need to go in there," he pointed to an open door to his right, through which she could see a large bed. Tingles washed across her body and her panties heated with dampness. *Yes, please.* She turned toward the door to comply, and he continued speaking. "And as soon as we reach port, I want you off my ship."

She halted, looking over her shoulder. "Wait, what?"

He stood in the same spot, hands clenched into fists at his sides. "I can't have you around me."

Understanding dawned on her. She slowly turned to face him, her desire burning into anger. "What is it you're afraid of, Kashatok? Is it all women, or is it just me?"

His eyes sparked with repressed anger. "I am not afraid of you. I'm afraid *for* you. Do you have any idea how close you were to destruction a few moments ago?"

"No, because you won't tell me." She crossed her arms. "This could all be resolved by talking."

He bared his teeth. "You want me to tell you? All right. How's this? The denaidan mating ritual is deadly to humans."

Her mouth fell open. *Well, that was unexpected.* "Uh, mating ritual?"

"During intercourse, my species creates an empathic connection so strong, it kills non-denaidan females." His gaze was so intense she almost believed him.

Almost.

She shifted her weight to one hip. "So that explains you banning human females. But why don't you just bring denaidan women on board?"

He looked longingly at the rum bottle sitting on the desk. "Our females are all dead."

Her brows drew together. *All* dead? Gassy'd told her a bit about the destruction of his world in between the last couple of burn cycles. She still had trouble believing Syndicorp would do such a thing, but he was fairly convincing, and she'd grown to trust the old man in the short time she'd known him. Strange that he'd neglected to mention this business about mating rituals, especially since he apparently knew her secret all along. "Are you saying all your women were destroyed with your planet?"

"Our women's empathic abilities were too sensitive. They were incapable of interacting with other species. There were none off-planet."

She realized she should be recording this and engaged her camera. "Have you ever actually reported any of this?"

He scowled. "Not personally."

"Then humor me." She took a step toward the desk. "I'll make sure the galaxy knows."

His eyes tightened, and he held up one palm. "Stop right there. How about you humor *me*, first? It took a lot of nerve to disguise yourself as a boy and board my ship after being warned about the consequences. Why do you want to film us so badly?"

She stopped. If keeping her distance got him to talk, she'd shout from the moon. Not that she felt she could stay away from him for long. He drew her like a magnet drew iron filings. "I'm a reporter. That's my job."

"No. You're a mechanic. A damned good one if you're keeping up with Gassy. A real reporter would've had her camera running this entire time. You just began recording a moment ago."

The heat infusing her face grew nearly unbearable. How did he know? "I… was trying to be polite."

He laughed. "A polite reporter. I buy that even less than your disguise."

She put her hands on her hips. "Hey! It took several days and a jump across open space for you to figure it out."

"I was drunk." He picked up the nearby bottle and rolled it between his hands. "Besides, Gassy figured it out."

"He's smarter than you are." The dig made him blanch. *Good.* He needed to learn she wouldn't put up with bullying. Jhikik tapped her pant leg with one paw and she bent to pick him up. "I've told you the truth. Lock me up if you need to."

He looked up from the bottle, one eye twitching slightly. "I just tried to, and you refused."

"You did?"

He gestured toward the bedroom.

"Oh. That. I thought you wanted me in there for another reason."

Now it was his turn to blush, an adorable bluish green. *Had she seriously just thought this fierce alien pirate was adorable?* He cleared his throat. "Now you know better."

She watched the blush fade. "That other captain you just talked to. He had a woman on board."

The softness that had come with Kashatok's blush solidified into the familiar angry lines she was used to. "Not you, too."

"Me too, what? Does this have something to do with the nanites Gassy was talking about?"

"The nanites are a false hope." Something about Kashatok's expression made her think he wanted that hope, even if he kept pushing it away.

Much as she wanted to smooth the furious lines from his face, she knew better than to approach him. Instead, she plucked a leaf from inside the cage and offered it to Jhikik. He nibbled it delicately, purring in her ear. "Please don't stop talking."

He exhaled slowly. "Stop recording."

She'd forgotten she was. Nodding, she stopped her camera. Her personal curiosity was stronger than her need to film.

Looking closely at her face, he seemed to decide she'd done as he asked. "That woman you saw supposedly stole some Syndicorp biotech that made her telepathic to computers or some such bullshit. As a side effect, the nanites changed her synapses enough to allow her to bond with a denaidan."

Joy broke into an involuntary grin. "That's great news! How many of you have bonded?"

"She's the only one. And she almost died during the process."

"Oh." Joy bit her lip and noticed his gaze shift to her mouth. Her stomach fluttered. "Have other women tried?"

Kashatok turned away. "Not that I'm aware of. But it's not like I'm tracking it."

"But you're wanting women to try."

"*I'm* wanting nothing." He slammed a palm against his desk, shaking the nearby bottle. "Now, can we stop talking about this?"

She gave Jhikik another leaf and ran her fingertips over the maroon petals of a flower, watching it close in response to her touch. She'd get no more out of him right now. "Thank you for telling me."

"Will you lock yourself up now?"

"No." Joy raised an eyebrow. This guy had a single solution for everything. "But I will go to engineering and wait for the other ship."

When the boarding tube connected, she planned on being front and center. She had a few questions for this Captain Qaiyaan.

Kashatok paced the room, waiting for an update from the other ship. Every few minutes he strolled down the corridor and past the open door to engineering, worried about Joy alone in there with his crew mucking about. He'd warned her to keep up her disguise as she'd left his cabin, but for all he knew, Gassy was babbling the secret to everyone in his drug-induced stupor. The old engineer had been sound asleep every time he passed the med bay.

Damn that woman. She had no idea how close she'd come to becoming a turnip with that kiss. The memory of it laced a fiery trail through his veins and settled with low, hard heat in his cock. It had been hours, yet he throbbed against his pants. If he hadn't been interrupted, he had no idea how far he might've taken things.

How long had it been since he'd even wanted a woman? Really wanted one? The few he had to interact with while in port never lingered in his mind. He glared at the bottle on his desk. Then again, he usually drowned himself in rum. He knew how to ride a fine line with the intoxicant, drinking enough to dull his desires but keep him functional for duty.

But desires were easy to dull when the object of them was far out of reach, and he made a point of never staying in port long enough to crack his reserve. With Joy right here on the ship, it was all he could do to keep himself from storming into engineering and taking her hard against the control panel. Or in the parts locker. Or on the floor... He glanced into his open bedroom and imagined her splayed out on the crisp, clean sheets.

Whirling, he grabbed the bottle and threw it, shattering it against the far wall. Even sober, he could barely keep his mind and his hands off her. He couldn't afford to have the stuff sitting around taunting him.

Closing his eyes, he sighed, remembering her slight frame pressed against his back during the jump between ships. Now he had the sensation of her limbs seared against his front as well, her soft belly pressed against his raging hard-on. The wet and willing pressure of her mouth—oh, her mouth—he wanted to devour her.

If he wasn't careful, he would.

One wrong move from him would empty her mind of all its contents forever. Much as he preferred not to, he forced himself to picture Aiyana's blank stare. Why couldn't he remember her face? When he tried to recall those dead eyes, that slack mouth, all he could see was Joy's liquid brown eyes and the delightful way she was always chewing her bottom lip. Very alive.

Jhikik, sensing his distress, chirped and clawed his pant leg. Out of habit, he picked the little creature up and set him on his shoulder. The long tail with its suction cups curled up under his arm and gripped his chest, making him think of Joy's hands against his sides. What if the nanites worked? Could they possibly make her strong enough to withstand the passion of a killer like him?

No. The idea was nonsense, and thinking about it would only invite trouble. As soon as Captain Qaiyaan arrived, Kashatok would transfer her. Get her out of danger. She was a talented mechanic. Maybe Qaiyaan would swap his engineer for her.

As soon as Kashatok came up with the idea, he rejected it. No way he'd put her in Qaiyaan's hands with the nanites right there. What if the bastard slipped them to her? The man was obviously dead set on making mates. Those damned Syndicorp machines could fry her brain as easily as Kashatok would if he took her on the floor in engineering.

The comm pinged. Kashatok stalked to his desk, his mind in a fury.

A bearded face appeared on-screen. "Captain Kashatok, we're approaching the asteroid belt."

Holding back a string of unwarranted curse words, Kashatok replied, "Acknowledged, Captain. I'll turn on our locator."

Qaiyaan ran his fingers down the twin braids under his chin. "Have you discovered any information about that lab?"

Uminaq. The lab. Back when Captain Qaiyaan first contacted him with the request, Kashatok'd done a quick overview of his informant's notes, mostly out of personal curiosity. But he hadn't bothered to actually offer to pay the cartel to dig up the information not already out there on the darkweb. That kind of intel was expensive, and Qaiyaan wasn't a wealthy captain. Even his bucket-of-bolts ship was worth less than Kashatok's usual payout.

Now the *Hardship* was going to pull his ass out of the fire. He guessed he owed him. "My initial assessment doesn't show excessive trooper activity in any of the systems that might indicate they're guarding a secret lab. I do recall a couple that have a suspicious *lack* of Syndicorp traffic. Sometimes that's as good an indicator as excess vessel movement. I'll ask my informants as soon as I reach a port."

Qaiyaan's eyes narrowed. "Is this the first you've looked into it? You know how important this information could be. Not just to me. To all of us. We need a renewable source of nanites."

Kashatok cleared his throat. "Yeah. Have you infected any other women yet?"

A muscle in Qaiyaan's jaw bulged. "No. And it's not an infection."

"My mistake." Kashatok didn't hide the sarcasm in his tone. As he'd suspected, the nanites were a hoax. Still, if information was what the guy wanted, it was a fair price for a ride out of here. "I'll contact you when I have information."

"That's what you said last time." Qaiyaan's holographic face grew larger as he leaned forward. "How about you send out that request right now? I'll wait."

Sighing, Kashatok shook his head. None of the so-called pirates in the fleet really understood what it meant to be a criminal. "I never put cartel requests out via comm or the darkweb. Not even on secure channels."

"Awful convenient excuse. Maybe I should leave you here to think about it while I go track down your part. How much juice do you have left for life support?"

Kashatok grit his teeth. He had to admit, he'd basically ignored Qaiyaan's previous request. He wasn't exactly a pay-it-forward kind of guy, and he'd owed the captain nothing. "Listen, that intel's going to be expensive. I couldn't front the money when you asked before. This time I owe you, so I'll make sure I follow up. The sooner you get us out of here, the sooner I can work on it. If there's a Syndicorp lab around here, you'll know in a few days."

Qaiyaan cast him a disgusted look over the holo, gave a curt nod, and cut the transmission.

Kashatok stood staring at the empty space above his desk for a moment, then he hit the comm and told the bridge to engage the ship's locater. He prayed Qaiyaan didn't make him wait out of spite.

CHAPTER EIGHT

Joy'd been mulling over her options for hours while she puttered in the cargo bay waiting for the other ship. Kashatok's sudden and urgent kiss had left her breathless. Never had a guy as hot as this broody alien pirate even batted an eye in her direction. He made her feel stupid and giddy, like she was thirteen again with dreams of movie star boyfriends.

Don't get involved. He'd just kissed her because she was the only woman around. She wasn't glamorous. Even Mother called her plain. Her few sexual encounters had been nothing worth mentioning, and she had no spectacular skills in that department. Give Kashatok a selection of other women and she'd surely be the last pick.

Besides, on board this ship, she was a reporter, and she needed to think like one. How many filming opportunities had she missed already? No more. If she had to keep her camera rolling until the resulting headache knocked her out, she would. Her gritty pirate exposé had shifted, becoming the heartbreaking story of a species' hopeless cause, of cover-ups and revenge, of stolen technology and sex. It was going to blow her ratings off the charts. As for the nanites, well, if the chance came along, she'd take it. The mechanic in her was intrigued by the little robots. She'd thought her camera was the coolest thing ever when it was installed. What would it be like to have tiny computers at her beck and call?

The comm lit up with a call from the bridge. "All hands, prepare to be boarded."

Excitement surged in her chest. She wiped her hands on a nearby grease rag and engaged her camera. Two pirate ships meeting had to be something special, and she wanted to be sure to capture every interaction. Hurrying to the cargo bay, she joined the rest of the crew. As she panned their faces, she realized that although they seemed relaxed, every one of them was armed.

Kashatok strode between them without a glance in her direction and proceeded to the bay door just as it hissed open. Her ears popped at the sudden change in pressure.

A tall, shaggy-haired man she recognized as Captain Qaiyaan stood on the boarding tube's other side, just as broadly imposing as all the other denaidans. "Permission to come aboard, Captain?"

Her captain was armed, as well, she noted. "Granted."

Qaiyaan crossed over, followed by a younger denaidan with hair as copper as his skin.

Joy focused in on the younger man's bare feet, curious, panning upward to meet his gaze. He grinned at her, and she couldn't stop herself from grinning back.

Captain Qaiyaan asked, "Who's your engineer?"

Kashatok shook his head. "Gassy was injured." He gestured Joy's direction without looking at her. "The kid and I've taken the repairs as far as we can."

The younger copper-skinned man strode right over and stuck out his hand. "Hi, I'm Tovik. You're an engineer? *Assirpaa*!"

She didn't know what *assirpaa* meant, but he seemed genuinely excited. "Mechanic, actually," she said, holding out a hand. "Name's Joey."

"Nice to meet you, Joy. I thought Kashatok didn't allow women on his ship!"

Joy froze, her attention sliding to Kashatok. The entire cargo bay went silent, and the crew seemed to turn toward her in slow motion.

She felt like a mouse in a den of cats. Apparently oblivious, Tovik kept grinning, and she realized she still held his hand. She dropped it and backed up a step, scrambling for a comeback. "You trying to insult me?"

But it was too late. Cooper and Moore had their heads together, muttering. Manopup's tentacles writhed like snakes around his chin. Aleknagik stared at her with predatory eyes. Chignik laughed and slapped Ekwok on the back. "I thought there was something off about the kid."

Kashatok closed in, forcing Tovik to take a step back. "How did you know?"

The poor young man's mouth hung open. He looked over his shoulder at his captain. "Isn't it obvious?"

Qaiyaan took a step forward. "Come here, Tovik."

Tovik slumped back toward his captain. "I knew I should've just stayed in engineering. I'm never going to find a mate."

All around her, the crew continued murmuring. The word "nanites" surfaced several times, along with "sex" and several more obscene references.

"So who does she belong to?" Qaiyaan asked, looking around at the denaidans.

Joy stiffened. "Belong to? I belong to myself."

Qaiyaan looked from her to Kashatok and back to her as if verifying she was telling the truth. Then he dipped his head toward her. "My apologies, Joy. Knowing Kashatok, I assumed…"

"You assumed wrong," Kashatok said.

Joy's stomach churned. Knowing Kashatok? What did that mean? She looked at her captain, but he kept his focus on Qaiyaan, his fists like hammers at his sides. She'd have to grill him for answers on that later. For now, she stepped in between the two captains. "It's a long story, Captain Qaiyaan. But I'm the closest thing the Kinship has to an engineer right now." Reminding the crew of how important she was couldn't hurt. "How about I escort Tovik to our engine room and start working on getting us out of here?"

"I believe Tovik needs you to go with him first." Qaiyaan stepped to the side and held a hand out in invitation. "To go over our ship's burn schematics so you can match up during piggyback. I'd hate to get the alignment wrong and fling you into another galaxy."

"If you send the schematics over, we can review them here," Joy said.

Qaiyaan shook his head. "We won't release specific details about our ship." His gaze cut toward Kashatok. "Especially not to a cartel informant."

Gassy'd mentioned Kashatok was the only cartel member in the fleet, but Joy hadn't realized there was animosity about it. Shrugging, she took a step forward.

Kashatok's hand on her arm halted her. "I'm coming, too."

Qaiyaan thrust out one hand, his other close by his pulse pistol. "I'd prefer you stayed aboard your own vessel, captain."

Kashatok's grip on her arm grew firmer. "I'm not comfortable letting her go alone."

Joy gently pried his fingers loose. "I'll be fine, captain."

He dropped his hand, but she could see by the heaving of his chest he didn't agree. Spearing her with a dark look, he said, "I need to speak to you. Now."

"Of course." Acting more self-assured than she felt, she followed him to the far corner of the cargo bay. Ekwok bobbed his tawny head thoughtfully as she passed by, his eyebrows high. She refused to notice anyone else, but she could feel their attention like lasers following her movement.

Rounding the nose of the shuttle, Kashatok turned and gripped both her biceps. "I don't trust him not to take off with you once you're on board. Without functional drives, I can't follow you."

At the physical contact, her nipples had hardened involuntarily, yearning for his thumbs to spread inward and tease them. How did this man banish all sense of reason within her? Perhaps his caveman-like attitude was pushing her biological buttons. Whatever it was, she liked it, but now wasn't the time for such things. "Why would he take off with me?"

"He has the nanites."

She waited for more explanation, but he apparently believed he'd said enough. Shrugging free of his grip, she tried to give him a reassuring smile. "Kashatok, there is no reason he would steal me away. There are countless numbers of women throughout the galaxy he can give nanites to."

"The nanites are stolen Syndicorp tech. He can't just give them to anyone."

"If that's true, he won't force them on me. Stop trying to hide me away."

His jaw muscles bulged as he ground his teeth and his chest still heaved, but he obviously couldn't argue. "I don't like it."

A warm feeling welled up inside her. She'd never felt protected by someone before, had never thought she'd like it, especially since her mother was so overbearing. But Kashatok's emotion was so raw and genuine, it wasn't about control for the sake of control. He was truly worried about her.

She checked over her shoulder to be sure no one could see, then playfully tugged the end of his beard. It was too bad he'd left Jhikik back in his cabin; the little netorpok might've given him comfort. "I know you just want to keep me safe, but Captain Qaiyaan came all the way here to help us before he even knew I was aboard. I don't think he'll harm me."

"What if he doesn't let you come back?"

"Why would he do that?"

"The other pirate captains don't trust me."

Joy tilted her head. "But he came to help you."

Kashatok rubbed his forehead, his face tight. "Denaidans help other denaidans. There're too few of us left not to. But they don't trust me with women, and for good reason."

She made a show of turning off her camera. This was something personal, and she wanted him to feel free to talk. "Tell me why. Please."

Tiny muscles twitched on his cheeks as if it took everything he had to keep himself in check. "It's complicated. Now's not the time or place."

She leaned closer, making sure she had full eye contact. "When I get back?"

He closed his eyes, letting out a shallow breath before nodding sharply.

"All right. I have an idea." She leaned around the shuttle to look at Qaiyaan. Aleknagik had moved forward and was talking to the other captain. Tovik laughed at something they said, and the rest of the crew joined in. She turned back to Kashatok. "Ask him to leave one of his other crewmen behind as collateral. He won't abandon his own man."

Kashatok inhaled slowly and released it. "You're suggesting a hostage, of sorts."

He didn't move for a long moment, just looking at her, and her heart threatened to beat out of her chest. It felt like he might want another kiss. He smelled so good, like nutmeg and smoke. She licked her lips.

Gazing at her mouth, he reached out and brushed her lips with one thumb. "Don't let them talk you into anything stupid. All right?"

She nodded, every nerve ending alight with his nearness.

Then he pulled away and stalked toward the gathered crew.

Regaining her presence of mind took a moment. When her legs felt steady, she hurried to catch up, trying hard not to stare at his amazing backside. The irony wasn't lost on her; she was ogling him while the crew was obviously thinking similar things about her. Sweat prickled her skin under the crew's watchful eyes, but she kept her head high.

Kashatok stopped several feet from the other captain. "She'll go with you, but we need one of your crewmen to stay here while she's gone."

Moving into place at Kashatok's side, she caught Tovik's eye and winked. The stiffness in the young man's shoulders eased, and he winked back. This could all be worked out if she could just keep them talking.

"Agreed." Qaiyaan tapped a spot below his ear. "Noatak, you're needed on the *Kinship*."

Kashatok added, "And don't mess with her head. She's my only engineer."

The warmth she'd felt earlier cooled a little. Engineer. Right. That's why he needed her safe. She'd been reading way too much into the kiss.

Noatak arrived—a big denaidan with thick black hair kept in check with wide silver bands along its length—and after a moment of hushed discussion between him and Qaiyaan, Joy followed Tovik aboard the *Hardship*.

A hard lump blocked her throat as she crossed the boarding tube. She entered the much smaller cargo bay of the *Hardship* close on Tovik's heels, expecting him to continue toward the stairs leading to a grated catwalk ahead. Only a few steps inside, he spun, stopping her short. "Orders, Captain?"

Qaiyaan cycled the atmosphere shield up behind them, hazing out the view into the *Kinship's* bay. Joy's stomach clenched, and not only because the gravity on this side was lower than she was used to. Kashatok might've been right. "What's going on? I thought we were going to look at schematics."

A charcoal-haired woman bounded down the catwalk stairs, spotted Joy, and slowed. Joy felt a strange desire to cringe. To turn tail and run back down the boarding tube. The woman was even more stunning in person than she'd been on the holo-screen, wearing a form-fitting tank top and black leather pants, rounded in all the right places. Her perfect, heart-shaped face and creamy skin made Joy feel absolutely swarthy. Joy brushed both palms ineffectually down the front of her shirt and onto her thighs, as if that might magically change her grease-stained work clothes into a pirelux suit.

The captain held an arm out and the other woman ducked under it, wrapping her arm around his waist. He said, "Joy, meet Lisa, my mate."

"A woman?" Awareness dawned on Lisa's face and she scrolled her gaze down Joy's body. "I thought you said this Kashatok fellow didn't allow females on his ship?"

Joy glared at the woman. She'd met this type plenty of times; sexy, confident, and dismissive of those they considered beneath them. Her mother was that way. Joy stood taller, looking down at the shorter female and lacing her words with sarcasm. "A pleasure to meet you, too."

The woman's pale skin flushed pink, and she lowered her gaze. "I'm sorry. I didn't mean to be rude. It's just that I didn't expect you." She raised her eyes to meet Joy's. "Can we start again? I'm Lisa."

Joy nodded politely. She didn't trust this woman any more than she currently trusted these men. "Why did you bring me over here?"

A clean-shaven denaidan appeared at the top of the stairs and leaped down what had to be fifteen steps in a single bound. His eyes widened as he approached. "A woman?"

Lisa elbowed him. "Be polite."

What was it with this crew and their rude introductions? Joy thrust out a hand. "I'm Joy. Interim engineer for the *Kinship*."

"Mekoryuk, but you can call me Mek." He took her hand, a smile toying with his lips. "I'm delighted to have you aboard."

"Now that the introductions are over, I need to get back to the *Kinship* and finish repairs."

"Take a breath," Qaiyaan said. "You're safe now, and welcome to stay. Kashatok can't hurt you here."

"Kashatok would never hurt me." Joy realized as she said it how much her opinion had evolved in only a couple of days.

The three men exchanged a glance.

"What?" Joy asked.

"Kashatok has a reputation," Qaiyaan said.

"He leaves dead women at every port!" Tovik's green eyes went wide.

Joy's hand fluttered to her throat. His words a short while earlier floated through her mind; *they don't trust me with women, and for good reason.*

"Not dead, Tovik," Mek said. "Comatose."

Comatose—were they saying Kashatok was trying to mate with women in every port?

"Same thing." Tovik scowled. "They ain't getting up again, are they?"

Not Kashatok. She didn't believe he was capable of such a thing, not with how he kept pushing her away. Not with how he wanted to protect her. Joy found her voice. "You must be mistaken. Kashatok would never do that."

"You know about our mating effects?" Mek tilted his head as if reassessing her.

She nodded firmly. "Kashatok told me all about how you can't be with women and how the nanites are supposed to fix that."

Qaiyaan crossed his arms. "Asked you to get them, did he? Probably wants a toy with a longer battery life."

Joy gritted her teeth. "I'm not a toy. And no, he didn't ask me."

The captain's cocky attitude turned to confusion. "He didn't?"

"He told me to stay away. Wants me off his ship as soon as possible. If he didn't fear you'd infect me with nanites against my will, he'd ask you to take me off his hands for good."

Mek held both palms out. "Let's be clear here: the nanites are not an infection."

"And we'd never do anything against your will!" Tovik insisted.

All the men started talking at once until Lisa put her fingers in her mouth and emitted a sharp whistle. Joy's assessment of her improved another notch. "All of you, be quiet."

The men grumbled but quieted.

Lisa put her hands on her hips. "What's important here is what Joy wants." Lisa turned to look Joy in the eye. "So let her speak."

Joy's throat went suddenly dry. What did she want? These pirates had stumbled upon top-secret Syndicorp tech that could allow them to hack into galactic banks or steal military secrets, and yet all they wanted to do with it was to create mates. If she was honest with herself, she no longer cared about the exposé. She hadn't even turned her camera back on after talking to Kashatok. She honestly wanted to fix the *Kinship* and make Kashatok value her enough to keep her aboard. And maybe, just maybe, explore this mating ritual thing.

But to do that, she'd need the nanites.

Her pulse thundered in her ears as she said, "I'd like to know a little more about those nanites, please."

CHAPTER NINE

Kashatok paced the big bay, pretending to catalog non-existent cargo while he waited for Joy to return. At the back of the cavernous space, his crew sat around a cargo-container-turned-card-table playing the slowest game of Ongaru Flip Kashatok'd ever seen.

The *Hardship's* first mate had fit in among the men as easily as if he was one of them rather than what amounted to a hostage. The thick bands of silver in his long hair made him stand out among the slightly rougher crew, who seemed to hang on his every word while he spoke animatedly about the nanites. "It took me awhile to believe it, too, and I was right there. But believe me, if you could hear the noise coming from the captain's quarters every night, you'd believe it's possible, too."

Chignik tilted his head back and groaned. "*Ellam Cua*, to experience a woman again."

Nodding in agreement, Ekwok leaned forward. "Noatak, please, will you give the nanites to our female?"

Kashatok bristled at the term "our." This was just what he'd feared; the crew wanted her. Were already plotting to have her. *She's mine.* The thought rose up inside him in a primal wave, and he clenched his fists at his sides, trying to squash it down. He was no better than they were if he thought like that. He needed to keep himself and his crew in check. Perhaps he should ask Captain Qaiyaan to keep her on board the *Hardship* and avoid the whole thing. But once again, that primal possessiveness rose inside him. *Mine.*

Noatak continued, "The choice is up to her. I doubt she'd want them if she's not attached to a denaidan."

Jhikik appeared out of nowhere, digging his claws into Kashatok's pant leg and scurrying to his shoulder. The little *tunrak* must've escaped through the vents again, but for once, Kashatok was glad. He needed the little guy's calming effect. He stroked the soft tail as it hugged his neck. "Don't worry, Jhik. She'll be back."

Jhikik made a high-pitched noise and settled into a crouch.

At the game table, Cooper slapped a card on the center pile, waving away the bottle being passed around. "I'm glad I don't have to rely on some damned microcomputers to get lucky. Wonder if the captain will let her stay on board a while?"

Moore snorted and shuffled his hand. "I'll wait for the next brothel, thank you. I prefer my bed partners to look like women."

A few of the men laughed. Chignik shook his head. "She's not that bad."

"You have obviously not been around women much," Manopup said, his tentacles waggling suggestively.

"One more thing," Noatak said, playing his turn. "Not every woman's brain structure will be suitable. The nanites could be deadly."

Aleknagik finished a long swig of rum and thrust the bottle at Moore. "I don't care a damn about her brain structure, as long as her girly parts are in the right place."

Without thinking, Kashatok all but leaped across the bay to the table, looming over the players. The chatter cut off. "There will be no more talk of Joy's girly parts, and she's not going to take the nanites, so get her out of your mind."

The astonished faces broke eye contact with him one by one. All but Aleknagik. "Interesting that you gave her the option for a solo bunk room, captain."

Kashatok's dual hearts slammed hard against his ribcage while his crew exchanged questioning and suspicious glances. *Hadn't Aleknagik offered her that deal?* Kashatok honestly couldn't remember. He took a menacing step toward his first mate. "Just what are you suggesting?"

"Difficult to respect a captain who breaks his own rules."

"Hey, now, hey!" Noatak rose from his seat, making calming motions with his hands.

Just then, a hiss indicated the boarding tube shield had dilated.

Joy stepped into the bay.

Joy's mind buzzed with nanite activity. That was the only way to describe the sensation in her head. They were having a party along her optic nerve, right where her camera interfaced with her cerebral cortex. After she'd learned more about the nanites, the mechanic in her was even more fascinated. The things were supposed to allow her to hack into computer systems, of all things. Imagine how easy diagnostics could be with that kind of tech in her head? Not only that, she wanted to see if that kiss Kashatok had given her meant anything. If it hadn't, she'd at least be helping these men increase their supply of nanites and doing something to make up for the damage Syndicorp had done to these people. Not that they could ever know she was in any way affiliated with the corp'. That was one secret she needed to keep fully and completely.

Because of her cybernetic implant, Mek had been able to streamline the synaptic insertion. He'd wanted to keep her aboard the *Hardship* for observation, since she'd just received one of the two remaining nanite samples in their possession. But Joy knew Kashatok was probably blowing a gasket by now, so she'd made a deal to bring Tovik along so he could monitor her.

She stepped off the boarding tube and into the *Kinship*, leaving Tovik to maneuver the hover container carrying specialty parts across the walkway. The moment she emerged, Jhikik came bounding across the deck and leaped into her arms. "Hey, little guy. I missed you, too."

Looking up, she met Kashatok's concerned gaze across the wide bay. Behind him, his men had risen from their seats around a cargo container. Several game cards fluttered to the floor.

In a burst of motion, Kashatok strode over, his face once more bearing his usual scowl. "Well?"

She'd meant to tell him she'd taken the nanites, but hadn't pictured an audience. Instead, she gestured behind her, where Tovik was emerging from the boarding tube. "Tovik wants to install a burn harness, but I'm nervous about trying without Gassy's help." More than nervous, actually. A ship that got caught in another ship's burn wake could be flung to an unknown location, even another galaxy—and not always in one piece. The harness would create an invisible field that aligned each ship's frequency and, in effect, turn the two ships into a single unit, at least for purposes of the burn. "I'm not an engineer. What if I mess something up?"

Tovik stopped beside her, his bare feet and easy smile out of place among the crew. But the kid seemed to have eyes only for her. "Aw, you got this, Joy. I'm here every step of the way."

"I appreciate that." She smiled back gently. Tovik was obviously in puppy-love, and just as obviously had little experience with women. She wanted to tread carefully around him.

Kashatok wasn't as gentle. "She and I can handle it. Dismissed."

Tovik's face fell. "But you need to pilot the ship."

"Aleknagik can handle it."

"Damn straight," his first mate agreed.

Tovik's eyes darted nervously between the two men. "I'm also supposed to stick close to her in case the nanites go haywire."

As if with one breath, the surrounding crew seemed to gasp. "She took 'em."

"I thought they were dangerous?"

"What happens now?"

Joy's gut clenched, and she bit down hard on her lower lip. This was not how she'd wanted Kashatok to find out. And it'd definitely not been her intention to tell the entire crew.

Kashatok met her gaze, his eyes roiling with a maelstrom of horror, anger, and… hope? "I told you the nanites were dangerous. Why would you take them?"

Joy nibbled her lip, stopping self-consciously as his eyes followed the movement. "I already had a cybernetic implant, so my brain's used to interfacing. Mek says he thinks it'll be easy for me."

The Hardship's doctor had also pointed out that since she'd be surrounded by denaidans, the nanites would protect her if someone got "a little rowdy," as he put it. He'd also given her a small pulse pistol, which she now wore at her belt.

Kashatok let out a string of curses in that guttural language the denaidans spoke. She thought she heard both Qaiyaan's and Mek's names squished in there.

Chignik moved toward her almost reverently, causing Jhikik to scurry from her arms and perch on her shoulder. The netorpok bared his blunt teeth and Chignik halted, his gaze never leaving Joy's face. "How do you feel?"

Tuliak, usually so quiet he was forgotten, murmured, "Hopefully horny."

The burst of laughter from the crew cut off as Kashatok rounded on the group behind him. "Anyone who touches Joy without her permission will get worse than space-locked."

Tovik's eyes were nearly bugging from his head. "What could be worse than space-locking?"

Leaning close, Kashatok nearly breathed fire with his next words. "You don't want to find out."

Joy made a cutting motion between Kashatok and the young engineer. The tension was making the slight headache from the nanites worse. "No one's touching me and no one's getting space-locked. We have much bigger issues at hand." She grabbed the handhold at one corner of the hover container. "Qaiyaan detected a trooper ship back in the area, so we need to get this thing installed and burn out of here before they find us."

Kashatok's snarl relaxed enough to be called a scowl once again. "*Uminaq.* Fine. You two get to work. I'm going to have a word with

Qaiyaan." He bored into Tovik with a gaze that could cut through hull plating. "I'll be back soon."

To his credit, Tovik stood his ground.

The denaidan who'd stayed aboard the *Kinship* stepped forward. "I'll escort you over." The big man slowed as he passed Joy, his gaze curious. "Got to say, you're one ballsy woman, coming back here. I'd keep a blaster close if I were you."

Joy didn't answer him. She wasn't sure if she was ballsy or just plain stupid.

Kashatok focused on Joy before he headed toward the docking tube. "You're my mechanic. Remember that. Do not put up with any *anaq* from the others."

This time, the way he called her "my mechanic" filled her with a new flutter of hope. His words felt possessive. Personal. A lightness seemed to blossom right below her heart, filling her stomach with butterflies. Unable to help herself, she beamed at him and pulled the hover container between the surrounding crew toward engineering.

Entering the familiar space, she paused. The room seemed full of motion, even though there were no moving parts within view. Was it the nanites increasing her awareness? Lisa had told her she might begin to sense computer systems as the nanites populated her synapses, but she shouldn't expect any immediate changes. Like her camera implant, it would take time to train her brain to use the nanites once they began working. She tried to focus on the console across the room but received nothing out of the ordinary, so she moved toward the workbench and helped Tovik unload the elaborate contraption of metal and flux tubing he called a harness. He stroked a palm over the part's shiny metal face. "We'll need to splice this into your main burn drive. Is the power supply off?"

She turned to the nearby console. Without even calling up the information, she knew the circuit to the burn drive was disconnected. Excited, she swept her gaze over the controls and received a reading from the gravity generator telling her all systems were within acceptable parameters. *Wow.* These nanites were going to be useful.

Still unsure it was all real, she tapped the controls and manually reassured herself that the system powering the burn drive was off. "Ready."

Together, they manipulated the harness between the mess of pipes in the jungle. Halfway through securing the harness, she had a new understanding of why Gassy called it a jungle. Both she and Tovik had to invent new ways to bend and twist to access the connections, while Jhikik clambered among the conduits overhead, seemingly unwilling to let her out of his sight. Currently, she lay on her back on the floor beneath a large duct, stretching one arm overhead toward one cable while holding two other cables near her belly button to keep them from escaping. She couldn't quite reach her target. "Damn it, I could use a third arm in here."

On his hands and knees, Tovik squeezed his wide shoulders into the small space next to her. "You sure you're on the right set of circuits?"

With a sudden yelp, he toppled forward. Just as abruptly, he was yanked backward out of the hole.

"What the hell do you think you're doing?" Kashatok's low voice rattled the metal duct above her face.

"*Anaq*, dude!" The sound of scuffling reached her. "We're just modulating the shield phasing. You want us to crack each other like eggs on our first piggyback?"

Letting go of her cables, Joy wriggled herself free. Kashatok's fists held Tovik's tunic and the black expression on his face would be enough to make a rakwiji male go limp.

"Kashatok, it's okay." She moved forward to stop him.

The captain gave Tovik a hard shove, sending him stumbling backward against the nearby console. The panel lit up at the impact, and a wave of data hurtled outward. It slammed into Joy's mind like a pulse blast. Out of habit from over a year practicing with her camera, she threw up her data override protocols. But the incoming wave was huge.

Her vision went dark. Tovik's angry response to Kashatok was lost to her as she stumbled backward, blinking.

Blinking.

Blinking.

She pressed both palms against her eye sockets and released them while information twittered incomprehensibly through her consciousness. Her veins slowly turned to ice. She felt like she could no longer breathe under the onslaught. Just before her legs collapsed beneath her, she gasped, "Kashatok, I can't see."

CHAPTER TEN

Kashatok hovered over Mek's shoulder, watching the doctor run a scanner over Joy's head for at least the fifth time. She lay unconscious on the cot in the *Hardship's* medical bay while Jhikik, refusing to stray more than an arm's length away from her shoulder, clicked a warning every time the doctor's hand moved closer to her. Kashatok knew how he felt.

The instant Joy'd collapsed, he'd scooped her up and rushed to the *Hardship's* medical bay. Qaiyaan and Lisa had met him at the boarding tube and now the couple stood close together at the far corner of the medical bay, murmuring softly together. The part of him that wasn't intent on the dire situation envied the way they seemed to act as extensions of each other.

Mek set the scanner aside and turned to face Kashatok and the others. "I can't yet determine if the damage to her optic nerve is permanent."

Kashatok needed to punch someone. Or he needed a drink. "Why didn't you warn her this could happen?"

Mek stared at his scanner. "I warned her there would be side effects, but we didn't count on the nanites populating her synapses this fast. She's nearly fully integrated already."

Lisa sighed, her face flushed pink. "I should've remembered. At the Syndicorp lab, people with existing cybernetics stabilized at least ten times faster than people like me. My brother was using the nanites to hack the lab's computer the very next day."

Kashatok examined the soft curve of Joy's face. *Ellam Cua.* He wanted to touch her, to physically make sure she was still breathing. His gaze slid to her chest where her breasts were barely noticeable mounds beneath her tunic. She wasn't pinup-girl curvy, but she was definitely female. How could he have ever thought otherwise? Dragging his attention away from her breasts, he shoved his hands in his pockets and satisfied himself with the reassuring beat of her heart through his ionic senses. "When will she wake up?"

"I'm not sure," Mek said. "Her brain waves indicate she's cognizant of what's going on and it appears the nanites are working in tandem with her cybernetic implant. I'm hoping that's a good thing. But awake or not, she's going to need to stay on the *Hardship* for observation."

Of course. They'd probably planned this all along. Well, he wasn't leaving her. Kashatok settled back on a nearby stool. "Just tell me what I need to do."

"Go back to the *Kinship* and get ready for piggyback," Qaiyaan said. "Those troopers are scanning the asteroid field only a few kilometers away."

"My first mate can handle the *Kinship*." Kashatok crossed his arms. "I'm staying here."

Mek and Qaiyaan exchanged a glance.

Anticipating an argument, Kashatok found himself off balance when, instead, Lisa gently took Qaiyaan's hand. "He's worried. Let him stay." She tugged her mate toward the door. "We need to bring a nav-grav buffer in here, anyway."

The two left the room and Kashatok stared morosely at Joy. The woman must have a death wish with the choices she made. He shouldn't care, should leave her here to deal with her own consequences. Hell, he should've locked her in her room when he'd first learned her secret. But he'd let her convince him she was needed. He'd been a fool.

Mek took more blood samples, filing them away in a stasis locker. For a small ship, the *Hardship's* med bay was remarkably well equipped. Jhikik continued to click, tail twitching as if ready to slap the doctor's hands away.

Unsure of what to do with himself, Kashatok asked, "What are her options now?"

Mek placed a second set of samples in a centrifuge. "The nanites act like seed cells. Over time, they make synaptic changes that will provide resistance to denaidan mating frequencies. But if allowed to progress too far, the nanites take over completely. I'm monitoring her levels. Short of terminating the nanites early, we have to wait and see."

Terminate the nanites? Kashatok bolted upright. "You mean the nanites aren't permanent? If you can get rid of them, do it now!"

Mek leveled a serious gaze at him. "There is only one way to get rid of the nanites, Captain. The denaidan mating frequency."

A lump rose in Kashatok's throat. To be rid of the nanites, Joy would have to have sex. Glorious, fulfilling, mind-boggling sex. An act Kashatok could never take part in. "You've got to be kidding. Was Joy aware of this?"

"I told her. She was remarkably unconcerned."

"*Uminaq!* Who did she..." Kashatok scrubbed his palms over his cheeks, the heated memory of kissing her washing over him. Had she envisioned him as part of the process? *Ellam Cua,* he should have made it clear that he absolutely wasn't an option. "She can't. She's unconscious."

Rubbing his nose and mouth as if reluctant to say his next words, Mek said, "She... doesn't need to be conscious."

Kashatok took a menacing step toward the doctor. "No one is touching her without her permission."

Mek stood straighter and narrowed his eyes. "You'd rather she died?"

"Of course not. But..." Kashatok scrambled for solutions. "We could engineer a frequency pulse simulation."

"Hm." Mek drummed his fingers against his chin. "We never considered we might need such an option. Truthfully, Tovik may be able to, given enough time." The doctor shook his head. "But he has his hands full overseeing the piggyback."

Kashatok wanted to volunteer. But he didn't know enough about engineering, and Gassy was out of commission. If Joy was awake, they could probably figure something out together.

"She's your crewman, so the choice is yours," Mek said. "She made it very clear that she trusts you. Maybe even more than trusts."

Kashatok didn't realize he was backing up until the stool hit the back of his legs. "Even if she was awake and asked me to, I couldn't. Can't." His heartbeats warred with each other inside his chest. In a rush, he blurted, "I'm a *carayak!*"

The word hung in the air like a toxic cloud. One, two, three heartbeats.

Mek's attention drifted toward Kashatok's groin, and Kashatok knew what he was thinking. *Why isn't he castrated?*

A small voice punched through the tension. "What's a *carayak?*"

Kashatok about jumped out of his skin. "You're awake!"

Joy's eyes remained slit, as if she was having trouble in the bright light, while Mek waved a scanner above her head. "Still no sight?"

She shook her head. "Nothing. Tell me what a *carayak* is."

"A denaidan male with an extraordinarily rare genetic condition which causes incompatible mating frequencies." Mek jerked his hand back, barely in time to avoid Jhikik's teeth.

"Deadly frequencies." The words felt like lava crawling up Kashatok's throat. "Even to other denaidans."

"Deadly?" she whispered, raising one hand to her lips. Lips he remembered kissing all too well. "But you kissed me."

"The harmful frequency is created during climax," Mek said, his voice annoyingly clinical. "It doesn't kill the female, just destroys her consciousness. Most *carayaks* discover the condition during puberty, unfortunately during their first sexual encounter." He turned to Kashatok. "I've never heard of an un-castrated adult *carayak* outside of a monastery. Have you been tested?"

Kashatok half grunted, half laughed. "Only the old-fashioned way."

The truth was out now, and no amount of rum could ever hide it again. He numbly stared into Joy's blind face, hating her unfocused eyes; they reminded him of Aiyana. But he was also glad Joy couldn't see him. He wanted her as far away from this horrible side of himself as she could get.

"That's why you don't want women on your ship," she said softly.

Mek leaned back against the counter and crossed one leg over the other, but the leisurely motion somehow only exacerbated the tension. "Captain, I have to ask. Are the rumors about you true?"

Dredging up these memories had created a hollow pit inside Kashatok's gut, like the sudden emptying of a pond that left nothing but stinking, rotting sludge behind. He may as well purge himself of all of it. "Yes. I was sixteen and her name was Aiyana." He refused to look at Joy, the hopelessness in his chest a raw wound. "And for the record, I loved her."

"And the others?" Mek asked.

"Others?" Kashatok frowned.

"The comatose women you leave in every port."

Kashatok straightened. He knew people considered him a monster, but he'd never heard that rumor. "I would never! I don't even allow women on my ship."

"Then how did you end up with her?" Mek nodded toward Joy.

Kashatok recalled the first moment he'd seen Joy, a wide-eyed, olive-skinned face in a cantina. How spunky she'd been arguing for her cut of the profits. Even though he'd thought she was a boy, something about her had drawn him.

"My fault." Joy raised her hand as if asking permission to speak in class. "I disguised myself as a man."

"I didn't find out until we were well underway," Kashatok added. "Or I would've dropped her off at the next port."

Mek scratched his cheek, his nails loud against the stubble, tilting his head to regard Kashatok. "And what about now?"

Kashatok swallowed. *What about now?* He liked having Joy around. Yet having her near could only end badly. Hell, it already had. She was fucking blind. And nanites or not, she couldn't remain on his ship. "A blind mechanic's useless to me."

From the bed, Joy sucked in a breath and turned her face away. Kashatok wanted to pound his own skull against a bulkhead. Why'd he say such a thing?

Jhikik chirped and stroked Joy's cheek with the furry side of his tail.

"I see." Mek straightened. "Well, you won't need to worry about her from here on out. She's welcome to stay on board the *Hardship*. I know Tovik won't mind."

The little voice inside Kashatok's head was chanting *mine* over and over. Another voice repeated he could never have her. Then a thought occurred to him. "Wait. Are you suggesting all she's good for now is mating?"

Mek shrugged. "Mated or not, we'll take good care of her, even if she's blind. But she'll eventually need to get rid of the nanites with someone."

Kashatok realized he'd moved to the bed as if to shield her. His ionic sense could feel her trembling, hitching, fighting tears. Tears he'd caused, and he hated himself all the more for it. "She's good at engineering. Maybe I can be her eyes and help her come up with an alternate plan to zap the nanites."

The doctor raised his brows. "As long as she allows me to draw a small supply of the nanites to inoculate future mates, we're completely open to any alternatives." Mek tapped a finger against his chin. "You know, *carayaks* are extremely rare. If you are one, you might help us understand how our mating frequencies interact with other species. Will you allow me to take a tissue sample?"

Balls tightening as he thought of the tissue Mek wanted, Kashatok considered agreeing; castration would make him safe for Joy to be around. Then he imagined the overweight, soft-voiced monks from his childhood. *No fucking way.* He turned so his shoulder faced the doctor, keeping his groin well out of reach. "I happen to like my balls right where they are."

"Not your genitals." Mek pulled a swab from the cabinet and held it up. "I just want a few tissue cells from your mouth."

Kashatok regarded the harmless swab. After a moment, he shrugged. "Fine."

Mek had just finished swabbing Kashatok's mouth when Qaiyaan entered the room carrying the bulky headset from a nav-grav chair. Behind him, Lisa shouldered a loop of wiring, stringing it along behind her. Qaiyaan set the headset on the countertop. "Captain Kashatok, you're wanted aboard the *Kinship*. Something about your engineer?"

Kashatok's hearts skipped over each other. Next to him, Joy's heartbeat ratcheted up as well. Why hadn't someone called his implant? Eyeing Qaiyaan suspiciously, he tapped below his ear. "*Kinship*, this is the captain. Status update."

Within moments, Doc's voice filled his head. "Captain, you need to come now."

He felt the blood drain from his face. "On my way."

Joy groped for Kashatok's hand. "Gassy?"

The comfort of her touch made him want to stay. Or keep her by his side. But he couldn't. He had to leave her here, not just now, but always. With his other hand, he brushed a loose curl from her forehead. "I have to go."

She squeezed his hand. "Yes, go."

"There's nothing you can do here, anyway," Mek said. "I'll keep you updated."

Kashatok ran a palm over Jhikik's furry head. "Take care of her, Jhik." Then, unable to stop himself, he ran the back of his knuckles down Joy's satiny cheek one last time. "I'll be back."

Staring Mek in the eyes, he reassured himself the doctor had everything in hand before hurrying to the boarding tube. For the first time in over a decade, he sent a prayer to the denaidan god.

<h1 style="text-align:center">CHAPTER ELEVEN</h1>

With Kashatok gone, Joy shivered, overwhelmed by all that was happening. Gassy might be dying. Would she ever see him again? She held back a sob as the question floated through her mind. She may not *see* anyone *ever again*. Kashatok didn't need a blind mechanic. Remembering his words made her want to vomit.

She kept telling herself the blindness was a temporary side effect, like when she'd received her camera implant; migraines had kept her holed up in her apartment with the shades drawn for days. Yet despite the self-talk, panic pressed down on her chest. Kashatok didn't need a blind mechanic. *Don't let it be permanent.*

Fighting tears, she pressed the heels of her hands against her eyes.

Somewhere to her left, Captain Qaiyaan directed Lisa in positioning some equipment. She could tell when Qaiyaan drew too close because Jhikik stiffened and his teeth clacked. His fur was reassuring and warm against her neck.

Qaiyaan asked, "How're we going to get that creature out of the way?"

"He's not hurting anything. Here, let me," Lisa said. "Joy, I'm going to attach the frequency modulator diodes, all right?"

Joy felt cool hands press the small pads against her temples. Next to her ear, the netorpok vibrated with warning but didn't lunge or bite.

Regaining her composure, Joy asked, "What are you guys doing?"

"When I had the nanites, they were extremely unstable under certain frequencies," Lisa replied. "Especially when we engaged the burn drive."

"Don't worry, Joy." Tovik's voice startled her. "I modified the nav-grav buffers specifically for the nanites. I'll protect you."

Much as she appreciated him trying to help, she wasn't in the mood for his puppy love. "I'll be fine."

"You're still likely to experience some discomfort," Lisa said. "Piggybacking a K-class ship will make things a little rough."

The nanites had settled into a low buzz she could barely hear over Jhikik's purr. For some reason, the influx of data on the *Kinship* had energized the little machines, given them a purpose, and they'd tried to hijack every synapse in her brain to process the information. Since going blind, she hadn't been unconscious so much as *busy*. The mechanic in her had sought to develop a mental "kill switch" of sorts —not anything that would disable the nanites completely, but something to stop their process. She'd succeeded, at least for now, but she had no idea what might bring the machines unexpectedly to life once again.

"Tovik," Qaiyaan said, "get your ass to engineering and finish preparations. Lisa, I need you on the bridge."

Lisa squeezed Joy's hand. "Hang in there."

Footsteps. Then the room was silent. Being blind sucked. "Hello?"

"Don't worry, I'm still here," Mek said. She could hear him moving about on the other side of the room.

Joy stroked Jhikik's shoulder, feeling completely helpless. She longed for Kashatok's reassuring presence. "How long until we burn?"

"Shouldn't be too long. They'll announce it."

Joy took a few more breaths. She needed to focus on something besides her own fear. But the only thing she could think about was the nanites, which made her think about Kashatok. "Can you cure a *carayak*?"

Mek sighed. "No. We never discovered a way to suppress the gene. Then the Termination made continued research unnecessary."

She chewed her lip. "So, there's no hope for him?"

"Not if he's a *carayak*."

"You think he might not be?" She couldn't keep the edge of hope from her voice.

"I can't say. Hopefully, I'll be able to tell from the tissue sample he gave me."

Keeping the tremor from her voice took every ounce of strength she had. "What about his idea about creating an artificial frequency that destroys the nanites?"

The sound of a stool sliding across the floor. Mek finally answered, "The idea has merit, and I've already begun preliminary research. Ionic frequencies are very complex. For mating purposes, they're accompanied by pheromones and hormones within both participants. I'm not sure we'll have time to create and test a procedure before you run out of time."

Her throat tightened. Although Lisa had warned her about the time limit on the nanites, Joy had never imagined the things would take over this fast. She was supposed to have time to prove herself to Kashatok. Not just as a mechanic, but as a woman. Although she'd never thought of herself as attractive before, after he'd kissed her, she'd believed she might be able to tempt him.

If only she'd known.

Footsteps approached the bed. "You can have your pick from our crew—probably either crew—when the time comes."

Just not Kashatok. She turned her head away, needing to grieve in private. "I'm going to try to take a nap. Maybe the blindness will wear off."

"I'm here if you need me." He patted her hand, and she heard his footsteps once again move to the far side of the room.

Her nanites were heating up—an almost prickly sensation inside her head—possibly because of her agitation. God, what was she going to do? As sweet as Tovik was, she felt no desire for the ginger-haired denaidan. None of the men on either ship had ignited her imagination like Kashatok had. A small voice in her head sounded like her mother saying *I told you so*. Her chest tightened.

What if she contacted Mother?

The CEO of the corporation that had created these nanites could probably tell her how to purge them. She'd bet the corp' already had a machine to do it. But contacting her mother without the pirates finding out would be a challenge. How would Joy even locate a comm if she couldn't see it?

You have something stronger than your eyesight. The thought made her heart pound. In engineering, she'd received information from the console from clear across the room. What if she could use the nanites to access a comm? Dare she?

Envisioning the comm's circuitry in her head, she released the brakes on a few of the nanites.

Amidst all the bits of information hammering at her from cyberspace, the comm connection lit up like a firework.

She shifted, wishing she could see what Mek was doing. Could he see her? Would he know if she tried to make a call? And how could she make a call without talking out loud? Would her thoughts translate into words on the other end?

Deciding she had little to lose, she sent a request to connect to her mother's private polycom, adding her own personal identification tracer so Mother would know it was her.

Mother's thin face came into focus as if Joy was looking at a screen. Joy bit down on her lip to keep herself from calling aloud. Mother had never been a nurturing type, but her familiar face provided some comfort.

"Joy? What's wrong with your connection?"

Concentrating, Joy sent, "Mother, I need your help."

"What kind of help?"

Mother could hear her!

The lines on Mother's face deepened as she brought the polycom closer to her face. "And why aren't you on video? Aren't you supposed to be a reporter or something now? You need all the practice you can get."

Joy's relief twisted into the more familiar sensation of self-doubt. "I'm undercover. I've been..." she chose Mek's preferred term, "inoculated with cyber-sensitive nanites from one of Syndicorp's test labs. I need to know how to get rid of them."

"You did what?" Mother's eyes widened. "That technology is still undergoing stage two testing. How did—"

"Never mind that. I don't have much time. Do you know how to destroy the nanites?"

"How did you even find our biotech lab? They told me it was undetectable beneath the gold mine. Well, that will teach you to poke around where you don't belong. I ought to leave you there to learn your lesson."

Joy clenched her teeth. Mother never helped just because Joy asked. "I'm not at a lab. I'm doing an exposé on pirates. Now, are you going to help me or not?"

For the first time Joy could remember, her mother looked truly worried. "Pirates? Are they asking for ransom?"

Shit. I shouldn't have mentioned pirates. "I'm fine. I told you, I'm undercover. They're going to drop me off at the next space port. Please tell me—"

"Don't worry. I'm getting corporate security on this right away, honey. We cannot allow these dirty pirates any leeway. Stay on the line so they can start a trace."

"No!" Joy's eyes flew open, and she sat up, too late realizing she'd spoken aloud.

Jhikik chattered loudly, claws digging into her thigh where he'd latched on after her sudden move. She swore Mek's concerned face flashed before her eyes.

The doctor's voice spoke from her right. "Are you hurt?"

Joy couldn't answer. Images were flickering through her brain; Mother, Jhikik, comm circuitry, Mek. Her head throbbed as if she was having a root canal done on her brain. What the fuck was going on? She gritted her teeth and focused on one command. *Kill switch!*

Kashatok crossed the boarding tube in a single stride and passed through the empty cargo bay as if he was flying. Where the hell were his guards? If there was one thing being in the cartel had taught him, it was never to expose your back, not even to a fellow pirate. He had some words for Aleknagik the next time he saw him.

As he passed the weapons locker, he thought of Joy, blind and unprotected on the other ship. Yet jealous as he was of Tovik, the kid would watch out for her and his gut told him she was better off with a doctor who knew what he was doing. *Damn her for taking the nanites, anyway*. He'd known the Syndicorp tech could be nothing but trouble. Right now, he had to think about Gassy.

He took the corner into the *Kinship's* med bay so fast, he had to hold the doorframe as he entered. The room stank of disinfectant and blood. His gaze scoured the room, finding the old engineer alone and lying beneath the sterility shield just as before. "Gassy?"

Gassy opened his eyes. "Hey."

Settling on the tall stool beside the bed, Kashatok assessed the steady heartbeats on the vitals monitor. He wasn't a doctor, but the lines and numbers there seemed the same as before. "Where's Doc? I got a call that something was wrong."

"I heard a bunch of noise earlier, but no one came in here."

The back of Kashatok's neck prickled with ionic awareness and a sickening weight settled in his gut. Someone stood behind him. He rose slowly and turned toward the door.

Aleknagik stood just inside, legs wide and arms crossed. In the corridor behind him, Doc and Manopup held pulse pistols.

"What the fuck?" Kashatok ground out, blood running cold.

"Crew's voted you out," Aleknagik said.

Behind him, Gassy coughed wetly. "Why didn't I hear about a vote?"

"This is mutiny." Kashatok took a step forward, halting when the two men in the corridor trained their pistols on him. "Aleknagik, tell them to stand down."

"This isn't a trooper ship, Captain." Aleknagik raised one eyebrow. "We're pirates. We all have a share. We voted. You betrayed us by breaking your own rule."

"You son of a rakwiji whore." Kashatok clenched his hands. "You had as much part in hiring her as I did."

"Yep. And I'll bring her aboard again, just as soon as the nanites are done with her." Aleknagik grinned. "Different captain, different rules."

Kashatok jutted out his chin. His first mate had nothing good planned, but perhaps the rest of the crew could see reason. "She can't be your mechanic. She's blind. Useless."

"Nobody's useless." Aleknagik's grin widened, and he placed a palm to his chest. "Besides, she's crew, wounded in the line of duty. We take care of our own." The first mate flicked a glance over his shoulder at his men. "Right?"

"I am sure she will find new positions among the crew." Manopup's tentacles writhed. Someone Kashatok couldn't see snickered from the corridor.

"I'll kill you all first." Kashatok took another step.

A pulse blast hit him in the shoulder, spinning him around. Men moved into the room. Gassy called out from the bed. "Stop!"

The cold, hard point of a pulse pistol jammed into Kashatok's lower spine. He struggled against rough hands. The pulse blast had left his entire arm unresponsive. Aleknagik cinched a zip tie around his wrists. "We need you alive—at least for now. But if you do or say anything we don't like, Gassy gets it."

At the bedside, Manopup held his pistol loosely trained on the engineer.

"Doc," Kashatok twisted, boring his gaze into the denaidan who'd remained in the corridor. "How can you do this?"

Doc shrugged without meeting Kashatok's eyes. "The crew voted."

"To the brig." Aleknagik shoved Kashatok toward the doorway, sending a flare of pain through his shoulder.

"The *Hardship* won't hand Joy over once they find out what you've done," Kashatok said as he moved down the corridor.

They rounded a corner and Aleknagik yanked Kashatok close to hiss in his ear. "You think I really give an *anaq* about the female? I have a fresh piece of ass in every port." Aleknagik jammed a hand between Kashatok's shoulder blades and sent him reeling into the tiny room used for a brig. "The men want her aboard. And a good captain listens to his men." The door shield engaged with a subliminal crackle. "It's about time the *Kinship* had a worthy captain."

"You will never be worthy," Kashatok righted himself and stood tall in front of the glimmering shield, glaring at his first mate. How could his crew do this? He'd never been tight with his men, but they'd always respected his authority. *Or wanted your cartel connections.* After the most recent failed job, they obviously wanted him gone. *Uminaq*, a drink would go down well right now.

Aleknagik leaned forward, his face millimeters from the door shield. "Tell you what. Make this easy for me, and I won't insist on bringing the female over."

Kashatok grit his teeth and clenched his fists. "You want me to hand over my ship."

Nodding his shaggy head, the first mate looked as pleased as an ohn-cat who'd drunk all the cream. "Just keep things friendly with the *Hardship* until they cut us free."

"And what happens to me when this is over?"

"Hm. The punishment for bringing a woman on board is space-locking, I believe?" Aleknagik grinned. "But if you're good, I'll try to make sure we're within hailing distance of the *Hardship* when we do it. Perhaps they'll pick you up."

Chignik's voice came over the ship-wide comm. "We burn in six. Stand ready."

"The captain's needed on the bridge." Aleknagik shot Kashatok a mocking glance. "Oh, that's right. That's me."

With that, he turned on his heel and disappeared down the hall.

Still reeling from the pulse shot and burning with fury at his crew, Kashatok stabilized himself for burn.

Joy had been through countless burn cycles in her life, but never one that'd felt like this. Even with the nav-grav buffer, the burn drive emitted a frequency that drove her nanites crazy. The little machines seemed to spin and swarm like insects looking for a hive. Whenever the machines touched each other, they arced, creating strange flavors in her mouth, making her skin heat and cool, speeding or slowing her heartbeat. Her camera flickered on and off in a random pattern that felt like it would send her into a seizure at any moment. How had Lisa survived this chaos?

Clutching the bedsheets at her sides, she squeezed her eyes shut and concentrated on the 3D layered structure of one of the nanites along her optic nerve. The things were acting like the actuators in a bio-responsive holo-suite she'd once repaired. Sure enough, the gel-metal composite in the one she examined was flexing in response to the ship's burn frequency. What if she lined up its molecular structure with a second nanite? Could she alter the frequency receptors?

The two tiny machines clamped onto each other like puzzle pieces, calming immediately.

She lined more nanites up. Behind her closed eyelids, steady pinpricks of light, like illuminated micro-pixels, appeared. Opening her eyes, she was disheartened to see only the same colorless pixels. She needed more nanites engaged.

There were thousands, however—hundreds of thousands. She'd barely begun and was already sagging with fatigue.

As suddenly as it had begun, the burn frequency cut off. The nanites slowed. Settled. Joy's head throbbed as if someone had taken a jackhammer to it, but she let out a gusty sigh of relief. She had some time to recover.

A voice from the comm pierced through her headache. "Mek, how's our passenger?"

"Joy, you still with us?" Mek asked.

"Working on it," she mumbled, surprised she still had control of her tongue.

"Excellent." His hand patted hers. "The buffers appear to work, Captain."

"That's good news. But I have some not-so-good. Troopers somehow picked up our trail as we left the asteroid belt," Qaiyaan said. "We need to burn again immediately."

Joy couldn't be sure, but she thought she heard herself whimper. For a moment, she actually yearned for the troopers to catch them; she was the daughter of the CEO, after all. It would be like running home to Mother. Then again, the troopers hadn't paused to talk when they'd approached the slave ship before trying to blast the *Kinship* out of space. She bit her lip, trying to be brave. The only way to survive this was to keep going.

Mek moved quietly beside her, checking monitors. "You heard him. Need anything before we go?"

The nanites were relaying her medical information from the sensors. Elevated blood pressure, high levels of cortisol, increased respiration. Would another burn cycle kill her? She didn't think so. "Just get it over with."

"Ready when you are, Captain."

Her nanites jolted once more into chaos.

CHAPTER TWELVE

The first burn was short, exactly what Kashatok expected for a piggyback. Arm and hand still tingling from the pulse shot to his shoulder, he dropped his ionic shielding and began prying open the door's force shield control panel. He didn't trust Aleknagik to keep any promises, not about keeping Kashatok alive, and certainly not about Joy. Getting out of this cell was top priority.

Suddenly, his balance was yanked out from under him and his vision went blurry. He staggered sideways, hitting his head on the wall. His knees buckled and his stomach heaved as space folded in on itself and the ships' frequencies adjusted to the new location. A second burn? *Ellam Cua*, why hadn't anyone announced it?

Raising his ionic shield, he sat on the floor with his back pressed into a corner, head throbbing as he rode out the burn. Such a quick cycle could only mean trouble. Was Joy all right? Was the *Hardship's* crew onto Aleknagik? Had the troopers managed to catch their trail? He loathed not knowing; not being able to make decisions.

When the burn ended, Kashatok crawled to the door's force shield and peered down the hall through the glittering curtain. "Hey! Someone?"

A cut from his scalp trickled down his forehead, dripping blood into his eye. He swiped at the sting, hand coming away turquoise. A soft chirp to his left drew his attention.

"Jhikik?"

Another chirp rose from a floor vent no bigger than his palm. He crawled over to find two glistening eyes staring up at him through the grate. Poor little guy. The netorpok generally sat on his shoulder during burn, wrapped in Kashatok's ionic shield. Or cuddled up to Joy. Why wasn't Jhikik with her? Had Mek or Qaiyaan chased him away? Anger simmered in the pit of Kashatok's stomach.

Siphoning what little ionic power he could dredge up past his nausea, Kashatok yanked the grate free.

Jhikik squeezed through the opening, tail clutching a sock behind him. He scampered up Kashatok's arm and nestled against his neck, trembling.

"Caught you unaware, too? Why are you here?" He stroked the creature's downy head.

The tip of the netorpok's tail raised the sock in front of Kashatok's face like a peace flag, the fabric full of shredded holes. Jhikik chirped again.

Guilt swept through him. "*Anaq.* You're hungry, huh?"

When was the last time he'd fed his pet? Hell, when was the last time *he'd* eaten? Too much had been happening too fast. Legs unsteady, he rose, praying there wouldn't be a third burn without warning. At the door, he resumed efforts on the shield control panel. A shadow of movement from the corridor made him thrust his hands into his pockets a heartbeat before someone rounded the corner from the cargo bay.

Chignik. The denaidan carried an open bottle of rum, his multiple braids hanging limp and a line of blood darkening his chin. "Hey, Cap."

Kashatok glared at the man, betrayal washing through him all over again. He crossed his arms. "You going to tell me what's going on?"

Chignik took a long swallow from the bottle, swaying just a little. "I voted against it, just so you know."

Exhaling slowly, Kashatok met his crewman's bleary gaze. Not all his men had mutinied. There was still hope. "Get me out of here, then."

"Can't." Chignik shook his head. "Aleknagik revoked my codes."

Kashatok closed his eyes a moment, previous hope stretching thin. "Anyone else on our side?"

"Gassy, but he's not good for much right now. Ekwok maybe." Chignik took another drink. "He abstained from the vote. Cooper kept saying he didn't like it, but in the end, he voted with Aleknagik."

Kashatok paced in front of the door, legs still unsteady. Aleknagik had always been good at dominating the crew. It was part of what made him a good first mate, or so Kashatok'd believed. "Why'd we do a second burn so soon?"

"Troopers caught our signature and were hot on our tail. Aleknagik says they're after your woman."

Kashatok paused, only halfway registering that Chignik had referred to Joy as his woman. "Why would they be after her?"

Chignik blinked slowly, lids slightly out of synch. "Her mother broadcast a reward. Moore caught it on one of the Syndicorp channels he was monitoring from the slave ship."

"Mother?" For some reason, he hadn't pictured Joy with family, let alone a mother with enough power to put an entire trooper ship into action.

"She's offering one point five mil to anyone who leads the authorities to Joy's kidnappers."

Kashatok clenched his fists. Joy's family assumed she'd been kidnapped. But what kind of family could offer a one point five mil reward? That was an *anaq*-load of creds, worth the crew's total shares for an entire solar year at least. "Who the fuck is she?"

"Syndicorp's CEO. Joy's last name is Mulholland-Aird." The words felt like pulse blasts coming from Chignik's lips, stunning Kashatok for a few heartbeats.

He ran a hand down his beard. He'd never bothered with last names among his crew. "That's ridiculous. It can't be."

Shrugging, Chignik dabbed at his bloody lip with the back of his hand. "She called Joy by name and had a picture of her with longer hair."

Kashatok put one hand against the wall to steady himself.

Syndicorp? How was that possible? And how did that play into Joy seeking a spot on his crew? Had she been after the nanites all along? Fuck, he needed a drink. He was about to reach through the damned door shield and rip the bottle from Chignik's fingers.

Next to Kashatok's ear, Jhikik purred softly. Kashatok absently rubbed the soft fur under his pet's chin. There had to be a good explanation. Joy might've disguised herself to get on board, but she wasn't a very good liar. She'd told the truth about her name; he'd chosen to mishear it. When Gassy first mentioned the nanites, she'd been completely clueless. And she'd flat-out told him she wasn't a Syndicorp spy. He believed her.

But the others didn't and now she was alone on the other ship. *Uminaq*! He straightened, staring helplessly through the door shield. "What did Captain Qaiyaan say?"

Chignik shook his head. "Don't think he knows. Aleknagik wants to keep it that way." A queasy look came over the big man's bearded face. "He says after we have our fun, the ransom is ours."

Both of Kashatok's hearts slammed against his ribs. There was absolutely zero chance Aleknagik would honor his promise of leaving her aboard the *Hardship* now—if he'd ever intended to in the first place. "You can't let Aleknagik and his men get their hands on Joy." His insides tightened as he thought of her at Aleknagik's mercy. What would Qaiyaan and his crew do once they found out she was Syndicorp? At least they valued her for the nanites. "Think you can get a message to her?"

"Like I said, my access codes are no good," Chignik said. "But maybe I can sweet talk Ekwok into doing it. Or get Gassy up long enough to send one."

"You have to try."

Chignik turned to go and Jhikik chirped again, tail in a stranglehold around Kashatok's neck. *Still hungry.* At least he could try to get Jhik some food.

"Chignik?" Kashatok called after him. "Open the hydroponic gate in my cabin so Jhikik can eat?"

None of the crewmen liked the netorpok, but Chignik looked over his shoulder and nodded. He disappeared unsteadily around the corner, leaving Kashatok and Jhikik alone once more.

Kashatok pulled Jhikik off his shoulder and placed him near the grate. "Feast while you can. Aleknagik'll probably toss you out the airlock with me."

Jhikik chirped with alarm, tail clinging to Kashatok's wrist.

For the first time in a long time, Kashatok realized he might regret dying. He'd probably never see Joy again. The thought created a void inside him that wanted to fold in on itself. "I know, buddy. Go back to her if you can."

Then an idea occurred to him—maybe Jhikik could go back. He could carry a message to her. Kashatok patted his pockets and glanced around the barren room as if he might find something to write on. Or with, for that matter. Nothing. Blinking, he wiped a dribble of blood from his forehead with his sleeve, absently noting the stark turquoise blood against the white fabric. He may not be able to write a message, but he could send a warning.

Tearing a strip of fabric from the shirt's hem, he dabbed it against his forehead, then tied it like a collar around a squirming Jhikik's neck. *Anaq*, did she even know his blood was turquoise? As if she could even see it. She was blind for *Ellam Cua's* sake. Yet it wasn't as if he had any other options. Perhaps Mek would notice the collar and say something.

Nudging his companion toward the grate, he said, "Take it to Joy."

The netorpok looked over his shoulder at Kashatok for a moment, then disappeared down the black hole.

Kashatok prayed like hell the creature didn't get distracted by the open hydroponics cage.

The burn ended, and Joy sagged with mental relief. She'd aligned enough nanites that the tiny machines could continue stacking on their own, like a chain reaction. She'd always had a knack for mechanics, but the nanites were painting a more rounded picture of the ship's systems than she'd ever imagined possible. She could sense the slight variation in the gravity system Tovik had chattered to her about. Knew Mek's centrifuge needed balancing. Next to her, she detected the report on her biological systems from the scanner Mek held close to her ear.

But the volume of information was also exhausting, and it took everything she had left to shut it out. She'd never worked so hard in her life. Deep in her chest, she trembled with fatigue, her eyes glued shut as if each lid weighed a thousand pounds. Even her hands ached as if she'd been wielding a wrench for hours on end. She could fall asleep for days and still not feel rested, yet a small part of her refused to let go of consciousness in case the nanites decided to get frisky once again. If they returned to chaos, she'd drown under the onslaught.

The emanations from Mek's scanner changed frequencies, and she groaned.

"How're you doing, Joy?"

"Can you not do that?"

"Sorry." The scanner ceased, but Mek jabbed her arm for what felt like the millionth time. "I'm taking another sample."

Something beeped, and the nanites jittered like toddlers refusing to take a nap. She heard Mek shuffling around the room as she lapsed back into semi-consciousness.

"I have some good news for Captain Kashatok about his DNA test." The doctor's voice startled her alert.

Then she realized what he'd said. *News for Kashatok*. As if responding to her curiosity, her nanites sifted through the nearby information, returning the DNA results; Kashatok did not have *carayak* disorder. Her eyes flew open. Bright whiteness sliced into her brain, and she slammed her lids shut again. *What the hell?*

She must've made a noise, because Mek asked, "Joy?"

Carefully slitting her right eye, her heart fell. Black void. Shutting it, she cracked open her left lid and winced as a crescent of light filtered through her lashes. *Filters*, she ordered out of habit. Her camera responded by dialing down the lens receptors. The light became bearable. She opened her eye the rest of the way.

The brilliant overhead light of the med bay came into focus amidst the grooved ceiling panels. Her heart skipped several beats, and excitement filled her limbs. She wasn't blind! Then everything grew fuzzy again, and she wanted to cry before she realized things were fuzzy because she was crying. She lifted her hands and pressed away the tears, letting out a sobbing laugh. "I can see!"

She turned her head to find Mek beside the bed, a grin splitting his face. "That's wonderful news! I have to admit, I was worried your optic nerve was permanently damaged."

He grabbed a scanner and pressed it to her temple. She winced as the nanites did their dance, but bore it. This was worth the discomfort.

Mek's face grew serious. "You're sure you can see? Your optic nerves are still non-responsive."

She closed and opened her left eye, confirming her suspicion. "It's my camera."

Even as she said it, she bit her lip. She was still blind. Her camera would never be the same as her real vision. For one thing, it was only in one eye. For another, extended use brought on a migraine.

"Let me run some tests." Mek pursed his lips as if mulling something over, then turned to his workstation.

Joy knew she should turn the camera off. Reserve using it for when it was needed. But she was too relieved and excited. "I want to tell Kashatok."

"I just tried to call him. His crew says he's occupied, but he'll call back as soon as he can."

She fumbled with the nav-grav harness securing her chest and legs to the cot. Her fingers didn't want to obey commands for fine motor skills.

Mek gave her a warning frown over his shoulder. "Slow down, Joy. More than just your eyesight is being affected."

"I'm tired of lying here helpless." Inside her head, the nanites responded to her agitation and excitement with another monster headache.

A tiny weight landed on her legs, and she glanced down to find Jhikik scampering toward her.

"Jhikik! I can see!" She spotted a rag tied around his neck. He'd never worn a collar before. Reaching out, she tried unsuccessfully to untie the knot. "Who did this?"

"What?" Mek asked.

"There's something tied on him. Can you help get it off?"

Mek raised an eyebrow. "I don't think he likes me."

She rubbed behind Jhikik's ears. "Jhikik, will you let the doctor get that thing off you? For me?"

Jhikik purred, closing his dark eyes.

Mek sighed and moved closer. Jhikik's purring turned to warning clicks, but he allowed the doctor to worry the knot free. Mek held up the white and turquoise scrap of cloth. "This appears to be blood."

A chill settled into Joy's veins. She took the cloth from him, fingering the soft pirelux fabric. Kashatok's shirt had been made of the same material. "Try to call Kashatok again."

Mek nodded and walked over to the comm. "This is Mekoryuk on the *Hardship*. I need to speak to Captain Kashatok immediately."

Aleknagik's voice came back. "Is it about the female? I can give him a message."

Joy's hackles rose. Kashatok had warned her his crew was dangerous, but referring to her as if she was some sort of livestock rankled her. Jhikik climbed to her shoulder and clicked his teeth in agreement.

Mek said, "This is for Kashatok's ears only."

A pause. "I'll see if I can free him up. We'll call back."

Joy met Mek's eyes across the med bay. Something wasn't right. "Try his cochlear implant."

"You have the code?" he asked.

She didn't, but her nanites could get it. In fact, she could probably use her nanites to call him directly. "Let me try my nanites."

"No!" The urgency in Mek's voice stalled her. "Encouraging them at this stage could be dangerous. Lisa only escaped their control with her brother's help."

"But Kashatok may be in trouble." She held up the rag.

"That's different from trying to command them."

The comm came to life once again, this time with Qaiyaan's voice.

"Mek, can you leave your patient for a few minutes and come to the bridge? We've just received some intel and need to talk."

Joy swung her legs over the edge of the bed. "I'm coming, too."

The comm was still open, because Qaiyaan replied, "Crew only, Joy. Hang tight. We'll only be a few minutes."

Mek held up a palm. "Stay and rest. I'll get the code from Qaiyaan and when I get back, we'll call Kashatok."

She settled back against the pillow, but inside, she knew something was very wrong. Jhikik knew it too, pacing the mattress beside her as if asking her what she was waiting for. Kashatok needed her and there was no time to waste. She could feel it in her gut. In her nanites.

Once the doctor was gone, Jhikik hopped down and, with a quick glance over his shoulder, disappeared through the door. She swore she heard him say, *Come on.*

She swung her legs over the edge of the bed. The nanites were under control. It wasn't far to the boarding tube. She would just pop over with Jhikik, make sure Kashatok was okay, and come back.

Except her legs refused to support her. No way was she walking out of here right now. She slumped back to the cot. *Fuck.* If she could just reach Kashatok's implant, she'd feel better. The nanites could do it in mere seconds. She winked her camera eye, testing the microcomputers now embedded in the interface. She appeared to have full control. Surely one quick search and a comm call wouldn't be harmful? She'd managed with Mother easily enough.

Closing her eyes, she opened an interface to the comm.

A stream of information surged through her senses. She throttled the flow, focusing on what she wanted. Kashatok's implant. *There it is.* Easy as she'd imagined. But some kind of firewall stood between her and the connection. An intentional block within the *Kinship's* comm array. She recognized that signature from her work on the ship's systems.

He was in the brig.

What the hell?

"Mek!" she called out, hoping he could hear her from here. She had to tell him. Now. Realizing she was still connected to the comm system, she opened a line to the bridge.

The men were talking loudly, Tovik's voice overriding the others. "Kashatok probably *did* kidnap her!"

A sickening sensation filled her throat. They were talking about her. She should've known when Qaiyaan called for crew only. She concentrated harder, trying to make out who was saying what.

"Whatever the case," said Qaiyaan's deeper tone, "we can't just let her run around free if she's Syndicorp."

She stiffened, breath catching. How could they know?

"One point five mil creds is a lot," said a voice she wasn't as familiar with, but she thought might be the first mate. "If she's not matable, we should turn her in and collect."

"We can't let her go," Lisa said. "It'd compromise our search for the lab if her mother finds out about the nanites. My brother…"

But Joy was barely listening. The pirates knew because of Mother. With a surge of adrenaline, Joy found herself on her feet. Trembling, but upright.

Tovik's voice cracked loudly over the connection, "Are you suggesting we kill her?"

Holy shit, they were coming to murder her. Throat too tight to swallow, she cut the connection, not trusting her command of the nanites enough to use the comm and her camera at the same time. Forcing her feet to take one step after another, she stumbled to the door, gaining more motor control the closer she got to the boarding tube. Did the men on the *Kinship* know? Did Kashatok? Was he in the brig because of her? If she'd learned anything during her time on Kashatok's ship, it was that denaidans hated Syndicorp more than anything else in existence. These pirates would torture and kill her before ransoming her lifeless corpse back to her mother and the corp'.

Not Kashatok. He'd scared her at first, but she'd come to recognize the good behind his drunken, savage appearance. He'd tried to shield her, cared for her, made her believe he saw something special in her. Kashatok was the one man among all these pirates who might actually protect her, Syndicorp or not.

But first, she had to get him free.

235

CHAPTER THIRTEEN

Joy gripped the edge of the boarding tube and peered into the *Kinship's* cargo bay. At the back of the dimly lit cavern, Moore sat with his wiry back to her across one of the cargo crates from Ekwok. Without being sure if they knew about Mother, she couldn't risk being seen. But how was she going to get past them? They were obviously guards, and Ekwok had a clear view of the boarding tube.

The tawny-haired denaidan glanced up, then jerked his gaze back to his cards.

She trembled, bracing herself against the edge of the tube. He'd seen her. But a moment passed, then another, and he continued staring at his hand. Perhaps he had poor eyesight? She edged onto the deck and hugged the outer wall, hurrying toward the angular shuttle sitting in the starboard bay. Ducking behind the rear landing strut, she paused, leaning against the hard metal and panting. The nanites were going wild from adrenaline. She squeezed her eyes shut, imagining herself holding a spanner, tightening her hold on the little machines. The kill switch was not a preferable option; without the nanites, she'd be blind, and she wasn't quite that familiar with the *Kinship's* layout.

The single-cell brig lay around the corner just past the escape pods.

Would there be more guards there? She was unarmed, unstable, completely unprepared—what the hell had she been thinking, fleeing the *Hardship* without a plan? What had she been thinking when she decided to go undercover in the first place? Now she was trapped between two pirate crews with nowhere to flee except the vacuum of space.

Next to her, the shuttle door stood open as if inviting her to try. Not that she'd get anywhere that way; the *Kinship* would never open the landing bay door, and the umbilical to the ship's main diagnostic system was still connected to the shuttle's belly. But there were tools inside the shuttle. Carrying something as a weapon would make her feel better.

She crept on board, crouching so she couldn't be seen through the windows. On her hands and knees, she rifled through the emergency locker, tucking a screwdriver into her back pocket and gripping a large spanner. She turned to exit, but her gaze caught the open panel of the shuttle's micro-drive. She'd been calibrating the power coil's coolant system before they encountered the slave ship. If she adjusted it toward the negative end and engaged the shuttle's life support, the coil would overheat in about five minutes, sending an alarm to the console in main engineering. A very loud alarm.

That could be enough diversion to get her to the brig undetected. Without an engineer, the crew'd scramble to figure out what the noise was. On the other hand, if someone didn't figure out what was wrong and shut it down, the shuttle's innards would experience a meltdown. Possibly explode.

By then, you'll have Kashatok free. The brig's door controls should be a piece of cake to override using the spanner in her pocket. Together, they'd return to the shuttle and shut the power coil down. Hell, maybe they could actually use the shuttle to escape.

Sucky plan, but it was all she had.

She made the adjustment and crept outside, waiting nervously near the shuttle's pointed nose.

Heartbeat loud in her ears, she watched the mouth of the corridor expectantly for what felt like hours. The nanites seemed to surge in time with her pulse, making her camera's focus go in and out. She shut her eyes against the disorienting sensation, but only for a moment. She couldn't afford to be blind if someone came around the corner and spotted her.

Finally, a rolling wail echoed through the bay. She counted to ten before peeking around the nose. The guards had risen, and she caught sight of Ekwok disappearing into the far corridor. Moore remained at the makeshift table with his back to her.

She slipped from behind the shuttle and darted toward the door to the brig, sure she'd feel the bite of a pulse blast at any moment. Clearing the corner, she breathed a sigh of relief and took the last few steps. The door's force shield glimmered, making her camera's auto-filters roll through several settings before stabilizing. Once she could see again, she peered through the shield to meet Kashatok's furious gaze.

The alarm bell rolling through the ship was a perfect accompaniment to the confusion coursing through Kashatok's system. Joy was here, looking at him. His hearts warred with conflicting emotions. Joy could see again? Had she received his warning? If she had, why was she here? And the thing he really didn't want to know—was she actually a Syndicorp spy?

He said the only thing he could think of. "You shouldn't be here."

She jimmied the door's control panel loose and applied the spanner to the mechanism. "I got your message."

He glanced to the corner where Jhikik hunkered over a naujiar branch he'd dragged up the vent a few minutes earlier. "The collar was supposed to be a warning, not an invitation."

The glittering force shield sputtered and dissipated. Joy dropped the spanner and flung herself into his arms. "Did they hurt you?"

Any anger he may have been trying to summon vanished. She felt so good, so right. He'd lived aloof for so long, he'd forgotten the simple pleasure of being touched. Stealing a moment to return her embrace, he breathed deeply against her hair, filling himself with her essence.

The alarm cut off as suddenly as it began. He pushed her away. "You're in danger. Go back right now."

"I can't." She was trembling, her liquid brown eyes tense. "Kashatok, there's something I need to tell you."

He wrapped one hand around her arm and pulled her from the brig, listening intently for approaching footsteps before turning toward the cargo bay. "You're Syndicorp, I know."

She stiffened. "I'm not, though."

He took a deep breath. He didn't have time to argue. Whatever was occupying the crew wasn't likely to last. Looking over his shoulder, he said, "Either way, you're not safe here."

"Neither are you. They locked you up because of me, didn't they? Are they planning to kill you?"

He continued pulling her forward. "We don't have time to stand here and—"

A pulse blast whizzed past his shoulder. He grabbed Joy around the waist and dashed into the cavernous bay, sidestepping around the corner. Setting her down, he scanned the open space for other attackers. The shuttle blocked his view of the boarding tube, but the rest of the bay appeared empty.

He looked at Joy's empty hands. "Did you happen to bring a weapon?"

She cringed. "I dropped the spanner back there." Pulling a small screwdriver from her back pocket, she held it out. "This is all I have."

"*Uminaq!*" Ignoring the screwdriver, he turned to face the mouth of the corridor. Standing between their attacker and Joy, he could protect them from one pulse blast with his ionic shielding. He prayed no one crept up on them from behind the shuttle. Joy moved in close, her warmth reassuring against his back.

Aleknagik's shaggy head poked around the corner several feet away, followed by a pistol leveled at Kashatok's chest. The mutinous first mate stepped into view as casually as if he were saying hello. "I wondered if I might find you together. Good to see our little female in working order again."

"Leave her alone." Kashatok balled his fists, daring the man to come within range.

"Can't. Turns out you not only brought a female on board but a Syndicorp spy. Captain Qaiyaan's eager to talk to the lady in question."

Kashatok maintained his shield, glancing desperately around the big bay. If both crews knew Joy was Syndicorp, neither ship was safe for her. But there was a third option. "Let us take the shuttle, and I'll relinquish the *Kinship*. Yours, free and clear."

Joy's breath fanned over his shoulder blade. "Kashatok, I don't..."

A new voice echoed through the cargo bay from the comm. "Captain, I'm detecting troopers on long-range sensors. They've found us again."

Aleknagik extended his free hand forward. "Tell you what. Hand her over and I'll let *you* take the shuttle."

"Fuck you." Kashatok snarled.

The sound of raised voices echoed from beyond the shuttle, Tovik's youthful voice carrying through the bay. "I don't think you understand how serious this is. Just let me help look for her. She's probably in engineering."

"Captain gave me direct orders not to allow you on board. Now get off our ship." Moore's gravelly retort left no question about whose side he was on.

Aleknagik's nose flared. "Sounds like she has that little punk as duped as you are, Kashatok."

The comm crackled again. "Troopers are coming in fast. The *Hardship* says we have to burn in three."

"She's not a spy," Kashatok said, putting as much surety behind his words as he could muster.

"Are you sure?" Aleknagik tilted his head, eyes narrowed. "The troopers have tracked us through two burns."

Tracking a ship through burn was difficult, to say the least; the frequency alignments that allowed a burn drive to fold space were very precise. A spy on board the *Kinship* would make the troopers' arrival much more plausible. Deep inside, Kashatok fought to contain his doubts. Was Joy responsible?

More arguing echoed from the other side of the shuttle. Tovik sputtered, "If she's not buffered when we burn, the nanites could kill her!"

"You hear that?" Aleknagik tilted his head toward the shuttle. "We don't have much time. Step aside, and I'll make sure she gets stabilized. We'd all prefer to keep her..." His teeth flashed in a grotesque leer. "Functioning."

Joy's fingertips dug into Kashatok's sides, and he could sense her heart racing. Every instinct told him to protect her. But what could he do?

"Two minutes," the comm announced.

Kashatok ground his teeth. Even if Joy ran, she'd never get herself positioned into a nav-grav seat in time. Burning was no longer an option—they had to stand and fight. He took a deep breath and shouted, "Battle stations!"

From the far end of the bay, Ekwok appeared from the opposite corridor. He stopped and gaped. "Captain?"

At Kashatok's back, Joy's warmth faded. She must've moved. If she wasn't directly behind him, she'd be vulnerable to a blast from the pulse pistol. "Joy, stay close." He took a step backward without taking his gaze off Aleknagik. Speaking loud enough to be heard throughout the bay, he said, "Are we going to run like scared dogs forever? We stand here with two ships. Two crews. It's time to stand and fight!"

Aleknagik aimed the pistol barrel at Kashatok's head.

Kashatok focused all his power to the front of his ionic shield.

The comm announced, "One minute to burn."

It was too late. Too late for everything. Kashatok's entire sorry existence flickered before his eyes. Yet damned if he wouldn't go down fighting. He coiled himself to pounce as a clunk and a hiss came from behind him, followed by a rush of stale air.

Joy's hand gripped the back of his waistband, yanking him backward through the narrow opening of an escape pod. He sensed a pulse blast headed his direction. Reality became slow motion as he grappled for the pod door. His fingers wrapped around the door's airlock wheel. A pulse blast struck him straight in the chest, knocking him off his feet.

And his world went black.

CHAPTER FOURTEEN

Kashatok opened gritty eyes, his head pillowed against warm skin. Above him, a brushed metal ceiling glowed with ambient light. Green and amber alerts blinked somewhere in his peripheral vision. His ribcage felt like he'd been used as a punching bag. He let out a slow breath, his ionic senses detecting a beating heart to his left just as a cool hand cupped his cheek.

Joy's face moved into his line of sight. "Kashatok? Are you awake?"

For a moment, he simply drank in her smooth olive complexion, the short dark ringlets surrounding her face, the liquid quality of her eyes. "What happened?"

A shiver coursed through her, and he realized his head was cradled on her lap. "You grabbed the escape pod's door handle just as you were shot. The blow shoved you backward, slamming the hatch shut. I hit the seal and ejected."

He remembered now; they'd been within seconds of burn. An escape pod caught by the edge of a ship's burn frequency was either pulled along, torn apart, or flung into a random sector of space. A pod could even end up in another galaxy, although no one had ever returned to prove it true. "What are our coordinates?"

She shook her head. "I can't tell."

Then he realized she wasn't looking at him. She wasn't looking at anything. His stomach tightened, and he reached up to caress her velvety cheek with the back of one hand. "Are you blind again?"

Her eyes performed a hard, slow blink, then she met his gaze. "My eyes can't see, but my camera can. I get a headache using it for too long. And I can only use the nanites for one thing at a time. I was reading the ship's systems just now."

He wasn't sure whether to be grateful or worried. "We have to get you to a doctor."

Although he wanted to remain in the comfort of her lap, he sat up, one hand pressed against his bruised ribs. The pod was literally that: a metal hexagon with passenger seats on four sides and a viewport with a rudimentary control panel on the fifth. Sprawled on the floor, he took up the entire space. No wonder he'd been on her lap.

On hands and knees, he moved to the panel, muscles still spasming with the aftershocks from the deflected pulse blast, and knelt in front of the controls. A green light next to the comm indicated the emergency beacon had automatically engaged after they ejected. Life support was also green. The navigation system blinked amber, unable to correlate their current position with any locations in its databank. Not that it really mattered; the pod had the maneuverability of a rowboat.

Swallowing, he did a sensor scan of the surrounding space. Emptiness. "How long was I out?"

Joy scooted over and knelt behind him, one soft breast brushing his shoulder as she leaned forward to view the panel. "A few hours, I think."

A few hours and no one had responded to their emergency beacon. This did not bode well. He relaxed onto his heels.

Joy settled back to make room, her breath fanning his shoulder. "Where are we?"

"Nowhere."

For long moments, they both stared at the blinking control panel. They were out of tools and out of alternatives.

"How long can we survive in the pod?" she whispered.

He'd been asking himself the same thing. Turning, he sat cross-legged to face her. "It's designed to keep three or four crewmen alive a few days. We might have a week with only two of us."

She grimaced. "And you didn't detect any nearby systems?"

He shook his head. He could feel her heartbeat racing and smell her warm citrus scent filling the pod's small space. Watching as she chewed her bottom lip in that distracting fashion of hers, he was filled with the desire to run his thumb across her mouth, to press inside and feel her teeth and tongue and…

How could he be thinking about these things when they were facing imminent death? He forced himself to look away.

"Are we going to die out here?" she asked.

He swallowed. No sense hiding the truth. They were in this together. "Probably."

She inhaled and blew it out in a long breath. "Then I have a final request."

He dragged his gaze back to her face, meeting her liquid brown eyes. The intensity there was shocking, sending sparks directly into his bloodstream.

She licked her lips, leaving them moist and rosy. "Make love to me."

Her request about knocked him flat. What was she thinking? She knew he couldn't. Yet her heartbeat fluttered, her breathing quickened, and her body temperature rose in what could only be classified as arousal. *Uminaq,* even her scent told him she wanted him at least as much as he wanted her. "You know I can't."

"I think you can. Mek said he had good news for you before everything fell apart. I'm pretty sure it was the results of your DNA test." She smiled tremulously. "You're not a *carayak.*"

Her words made no sense. For almost two decades, he'd lived without sex, defining himself as a monster. Mek's test had to be wrong. *Wrong or right, you still can't be with her.* She was human. He was denaidan. "*Carayak* or not, I can't be with you."

She seemed to shrink, her shoulders drawing up. "You don't want me?"

"Of course I want you!" The words were out before he could rein them in. Even his cock surged to life, as if affronted that she'd suggest such a thing.

With a trembling hand, she touched his knee. "Then what's stopping you? I have the nanites."

It was as if she'd flipped a switch directly tied to his groin. His hearts pumped rhythmically in his chest, the increased blood flow heightening his awareness of her through every sense. Could he be with her? Dare he? Memories of Aiyana surfaced, but her face was blurred by time, more like a nightmare than a memory. Fresher was the recent memory of Joy's heated kiss in his cabin, her tender mouth beneath his, her soft breasts against his chest.

He scrubbed both hands over his face. "I couldn't bear it if you died. Especially like… that. With me."

"We're likely to die, anyway." Her voice was firmer than he'd expected, and her gaze remained steady. "Let's go out in a blaze of pleasure."

"*Ellam Cua*, woman." But he couldn't deny her. Not her words, not her body, and not her plump and inviting mouth. He reached out and wrapped both hands around her hips, pulling her forward to straddle his lap. "I'm not in control. If I take you, it won't be gentle." His voice sounded like he'd eaten broken glass.

"Let's try." Her fingers threaded through his long hair, forcing his head back ever so slightly. She leaned in and brushed her lips against his like a breath of wind, then her tongue teased the seam of his lips.

He opened his mouth against hers, one hand running up her back to cup the nape of her neck as he savored the kiss. Still, a part of him held back. He murmured against her lips, "I won't be able to stop once I start."

She rocked forward on top of his erection, then back again before sliding one hand down his shoulder and over his hip. Her fingers dipped inside the waistband of his pants, brushing the tip of his throbbing cock. He sucked a breath through his nose, trying with every ounce of strength to control himself. Her hand moved deeper, fingers sliding down his shaft, cupping his balls. He stiffened, unable to breathe as he hardened to the point of pain. His chest burned and his vision hazed. Never had anyone touched him like this.

With a growl, he lifted her off his lap and laid her back on the floor. In the blink of an eye, he'd torn her tunic down the front, exposing the bindings around her breasts. Her nipples poked hard and sharp through the layered fabric. He yanked the binding free, lowering his head to one nipple. The hardened peak against his tongue was ecstasy. A gasp escaped her lips, and she arched into him, nearly toppling him over the edge. He ran his tongue over the silken mound of flesh, nipping and suckling until he reached the other. There, he drew the nipple hard between his lips and she cried out, her fingers digging into his shoulder blades.

His cock throbbed painfully against his pants, but he knew the moment he exposed himself, all would be lost. Instead, he grabbed hold of her waistband, tugging the clothing over her hips to expose her downy sex.

He could have cried with joy. The beauty of her olive skin, the perfect V of curls, the scent of arousal reaching his nostrils was like a taste of heaven. *Ellam Cua*, he'd heard his men speak of tasting a woman. He was going to do more than taste. He was going to devour her. Yanking her legs free, he flung her pants aside before sliding his hands beneath her knees. He drew her legs up and apart, diving into her warm center like a man who'd found an oasis in the desert. She was as savory as honey. He lapped at her folds, her fingers threading into his hair while he stroked his thumbs along the creases of her thighs and feasted.

She moaned, a song that soared through his bloodstream like a drug.

Grabbing hold of the nub of her clit with his lips, he suckled, teasing until she was swollen and throbbing. Her slickness filled his senses. He wanted to feel every part of her. To make her moan his name as she came around him again and again. Sliding one long finger against her opening, he delved inside.

She bucked against him. "Kashatok!"

His name on her lips was like a prayer. He delved again, and she widened her legs, giving him access to the ridges within her. Her essence coated his hand, filled him with a pleasure he'd only imagined for over fifteen years. Everything was so much better than he remembered. He added a second finger, stroking in and out while he circled her clit with his tongue. He could smell her arousal reaching its peak. Feel her tightening around his fingers. There was nothing in the galaxy better than this, and he'd denied himself too long.

She began to quake and shudder. He slammed his fingers into her again and again, his palm now smacking her sex as he lifted himself on his other hand to peer at her flushed face. She arched against the floor, her bared breasts quivering as she rose to meet his thrusts. His cock surged and jolted, demanding its release. But he couldn't be sure he'd last long enough to finish her, and she deserved pleasure.

A scream erupted from her panting lips, and her core clamped down around his fingers. He didn't stop. He continued driving into her until she sagged, her legs relaxing and her shudders easing. His cock was so hard now, so painful, he doubted he could come if he tried.

She opened her eyes and lifted both hands to reach for him. "I want you."

He needed no more encouragement. With a flick of his fingers, his buckle came loose, his fly was open, and his cock sprang free. Her hands helped ease the waistband down around his hips, the air cool on his exposed flesh. He positioned himself at her entrance, eyes closing as the delicious friction of her heat enveloped the blunt head of his cock.

"*Ellam Cua*," he swore again as he slipped centimeter by centimeter inside her.

She was wet and tight, wrapping him in an embrace he'd never imagined experiencing again. Once he was fully seated inside her, he sighed and remained locked in place for a few moments, reveling in her pulsating heat.

When he opened his eyes, she was looking at him intently, pupils dilated with desire.

She slid her hand beneath his shirt, caressing up his abs until she reached a nipple. She pinched it lightly, sending rockets of pleasure through his nerve endings. Who knew his nipples could be so sensitive?

Slowly, tentatively, he began to move. It was nothing like he remembered from his singular previous experience. Joy was perfect. Joy was pure. Joy was *his*. Her breath washed over him and he took it in, buttocks tightening as he ground against her.

She gasped his name, clinging to him, their gazes locked in what could only be a melding of souls. He increased his speed, pleased when she matched him. Without warning, he became a rutting beast: a primal thing, pounding into her relentlessly, teeth clenched and muscles taut.

He could feel her everywhere, not merely on his cock. Her legs around his hips. Her hands on his torso. Her gaze locked with his. A connection solidified between them, something beyond the physical, beyond the mental, and every stroke hardened the bond.

Even without words, he knew Joy felt it, too. Her eyes were bright with pleasure and love.

Her mouth gaped in a silent scream and she threw her head back, eyes closing as rapture swept through her.

Fear sank its claws into him one last time. "No," he gasped. "Look at me."

He needed to know she was with him. That she wouldn't leave him.

Her lids flew open, and she nodded, still spasming around him. He pumped unrelentingly, driving her through her pleasure. She gripped his shoulders, and he focused his concentration more than he'd ever done before, willing her to rise even higher. To meet him at the precipice. To push him over the edge.

When she crested again, he couldn't stop. He let go, light behind his eyes exploding into pleasure he'd never dreamed possible.

And in that moment he sent his ionic sense into her mind, piercing through the veil that shrouded her thoughts. In that moment, she was his completely.

Every synapse in Joy's mind had seemed to alight at once with her orgasm—or was it his? Her senses were flooded with Kashatok, an essence so pure she didn't know where he ended and she began. She could sense his every thought. Every emotion. Right now he was desperate, terrified, full of adrenaline. "Joy, don't leave me. Joy!"

Much like when the wave of data had hit her on the *Kinship*, she was unable to control her body. Her insides still fluttered from the shattering physical release. But she took comfort from the warm arms around her, relaxed into the heated breath against the crook of her neck, breathed deeply of a sweet yet masculine scent that reminded her of rum.

Kashatok.

Slowly, painstakingly, she untangled her thoughts from his, calming her ragged breathing. She opened her eyes, turning her head to meet his gaze. "I'm right here."

He sucked in sharply. "*Ellam Cua*, I thought..."

He shuddered, then his mouth was on hers, his need more emotional than physical. Breaking the kiss, he rested his forehead against hers. "The nanites worked? Praise *Ellam Cua*, you're safe."

She smiled, her camera focusing on the thick fringe of his eyelashes dominating her field of vision. She'd assumed that with the nanites gone, her camera would stop functioning. "I can see."

"That's wonderful." He kissed her again and rolled onto his back, carrying her with him so she rested against his chest. She could hear his dual-beating hearts, strong and sure against her cheek.

"But the nanites should've been destroyed." She peered inside her mind, concentrating on the microcomputers. They no longer floated free about her system. Every single one of them had aligned, coating the myelin sheaths around each nerve cell like armor. The ones on her optic nerves tingled as they transmitted data from her camera, while others had settled into various dormant positions as if awaiting tasks she had yet to assign. Through it all, every one of them thrummed with awareness of the ionic frequency of the man lying beside her. "They're still active."

He stiffened, the hand that had been stroking her back halting sharply. "How can that be?"

She shook her head. She had no idea. Except that in the last moments of climax, something had changed. He'd opened up to her, and she'd glimpsed his essence, the core of his being. And at that moment, she'd become more than herself.

The nanites had changed with her.

He sat up, keeping her on his lap and holding her shoulders to look deeply into her eyes. "*Uminaq*, you need a doctor."

She placed her hands on either side of his bearded face, heart swelling with love for this gruff, protective pirate captain. She wasn't afraid. The machines were a part of her now, as much as her breath or her pulse or her soul. Something she couldn't control yet had become vital to sustaining life. "I don't think they're a danger anymore."

"They're fucking Syndicorp tech. We need to destroy them."

She licked her lips, giving him a mischievous smile, and stroked a finger down his copper-skinned chest toward his navel. "We could try again."

His skin twitched beneath her touch, and from the gap of his open fly, his cock swelled back to life. His pupils dilated as his gaze shifted to her mouth and back to meet her eyes. "I never thought I'd hear a woman say that."

She grinned, wiggling her ass against his legs. Her tunic was ripped to shreds, hanging from her shoulders, so she shrugged out of it. Then she lifted his shirt over his head, exposing his broad chest and muscular shoulders. Damn. Even sitting, the man had washboard abs, his long beard dangling between his pecs.

Pushing him back against the deck, she yanked his pants free. His narrow hips and rock-hard thighs reminded her of the ancient Greek statues Mother'd forced her to study after Joy'd professed a desire to be an artist. While the statues had been drool-worthy, Mother's drive for perfection had nipped Joy's love of art in the bud.

Now she regained her appreciation, running her palms up Kashatok's naked legs, pausing where his groin rose into a massive erection unlike any she'd ever seen on a Greek statue. Her pussy tightened, its soreness reminding her of the Earth-shattering orgasms she'd just experienced. Despite the ache in her core, she wanted another one.

She lifted a leg and straddled him, continuing to smooth her palms up his chest to his shoulders.

He grabbed her hips and pulled her down, trapping his erection between them. She tilted her hips, and he pulled her tighter, grinding his length against her clit. A shudder raced through her, and she lifted her chin in an involuntary moan of pleasure.

Sitting up again, he slipped his broad hands around to cup her ass, fingertips feathering the outer edges of her sex. She was slippery, throbbing, heated. Leaning in, she breathed in his masculine scent. He met her move, biting softly at her bottom lip before claiming her in a kiss that made her nipples harden and her nanites fire with anticipation. Each stroke of his tongue within her mouth built the fire within her higher and hotter, until she was rocking against him, her lower lips embracing his length in tantalizing strokes.

Lifting her as if she weighed nothing, he settled her back down, spearing her with his cock. She gasped as his thick head pulsed deep inside her. Holy hell, she was going to come again, and they'd barely started. Her hips twitched, needing to move, but he ground her firmly against him, his mouth devouring hers. Whatever he was doing was building a pressure deep within her like she'd never experienced, as if his cock was growing in size, stretching her to the fullest.

When he finally relaxed his hold, allowing a breath of space between them, the delightful friction sent micro-orgasms shuddering through her.

Then he began to undulate his hips beneath her, rocking side to side. "Kashatok," she gasped, meeting his rhythm, eyes locked on his.

He lay back, bringing her with him. The shift deepened his penetration, hitting a spot just below her navel that made her shiver. She rocked her hips, building to a frenzy while bracing herself with both hands against his rock-hard chest.

He slid a hand between them, thumb circling her clit.

Jolts of pleasure fired through her, igniting her nanites to new levels of awareness, additional levels of pleasure. She settled into a rhythm that drowned out all else, riding him until it felt as if every synapse would explode.

"Joy," he grunted, his hands running up her sides to cup her breasts. He pinched her nipples ever so lightly, but the added sensation sent fire through her bloodstream. Every muscle in her body convulsed with her orgasm. His release took him at the same moment, filling her with his heat and leaving her breathless.

CHAPTER FIFTEEN

Hours later, Kashatok roused as Joy's warmth left him, and she moved to the lavatory. Much as he reveled in watching everything she did, he rolled over, cradling his head on his wadded-up shirt. The elated contentment pulsing through him felt as if his body was trying to catch up on fifteen years of deprivation. It almost masked the hopelessness of the situation they were in.

Joy returned, shivering in the chill of the pod's struggling life support system. How long did they have before the energy cells were depleted? He pulled his shirt from beneath his head. "Here, put this on."

The hem fell almost to her knees. His cock stirred yet again. He couldn't get enough of her. "I like you in my clothes."

She pursed her lips, fighting back a smile. "Are you warm enough?"

"Never better." He held an arm up, inviting her to snuggle against him.

He wrapped both arms around her, spooning against her while he breathed deeply against her hair. It felt as if he might wake up from a dream at any moment.

She kissed his forearm. "I'm sorry I got you into this."

He could honestly say that if he died now, he'd die content. But the thought of Joy's life being extinguished was nearly unbearable. "It's not your fault. I think you merely provided Aleknagik with an excuse to do something he's wanted to do for years. Finding out you were Mulholland-Aird's daughter was just something he capitalized on to rally the crew against me."

Her hands clenched into fists. "My damn mother."

His arms tightened. He'd told her he believed she wasn't Syndicorp, but how could she not be? "So... how *is* the CEO's daughter not with the corp'?"

Joy sighed, her breath tickling his arm before she sat up to face him. She drew her knees inside the shirt and hugged them against her. "Mother and I have never seen eye-to-eye. She wanted me to follow in her footsteps, yet I was never pretty enough, charismatic enough, or even worse, *dedicated* enough in her opinion. The entire reason I became a reporter was because I thought if I made anchor, she'd have to respect that. She watches the news all the time. She knows more about what's going on in the finofan bureaucracy than she does about her own family. She didn't even realize I was gone until I called her."

His stomach did a flip-flop. "You called her?"

Joy blanched, then nodded. "Like I said, this is all my fault."

Kashatok sat up to face her. "So, you *were* reporting to her?"

"No!" Joy's eyes widened, and he felt her blood pressure spike through their lingering ionic connection. "I just... after you said you were a *carayak*, I couldn't stomach someone else... destroying the nanites, so I hacked into the *Hardship's* comm and called Mother, thinking she would know where to send me for help."

Any growing rancor he felt about her subsided. She hadn't wanted anyone but him. It was one thing to dangle love before him and snatch it away once. But twice? *Ellam Cua* couldn't be that cruel. "Any chance your mother's sending help now?"

Joy shook her head. "I don't think she even knows which quadrant I'm in. I cut the connection as soon as she suggested sending troopers. And the emergency beacon is only sending a generic long-range transmission. She has no way to know I'm on board."

He waved a hand at the star-studded void outside the small view screen. "For all we know, there's a space station just out of sensor range."

Chewing her lip, Joy stared at the view screen. "We need to boost our signal." She scooted forward and popped open the compartment below the control panel. "If I up the amperage and integrate the sensors to latch onto any nearby signals, we may be able to increase our range." She paused and looked over her shoulder at him. "But it will use up all our extra juice. Our life support will be reduced by days. What if no one hears us? Or they do, but can't reach us in time?"

For a long moment he looked at her, the woman he loved. The future he'd never have. Their chance of surviving was already slim to nothing. Was there a wrong choice in this situation? "I think we should try."

She nodded and pointed at the compartment holding the pod's tools. "Hand me the smallest spanner you can find."

After several hours of tinkering, Joy wiped her hands on the rags of her shirt and disengaged the pod's gravity to save energy. "We're broadcasting." Her short hair made a halo around her head as she floated free of the cabin floor. "I'd say we have less than half a day of power using these levels."

Kashatok pulled her close, wrapping both arms around her middle and spinning lazily in the center of the cabin. "I'm not ready for this to end."

"I know. Me either." She grabbed his beard, tugging gently to bring his mouth down to hers. The kiss she gave him lingered long and slow, heating his blood with a soft tenderness they'd not indulged in previously. Breaking the kiss, she looked deeply into his eyes. "Do you believe in an afterlife?"

Although he knew she could only see him through her camera, she saw the real him. She knew his darkest secret and didn't shy away. The mate bond—something he'd given up ever hoping could be his—had created a tangible thread between them. "*Ellam Cua* promises when we find our mates, the bond will be true and after death, we'll be united to experience new dimensions, new purpose."

"That's a lot to hope for." She let out a trembling laugh. "Now that you're not a *carayak*, you can have your pick of women with nanites. Sure you don't want to trade me in for a better model if we make the next port?"

If he hadn't been so attuned to her, he might've mistaken her words for a brush off. "You're the most beautiful woman in the universe, Joy. My mate. My heart. My everything."

Her entire body heated within his embrace, her face lighting with a smile. "I love you, too."

He ran one hand up her back and threaded his fingers through her short hair, memorizing her face, enjoying her closeness for what might be the last time. "This has been the happiest time in my entire life."

"Mine, too." Joy's eyes widened abruptly, her gaze drilling past him toward the view screen. "Holy hell, Kashatok, there's a ship!"

Kashatok twisted, looking out the port. His breath caught at the oblong module covered in Syndicorp markings. "Troopers."

Pawing her way through the air toward the viewport, Joy pressed her face next to his. "We're saved!"

Gritting his teeth, he nodded. He was a wanted man, sure to be executed at the next port—if not immediately. Syndicorp gave no quarter to pirates.

As if sensing his concern, she asked, "What's wrong?"

"Nothing, my love." He ran his knuckles along the side of her face. "You're saved, and that's all that matters."

"Oh, shit." Her face paled. "You're a pirate."

He nodded, giving her a resigned smile. "I always assumed I'd die in a firefight, not under a Syndicorp executioner's needle."

"That's not going to happen. You saved me. My mother has to pardon you." She elbowed him aside and switched on the comm. "Trooper vessel, this is Joy Mulholland-Aird on board the escape pod. Do you copy?"

Long moments passed with no answer. Outside the view screen, the trooper ship drifted against its background of stars, as if oblivious to their presence.

"Is it possible they don't know we're here?" she asked.

"Try another channel."

She cycled through the three distress channels, each with no response. Pulling herself downward to the base of the console, she traced the exposed wiring beneath the control panel. "Everything looks fine here." She lifted her head and looked out the view screen again. "Maybe they're having trouble with their sensors? We're hardly bigger than space dust in this pod. We might be out of visible range."

He nodded slowly. Something wasn't right. Trooper protocol was to check for survivors. "I think we should move in. Get close enough for them to get a visual."

"We don't have enough power for thrusters."

"Yes, we do. It just reduces our life support from hours to minutes." He hated to put them in further jeopardy, but there was the possibility the other ship could move on at any moment. "We have to do something." He hooked the toes of his boots at the base of the console and engaged the thrusters to swing the pod toward the troopers.

At the edge of the view screen, another ship appeared. Kashatok's heart caught in his throat. The *Hardship*. Captain Qaiyaan had come for them after all. *Come for Joy.* The other pirate owed nothing to Kashatok.

Purple bolts of light flashed over the trooper's hull. "God, is that the *Hardship*?" Joy asked. "They're firing at each other!"

The familiar shape of Captain Qaiyaan's ship dodged around the other vessel, evading its blasters while pummeling the troopers with its smaller gunfire. A stray blaster bolt bathed the view screen in a florescent glow.

"*Uminaq!*" Kashatok reached for the controls to guide them away from the fight.

Every light on the console flickered and went out. Then the low hum of the air scrubbers went silent. Using the thrusters had killed the last of the power reserves. Kashatok bellowed, "No!"

Bursts of light from the battle outside lit Joy's terrified face with deeply cut shadows. He could feel her trembling and pulled her into his arms. "We're heading straight into the line of fire."

She pressed her cheek against his chest. "Are we close enough to use your cochlear implant to call out?"

The implant had a short range, but it was worth a shot. He tapped below his ear. "This is Kashatok aboard the escape pod. Does anyone copy?"

"We read you, Captain!" Qaiyaan's voice came back immediately. "What the hell do you think you're doing? Reverse thrusters, now!"

Kashatok's hearts thumped as if they were knocking together. "Thrusters are down! Stop firing! Tell the troopers Joy's on board."

"Those aren't troopers, Captain."

Kashatok gripped Joy tighter. "Who are they?"

Tovik's voice cut in. "Kashatok, you have to evacuate the pod!"

"I told you, Joy's with me," Kashatok nearly shouted. "We have no vacuum suits."

"You'll only have to hold your shield around both of you for a few minutes. Push off the pod perpendicular to us with every bit of ionic power you can spare. We'll keep Aleknagik occupied and hopefully he won't notice. Then we can give him the pod while we sweep by and pick you up."

The pod shuddered as a blast passed close by. "I don't understand. How is Aleknagik shooting at us?"

"He commandeered the fucking trooper ship!" Qaiyaan said. "Now either evacuate or prepare to be blown to cosmic dust."

"We can do this, Kashatok," Tovik said. "I won't let you two die."

Kashatok believed the kid. Seemed to be a habit of his to believe people lately. He took a breath and pushed Joy off his chest. "They want us to evacuate."

"How?" The look on her face was almost comical in the strobing purple light.

"My ionic shielding. Like we did when we jumped off the slave ship."

She swallowed loud enough for him to hear. "Are we near enough to do that?"

"No. But Tovik says he has a plan."

"Much as I like Tovik, jumping into space without a suit and nowhere to land sounds like the stupidest plan ever."

A crazed chuckle rumbled through him. He felt absolutely insane right now. "They want us to space-lock ourselves."

She took a deep breath. "I trust you. Just tell me what to do."

They might die out there, but they were definitely on course to die if they stayed here. He turned around. "Hop on my back."

She wrapped her legs around his hips and gripped his shoulders.

He wrapped his hands beneath her knees to hold her against him. "Take a bunch of quick breaths, like you're hyperventilating."

He followed his own advice, saturating his bloodstream with oxygen before raising his shield.

"Popping the air seal now," he said into his implant.

The small cabin evacuated its atmosphere like a sigh. Against the velvet blackness, the two ships looked like toys in the distance.

Kashatok bent his knees and jumped.

He probably should've put more force behind his leap, but he wanted to be sure he reserved enough strength to maintain his shielding. Far out to his left, the troopers and the *Hardship* seemed evenly matched, purple pulses of light strafing the blackness between them. Both vessels wove around each other in evasive maneuvers. How could Qaiyaan possibly break away before Kashatok ran out of energy for his shield? Locking his forearms more firmly beneath Joy's knees, he prayed to *Ellam Cua* for a miracle.

J oy clung to Kashatok's back, unsure if she needed to hold her breath. Just to be safe, she did. Far off to her left, the two vessels continued exchanging fire. The vastness of space surrounding them felt like a monster's jaws, ready to swallow them at any moment. She'd hoped Kashatok's super-power included some kind of propulsion, but he only drifted in the direction he'd jumped, his arms clamped around her knees.

Then the *Hardship* suddenly spun on its axis and darted straight for them. A bolt from the trooper ship's long-range cannon whizzed past, too close for Joy's comfort. A sip of air escaped her lips, and she clamped her mouth closed to contain what she had left in her lungs.

Then a crushing hand seemed to grab hold of her, freezing every limb in position. *The tractor beam? Oh, God.* It was designed to move metallic structures like ship hulls, not living flesh. She hoped their young engineer knew what he was doing.

The *Hardship* seemed to double in size. Then double again. Without warning, the tractor beam cut off, releasing the bone-crushing pressure. The ship continued to rush toward them, the open maw of the cargo hold several ship-lengths away. Whoever was piloting the ship had better have a damn steady hand, or she and Kashatok would end up as nothing but smears against the hull.

She pressed her cheek to the side of Kashatok's neck, wishing she could take one last breath, smell him one last time. The hatch was nearly within reach now, the opening hazed by a sparkling atmospheric force-shield.

Three meters.

Two.

Kashatok ducked, his top-knot almost brushing the bay's door frame as they shot into the lit interior and slammed into a cargo net strung inside the hold. Joy's breath exploded in a giant rush, her hold on Kashatok broken. Like a slow-motion rubber band, the netting stretched...

The rebound flung her back in the direction they'd come from. Terror that she might be ejected through the open door seized her; instead, she crashed into the opposite wall of the cargo bay.

The impact felt like it had bruised every inch of her body. Her camera winked out. Barely conscious, she felt someone lift her.

"They're in," Mek said.

Next thing she knew, she was lying on a mattress. Hands pressed diodes to her temples. A familiar furry body brushed against her cheek, settling at the crook of her neck and shoulder.

"Jhikik?" she slurred, unable to open her eyes.

The netorpok purred softly, nuzzling his head beneath her ear. Where was Kashatok? Before she could rally the strength to open her eyes, the familiar vertigo of burn twisted her inside out. Nausea rose and fell, her muscles quivered, every vein in her body seemed to be filled with lava. After long, excruciating minutes, the sensation ended.

She let out a sigh. Her body throbbed from hitting the cargo wall, but compared to the last couple of burns, her head didn't feel so bad. Even the nanites had remained sane. In fact, they were silent as the grave. Curious, she commanded, *Camera*.

Light stabbed into her brain and she squeezed her eyes shut, adjusting her filters before trying again. Next to her ear, Jhikik clacked his teeth.

Kashatok's voice came from somewhere near her feet. "How is she? I need to see her."

She lifted her head, noting the familiar surroundings of the *Hardship's* med bay. Kashatok leaned on the door frame, looking haggard as hell, but alive. *Thank God.* She dropped her head back against the pillow. "I'm okay. A little beat up, but alive." She extended a hand toward him. "How're you?"

He moved up the side of the cot, the furious lines of his face softening. Behind him at the computer, Mek watched them with his arms crossed.

Kashatok wove his fingers between hers. "I can't believe that worked."

"Me either." Her heart felt so full, it hurt almost as much as her bruised body.

Jhikik scurried over their connected hands, perching on Kashatok's shoulder. A contented purr filled the room.

"Good to see you, too." Kashatok rubbed the netorpok beneath the chin.

Joy sighed. "Do you know what's going on?"

"Maybe *you* can tell *us*, Ms. Mulholland-Aird." Noatak's voice cut through the room like a laser.

Her heart leaped into her throat. *They're going to kill me.* But they wouldn't go through the effort of rescuing her only to kill her, would they? Not before they harvested the nanites.

Kashatok widened his stance, standing between her and Noatak. "Back off."

Tovik tore around the corner into the med bay, his face alight. "*Anaq*, you guys! That was *awesome!*"

"Not now, Tovik," Noatak warned without taking his gaze off Joy.

Mek pointed to Joy and Kashatok's joined hands. "They've mated."

Heat crept over Joy's face while Kashatok strengthened his grip on her hand. "Yes."

Noatak's face darkened. "So the nanites are gone?"

"Oh, crap," Tovik said. "Qaiyaan's going to be pissed."

Mek picked up a syringe. "Perhaps I can still learn something from her blood."

Even without ionic senses of her own, Joy felt Kashatok's power expand. He let go of her hand and snatched the syringe from Mek's grip. "No one touches her."

Joy pushed the diodes away from her head and sat up painfully. "Kashatok, it's okay. Let him take a sample." She held her arm out to Mek. "I know you said the mating frequency would destroy the nanites, but they're not gone."

Mek's gaze sharpened. "Interesting. Let's take a look."

She looked away while he pressed the sample gun against her arm.

Qaiyaan rounded the corner and stopped in the doorway. "Mek, Lisa needs your attention before we can jump again." He stiffened, eyes narrowing as he looked at the gathered men. "What's wrong?"

"She's mated," Noatak clipped out.

"But I still have the nanites," Joy added, willing herself not to turn away from Qaiyaan's furious look.

"I'll know in a moment," Mek said, plugging her blood sample into his diagnostic machine. Joy's camera jounced in time with her heartbeat while she waited. After a moment, Mek shook his head, turning back to face the room. "There are no nanites in her bloodstream."

"What?" Joy could barely form words. She didn't want to think of what might happen to her if she didn't have the nanites to bargain with. "There has to be. My camera's working."

Face doubtful, Mek pulled a scanner from the cupboard. "Most likely, your optic nerve has simply returned to normal. Let me take a reading of your synaptic system."

Passing the scanner slowly over her scalp, he made a surprised noise and repeated the motion. Setting the scanner aside, he scratched his cheek. "I don't know how, but she still has them. It appears the nanites have secured themselves to her nervous system."

The entire room seemed to breathe a sigh of relief. Joy's sigh was loudest of all. "So that's good, right? We didn't kill them. Why aren't they showing up in my blood?"

Mek shook his head. "They're no longer free floating."

"What does that mean?" Kashatok grumbled.

"I can't harvest her," Mek said. "At least not the way I'd imagined."

The word harvest had Joy's blood racing, and she was grateful when Kashatok spoke with caveman-like protectiveness. "You're not harvesting my mate."

"Bad choice of words." Mek held up a placating hand. "I meant to say gather excess nanites."

Kashatok's fists knotted at his sides. "Whatever she has or doesn't have, she's my mate. I won't let any of you hurt her."

"Me either." Tovik glared at Noatak.

"She's Syndicorp, you fools." Noatak took a step forward. "Probably in league with Aleknagik this entire time."

Jhikik clicked his teeth at the advancing crewman.

Joy's jaw dropped. "Aleknagik's with Syndicorp?"

"No, fucking way," Kashatok shook his head. "He may've taken me by surprise with the mutiny, but if there's one thing Aleknagik is not, it's Syndicorp. He's just a bastard who subverted my crew and stole my ship. Where the hell is my ship, anyway?"

"We left it behind to rescue you," Qaiyaan said. "Are you sure he's not with the corp'?"

"Positive."

Qaiyaan shook his head, brow furrowed. "Aleknagik probably went straight back to where we left the *Kinship*. He'll be waiting, and we're no match for those trooper guns."

"Suicide mission," Noatak added.

CHAPTER SIXTEEN

S uicide mission, Kashatok thought, remembering Chignik's helpless confession to him in the brig. "Who's left on the *Kinship*?"

"Not sure. We didn't stick around for roll call," Qaiyaan said.

Tovik added, "Aleknagik took two guys with him."

Joy's hand slipped into his. "I'm worried about Gassy."

Kashatok nodded, his gaze locked with Qaiyaan's. "They're my *iluq*," he said softly. "I owe them my help." For the first time in over fifteen years, he realized he wanted that sense of brotherhood.

"I understand." Qaiyaan crossed his arms. "But if we let the nanites be destroyed, that's the end of any hope for future mates."

"If we don't make a point of protecting our fellow denaidans, we have no reason for mates," Kashatok pointed out. "Losing the men on the *Kinship* would be a major loss when there are so few of us left."

A pained look crossed Qaiyaan's face. He rubbed his forehead. "One impossible situation after another. First, my mate is wanted by the cartel. Now your mate is being tracked by Syndicorp. *Anaq*, we have terrible taste in women, Kashatok."

The men chuckled, and even Kashatok had to smile. "I'm just grateful to have found a mate at all."

Joy's brows furrowed. "But if Aleknagik's not with Syndicorp, how'd he end up in control of the trooper ship?"

Qaiyaan smirked. "We're pirates. It's what we do."

Kashatok squeezed her knee. "Superpowers, remember? We surprise and board ships that way all the time."

"Oh. Right." Joy groaned and pushed herself off the cot. "Tovik, is the piggyback harness still in place on the *Kinship*?"

"Yeah. Why?"

"If we catch Aleknagik between our two ships while engaging the piggyback, wouldn't it blow out his power coils?"

Tovik let out a low whistle. "Theoretically, yes. But that last piggyback knocked us apart. We'd need them to recalibrate."

"How do we do that when they're being guarded?" Qaiyaan stroked his beard.

"I could talk them through it if we were in comm range," Tovik said.

Noatak shook his head. "Aleknagik knows all our comm channels. He will be monitoring them."

"I have the nanites," Joy said. "I can connect straight into the *Kinship's* comm and walk them through the calibration without Aleknagik being any the wiser. Although…" She bit her bottom lip. "We'll need to be fairly close to do that."

"Our shields are no match for trooper cannons," Qaiyaan said.

"Let me handle the controls," Kashatok said. "I've piloted through worse."

Qaiyaan raised his brows. "I know your piloting is legendary, but are you sure?"

Imagining blowing Aleknagik to space dust, Kashatok grinned. "Just show me to the cockpit."

He was going to get his damn ship back if it killed him.

The makeshift nav-grav seat Tovik had rigged in engineering barely held Joy steady as the *Hardship* changed trajectories again. With her camera deactivated so she could use the nanites for the comm, blindness had her panicking every time the ship shuddered under impact.

"Whoa, that was a close one," Tovik reported from somewhere in engineering as he worked on calibrating the *Hardship's* drive. "How're things going over on the *Kinship?*"

Still reeling from post-burn nausea, Joy'd contacted Ekwok on the *Kinship's* bridge. Gassy was still down, however, and none of the crew knew much about engineering. Cooper and Chignik had been taking the instructions she was relaying on how to adjust the harness, but were now debating each other on the other end of the comm.

"Listen up," Joy strengthened the nanites' signal, needing to sound authoritative before she lost them all together. "Stop arguing and tighten the hex bolt another quarter turn, then send me the numbers."

Joy's heart raced as she waited for the data. How long could Kashatok evade Aleknagik's guns yet remain close enough to the *Kinship* for her to keep contact? And that wasn't even the hard part; once the harness was aligned, they had to maneuver Aleknagik's ship between the other two ships and hit the burn drive.

Data streamed over the comm, and she immediately relayed the information to Tovik's console. "Please tell me they've got it close enough."

Chignik's transmission through the nanites was asking the same thing. Tovik mumbled, "Maybe if I make an adjustment to our flux membrane…"

The ship jerked, lifting her from the seat before the chair's harness caught her and slammed her back against the padding. Tovik grunted.

The internal comm exploded with Noatak's voice. "Direct hit! Shields at eighteen percent. Engineering, you'd better have things ready soon."

No answer from Tovik.

"Tovik?" she asked. *Damn this blindness.* "You okay?"

His strained voice answered her. "Go ahead and let the *Kinship* know they're good." He cleared his throat. "Captain, we're ready to line them up."

"Chignik, Cooper, that did it," Joy sent. "Tovik says to hold on tight. Things may get rough over there."

She gripped the arms of the nav-grav chair and hoped her plan wasn't about to blow them all up.

Kashatok clenched his sweaty hands over the yoke, guiding the Kinship through evasive maneuvers while Noatak manned the co-pilot seat.

The tiny bridge could barely hold two men, and Qaiyaan had given up his seat to operate the ship's gun turret. Never would Kashatok have imagined having respect for a man who willingly relinquished his ship, but Captain Qaiyaan had managed to maintain his regard. He was a damn good shot with that gun, as well, taking down one of the trooper vessel's short-range lasers despite Kashatok's crazy flying.

"Captain, we're ready to line them up," Tovik sent over the ship's internal comm.

Kashatok was ready. He spun the ship on its axis, heading straight for the troopers. The smaller *Hardship* had great maneuverability, but he'd gauged that he'd need to get within meters of the trooper vessel to be in range of the *Kinship's* harness field.

Kashatok held the yoke steady, staring down the barrels of three lasers. His gaze flickered between the deadly menace and the range sensor on his dash. "Full shields to the forward panels."

Purple strobes of light hit the Hardship face-on and rendered the view screen temporarily useless.

Anaq.

Relying on sensors alone, Kashatok held his course.

Noatak's voice cracked from the co-pilot seat. "Forward shields holding at fifteen percent."

The wail of proximity alarms filled the cabin.

Kashatok's hands remained steady, even though his mind was screaming at him to pull up.

Two more heartbeats.

Now. Praying to *Ellam Cua*, Kashatok hit the burn drive and pulled up on the yoke.

The inertial force flattened him into the seat and made it hard to breathe. The familiar nausea of the burn drive swelled over him, but that feeling of being sucked through a straw never came. He squinted at his sensors and twisted the yoke to bring the ship back around.

Through the view screen, the *Kinship* floated as before, the familiar pattern of stars the only backdrop.

Aleknagik's ship was gone.

"Where'd they go?" Noatak asked, fingertips flying over the sensor controls.

Kashatok's insides contracted. That had been too easy. "Look for debris."

He called up the sensor readings on his own panel, backtracking through the data to find the precise moment he'd hit the burn drive.

Qaiyaan poked his head inside the cockpit. "What the hell just happened?"

"Trying to figure that out, Captain," Noatak said without looking up.

"I'm going to check on Lisa. She's been ill, enduring so many burns in a row."

Kashatok sucked in a breath and rose from his seat. Joy probably felt the same way, and he'd been focused on Aleknagik. He tapped the comm to engineering. "How's Joy?"

"I'm okay," her voice came from behind Qaiyaan. The big captain stepped aside and let her move into his spot. "Tovik's got a nasty bump, though."

Relieved as he was to see her well, Kashatok's throat tightened. "The bastard got away."

"What do you mean?" Her eyebrows drew together.

He slumped back down into the pilot's chair. She moved into the cramped space to stand behind him. He pointed to the burn data on his console. "I need more time to go over the details. We're in the same location, but there was a frequency dilation."

"*Anaq*," Noatak punched more buttons next to him. "He burned out of here?"

"Wherever he ended up, he's nothing more than flotsam now." Joy leaned over Kashatok's shoulder for a closer look at the screen. "The energy certainly arced out his power coils."

Kashatok reached up and cupped her other cheek. "I have what matters most. You're safe."

"And you can have your ship back." She squeezed his shoulders and pressed her cheek against his.

Kashatok nodded, still staring at the *Kinship*.

He hoped Aleknagik had ended up in the middle of a star.

CHAPTER SEVENTEEN

Kashatok strode across the boarding tube onto the *Kinship*. Waiting on the other side, Ekwok and Cooper pumped their fists while Chignik strode forward and clapped Kashatok on one shoulder. "You're one hell of a pilot, Captain." Nodding to Joy, who remained a little behind Kashatok, he smiled. "Good job talking us through those calibrations, too."

Kashatok sensed her stiffness ease, but she remained near the boarding tube, which Kashatok appreciated. She'd insisted on coming along and having his back, and Jhikik had insisted on coming with her, curled at the crook of her neck. Next to Joy, Qaiyaan stood with his hands near the pistols on his belt.

Cooper smoothed a big palm over his bald, tattooed head. "We want to say we're real sorry things went like they did, Captain. Aleknagik played us all against each other."

"Chignik was the only one he had nothing on," Ekwok added.

Kashatok glanced over the three men, his heart still hard over the mutiny. "You the only three left on board?"

"Gassy's in the med bay. We put Manopup and Moore in the brig," Chignik said. "They were still woozy from burn when Aleknagik jumped ship or they'd've gone, too."

"They'd been whispering mutiny for a long time." Cooper ducked his head. "I thought it was just talk."

The muscles in Kashatok's jaw tightened as he considered what he was going to do to the men in his brig. Space-locking seemed too kind.

"Gassy's been asking for you," Ekwok volunteered.

Joy stepped forward. "Is he okay?"

"I think so," Ekwok said. "But Doc's gone with Aleknagik, so I can't say for sure."

Their betrayal hurt, but at least they'd surrendered his ship back to him. He cleared his throat. "Qaiyaan," he turned to address his fellow captain, "may we borrow your doctor?"

"I'll send him over." Qaiyaan nodded and headed back to his own ship.

Kashatok extended a hand to Joy. "Let's go check on Gassy."

In the med bay, Gassy was propped against some pillows. He looked just as hellacious as before, but at least he was sitting up instead of lying there like a dying fish. Kashatok stopped just inside the med bay, noting the sterility shield over the bed was down. "You're breathing normal air again. How're you feeling, old man?"

"Couldn't take another breath inside that shield. I hear I better get my ass up and moving soon 'cause this little lady's after my job," he said with a twinkle in his eye.

Joy moved forward and took the old man's hand. "I could never replace you. You still have a lot to teach me."

"Don't worry, you're not getting rid of me quite yet," Gassy said.

Kashatok approached the bedside until his shoulder touched Joy's, loving the subtle way she leaned into him. "Qaiyaan's doc will be over soon to check you out."

"If anyone can make you well, Mek can," Joy added.

"Take it you've had reason to be in his med bay?" Gassy's astute gaze swept across their connected shoulders.

Joy flushed a delightful pink.

Kashatok couldn't help the grin that felt like it might crack his face in two. He lifted his arm to pull Joy firmly against him, resting his chin atop her head. Gassy'd always told him he should question the assumption he was a *carayak*. Never had Kashatok been so grateful to admit he'd been wrong. "You were right all along."

"'Course I was." Gassy's blistered face sobered. "Just remember, the rest of us aren't as lucky as you are."

Kashatok removed his chin from Joy's head, but kept his arm around her. He wasn't used to being one of the lucky ones. "We're going to help change that."

Joy nodded. "We're going to help Qaiyaan locate Syndicorp's secret lab."

Gassy tilted his head. "That's well and good. But you have other things to consider first."

It wasn't like Gassy to be negative. Frowning, Kashatok asked, "What do you mean?"

The old man shook his grizzled head. "With Aleknagik gone, you're going to need more crew. And you don't exactly have the best reputation in the galaxy."

Kashatok cringed, remembering how difficult it'd been to hire a shuttle mechanic. What would his reputation be like after losing three more crewmen, including his first mate? Looking at Joy, he realized things didn't need to be difficult; she was as charming as he was gruff. He grinned at her. "I have a new first mate who can do the interviewing for me."

Joy sucked in a breath, twisting to look up at him. "Me?"

"Sure," he said. "There's no one I trust more."

"What about Gassy?"

"Leave me out of this," Gassy said. "I'm old and one of these days I'll have enough money to retire in a cushy flat at some exotic port."

She scrunched her nose and seemed to consider. "Will your men even listen to me?"

The sound of a throat clearing behind him made him turn. Chignik stood in the doorway, the rest of the crew in the hallway at his back. "You busted our captain out of the brig, made a daring escape, then came back for more. I'd say you earned it."

The others nodded. Pride in Joy made Kashatok stand a little straighter.

Gassy coughed. "That settles it then. Now get out and let an old man get some rest, would you?"

Giving Joy's shoulders one last squeeze, Kashatok ushered her out the door. It was time to get his ship up and running.

Joy stared out Kashatok's cabin window on the *Kinship*, the faint outline of her reflection in the glass overlaying the jutting buttresses of the space station outside. She wore one of his billowy shirts, enveloping herself in his ginger-cinnamon scent. How many times had they made love since she'd become the *Kinship's* first mate? She felt like she'd finally found a place where she belonged, doing exactly what she was meant to do. Never in her life had she imagined feeling so complete.

As if to reflect her own happiness back at her, the leaves of the naujiar plant rustled, contented cheeps echoing among the foliage. Kashatok had given Jhikik open access to the plant to keep him occupied after Joy pointed out how fascinated the netorpok seemed to be by their intimate activities. And there'd been a lot of activity. She turned to face where he still lounged on the rumpled bed, one deliciously sculpted leg outside the sheets while he read his polycom.

But she needed to stay focused on their immediate problem. Qaiyaan'd towed them to the port, and she'd installed the new flux inverter, but they had yet to fill the empty crew positions. Kashatok's reputation was proving hard to overcome. She climbed onto the corner of the mattress and knelt, settling back against her heels. "People like stories about pirates."

"As villains." Kashatok's voice rumbled sexily as he lowered the polycom to his lap. She loved how he seemed to follow her train of thought, no matter how out of the blue her comments might be.

"What if we provided a different angle to the story?" She tapped her left temple. "Say… an exposé about pirate freedom fighters?"

He laughed, a sound she loved more and more the freer he became with his joy. He lunged forward and pulled her against him, flopping to his back with her resting on his hard abs. "Are you suggesting we start a revolution?"

She chewed her lip. She'd been thinking about it a lot, actually. After learning what Syndicorp had done, what her mother had done—not only killing off an entire race but covering it up—she'd become determined to blow the lid off the entire thing. "I'm suggesting we put out a call to action. I'm still on staff at RealTime News. I can spin the exposé into a thinly veiled advertisement to hire crew and find suitable candidates for denaidan mates."

His big hands stopped massaging her naked rump. "Advertise for mates?"

"There's no reason new crew members can't be female, is there? And if they find a love interest while they're here, even better." She pushed up, straddling his hips. "Let's put a call out to men and women who want to overcome the tyranny that's taken over every planet in the galaxy."

"An adventure in the swashbuckling world of black market trading and deep-space piracy?" His upturned mouth looked completely kissable as he teased her with the line from her original recording.

"I should've never shared that video with you." She smacked his chest and lifted a knee half-heartedly as if to dismount.

He grabbed her hips, securing her in place over the line of his growing erection, separated by only the thin layer of the sheet between them. "Ah, but there's only one rule on board my ship."

She narrowed her eyes. "Rule? You're not still trying to ban women, are you? Because as your first mate—"

"More of a request than a rule." He ran both hands up beneath the loose shirt to cup her breasts. "I want you to share everything with me."

His thumbs found her nipples and teased them to sensitive nubs. Her back arched involuntarily. For a moment, she simply reveled in the way he played her body. There was no need for words when he already knew her so well. She recalled something Lisa had told her over lunch yesterday. "Lisa said she and Qaiyaan can hear each other's thoughts. Do you think we'll ever be that close?"

His bottomless dark eyes drank her in. "Whether or not we ever can, you're my first mate, my only mate. There is no future without you."

She placed a hand against his chest, finding the twin thump of his hearts. Hearts that beat only for her. Being loved unconditionally was more beautiful than she'd ever imagined.

Leaning forward, she pressed her forehead against his, taking satisfaction that she had beaten all the odds to gain his love. "I will always love you," she vowed. "You are my mate."

One of his hands slid up to the back of her neck, pulling her into a kiss. His tongue teased open her mouth, swirling and stroking and building a heat within her while his rock-hard length grew more insistent between her legs. His other hand continued massaging her breast and nipple, moving to her ribs, down to her hip, and back up again in a teasing caress that made her skin tremble and twitch until the heat between them became a raging inferno.

"I need to be in you," he said.

"Yes," she breathed out, lifting herself so he could pull the thin sheet aside. She poised her opening over the blunt head of his cock. Then slowly, deliberately, she lowered herself against him, eyes locked with his in a connection so intimate, it wouldn't have mattered if they were touching or not. The delicious friction of his length entering her ran clear up her spine.

For long moments, she stayed locked in place, her gaze trapped by his. Reaching forward, she brushed her fingers against his cheek, then trailed them down the length of his beard.

Slowly, subtly, she began to move, rocking and lifting her hips at just the right angle to send flutters of ecstasy throughout her entire body.

He was right there with her, hips thrusting upward. His speed increased to match hers, ratcheting up her pleasure.

She was aware of him everywhere. Not just deep in her inner wetness, but pressed between her thighs, under her fingertips, sharing her air. His hands guided her hips, but it was as if he knew her every desire, anticipated every move before she even knew herself.

His eyes on her were bright with pleasure and love. "You're so amazing."

The first wave of pleasure hit her, shuddering through her body and nearly paralyzing her. But Kashatok didn't stop. He continued pumping upward unrelentingly, holding her hips and taking her past the first crest and onto another. Her mouth opened in a silent scream. She leaned forward and gripped his shoulders, her entire body throbbing with the connection. It wasn't like a psychic connection, but one of emotion. A bond solidifying between them like nothing she'd ever imagined possible.

His teeth were bared, his solid legs trembling. But his eyes never left her face. As he pounded into her, she felt almost as if she floated free of her body, tethered only by his gaze.

The euphoria or pleasure grew into a towering wave, hovering, promising to break. Her legs ached and yet she couldn't stop. Couldn't slow. Reaching that crest was all that mattered. In a curling, slow-motion release of pressure almost too great to bear, she caught the edge, rockets of sensation shuddering into the very core of her being.

Throwing her head back under the onslaught, she allowed the pleasure to wash over her. Through her. Fully aware of Kashatok's muscles tightening, his huge hands holding her hips firmly, his release pumping into her with a force that took her breath away.

She slumped forward across his chest, completely spent, her ear pressed over his paired hearts. They raced in unison beneath her cheek. In that moment, she knew the bond truly was forever. She'd found the only purpose that really mattered.

Love.

CLAIMED BY NOATAK

A STEAMY ALIEN ROMANCE

Marlis leveled her Blackstar E-11 and squeezed the trigger. The target at the end of the range flashed three times. *Bulls-eye.*

"Fuck them and their standards," she muttered, pushing the target back another meter. She took aim and fired several more shots, each one flashing success. The E-11 zero-recoil pulse pistol had been a gift for her eleventh birthday, and after fourteen years and many other weapons, it was still her favorite. "I was even on time this morning."

"Good shot, Marlis!" Marlis's AI chimed from her wristband. The artificial intelligence was supposed to assist Marlis with anger management and lapses in memory, but its trite encouragements did nothing to assuage her today.

"Shut up, Twerp." Marlis racked the energy coil's cooling module and set the pistol aside. Picking up her customized Renegade MCS6 rifle, she reset the target for long-range and sighted in.

The lanes of the Syndicorp cruiser's firing range were all occupied today, but she had eyes only for her target, imagining each bulls-eye as the face of the service recruiter assigned to her file. *I'm legacy, for fuck's sake.* Descended from a long line of trooper personnel with excellent records. And it wasn't as if she couldn't keep up during the drills. She could out-shoot, out-run, and out-wrestle every woman as well as most men in the squad. So what if she needed a little help to remember what day it was?

"Marlis!" a man's voice barked behind her.

Gut tightening, she whipped the rifle around.

Her father's narrow gaze flicked to the barrel, his mouth in a grim line as she lowered the weapon.

She refused to feel any regret about being battle-ready. Mom had died while she and Marlis had been on Pulati for a mother-daughter vacation. Ten-year-old Marlis had only survived the sudden terrorist outbreak by hiding beneath her mother's dead body for sixteen hours.

Marlis had no intention of letting her guard down. Ever.

Dad crossed his arms over his chest, covering the service ribbons on the lapel of his uniform. "You missed your date last night."

"That's tonight." Even as she said it, she realized she was probably wrong.

Twerp's feminine voice rose from her wrist strap. "I informed you of the engagement at seventeen hundred yesterday and again at seventeen twenty. You said you were in no mood to give someone a blow job and directed me not to remind you again."

Marlis's face heated to match the rising flush in her father's usually pallid cheeks. When would she ever remember to put in her earbud? Teeth clenched, she grated out, "Shut up, Twerp."

Dad squared his shoulders, looking Marlis straight in the eye. "He's a respectable young man, Marlis. From a good family. You couldn't ask for a better match."

"I don't want a better match. I want to join the troopers." She turned around and took aim at the target once more. "Get me a date with someone useful and I'll go."

"I can't rebuild the bridges you burn fast enough."

Refusing to be distracted, she let out a slow breath and squeezed the trigger in rapid succession. The target lit up on all but the final shot. She lowered the rifle. "I'd be a good soldier, Dad."

A gentle hand settled on her shoulder. "You blew up at your recruiter."

Marlis fuzzily remembered her rage at the small-eyed, beak-nosed recruiter who oversaw the drills the troopers used to weed out unworthy candidates. He was supposed to test the recruits' physical aptitudes. Instead, he'd thrown history questions at them. She seemed to recall a lot of swear words coming out of her mouth instead of answers. "What good is a history lesson going to do for me on the battle field?"

"He thinks you're a liability. They want to rescind your weapon carry permit." Dad's voice lowered with unaccustomed softness. "I'm sorry."

His words felt like a punch in the gut. Give up her pistol? *No way.* No longer able to focus on the target, Marlis shoved the E-11 into the holster built into the back hip of her pants and shouldered her rifle, turning to leave.

"Marlis."

She continued walking.

"Marlis. Your rifle case."

Face on fire, she halted; she might still have a permit to carry, but exiting the range actually welding a weapon, even on a military ship, was a big no-no. *Stupid memory.* Other AI models came equipped with a visual node to track items, but Marlis's therapist claimed that requiring her to remember some things on her own would help her improve.

Squaring her shoulders, she spun on her heel and retrieved the case, visually verifying there was nothing else she was leaving behind. Her father's watchful gaze made Marlis doubt herself. What else was she forgetting? *Dammit!*

Reacting to her elevated heart rate, Twerp vibrated against her wrist, encouraging her to remain calm, then came to the rescue with a reminder. "Marlis, you are scheduled for lunch with your sister in forty-three minutes. May I remind you that Attie is routinely early?"

"Thank you, Twerp." She offered her dad a weak smile. "I need to go clean up. I'll talk to you later."

Passing uniformed personnel as she moved through the carrier's corridors, Marlis silently repeated her mantra from years in therapy; *there is no danger.* Yet it was a hard mantra to believe when she'd just been told her right to carry a firearm was in jeopardy. She switched to *anger does more harm than good.* By the time she reached the family housing section and the modest quarters she shared with her dad and sister, Twerp had stopped buzzing.

She stowed her rifle and washed her face, then headed toward the mess hall on the lower deck where Attie probably already waited. Her big sister had been accepted into the troopers over a year ago, quickly rising to Private First Class. The job left Attie little time to visit with family, although she made a point of having lunch weekly with Marlis. No matter how routine it might be, Marlis's heart lightened at the thought of seeing her.

Uniform crisp and ash-blonde hair trimmed to short ringlets, Attie was already seated at their usual table. The huge room echoed with the predominantly human lunch crowd filling long tables, the homogeny interspersed by a few clusters of aliens. Attie's head was down, eyes scanning the screen of a polycom as Marlis approached. A new gold chevron adorned the epaulet on her shoulder.

"You made corporal?" Marlis asked, unable to drag her gaze from the emblem.

Attie set the polycom aside and rose, brushing her fingertips over the rank badge before rounding the table to give Marlis a hug. "I officially got the promotion today."

"Hugging's against regulation. They're gonna come take that chevron back." Marlis squeezed her sister, trying to summon a sense of humor instead of jealousy. Her sister was so together.

Attie rolled her eyes and once more took her seat. She glanced toward the long chow line. "You want to go first while I finish these reports?"

Nodding, Marlis got in line among the uniformed personnel. Prior to this moment, she'd always strutted into the mess hall knowing she was among her people; it was only a matter of time before she had her own uniform. Now it felt like everyone's eyes were on her; challenging her worth.

Putting two plates onto her tray, she selected the chicken curry and skipped the dessert section, opting for two coffees with cream instead.

Although Attie never asked, Marlis always came back with food for both of them. It seemed like a waste of precious sister-time to send Attie to stand in line all over again.

Returning to the table, Marlis set both plates down. "It was this or something that looked like cat vomit."

"Thanks." Attie picked up her fork and poked at a sliced tomato, edging it away from her chicken. "How're things with Dad?"

Something about the set of Attie's shoulders had Marlis on edge. "He's still trying to set me up with Colonel Yan's son. Why do you ask?"

Attie shrugged. "Is he cute?"

Now Marlis's warning bells began to chime. "Some people think so. Why?"

Taking a big bite, Attie chewed slowly before answering. "You turn twenty-six soon. You know what that means."

Of course she knew. At twenty-six, she'd lose her status as her father's dependent and all the perks that came with it. Unless she joined the troopers herself, she'd be sent to ground, forced to join the civilians on one muddy planet or another. Trapped, just like on Pulati. *Never, never, never.* "Of course I do. What does that have to do with Colonel Yan's son?"

"A lot of people enjoy marriage. It'd give you a partner."

"Marrying some douche bag I could beat at arm wrestling won't solve my problems."

Attie tapped her fork against her plate nervously. "Marlis, you need someone you can rely on."

"What do you mean? I have you. And I have Dad when he's not being a dick."

Setting her fork down, Attie took a deep breath, gaze locked with Marlis's. "I've been assigned to the flagship *Icarus*."

It felt as if someone had just opened the ship's blast doors, sucking away all the oxygen. Marlis's vision narrowed, the room fading around her. *Attie can't leave.* Her sister was her rock. The one person she could always turn to. Twerp buzzed almost painfully against her skin, telling her to calm down.

Attie leaned forward, speaking slowly. "It's part of my promotion. A great opportunity for advancement. I'll be serving on Admiral Olly's primary staff."

Marlis gulped. "I don't see you enough as it is."

"It'll be okay." Attie reached across the table and covered Marlis's hand with hers. "We can still talk on the vid. And Dad says—" She cut off, biting a corner of her lip as if she'd said too much.

"You told Dad already?" Marlis choked out. She'd always been Attie's confidante, the first to hear anything. "Before me?"

"He's worried about you, Marlis. You're his baby. He even called James."

Their older brother, James, had left when Marlis was ten, before she'd gone to Pulati with Mom. He was currently a Staff Sergeant on Aleigh. "What does James have to do with me?"

"He's trying to get you a dependency waiver. It's easier on planetary bases."

"You mean live with James?" Marlis shot to her feet, her blood on fire. "You're kidding me!" People at surrounding tables turned to stare. Twerp vibrated doggedly against her wrist. Still, Marlis couldn't keep her voice down. "And you agree with him?"

"No." Attie kept level contact with Marlis's eyes, exuding confidence. "Sit down, please."

"There is no danger, Marlis," Twerp added.

"Shut the fuck up, Twerp." There *was* danger. It was all around her, from places she never expected. "Dad says they're going to take away my weapon carry permit."

"What? They can't!" Attie's calm demeanor broke, and she rose to her feet.

Oddly enough, that made Marlis feel better. "I had an argument with my recruiter." Heat filled her face, and she lowered herself slowly back to her seat, scrubbing a hand over her forehead. "Do you think they'll let me petition for another try?"

Attie sighed, looking down at her little sister a moment before shaking her head no. "I won't lie to you. I've heard talk that you're unstable."

For the first time she could remember, Marlis felt tears prick her eyes. Actual, honest-to-god tears. She hated it. "What am I going to do?"

Picking up the polycom beside her plate, Attie began tapping in commands. "Since you can't live on board the carrier after your birthday and you don't want to live with James," she set the device on the tabletop and shoved it toward Marlis, "I think you should look for a job."

Marlis stared at the polycom, her pulse thundering in her ears. *A job?* As in something other than working for the troopers? Her brain refused to transform the blocks of text on the screen into meaningful information. "What is this?"

"Ads for jobs on Whylon Station. There are other options for you than military service. Legit shipping businesses looking for hired guns. Bodyguards. That kind of thing."

"Not through the troopers?" Marlis frowned. "Don't companies contract through the corp for those services?"

Her sister laughed and retrieved the polycom. "There's a world outside of Syndicorp—whole regions of the galaxy, in fact. Not everyone can afford troopers. You're fantastic with weapons, Sis. And you want to protect people. Let's find a way for you to do it." Attie stood. "I have to go or I'll be late for duty. I forwarded you the info." She took a few steps away, then looked over her shoulder and winked. "Oh, and don't tell Dad I suggested this, okay? I'd like to keep my reputation as the good daughter."

Watching her sister's retreating back, Marlis repeated her mantra. *There is no danger.* Yet she couldn't manage to take a full breath, let alone pull out her own polycom. *Work other than with the service?*

"Would you like me to assist?" Twerp asked calmly.

Grateful for any help she could get, Marlis nodded. "Yeah. Tell me about these shipping companies."

CHAPTER TWO

Noatak strode along the *Hardship's* corridor toward the cargo hold where Joy, the First Mate of the *Kinship,* was waiting in the shuttle. They were headed to Whylon Station to meet women who wanted to join their Resistance. *Resistance.* He grimaced as he walked. He still had his doubts about Joy's documentary attracting the right kind of people, but with both ships' captains off on a mission, that left him and Joy in charge of the interviews.

As he passed the med bay, Mek stepped out and held up a hand. "Before you go, we need to talk."

"I don't have time." Noatak scowled and shoved the medic's hand out of the way. It was enough he that could feel his ionic powers weakening every day; he didn't need to be hovered over like a newly hatched kemeg.

Mek trotted alongside him as he continued walking. "You need to strap into a nav-grav seat for the trip to Whylon Station."

That stopped Noatak cold. He spun on his heel to face the doctor. "No way. Nav-grav is for wimps."

"Your ionic levels dropped another six percent since my last scan." Mek pulled the med scanner from his belt and pulled up Noatak's record. "I ran some models, and it's only a matter of time before your secondary heart gives out completely."

"I strap in and Joy will know something's up. Soon as she knows, everyone will. Last thing I need is the entire universe knowing I'm weak."

"Let me put this into terms you'll understand." Mek lowered the scanner and focused on Noatak. "If you keep using your ionic powers, even for small things, you could die."

"Could is a lot different from will." Noatak rolled his shoulders. He'd faced death many times. But he'd always imagined going out in a blaze of glory, not dying from ionic failure like an old man. "Besides, aren't you looking into some procedure to fix me?"

"I am, but there isn't a lot of research available on denaidan physiology, especially with what's left of our planet under quarantine." The Termination had not only killed all females of their species, it'd also poisoned their home world beyond repair; no one had set foot on Denaida-daru in over fifteen years. Mek shook his head, lips pressed into a thin line. "Until I can determine a course of action, I recommend no shielding, no sensing enemy heartbeats, and definitely no burn without a nav-grav seat."

"What the fuck good am I for our cause if I can't do any of that?" Noatak crossed his arms. "Next, you'll tell me not to ping the women I'm about to interview." The applicants were going to join the pirates not only as crew, but potentially as mates; it was vital he select ones who would also be receptive to the nanites.

"Unfortunately, yes." Mek's stoic face softened. He opened his mouth as if to say more, then shut it again.

Noatak narrowed his eyes. Mek was usually abrupt. If he was holding back, it must be bad. "What else?"

Mek looked down, mouth pursed. "If these women accept the nanites, you'll need to avoid sexual activity."

The news was like a physical blow. They were about to bring a female crew onto the ship—the first ever—and he was being told not to touch? *"Ellam Cua."* His voice rose like a growl from deep inside his chest. "You're serious?"

"During sexual climax, your secondary heart automatically engages—"

"I don't need an anatomy lesson, doc. I get it." He let out a sigh, thinking about soft skin and pliant mouths and all the things he and the other denaidans had been dreaming about for fifteen years. Before the discovery of the nanites, non-denaidan females died during sex. Now it might be him. He rubbed his bearded chin. "Might be worth it, though."

Mek's eyes narrowed. "It's not only you at stake in that scenario, you know. If a mate bond were to form, you'd make her a widow before she even understood what was happening."

Noatak felt the blood drain from his face. He hadn't thought of that. Not every sexual encounter created a mate bond, but when it did happen, the bond was for life.

Mek put a consoling hand on his shoulder. "I'm sorry. I'll keep working on a fix."

Noatak shrugged the hand away, every muscle in his body tight. "I'd better go."

"Noatak," Mek called, but Noatak didn't slow down.

Numb from the shock, Noatak reached the cargo bay and climbed aboard the small craft, going through the motions for takeoff automatically. He settled into the pilot's seat next to Joy, unable to look at her—female, mated, a partner for Kashatok in every sense of the word. Noatak would never know what that felt like. *That'll teach you to hope.*

"You okay?" Joy asked, the camera in her eye dilating as she adjusted her filters to look at him. Filming, as usual.

"Yup." He flicked the controls to close the hatch and initiate the launch. "Have everything you need?"

She reached overhead and pulled the nav-grav harness over her head and shoulders. "I think so. There are a surprising number of people interested in the Resistance."

After being called a pirate for fifteen years, he doubted the general population would stop thinking of them as criminals just because they adopted a new name. "Or they just want to gawk at some real pirates. How many are we interviewing this time?"

"Eight or so. Some may bring friends."

He grunted in response, privately hoping there were a bunch of no-shows. After Mek's little talk, he wasn't thrilled about interviewing a bunch of women he could never touch.

Signaling the cargo bay doors to open, he maneuvered the craft out into space and began programming the burn frequency to jump to Whylon Station. The shuttle cleared the *Hardship's* perimeter, and he hovered a finger over the button to engage the burn drive. He glanced at Joy. No fucking way was he strapping in. Even a human could endure a short burn cycle without shielding. He'd have a killer headache and fatigue, but that was nothing new. "Engaging burn."

Before he could second-guess himself, he hit the button.

CHAPTER THREE

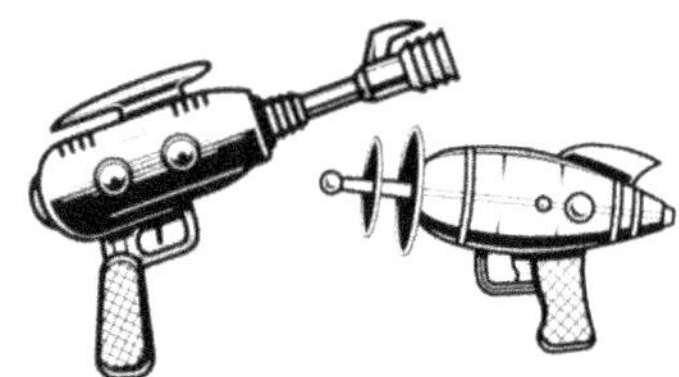

Fuming, Marlis waited at Whylon Station's public IGC booth, watching the finofan ahead of her extend and retract his ear fans as he spoke to the comm screen. He finished, and she barely let him escape the booth before pushing inside. The hard plastic seat was still warm from his backside, and the interior of the booth smelled like moldy lettuce, but she didn't care. She was going to murder her father.

Hours ago, she'd strutted into her first interview full of confidence. Attie'd set everything up, from the time and place of the meeting to information about the owner. Getting a job should've been a cakewalk. Instead, the portly owner had told her they were no longer looking for help. The receptionist at the second interview smiled condescendingly, patted her hand, and told her they didn't want any trouble with the law. By the time she walked into the offices of the third shipping company and the flushed young man at the desk told her she should call home, she'd pulled up her seldom-used charm and asked why not. Flushing even more, he'd shown her his polycom.

On her profile at a social media site she'd abandoned years ago, her face now appeared with the word MISSING and contact information for her father. She'd only set the account up because her therapist thought it would be good for her to interact with friends, but Marlis had no interest in pretending to like people's baby pictures and stupid quotes. Apparently, potential employers checked these sites and must've contacted Dad.

Scanning her credit chip, she punched in the code and waited for Dad to answer. The moment his pallid face appeared on-screen, she leaned forward. "How could you?"

He didn't bat an eyelash, as if he'd been expecting her call. "Come home now, Marlis. I'm making arrangements for you to have a job here."

"I could've had my pick of jobs here, except for your interference!" Marlis's blood was boiling, and the incessant thrum of Twerp's vibration against her wrist had all but numbed her hand. "What did you tell them?"

"You can barely remember to tie your shoes, Marlis. You're not ready to be out on your own. It's not your fault, considering what happened to your mother. Syndicorp's military division owes you for that. They owe us all. I'm going to make sure they take care of you."

She ground her teeth. "By take care of me, you mean let me push papers or scrub toilets for the other soldiers. No, thank you."

"Now, Marlis, everyone has to earn a living, and you can't be good at everything."

"I'm good at wielding a gun, Dad. Get me a job doing that."

"You've never been on your own. You have no idea what kinds of trouble you can get into."

"I'd be fine if you'd just let me."

"If you were going to school, maybe, or taking a retail position in a reputable establishment. But becoming a hired gun is ludicrous. I don't know why your sister would've suggested it."

"Because she knows it's the only thing I'm good at. The only thing I want to do." The little amber light at the corner of the comm screen began blinking that her time was nearly up, requesting more credits to continue.

Dad shook his head, frowning. "Come home and we'll discuss your options. I love you, Marlis. I only want you safe."

The burning in Marlis's gut was making her feel like she was about to spew acid all over the screen. She loved her dad, loved her family. But the one-way ticket to the station had cost her nearly her entire savings—which wasn't much, since she'd spent almost every dime she collected on weapon upgrades. If she went back now, she might never make it off the Syndicorp carrier again. The comm light shifted to red for the final ten-second warning.

"I'm staying here. Talk to you later, Dad." She ended the call and swung out of the booth, shouldering past the others waiting in line. She paused in the middle of the teeming corridor, drawing a blank on which direction to turn.

Ever-helpful, Twerp chirped from her wrist, "Do you wish to return to the hostel, Marlis?"

"Sure." Where else was she going to go? Her feet felt heavy as she considered how she was going to keep paying for a bunk without a job, let alone the rental for the weapons locker. The station frowned upon average citizens tromping around with MCS6's and pulse cartridges, although she'd kept her E-11 holstered beneath her waistband.

"Turn left," Twerp advised.

Marlis began trekking through the crowd, then changed her mind and shifted course toward a nearby cantina. Maybe a drink would settle her nerves.

Entering the bar, she passed a massive yanipa-nimayu bouncer kicked back on four of his six massive legs. One of his four eyes shifted to her holster, but he didn't stop her from passing. Inside, a sign flickered over the central bar—The Junk Heap. The soles of her shoes clung to the tacky floor, and the herbal stink of cirripi weed drifted from the back. Two human servers flitted among the scattered booths and high tables.

As Marlis looked for a seat, Twerp piped up over the music wailing from speakers in the ceiling, "I have taken the liberty of accessing the station's want ads and can locate no advertisements for guards or weapons specialists. Would you like me to look for alternate employment opportunities?"

On the barstool next to her, a thin man with grease-stained fingers looked at her from the corner of his eye, gaze flitting to her wrist before returning his attention to the bubbling drink in front of him. He was seedy, but not a threat, and Marlis settled onto her stool before lifting her wrist close to her mouth. "Not so loud, Twerp. Geez."

She'd forgotten her earbud on the carrier and didn't have the time or money to get a new one at the moment. Not that she ever remembered to wear it, anyway. She signaled the posungi bartender, who waggled his bright orange facial tentacles in her direction to indicate he'd be right there. While she waited, she spoke toward her wrist in a low voice. "Twerp, do any of the independent vessels post ads with the station? If I can't get a job with the shipping companies, maybe I can freelance."

"Checking."

The guy next to her looked at her again. "You'd be better off searching the boards." He lifted his chin toward the far wall. "Though a good-looking gal like you might make more money on her back than on a ship."

Marlis reconsidered her assessment of him, but when he shrugged and turned back to his drink, she decided her first guess had been right. Looking over her shoulder toward where he'd gestured, she spotted a bulletin board covered in haggard scraps of paper near the restrooms.

"How archaic," she muttered as she headed toward them. All manner of languages covered the pages, some typed, some scrawled. The few she could read in Corporate Common were selling items or services and one ad for a room rental. There were even two posters she could only assume were Cartel, offering bounties for information about a dark-haired woman and her brother. As she was attempting to decipher a splotchy note requesting someone willing to perform a sexual position she'd never heard of, an argument broke out near the restroom door.

"I said you mistook my words." A petite woman around Marlis's age was jerking ineffectually against the grip of a human male who looked like he'd taken one too many puffs of cirripi. "Just let me go."

"C'mon, baby, I just want to talk." He grinned, exposing a dead front tooth.

Marlis didn't like the way his fingers clamped around the woman's upper arm. She took a single step toward them, her right hand tensed to whip out her pistol if need be. "Everything okay?"

The brunette shook her head fiercely enough to bounce her curls, her wide eyes full of alarm. "No."

"Back off, Blondie," said the man with barely a look toward Marlis. "You ain't my type."

Marlis wasn't particularly good at hand-to-hand combat, preferring the sure results her E-11 provided, but she'd had some training. Lightning quick, she reached out and twisted the man's grip free of the woman's arm. The man fell to his knees. "Ow! What the fuck, woman?"

Pathetic. Not even worth getting angry over. She leaned in close enough to smell his reeking, weed-tainted breath. "She asked you to let her go. Now get out of here before I call that bouncer over there. Unless you think he'll be more polite?"

He pulled his arm against his chest the moment she let go, his hateful gaze still on her face. But she could tell he wasn't the type to put up a fight. Most likely he'd slink off to lick his wounds until he found another easy target.

The smaller woman watched the man scramble upright and retreat out the door, then extended a hand to Marlis. "Thank you. My name's Emmy."

"Marlis." Marlis accepted the handshake.

"Let me buy you a drink." Emmy adjusted her blouse hem around her plump hips. "It's the least I can do."

Marlis shrugged. "I won't say no."

At least she'd get a free drink. If she couldn't find a job, maybe she'd spend her time saving damsels in distress at bars. Marlis followed her to two empty stools at a high top table in the back. Nearby, a group of women held their heads close together while they murmured and glanced around nervously. A female posungi in the corner nursed a drink, her thin facial tendrils swaying in time to the music.

After the server took their order, Emmy smiled brightly at Marlis and leaned in to speak over the loud music. "Are you here for the interview, too?"

Marlis perked up. "I am looking for a job. Who's interviewing?"

"Oh," Emmy's face blanched. "You didn't get an invite? I just assumed..."

Her brief hope dashed, Marlis picked up the drink the server had just delivered and took a long, burning swallow. "That's okay. From your appearance, the job isn't likely for a Weapons Specialist, anyway."

"Wow!" An appreciative grin split the woman's face. "I've never met a Weapons Specialist!"

"What do you do?" Marlis asked, more out of politeness than anything else. She already couldn't remember this woman's name, and would probably forget all about this conversation by the time she left the cantina.

The woman's excited smile collapsed. "I trained as a therapist. But I'm looking for something else this go-round." She looked over her shoulder as if worried about being overheard. "I hear they're interviewing for all kinds of skills. I could ask them to include you."

Marlis leaned forward. Okay, so maybe she wouldn't forget this conversation that easily. "Maybe. Who would I be working for?"

Pulling out a polycom, the woman—*what was her name? Jenna?*—plopped it down on the table in front of Marlis and tapped the screen. "Here."

A video popped into motion of a charming, dark-haired woman speaking with the biggest, most copper-skinned man Marlis'd ever imagined. "Is that a cyborg?"

"No, they call themselves denaidans. Have you heard of them?"

The underlying thrum of conversation in the cantina changed tone, and Marlis glanced toward the door. A tall beast of a man blocked the light from the outside corridor. He scoped the area, then took the arm of a tall woman next to him and moved between the tables, directly toward Marlis's table. Marlis itched in that way that usually told her trouble was brewing, but this itch was centered low in her belly and had nothing to do with her trigger finger. "Holy hotness."

Jenna or Emma or whatever her name was looked up from the video and gasped. "That's them! I recognize the woman."

Now that she mentioned it, Marlis did recognize the woman as the one from the video, but she couldn't stop looking at the man. His black beard was plaited with small silver beads, and his long hair hung down his back in banded ropes. As he scanned the cantina, his eyes locked with hers, a steely, gunmetal blue that sent tingles straight to her core.

Against her wrist, Twerp vibrated gently to inform her of her increasing heart rate.

She picked up her drink and finished it in one gulp. That guy looked like he could hold his own in a gun fight, knife fight, or any other fight she could imagine. Against her will, Marlis could imagine other things she'd like him to hold, as well.

Without taking her eyes off him, she said, "I think I'd like to apply for a job."

CHAPTER FOUR

The interior of The Junk Heap was the same as Noatak remembered—cirripi-laced air and the thrum of scattered conversations. The headache from taking the burn without shielding made his head throb in time to the wailing music, and a familiar little voice in his head said, *nothing a hit wouldn't cure.* It took all of Noatak's willpower to look away from the jittery stim vendor skulking near the entrance. He hadn't felt this much need in a very long time. *Does it matter if you lapse?*

Keeping his hand lightly on Joy's arm, he focused on their task. He might not have a future, but his crew was relying on him for theirs. Not that he believed this bar was the place to find a decent crew, let alone suitable mates.

Joy leaned close and murmured to him, "We should order drinks to fit in. You okay with that?"

His gaze flicked to the stim vendor once more. The wiry human met his gaze with the bloodshot eyes of a heavy user. Noatak swallowed and turned toward the back of the bar. Alcohol was her captain's vice, not his, but a drink sounded pretty good right now. "Sure. Whatever."

Clusters of women had gathered at the tables in the back, and

Noatak's gaze came to rest on a stunning blonde. The holster on her hip made him raise an eyebrow. He'd met plenty of female soldiers during his service with the troopers, but she was by far the sexiest thing he'd ever laid eyes on. Rounded curves some might call top-heavy, yet strong in posture. Perfect alabaster skin marked only by a crooked scar on her chin.

You're not here to ogle the women, he reminded himself, turning to scan the rest of the room. Joy had hand-selected the applicants from the comments on her documentary, but that didn't mean there weren't any troopers or Syndicorp spies in the bar. Not to mention the crew of the *Hardship* had a Cartel bounty on their heads since they'd rescued Lisa from the Cartel's clutches.

Assessing the other cantina patrons, he noted a round table that hosted three scantily clad humans he guessed were sex workers, two female and one male. In the far corner slouched a mousy-type posungi female nursing a drink, her pale orange facial tendrils writhing. At the nearest table, a pair of human women sat side-by-side, spines ramrod straight, ankles crossed, and hands clasped in their laps as if they awaited an interview at a bank.

He selected a chair facing the cantina entrance, his back to the mousy woman in the corner. While Joy ordered drinks, he allowed his gaze to drift back toward the woman with the pistol, taking brief note of the small brunette sitting across from her. Both women met his eyes without hesitation. The brunette smiled lightly, nodding once in greeting. The blonde didn't smile, just took his measure. She wasn't threatening, just watchful. Cautious. Poised.

Anaq, she could probably take you in a fight. How warped was it that his groin stirred at the idea?

He turned to Joy. "Start with the blonde over there."

Joy shrugged one shoulder. "Fine by me."

Meeting the woman's tawny-eyed gaze once more, he crooked a finger to beckon her over. Her sculpted brows rose a fraction, then she whispered something to her friend and rose. Shoulders square, she strode toward him. From the sex-worker table, feminine voices complained they'd arrived first. He ignored them, watching the lithe way the woman moved. Her pale blonde hair was cut to shoulder length and gleaming.

Joy smiled brightly, gesturing toward the seat across from her. "We're glad you decided to come." She looked down at the polycom she'd pulled from her pocket. "I'm Joy, First Mate of the *PV Kinship,* and this is Noatak, First Mate of the *PV Hardship.* What's your name?"

The blonde sat. "Marlis Swan."

Frowning, Joy ran a finger over the screen. "I don't have your name on my list."

"I know." Marlis gestured toward the small brunette she'd been sitting near. "She told me about the interview. I need a job."

Instinct to use his ionic senses to measure her heart rate and breathing welled up inside Noatak. He wasn't used to making choices without it, especially about someone this intriguing.

Joy turned to him in uncertainty, but he kept his eyes forward. If he couldn't use his powers, he couldn't afford to miss a single cue, especially since he wanted to hire this woman on the spot. He leaned in slightly, nodding toward her gun. "What kind of work you looking for?"

Marlis pulled the E-11 from her hip and set it on the table, muzzle pointed away from them. "I'm trained in small arms and some hand-to-hand. Best shot in my class."

Pulling out the gun had been a bold move in the crowded bar. He liked it. She was straightforward. Honest. He slid a hand toward it. "May I?"

"Please."

He lifted the weapon. "Blackstar E-11 zero-recoil."

"Full-bore-plus with a custom trigger," Marlis added with obvious pride. "I have other models, but this one's my favorite."

"Nice." Noatak found himself nodding and handed the weapon back. "Where'd you train?"

Marlis took a deep breath and released it as if steadying for a sniper shot. "I come from a long line of troopers." She placed the gun back in its holster and lifted her chin slightly. "And before you ask why I'm not in the service, I'll tell you. I blew up at my recruiter. Kinda ruined my chances."

The hope that had been building inside Noatak took a nose dive. Captain Qaiyaan had specifically said to weed out anyone directly in service to Syndicorp or the troopers, and here he was talking to a legacy brat. *You have to turn her away.* Not a good sign for the very first interview.

Joy tilted her head, her camera eye contracting and expanding. "Why'd you blow up at your recruiter?"

"He wanted to turn drill practice into a history lesson." Marlis wrinkled her nose. "Let's just say I'm no good at history."

Beneath the table, Noatak nudged Joy's leg. This wasn't a documentary, it was an interview, and if they expected to talk to all these women, they didn't have time to play around. Hard as it was to pass Marlis over, Noatak forced his attention to the next applicant. "Sorry, Miss Swan. I don't think we need any more hired guns right now."

The tension in the air tasted like ozone, zinging against Noatak's senses even without him engaging his ionic power.

Marlis balled her fists in her lap, then nodded once and returned to her seat near the petite brunette. Noatak realized he was watching her firm backside when Joy poked him and hissed in his ear. "Hired guns are exactly what we need."

"Too dangerous. Her family's corp."

"So? Mine is, too."

She had a valid point; her mother was one of Syndicorp's top CEOs —but that didn't erase his captain's orders. "She wasn't even on your list. We didn't and don't have time to vet her. Running interviews for the Resistance right under Syndicorp's nose is dangerous enough. Let's move on."

Joy shook her head, letting out a frustrated sigh. "I'm keeping her name for future reference."

"Do what you like." Noatak signaled to a woman with brilliant blue hair sitting at the sex-worker table. The three rose together, but Noatak shook his head. "One at a time."

The second woman giggled, but she and the male sat down, allowing their blue-haired companion to approach. She jiggled in all the right places as she walked, taking a seat across from Noatak and leaning forward so her ample breasts rested on the tabletop. "Whatever you want, baby. I know how to play nice."

Noatak crossed his arms and leaned back in his seat to escape the cloying scent of her perfume. "Name?"

After verifying the woman was on her list, Joy asked several questions, then raised an eyebrow at Noatak. To be honest, he'd only been half-listening to the interview. Marlis had put him on edge in more ways than one, and he was seriously thinking about doing business with that stim vendor near the door. He met the applicant's half-lidded gaze. "You have any skills except for the obvious?"

Hardness rose in her eyes, her lips pressing into a grim line. She crossed her arms over her cleavage. "I gotta get off this station. Just tell me what to do and I'll do it."

Damn, he wished he could just ping her and be done with this. "You willing to leave your friends over there behind?"

Her nostrils flared, and she nodded. "Anything."

"Thank you. We'll be in touch." He dismissed her.

As soon as she was out of earshot, Joy leaned over and glared at him. "Are you discriminating against sex workers, too?"

He shook his head. "It's not her line of work I object to. She and her friends might act like they play nice together, but I suspect they'd stab each other in the back if the opportunity arose. Don't need that kind of loyalty."

Joy sighed and called the next woman over.

They continued the interviews while Noatak tried to keep his eyes off of Marlis. Unfortunately, the only other place he wanted to look was the corner where the stim vendor sat, and the growing desire within him was consuming all rational thought. He could forget everything for a little while so easily. *What are you waiting for?*

They began interviewing one of the amazingly boring bank women. Unable to take another obviously rehearsed answer, he rose. "Please excuse me a moment."

With purposeful strides, he moved toward the door, shouldering past the stim vendor and out of the confines of the cantina. If he didn't get away from temptation, he would suffocate. He closed his eyes and let his head fall back, breathing in the scent of roasted kemeg from a cart across the way.

Pull it together, Noatak. But the self-talk did little good. He was pissed. He wanted—needed—a distraction, and he needed it now.

As if in answer to his prayer, a gunshot cracked from inside the cantina, followed by screams and the distinctive zing from an E-11 pistol. He spun, realizing he'd left Joy alone. *"Uminaq!"*

The yanipa-nimayu bouncer was blocking the door, his six stocky legs planted firmly in Noatak's way. Calling up an ionic pulse, Noatak thrust him aside and stepped through the doorway, pulse pistol drawn. Between the milling bar patrons, Joy moved toward him, her face pallid. The brunette who'd been next to Marlis supported her under one arm while Marlis flanked her other side, pistol leveled toward the rear of the bar. Blood splotched Joy's light orange mechanic's shirt and coated her fingers.

"What the fuck's going on?" he asked as the trio reached him at the door. At the back of the cantina where they'd been sitting, people were shouting for medics.

"Just a scratch," Joy said through gritted teeth, her face pale and beaded with sweat.

The petite brunette helping her said, "I have some medical training. I'll get her to safety and check it out."

He nodded. "Thanks."

Marlis paused beside him, still alert for trouble at the back of the bar. "That posungi sitting behind her pulled an old-fashioned Bud-9 rimfire."

"Aiming for Joy? Or was she caught in the crossfire?"

"No idea, but I took the posungi down with a headshot." She shook her head. "I didn't think ballistic weapons were legal on a space station."

He raised an eyebrow. "They're not. The Cartel uses them, though, because they're concealable but not powerful enough to puncture hull plating."

A crowd had gathered outside the cantina doors, peering cautiously inside. Station enforcers were shouting at people to get out of the way as they tried to push through.

He glanced around. "If the attack came from the Cartel, we need to get off the station immediately. They all but own enforcement on this station."

Marlis kept pace with him all the way back to the shuttle, where she finally holstered her weapon.

"Thanks for the help," he said.

She tilted her head. "Still not in the market for a hired gun?"

"*Uminaq*," he grumbled. He owed her one, and he couldn't just leave her here to face the Cartel alone. Thrusting his pistol back into his belt, he held out a hand. "Welcome aboard the *Hardship*."

CHAPTER FIVE

Marlis wanted to run through the corridors to retrieve her gear, but she forced herself to keep to a brisk pace, trying not to draw attention to herself. After a quick idiot-check of her bunk at the hostel where she'd been staying, she hurried back to Noatak's shuttle with the reassuring weight of her rifle case against her back. She could hardly wait to call her sister to tell her the news. Who knew getting into a gunfight in a bar would be her ticket to the future? Her first ever live-fire combat had left behind an exhilaration that bordered on a drug, and Twerp hadn't stopped buzzing, but she knew her racing pulse was elation, not stress. *Let Dad try to stop me now.*

She stowed her gear and settled into a nav-grav seat next to Emmy, who'd also been offered a place on the crew. Emmy looked shell-shocked and pale, her blouse still stained with Joy's blood.

"You make a pretty good medic," Marlis said, trying to cheer her new friend up. Through the open cockpit door ahead, she could see the edge of Noatak's shoulder and muscular arm as he prepped to disengage from the station.

"Luckily, her wound doesn't appear to be life-threatening," Emmy replied, strapping in. "I didn't even see that posungi coming. I'm glad you were there."

Marlis grinned at the praise and shrugged. "Seems I excel at saving damsels in distress."

Emmy laughed and pointed toward Marlis's wrist. "You're buzzing."

Marlis sighed and looked at her wrist. "Calm down, Twerp. I'm fine."

"I feel obligated to tell you there is a fourteen point two percent risk of this endeavor leading to human trafficking," Twerp said. "I suggest removing yourself from this vessel at once."

"You have an AI!" Emmy twisted in her seat to look closer.

Trying to sound nonchalant, Marlis said. "It's just to remind me of appointments and stuff."

Twerp emitted an offended chirp. "I am a Wenzix model 15B, designed to provide space-time orientation through integrated biometric feedback."

Marlis clapped a hand over her wristband, muffling the AI's voice. She glanced toward the cockpit, relieved Noatak or Joy didn't appear to have heard. Would they change their minds if they knew about her condition? She couldn't afford to lose this job because of an AI with a big mouth.

"I worked with a client who had a 15B during my internship." Emmy raised her eyebrows. "Anger management issues."

Marlis let out a controlled breath. "Please don't mention it to anyone."

Emmy seemed to consider a moment, then nodded. "Of course. That's a cute name for an AI, by the way."

"Thank you," Twerp said brightly.

Grimacing, Marlis resisted the urge to bash her wrist against the nearest hard surface.

Emmy shifted her gaze to the cockpit, her amused expression shifting to worry. "I never considered we might be involving ourselves with slavers. They *were* only interviewing women."

Marlis looked at Noatak's broad shoulders and the way his muscles rippled beneath his thin shirt as he shifted in his seat to adjust controls. The alien practically oozed sexual tension, yet she didn't get the sense he was skeevy. Not that her hormones would give one flicker of objection if he wanted to throw her down in a wrestling match, preferably a naked one. She tended to have a good sixth sense when it came to danger. "I don't think Noatak's the type to run a sex ring." She patted her pistol against her hip. "And if he is, he'll regret it."

Outside the view screen, the pointed tip of one of the station's many communication arrays slipped past as they entered open space. Noatak's deep voice came over the comm. "Engaging burn."

The slightly nauseating thrill of the shuttle's drive rolled through her stomach. In what felt like a half a heartbeat, the cycle ended and the universe seemed to level out. *Huh, short burn.* They must not be too far from Noatak's ship. What'd he say its name was? Her sister was bound to ask.

Twerp reported. "Marlis, you'll be pleased to know your vitals have returned to acceptable levels."

"Twerp, I don't need a verbal report unless I'm in danger, okay?" Next time they stopped at a space station, she was buying a replacement earbud. She might not be able to shut the thing up, but she could restrict who heard its outbursts.

The cockpit's view screen was filled with velvety, star-studded blackness, and it took a moment for Marlis to spot the small, half-moon-shaped body of a D-class space craft blocking the pinpricks of light, its battle-scarred hull painted a dull black. A slice of light appeared in the darkness as the cargo bay doors opened. Noatak guided the shuttle slowly inside, settling to the deck with a slight thump. Behind Marlis's nav-grav seat, the shuttle's hatch hissed open with a rush of unfamiliar scents.

Noatak swiveled in his seat to look at his passengers. "Welcome aboard the *Hardship*."

Repeating the name to herself in the hope of remembering it for later, she rose and retrieved her rucksack and weapons. One strap over each shoulder, she followed Emmy down the ramp to the deck. This was about to be her new home. Her new purpose. How many people were on the crew? She was going to have to remember names. Protocols. Who knew what else? She focused on her breathing, keeping her pulse under control. The last thing she needed was Twerp piping up right now.

Compared to the vastness of the carrier she'd grown up on, the ship's tiny cargo bay felt almost cozy. The shuttle took up most of the space, butting up against a set of stairs connected to a grated catwalk overhead. A ginger-haired man with copper skin like Noatak's pounded down the catwalk at a run, slammed both hands on the rail, and in one swift move launched up and over the edge. Marlis didn't even have time to register shock before he landed gracefully on the deck in front of her.

"Hi! I'm Tovik!" He thrust an oil-stained hand toward Emmy, teeth gleaming in a self-satisfied grin.

Marlis blinked as the scent of flowery perfume wafted over her and stared at his bare feet. With that entrance, she wasn't likely to forget his name any time soon. He was younger than Noatak, but just as tall in a gangly fashion that promised more muscles to come.

Emmy smiled warmly and set her suitcase down to shake his hand. "Emmy Quick."

He turned to Marlis, and she accepted his handshake. "Marlis Swan."

"Wow. This is exciting." He continued pumping her hand and nodding, looking from Emmy to her as if he'd never before seen a human. Then he did a double-take at something behind her and dropped her hand. "What happened?"

Marlis turned to find Noatak descending the ramp, one arm around Joy's waist. Guilt flickered in Marlis's throat. A good crew member would've remembered to help.

Tovik surged forward and took up Joy's opposite side, sliding an arm around her. "*Anaq!* Joy! Are you all right?"

Joy smiled wanly. "I'll be fine as soon as Mek gives me some painkillers."

Tovik's brows drew together as he shifted his gaze to Noatak. "Kashatok's gonna kill you."

Noatak scowled right back at him. "She said she's fine, Tovik." His nose wrinkled. "Are you wearing perfume?"

The younger man's copper face flushed blue green, his gaze flitting to where Emmy and Marlis stood. "I heard ladies like flowers."

"Don't make me laugh, it hurts," Joy wheezed, her arms clutching her injured torso. "I think you've been getting some bad advice, my friend."

A third copper-skinned man arrived from the stairs, his clean-shaven face austere in comparison to Noatak and Tovik's well-groomed beards. He strode forward with a med scanner, completely intent on Joy until he saw Emmy's blouse. "You hurt, too?"

Emmy shook her head, seemingly at a loss for words as she craned her neck to look up at his face.

"Don't be rude, Mek." Tovik frowned. He turned to look at Emmy and Marlis. "This is Mek, our ship's doctor. He's not usually such a *terpak*."

Noatak released Joy into Mek's care. "You got this?"

Mek nodded, slipping an arm around the injured woman. He smiled tightly as he passed Marlis and Emmy on his way toward the stairs. "Sorry to be so abrupt. I look forward to talking to you later."

"Tovik." Noatak picked up the suitcase Emmy had set down and thrust it toward the younger man. "Drop their bags in the bunk room, then join us in the galley."

"Aye-aye." Tovik took Emmy's suitcase and held out a hand for Marlis's rucksack.

Marlis clutched her shoulder strap tighter. She didn't like to let other people handle her weapons. "I can carry my own bags."

"Suit yourself." Without preamble, Tovik bunched his legs and leaped into the air—if it could be called leaping. The move was more like a short flight, leaving the scent of perfume in his wake. He landed lightly on the catwalk above and turned to glance over his shoulder with a self-satisfied grin. "See you soon."

"Show off," Noatak muttered before leading them toward the stairs.

Marlis followed him up the steps, her boots ringing on the metal grates. "Are all of you so… nimble?"

"No." Noatak spoke without turning around, voice cold. "Don't let him fool you into thinking he has superpowers. Our species—most of our species—have the ability to manipulate ionically-charged molecules in immediate proximity to us."

Marlis had never been good at school, and his vocabulary took some pondering for her to unravel. While she did, Emmy pulled ahead of her to walk next to Noatak as they reached the catwalk. "Like telekinesis? That's fascinating!"

Telekinesis. That word she knew. How was she going to keep up with a crew that could move shit with their brains? Maybe Noatak'd been serious when he'd said they didn't need more hired guns.

They reached the hatch and stepped through into a narrow corridor. Noatak led them past several doors into a galley where a large oval table surrounded by chairs took up most of the space. He gestured to the seats. "Now that you're on board, we need to lay down some ground rules."

Marlis set her bags next to the nearest chair and sat, glancing around at the closed cabinets lining the walls. She wasn't familiar with the layout of D-class ships, but if this tiny galley served the entire crew, no wonder Noatak was extra picky about who he hired. Crew members had to get along. A flare of pride glowed in her chest; she'd made the cut.

Emmy took the seat to her left, hands clasped nervously in her lap as she watched Noatak move to the other end of the table. Marlis pulled out her polycom to take notes. Twerp recorded everything for her to review later if she wanted, but her therapist encouraged her to write things down for herself. She had to stay focused if she expected to prove to her new crew she belonged here.

"You'll both serve here on the *Hardship* until Captain Qaiyaan gets back." Noatak powered up a wall screen between the cabinets, bringing up the ship's data screen. "He and Kashatok may rearrange your assignments later, though."

While Marlis was jotting the names, the young denaidan who'd taken Emmy's bag burst in, chest heaving and eyes glittering. He yanked out the seat next to Marlis, looking over her shoulder at her polycom. She twisted her head to glare up at him. She hated it when people read over her shoulder. Her notes were none of his business.

Pausing with his backside half-lowered onto the chair, his smile faltered. Still, the kid was incorrigible, and winked before pushing the chair back in and moved down several seats.

Marlis swallowed, feeling a little guilty. She'd already forgotten the young man's name, and when she glanced back at her notes, she'd also forgotten who Kashatok was. *Dammit.* She'd written it down, so it was important. She needed repetition. Lots and lots of repetition. "Who's Kashatok again?"

"Captain of the *Kinship*." Noatak pointed to a K-class freighter on the screen. "Joy's his First Mate."

"And his mate-mate!" The young man chimed in, green eyes dancing.

"Enough, Tovik." Noatak glowered at him.

Tovik, Marlis repeated to herself, staring hard at him to ingrain his face in her mind.

The young man beamed under her scrutiny and Marlis felt herself flushing. *Fuck.* She was going to give this guy the wrong idea if she wasn't careful. She lowered her gaze to her polycom and put his name there with the words *don't shoot the puppy*. When she shifted her attention back to Noatak, he'd started a video rolling.

"You two have the honor of being among the first recruits for the Resistance. Our fleet is comprised…"

She wrote *Resistance* onto the polycom. Had they mentioned a resistance during the interview? She could ask Twerp about it later. For now, she had to assume that since she was here, she must've been okay with it. *Pay attention, Marlis.*

"I know the odds are against us, and the corporation is powerful. But more and more of their lies—"

Marlis was getting the feeling that this crew wasn't conducting the kind of legitimate business her sister'd had in mind. What had she gotten herself into? Throat tight, she raised a hand. "Are you talking about Syndicorp?"

Wariness flashed through Noatak's eyes. "Yes."

Emmy spoke up. "I was going to show her the video back in the cantina, but then the fight broke out. Maybe she could watch it now?"

Noatak's jaw worked as if he wanted to say no, but Tovik jumped up. "She hasn't seen it?" He tapped the screen on the wall. "Joy did a great job putting all the facts together."

A RealTime News logo appeared, followed by Joy's face.

Marlis forced herself to focus on the screen. She refused to believe her dad had been right about her getting into trouble. *Get all the facts, then decide.* That's what her therapist always urged her to do before she let her emotions get the best of her. Breathing in through her nose and out through her mouth, she settled back to watch.

Joy described a planet called Denaida-daru, where Syndicorp had been testing a genetically altered virus. Marlis'd never paid much attention to technology that didn't relate to weapons, and a lot of what Joy said didn't mean anything to her. She gathered that somehow the virus had mutated and created a cancer that killed off all the women and most of the men on the planet.

The emerald-green planet on the screen developed white spots, each spot widening and growing until the entire planet glowed like a small sun. "Rather than continue to work on a cure or make amends to the surviving population, Syndicorp sterilized the planet."

Marlis gasped out loud. She'd never heard of a populated planet being sterilized.

"You may be asking why you've never heard of Denaida-daru, also called K-4H10," Joy continued. "Because there would be backlash against the heinous act, Syndicorp started a war to divert attention. Remember Pulati?" The video cut to an all-too-familiar scene on what had been a lovely, tree-lined plaza. A plaza littered with bodies and blood and debris.

The floor beneath Marlis's chair seemed to wobble as she stared at the footage. Cut scenes from the war itself filled the room, making the walls close in around her. She heard her mother's scream cut off.

"… Not only did the people of Denaida-daru suffer genocide at corporate hands, but tens of thousands of Pulati colonists died fighting terrorists. Terrorists who were funded by Syndicorp."

While the voice on the screen kept talking, Marlis was no longer in the galley of a D-class ship. She was a ten-year-old girl lying beneath her mother's contorted body. Unable to breathe. Not daring to move. Gunfire sliced the air and trooper boots thundered against the earth.

Adrenaline surged through her veins. She couldn't breathe past the stench of blood or hear over the screams echoing in her ears. Flies tickled over her skin. Her wrist ached, and she had no idea why.

"Marlis, lower your head to your knees," a feminine voice floated through the chaos.

Marlis forced herself to focus, expecting to be staring into the muzzle of a trooper's rifle. Sure a hole would blossom in her head at any moment. *I need a gun.* She reached for her hip.

A strong hand encircled hers, gripping her fingers tightly. Keeping her from moving. Panic once again made her vision swim.

A woman's round face took shape in front of her, brown eyes concerned. "Marlis, it's just me. Emmy. It's all right."

I should know this person.

A disembodied voice chanted, "There is no danger."

The only important word in that phrase was 'danger.' Lurking danger. Marlis twisted against the grip still clamped on her hand and found herself looking into gunmetal blue eyes. Dark brows on copper skin. A beard decorated with metal beads.

Noatak's lips moved. "Cool your jets, soldier. You're safe here."

For some reason, those words cut through her fog. His hand on hers was like a lifeline. She took a deep breath. "Safe."

Cautiously and still maintaining direct eye contact, he said, "Everyone out."

The round-faced woman and another copper-skinned man with ginger hair backed out of the room. Noatak relaxed his grip on her hand, but to her relief, he didn't let go. He settled into the seat facing her. "Now tell me what this is all about."

How many therapists had asked her that? She felt like a robot as she answered, "I was in that battle."

His eyes narrowed. "You were a child when Pulati broke out."

"Yes, sir." For some reason, calling him sir made her feel calm. Like she was a soldier instead of a victim. "I was ten."

He raised a brow and slowly withdrew his hand. "You're from the colony? I thought you said you were legacy. Your family is with the troopers."

She let out a shaky breath. Her mind had started to clear a bit. "My mother and I went to Pulati on leave. The same day as the first terrorist outbreak."

Staring numbly at the screen, Marlis recalled her earliest memories; the ones that still, no matter how hard she squelched them, haunted her nightmares. *Troopers with guns. Trooper boots marching through the plaza full of bodies. A trooper looking down the barrel of her gun straight into Marlis's eyes.* No one had ever believed her before. Now she knew her memories were true.

The terrorist attack had been orchestrated by Syndicorp.

She turned to Noatak, his name like a pinprick of sanity in her chaotic mind. "Troopers killed my mother."

CHAPTER SIX

Noatak swallowed against the unfamiliar feelings welling inside him as Marlis described her hours on Pulati. How she'd faced down a young trooper who apparently hadn't had the stomach to finish the job and left Marlis half-dead beneath her mother's corpse. How she'd been in and out of consciousness for an entire day and into the night before rescuers arrived. How the media had put her on display as a victim without ever letting her speak.

"My first therapist said I misremembered the attack." Marlis's eyes were glassy, the scar on her chin a pale slash against her already pale skin. "Said my dad would lose his job if I told anyone and he'd be labeled a traitor. She blamed it on the damage to my brain, so I believed her. I changed my story. Troopers would never hurt innocents, right?"

She met his eyes, and he felt as if he'd just been sucked into a whirlpool. On instinct, he opened his ionic power, letting the feel of her heartbeat reach him, the subtle rhythm of her breathing. Sweet, feminine warmth and the subtle scent of musk from her skin caused a sense of protectiveness he'd never experienced before.

Uminaq, this wasn't the time or the place for softness. He was still trying to make up his mind about keeping her on board. His gut told him she was genuine, but his ever-doubtful logic insisted this had to be a complicated ruse. Why else would a legacy trooper end up in that cantina at that exact time?

As he worked to get himself under control, Marlis rose, hands clenched into fists at her sides. The wrist band he'd noticed earlier was emitting a low-frequency vibration. "They made me lie to myself." Her voice held outrage. Fury. Disgust. "I thought by joining the troopers I'd be protecting people."

"Most people think that." He watched her pace the length of the table. His admiration for her strength grew with every word she spoke. "I know I did."

She turned and stared at him. "You were a trooper?"

He nodded, leaning back in his chair. He wasn't proud of his trooper days, but he found himself wanting to tell her everything. "Joined up the moment I was old enough. Good pay, worthy cause, exciting adventures. All the stuff the recruiter was selling."

"Where'd you serve?"

"SNV Riley Blue, Galactic Ops."

Her eyes grew round, and she returned unsteadily to her chair, knees brushing his as she faced him. "What I wouldn't have given to join Galactic Ops."

His thigh muscles tightened with awareness of her closeness, like a proximity alarm racing through his bloodstream. He had to focus. "Not all it's cracked up to be, believe me."

The admiration in her eyes turned to distrust.

Once more, he found himself volunteering more information than he usually felt comfortable giving. "Almost all the denaidans still alive today were in the service. Joining up was one of the few ways to get off-world. The corp didn't know much about our physiology and while they studied my ionic abilities, they had me on almost constant recovery stims. After I went AWOL, I nearly killed myself getting off the stuff."

"You went AWOL?" Her tawny eyes widened.

He let out a sardonic laugh. Of course she'd care more about him going AWOL than she would about stim addiction. "Had to get away before Syndicorp could silence us." His nostrils flared as he recalled how many of his trooper *iluq* had come to mysterious ends immediately following his planet's Termination.

"Silence you for what?"

"They destroyed my home world, remember?" He frowned. Apparently, she'd been so engrossed in her own horrible memories she'd forgotten.

"Oh, yeah." The rosy flush on her cheeks was unaccountably appealing. She blinked several times, then put one hand over her forehead, gaze darting around the galley. "I need to call my sister."

That surprised him. Why this sudden urge for family? He crossed his arms. "Absolutely not."

Scowling, Marlis dropped her hand and leaned forward to look into his eyes, her heaving breath brushing his bare forearms. "She's a trooper. So are my dad and my brother. If I join your rebellion, what do you think might happen to them? I need to warn them."

He ran his tongue over his teeth. She had a point. Did this mean she was no longer a risk? Venturing another ionic pulse to test her sincerity, he asked, "You want to join us?"

She nodded, her jaw set. "Definitely."

He could tell by the steady beat of her heart that she meant it. But he needed her to fully understand what she was getting into. "You should also know that we're wanted for piracy."

Her delicate brows drew together. "As in, raping and pillaging?"

"Not exactly, although there were a few denaidans who went that far. The bulk of us just wanted revenge against the corp. Technically, I'd call us privateers."

She narrowed an eye. "Privateers, pirates, what's the difference?"

A feminine voice erupted from her wrist band. "Pirates attack anyone. Privateers only attack enemy ships."

She clapped her hand over her wrist. "Shut up, Twerp."

He'd been aware of the buzzing at her wrist off and on since meeting her, but this was the first time he gave it any serious regard. Now suspicion blossomed inside him again. "Is that a Syndicorp AI?"

"You may call me Twerp," the muffled voice said. "I am a Wen—"

"Shut up, Twerp!" Marlis lifted her hand and banged the wristband against the table.

The AI emitted an indignant chirp but did not resume speaking.

How could he have let himself be so careless? She'd brought a Syndicorp AI on board the ship. "Who does it report to?"

She blinked, as if unsure what he was asking. "Just me."

Twerp spoke up again, its chirpy voice a cheery contrast to Marlis's. "I have successfully connected to this ship's communication array. Would you like me to send a message to your sister?"

"Dammit! Not now, Twerp." The flush he'd appreciated earlier returned to Marlis's face. She unstrapped the thing from her wrist and offered it to Noatak. "Suppose I may as well tell you now. I have trouble remembering things and I get... frustrated... easily. Twerp keeps me in line."

"I don't give an *anaq* about all that." Noatak grabbed the band. "Tell it to disconnect immediately."

She stiffened, and he wondered for a moment if she was going to protest. Then she said, "Twerp, suspend all wireless connections, please."

The AI said, "If I am not connected to the ship, I will be unable to provide spatial data."

Marlis leaned forward to speak directly toward the device. "That's an order, Twerp."

"Disconnecting now. Please be careful when moving about to make note of your location."

Noatak gripped the wristband tighter. He wanted to smash the thing to smithereens, just to be safe. But Marlis'd complied with his request to disconnect. And she'd said something about a brain injury. "Can you get along without it?"

"I've had it since I was thirteen." Her pretty throat flexed around a swallow, and her lips were a pale line.

He rubbed his forehead. *Stop thinking of her as a woman and treat her like a soldier.* Even good soldiers sometimes needed assistance. She'd trusted in the corp, just like the rest of them, and her betrayal was real. That much he knew. But he didn't know about her AI. "I need to have it checked out before I can give it back to you."

She nodded and licked her lips. "What about contacting my sister?"

Could he blame her for wanting to be sure her family was safe? He'd do exactly the same thing. "I don't want to censor you, but we need to be careful about information leaks. What would you tell her?"

A furrow appeared between Marlis's eyebrows. "Fuck, she wouldn't believe me, anyway. I just don't want her to be caught unaware or punished because of my choices."

He reached out and put a hand on her shoulder. "Didn't you say your father and brother were also with the service?"

She looked stricken. "You think I might be a liability to this cause. That they'd be used as leverage against me."

He squeezed her shoulder lightly, unable to stop himself from imagining what her skin might feel like beneath his palm. *Ellam Cua, this woman is as addictive as stims*. He forced himself to release his grip. "We all have things that make us a liability." *Like my failing ionic heart.* "We just need to come up with something to tell them that won't connect you to the Resistance."

She drummed the fingertips of one hand on the table. "They're probably already wondering what happened to me."

"We'll work on a story together." He held up the AI's wrist band. "I'll get this back to you as soon as I can. Meanwhile, consider yourself on probation."

"Thank you for giving me a chance to prove myself." She rose and held out her hand. "You don't know how much that means to me."

He took her handshake, marveling at the fine bone structure engulfed by his grip. The perfect woman dropped in his lap when he was least able to make her his. He could picture *Ellam Cua,* their trickster god, laughing at him right now. He released her sharply, trying to reign in his stupid feelings, and grabbed her duffel bag. "I'll show you to your bunk."

She picked up her weapons case and followed him down the corridor to the women's bunk room where Emmy was waiting.

He left her there and headed for engineering to find Tovik. The young denaidan wasn't there, so he went to the med bay; if the kid wasn't in engineering, he'd be with Joy. Too bad that scoundrel, Kashatok, had claimed her heart, or the kid might've had his first taste of love.

As Noatak rounded the corner toward the med bay, he heard them discussing flux modulators. The two sat cross-legged on the single bed facing each other, Joy's legs covered by a sheet and her upper half in a medical gown. The screen behind her displayed her vitals in various colors.

Noatak frowned. "Aren't you supposed to be resting?"

"I can't, not when Kashatok's not here." She smiled sadly. Joy wasn't what he'd call pretty, but when she smiled, he could see why Kashatok had been attracted to her.

"Maybe you and Tovik can tackle this together." He held out the wrist band.

"What is it?" Tovik reached for it.

The AI's voice rose from the band. "Please return me to Marlis immediately."

Tovik raised his brows. "An AI?"

"My name is Twerp. I request your assistance returning me to my rightful owner."

Joy shifted her attention to Noatak, brows furrowed. "I heard she had a breakdown. Is she okay?"

Twerp chimed in, "I must have physical contact with my owner to provide biometric feedback and guidance."

Joy glanced from the AI to Noatak. "Um, thank you, Twerp. But I was asking Noatak."

Noatak shook his head. He'd never met a sentient machine, and he wasn't sure he liked it. "Marlis is fine. Turns out she has her own reasons for wanting to get back at Syndicorp. You want to know more, you can ask her." He pointed at the AI in Tovik's hand. "Can you make sure that thing's not bugged before I give it back to her?"

"I'll get on it right now." Tovik pocketed the device and stood up. "See you later, Joy."

She smiled at him. "Bye, Tovik. Let me know if you need any help."

The kid padded out of the room, his bare feet silent on the deck. Noatak remained, feeling uncomfortable as he looked at the monitor behind Joy's bed. He should say something, but apologizing wasn't his usual style.

"Don't worry, I'm fine." Joy stretched her legs beneath the sheets and leaned back against the pillow, closing her eyes. "It's not your fault, you know."

Given an opening, Noatak sat on the stool nearby. "I shouldn't have left you alone."

"I should've paid more attention." She shook her head. "I thought the Cartel would only be targeting Lisa. In hindsight, Whylon Station probably wasn't the best choice for a meeting."

Just then, Mek came around the corner into the med bay. "I just passed Tovik in the hall. He said Marlis has an AI. Is it a medical unit?"

"You'll have to ask her. She mentioned having a previous brain injury."

"Interesting. I'd like to check her out." Mek looked toward the door as if intending to call her in this very moment.

Noatak's throat felt suddenly dry as he imagined the doctor examining Marlis. Would he ask her to undress? He'd never before considered that Mek had an unfair advantage. *Stop being possessive about something you can't have.* He forced himself to shrug and kept his gaze on Joy. "You're the doc."

"Should we keep her on the crew?" Joy asked.

"She'll make an excellent crewman," Noatak snapped back before Mek could respond. "And she saved your ass. I could use someone like her at my back."

Joy chortled. "I think Noatak may have a crush on our new Weapons Specialist."

He glared at her. "Appreciating a skilled gunman is its own thing."

She scrunched her eyes in a snotty little sister kind of smile. "Uh, huh."

"Marlis's brain damage would be an interesting study." Mek tapped his forefinger against his chin. "I wonder if the nanites would repair her?"

The microscopic nano-computers were designed to alter brain structure and create something called cyber-sensitivity in humans—the ability to access computer systems remotely without any additional hardware. They were also the only thing that allowed the denaidans to have mates. Noatak didn't know whether to be excited Marlis might be the next candidate for the nanites or pissed. If she began the process now, someone else could end up bonding with her before his heart was fixed. "We only have one sample left, right? Maybe you should use it on a more steady patient."

"The sample's degrading quickly," Mek answered. "We need to inoculate a new host as soon as possible. And in Marlis's case, the nanites will serve a dual purpose."

"You still can't get my samples to survive?" Joy asked.

"No matter what I do, when I separate them from your dendritic tissue, it corrupts their operating system. They become completely inert." Unlike Lisa's nanites, which had died off completely during her mating with Qaiyaan, Joy's nanites had fused to her nervous system when she'd joined with Kashatok.

"We should at least wait to decide until Qaiyaan and the others get back," Noatak said. "Let her meet the rest of the crew before she commits to something as serious as the nanites."

Mek shrugged. "The longer we wait, the less viable the sample becomes."

"If they come back with Doug, we'll have all the samples we need," Noatak argued.

"And if they come back with nothing?"

The captains had gone to meet a black-market contact for information about the secret Syndicorp lab where Lisa's brother, Doug —the original nanite test subject—was being kept. But they'd come back from previous meetings empty-handed. Mek's sample might be their only hope for mates.

Pacing the short distance to the door and back, Noatak balled his hands into fists at his sides. He wasn't ready for things to be moving so fast. "We don't even know if the nanites will help her. They nearly killed Lisa." He spun and thrust a finger in Joy's direction. "And she'd be blind now if it wasn't for the camera implant."

"Calm down, *iluq*." Mek made a calming motion with both hands. "We let the nanites grow too close to critical saturation in previous instances. Next time, I plan to keep the host under constant supervision."

The host. It sounded so cold. So clinical. When they'd first come up with the plan to hire women and inoculate them, it'd been tactical. A means to an end. Now that they were talking about Marlis, it had become personal. "This isn't a Syndicorp test lab. You're talking about a person."

"Guys." Joy tilted her head. "We haven't even asked her yet. She could say no. Don't get so riled up."

Mek pursed his lips and gave Noatak a meaningful look. "I think she's the best candidate right now, regardless of any extenuating circumstances."

"*Anaq.*" Noatak blew out a breath and looked at a spot on the wall near Joy's monitor. "Fine."

They needed a host. He couldn't deny it. The future of his entire race depended on it.

And unless Mek came up with a solution for his heart, Marlis would end up pairing with someone else.

Marlis had grown up sharing a room with her sister, but the accommodations on the *Hardship* were a little ridiculous—barely more than a walkway between two sets of bunk beds. Inside the lower bunk compartment on the right, Emmy'd hung a picture of herself with a golden retriever. A menagerie of tiny stuffed animals dotted her pillow, and several articles of clothing lay scattered over the blanket in the process of being folded.

Tossing her rucksack onto the bunk above Emmy's, Marlis asked, "Do we have roommates?"

"I think we're the only ones in here so far."

Fewer names to remember would be good. She examined the compartment that would be her bunk. Two inset shelves took up the entire wall inside, yet seemed hardly adequate for her clothing, let alone any other gear. "Where can I stow my weapons?"

Emmy cocked her head. "They probably have a weapons locker to store guns."

"I like to keep my weapons at hand." Marlis thrust her rifle case across the mattress.

Rising from the bottom bunk, Emmy's head barely cleared the top edge of the mattress. "Are you going to try to fit everything in here?"

"I keep my E-11 beneath my pillow. Maybe I can install a mounting bracket at the foot to hold Fanny." Marlis stroked her MCS6 rifle.

"So…" Emmy cleared her throat. "Exactly how many gun fights have you been in?"

Marlis flushed. "That was my first, actually."

Emmy widened her eyes. "Wow. You reacted so fast, I assumed you did that sort of thing all the time."

"Thank you." Marlis's reflexes were the one thing her brain damage never seemed to adversely affect and the only good thing the recruitment trainer'd ever said about her.

"Do you think you killed Joy's attacker?"

A vague recollection of a pulse blast leaving her gun in slow motion and connecting squarely with the posungi's forehead intruded on her thoughts. Marlis's throat felt unaccountably thick all of a sudden. Until the cantina, she'd only engaged in mock exercises, shooting at digital targets. *Damn memory. Only comes back at the worst times.* She swallowed and answered, "I… I guess so."

"Is that why you were upset in the galley?" Emmy put a gentle hand on her forearm.

"Not exactly." She'd just told Noatak everything, and for the second time today she realized how odd it felt to be talking to people who didn't already know what she'd been through. People who didn't automatically categorize her as unfixable. If she and Emmy were going to be co-workers, bunk-mates, hopefully even friends, Marlis might as well tell her everything, just like she had with Noatak. "We're all in the Resistance together, so I guess it's only fair you know."

"Okay." Emmy swept some scattered lingerie aside and sat on her bunk, looking up expectantly.

Wishing for Twerp's reassuring buzz, Marlis thought, *There is no danger.* She sat on the bunk and leaned back against the footboard, pulling one knee up. As she related her time on Pulati, new memories cropped up, bits and pieces of detail she'd never dared voice. "My therapist kept asking if I was angry with my mother for failing to protect me. But all I recall is being happy Mom wouldn't be on duty, so I'd have her all to myself."

Her voice cracked. Every inch of her body trembled and her hand itched for the comforting grip of her E-11.

Emmy reached behind her and pulled a stuffed unicorn from her pillow, dropping it onto Marlis's lap. "Here."

Marlis stared at the plush toy, then back at Emmy. Did Emmy think Marlis was being a baby? "What's this for?"

"I just noticed you were clenching and unclenching your hands. Sometimes having something to hold on to helps when you're talking about stressful stuff. If you don't want it, that's okay."

"Why did you even bring these?"

"I'm sentimental, I guess, and I had room. They remind me of happier days."

The plush toy did remind Marlis of how innocent she'd been before the trauma. Of a childhood that had been cut off too soon. Her breath shuddered as early memories crowded her thoughts. "Mom was trying really hard not to be a soldier so we could have fun." Marlis felt a wistful smile tug the corner of her mouth. "She said someone else could police the universe for a few days and even joked with some of the troopers the morning before it all happened." She looked up into Emmy's eyes. "The same troopers who then shot her at point blank range and left me to die."

Emmy gasped, eyes glistening with tears. "That's awful."

Marlis dug her fingers into the unicorn's soft curves, wanting to rip it in half. "How could I forget that?"

"We're told to trust troopers from the moment we can walk. And Syndicorp wanted you to forget. You'd probably be dead right now if you'd remembered."

"You think these pirates can really mount a resistance? That there's any hope of making Syndicorp pay for what they did?"

"I certainly hope so." Emmy frowned. "Although I'm not sure exactly how I'm going to be able to help."

"You did a great job patching up Joy." The change in focus felt good, like the ship's gravity had just lessened. "Maybe you can help the doctor?"

"I had to do a medical rotation for my psychiatric internship, but blood makes me woozy." Emmy shuddered theatrically.

Marlis raised her brows. "Really? I never would've guessed. You did great."

A knock at the doorframe drew their attention, and Noatak leaned into the room. "Settled in?"

"I think so." Emmy smiled at him and pointed to the bunk above their heads. "Although Marlis really could use some space for her extra guns."

"I don't have *extra* guns." Marlis glanced at the unicorn in her lap and quickly thrust it back toward Emmy. "And Emmy's not going to have anywhere to sleep with all these stuffed animals."

Noatak's gaze flickered over the unicorn before pausing on something near Marlis's knee. A twitch of a smile lifted the corner of his mouth. She followed the direction of his gaze to a lacy orange pair of panties—definitely not trooper issue—but even though they weren't hers, she flushed.

"You can each have a locker in the cargo bay for extra items." His smile faded, and he stepped back into the hallway. "Marlis, do you have a few minutes? The doc would like a word with you."

"The doctor? Why?" Did this have something to do with her breakdown in the galley? Damn it all if she'd disqualified herself from yet another job.

Noatak rubbed his temple. "He saw your AI. Wants to talk to you about it."

Twerp. Even when she wasn't wearing it, the AI was a source of trouble. Swallowing, she nodded and slid out of the bunk. Shooting a worried smile at Emmy, Marlis followed Noatak down the corridor to a small med bay.

The doctor sat on a stool inside, his back to the door as he scrolled through computer files. He must've heard their approach because he swiveled to greet them. "Marlis. I'm so glad you're here." He patted the exam table. "Please, sit."

She perched on the foot of the bed, facing the doctor. She'd been through so many physical exams, it almost felt like home again. Except that Noatak remained stiffly just inside the door. Was he worried about her? Although he'd basically said she was on probation, he seemed to want her on the crew. Hopefully, he was sticking around as an advocate, especially since she couldn't for the life of her remember the doctor's name.

"Are you familiar with nano-bots?" the doctor asked.

"Sure," she answered with a shrug. "Itty-bitty computers, right?"

"Has anyone mentioned that humans and denaidans cannot engage in sex?"

"Uh, okay. Good thing that's not what I'm here for." She found her gaze sliding toward Noatak near the door. She had no idea where this conversation could be going. Was her brain damage getting worse? She reached for her wrist, seeking Twerp's comforting presence. *Gone.* "I thought you wanted to talk to me about my AI."

Noatak made a grumbling noise and took a small step into the room. "Mek's doctoring ability is far better than his conversational skills. He's trying to say he thinks he can fix your brain damage with nanites."

"The same technology that makes a human a compatible mate for our kind," Mek added, as if that was the most important part of this conversation.

She gaped at the doctor, Twerp's warning about sex trafficking coming back to mind. "You want to mate with me?"

Mek raised both palms. "No! I mean, not me, personally. I mean—"

Noatak cut in, his huge frame somehow a threat and a comfort at the same time. "No one would dare touch you without your permission."

"Of course not!" The doctor blew out a breath. "Sexual compatibility would simply be a side effect in this instance. Our primary objective is to restore full capacity to your central nervous system."

She straightened. "You're saying the nanites can actually heal me? Restore my ability to remember stuff?"

The doctor answered, "I can't make any promises, but yes, the nanites might restore cognitive function lost due to brain damage."

"Let's do it!" She looked at the two men expectantly. "What do I need to do? Sign a waiver? What?"

The doc held up a hand. "Not so fast. I'll need to get a baseline scan first. Plus, I want you to be fully informed before we proceed. We have some requirements of you during the process."

The prospect of being healed—being normal—was making her giddy. "Whatever it takes. Let's get on with it."

"First of all, you must promise *not* to have sex while you're under treatment."

Her gaze slid inadvertently toward Noatak. "But I thought you said the nanites would make me compatible?"

The intensity that met her in Noatak's eyes felt like a tractor beam. She recognized that hunger, but never before had it caused heat to pool between her legs as it did now. Dragging her attention away, she attempted to focus on what Mek was saying.

"The nanites will change your brain structure and chemistry, making you a viable mate for denaidans, but the culmination of the sex act itself will destroy the nanites," Mek said. "This offer isn't completely altruistic—you'll be a host to grow the nanites and provide us additional inoculations, and for that, we need time."

"Oh." This was getting confusing. She needed Twerp more than ever. "When can I have my AI back? She interprets this kind of stuff for me."

"Tovik's almost finished with his check and then we'll return it," Mek said. "We want to be completely transparent about what you can expect. Rest assured that I'll monitor you closely for any adverse reactions."

"Adverse reactions? You mean side effects?" This was starting to sound less and less like a sure thing.

"You could call them that. The nanites were developed as an experiment in cyber-sensitivity. You'll likely become hyper-aware of the computer systems around you and may experience blackouts, but I believe with proper monitoring I can minimize those events."

Now Marlis was getting really confused. "I thought you said these nanites had something to do with denaidan mating. Now you're saying they were developed for something else. Where did this technology come from in the first place?"

The two men exchanged an uncomfortable glance and Noatak answered, "We got it from a secret Syndicorp lab experiment."

That didn't surprise her. Marlis rubbed her temples. The temptation to just say fuck it and agree was strong within her. She wanted to be healed. To be normal. But with this much information, she didn't trust herself to make a sound decision.

"You don't need to give us your answer now," Noatak said, shooting the doctor a glance.

Mek nodded slowly. "Correct, although sooner is better. My remaining inoculation is degrading quickly and will soon be useless unless we can find a new host." He pulled the med bay scanner from the wall toward the exam table. "Marlis, if you don't mind, I'd like to begin non-invasive baseline scans right away. That way, if you decide to proceed, we can inoculate you without delay."

"Isn't there one more thing you need to tell her?" Noatak asked in a monotone.

"Oh, right." A greenish flush crept over the doctor's face. "I get ahead of myself. We need to walk a fine line between allowing the nanites to finish the job without letting them take over your system entirely. They will need to be terminated before they reach critical saturation."

"Critical saturation? That sounds… bad." She swallowed, casting a glance toward Noatak once more. It felt as if heat waves radiated off of him, his gaze once more pulling at her like a tractor beam.

Although he was focused on her, Noatak's words were for Mek. "Could you be more obscure, doctor?"

"I'm trying not to be crude, Noatak." Mek crossed his arms.

This time, Noatak did speak directly to her. "The only way we currently have to terminate the nanite replication is with sex."

To her surprise, relief flooded her. "Oh, is that all?"

CHAPTER EIGHT

Noatak rolled over in his bunk, unable to force sleep to come. *She was going to accept the nanites.* He knew it, could sense it in her eyes and confirmed it with an ionic pulse, despite Mek's knowing glare. Noatak couldn't help it. The instinct was just too strong. What he'd discovered was that Marlis wasn't afraid, not even of the idea of mating. She was the perfect candidate. When the *Kinship* returned, the crew would be falling over themselves to court her, and he didn't think he could bear watching her accept the advances of another man.

A knock pulled him from his half-doze and his heart leaped. *Marlis?* "Come in."

Mek stepped inside, closing the door behind him. "Just what do you think you're doing?"

"Trying to sleep," Noatak grumbled, pushing down disappointment. "How's Marlis?"

"I'm not here to talk about her." Mek pointed a finger at Noatak. "I felt you ping her in there."

Throwing back the blanket, Noatak rose to grab his pants. "Asking a denaidan not to use his powers is like asking a *qilzri* bird not to fly. Spreading my wings is a reflex."

"You can't be with her." Mek crossed his arms. "I'm sorry. I know you like her, but you can't."

Noatak fastened his pants and leveled his gaze at the doctor. "It's possible I could survive mating, you know."

Mek sighed. "Or you could leave her a heartbroken widow. I know you don't want to hear it, but it's my job to remind you of the consequences."

He glared at the doctor. "*Ellam Cua*, I know the consequences. Now go back to your lab and find a way to fix me." Half a heartbeat later, he added, "Please."

"You're one stubborn *terpak*." Mek threw up his hands and turned to the door. "I'll see what I can do."

Alone in his cabin once more, Noatak knew sleep was impossible. He'd spent many sleepless night cycles wearing himself out on the punching bag in the cargo bay, trying to forget his craving for stims. Maybe it'd get his mind off Marlis, too.

Not bothering with a shirt, he entered the dimly lit corridor, the ship nearly silent during the sleep cycle. Even the hum of the engines was barely audible. He reached the intersection between the galley and the women's crew quarters, pausing momentarily as he imagined Marlis curled up on her bunk, her hip forming a luscious curve under the blanket. She probably slept with that E-11 in hand, long lashes fanned against her cheeks and a slight smile on her lips. What would it be like to slip in and kiss her awake?

Uminaq. He shook his head and pivoted toward the cargo bay. That woman had gotten into his blood.

He didn't bother to brighten the bay lights. He knew every square centimeter of this ship and had boxed in the muted light before. More often than not, one of his *iluq* sensed his unrest and came to join him, lending unspoken support.

A small ring of empty containers in one corner of the bay cordoned off a section of the bay for training. Several handholds had been secured high on the wall and ceiling for use during anti-grav training, and a weapons rack held a few knives and small hand-to-hand weapons. In the corner, a punching bag had been set up, its worn padding repaired too many times to count. He rolled his shoulders and performed a few dummy punches before slamming his bare knuckles into the thing. He'd been working for about fifteen minutes when a woman's voice jarred his focus. "Mind if I join you?"

Turning, he only barely prevented his mouth from dropping open and drooling. Marlis stood there in nothing but a tank top stretched across her breasts and a loose pair of pants that hung just below her knees. He sucked in a deep breath, telling his cock to calm down.

"Trouble sleeping?" he asked.

She rubbed her wrist. "Yeah, I miss Twerp."

"Sorry Tovik's taking so long. I'll get it back for you first thing in the morning."

"Thank you. She's a pain in the ass, but you kind of get accustomed to her reporting to you all the time."

He watched her fingers encircle her slender wrist. "She?"

Marlis smiled wryly. "I know Syndicorp says computer programs don't have rights, but AIs *are* sentient, and Twerp's been my most steady friend."

There it was again; that loyalty he admired. He nodded in understanding.

She moved to the weapons rack and pulled out one of the knives, testing the blunted edge with a thumb. "You guys have a PT routine on the ship?"

"Not formally."

She tossed him the knife and picked up a second one. "How about you show me what you got?"

He grinned, widening his stance. Every cell in his body yearned to fill with power, to really show what his ionic strength could do. He tamped the urge down. Not only would he harm himself, using his abilities against a human would be unfair during training. "Think you can take me?"

She raised a brow, then spun the knife expertly between her fingers before solidifying her grip. "What do we count for points? Back on the carrier, we had electric vests that registered strikes during training."

"You're not wearing a vest." He couldn't help glancing at her chest.

She pushed her shoulders back, and by the look in her eye, he was certain she knew exactly what effect that had on him. "So, what do you suggest?"

"Practice disarming. First one to drop the weapon scrubs the galley tomorrow."

"I have a better idea." She twirled the knife. "If I win, you let me call my sister."

Between the glinting blade and the twinkle in her eyes, he was mesmerized enough to agree to almost anything. Almost. "I told you we need to wait until the captain returns."

"It doesn't have to be a two-way conversation. She has a new position and is likely to be busy, anyway. I only need to leave a message that I'm safe. I'll tell her I have an exciting new job with a cargo ship and she'll just figure I forgot to mention details."

He sighed. That was reasonable. "So, if you win, you get to call your sister. What if I win?"

She pursed her pink lips seductively and shrugged, making her breasts jiggle. "What do you want?"

He narrowed his eyes, a fire burning in his belly. He liked how direct she was about her goals; to get this job, to call her sister... to have him. *Ellam Cua*, he was staring at his perfect mate, and by the way she met his gaze, he was sure she wanted him, too. The urge to ping her again surged in his chest, but he tamped it down, growling, "Mek wouldn't approve of what I want."

"I know we're not compatible... yet. But it could be fun finding out how compatible we *might* be."

His cock surged against his fly. He made a slightly strangled sound in his throat, but he was somewhat aware of nodding like an idiot.

With a naughty grin, she lunged at him.

He regained his senses with barely enough time to twist out of the way, swinging around to spank her ass with the flat of his blade. His swipe only caught air. Facing her again, he grinned. "Feisty little *tunrak!*"

She laughed and thrust out her chin, eyes sparking. "Yes, I am."

He feinted a grab for her knife. She ducked and swept out a leg, trying to take him down. He seized her ankle, but she managed to twist free, facing him once more. They dodged and lunged for another few minutes, working up a sweat. He had to admit, she was good. She'd give anyone in Galactic Ops a run for their money.

Crouching, he coiled himself and launched forward, thinking brute force might tackle her. She brought up a knee, making contact squarely against his jaw. He saw stars, but didn't slow, carrying her to the decking.

They hit the floor hard, but she rolled out of his grasp, regaining her feet almost immediately.

"*Assirpaa!*" He gripped his knife and leaped upright to face her once again. "You must really want to call your sister."

"I do." The playfulness in her expression hardened. She lowered her guard as if about to say more.

Before she could speak, he lunged.

She must've been bluffing, because she leaped at the same moment, rolling herself across his back and locking onto his weapon hand. Hammering her knee against his arm, she tried to dislodge his knife. His hand went numb as his elbow bent the wrong way. The woman was strong and knew just where to apply pressure. But he was stronger. Flexing his biceps, he wrenched free. Before she could dodge away, he clamped both arms around her. He yanked her backward against his chest, keeping the blade of his knife pointing outward.

She elbowed him in the ribs, forcing him to exhale with a grunt. He was going to have bruises tomorrow, but he held tight. Keeping one arm locked around her waist, he used his other hand to pull her knife arm toward him. If he'd been using his powers, he'd've sent a little jolt into her arm to make her release the weapon. As it was, he had to rely on his fingers applying pressure against her tendon.

She was breathing hard, writhing against his grip, and the thin film of sweat on her skin smelled deliciously of fresh linen and musk. He breathed deeply, mesmerized by the slope of creamy skin exposed by the neck of her tank top. The way her soft hair tangled against his beard. She arched her back, panting as she attempted to wrestle free.

Her ass wiggling against him drew a different reaction than the urge to fight, however. Every flex of her muscles forced him to steady her tighter against him and made his cock grow harder. She arched again, rolling her hips downward in a way that had nothing to do with escape.

She wasn't fighting fair.

Anaq. If she was going to fight dirty, so was he. Lowering his mouth, he ran his tongue along the shell of her ear and pressed a possessive, wide-mouthed kiss against her throat, tasting the soft salty tang of her skin. She gasped and shuddered, her rolling hips freezing in place. "That's cheating!"

He wrapped his other arm around her hips, grinding his hard-on against her ass. "Is it?"

She struggled against his hold, and the scent of her arousal reached him, drowning him in pheromones and heat. Instinct rose inside him, the need to open his senses and verify she was a viable mate. Instead, he flicked his tongue against her ear once more and spread his palm flat over her ribcage, just below the weight of a breast.

"We're supposed to disarm each other," she panted. She arched her back again, centering the crack of her ass over his erection. "That's our deal."

"So, disarm me." He pressed the rounded knob of his knife's hilt into the juncture between her thighs.

She gasped and bucked, releasing a shaky breath that nearly had him undone.

Anaq. Mek was going to murder him. But Marlis was the sexiest woman this side of the galaxy, and every atom of his being urged him to make her his any way he could.

"Do you always fight this dirty?" Her voice was a husky whisper.

In answer, he flexed his hips, pressing his cock against her while sliding the smooth hilt in and out between her legs, massaging her clit through the fabric there.

She shuddered and clamped her thighs over the knob. "I'll take that as a yes."

With her free hand, she reached behind her, flattening her palm against the side of his buttock and urging him closer. Then she began a sinuous, rolling motion, pressing and releasing, pressing and releasing. He wasn't sure if she was doing it to feel his erection on her backside or to rub the knife hilt over her clit. Either reason was enough to drive him insane. Her musk filled his senses again, and he groaned.

Sliding the hand on her ribcage upward, he cupped her breast, finding the nipple hard through the material of her tank top. He rolled the bud between forefinger and thumb until it drew to exquisite tightness. She let her head loll back against his collarbone, exposing her throat, and he used his teeth to pull the strap of her tank top off her shoulder, rubbing his beard along the exposed skin.

She turned her face toward him over her shoulder, lips slightly parted, tawny eyes hooded. An invitation. He captured her lips. The need to feel her, to caress her, to taste every inch of her overwhelmed him. Flinging aside his knife, he drove his fingertips between her thighs to cup the damp heat pooling there. *Assirpaa!* How long since he'd touched a woman? And Marlis wasn't just any woman; she was perfect in every way.

In a sudden twist, she spun to face him, their lips still locked, her tongue flicking against his teeth. His blood turned to magma, his very essence on fire with need. His secondary heart slammed out a frantic counterpart to his main heart's beat. *Claim her. Claim her. Claim her.*

Resisting his ionic instinct, he focused on her needs, gripping her ass with both hands. Her body was a play of contrasts, muscles beneath soft feminine curves, strength underlying an utter submission to his ravaging tongue. He plunged into her mouth, tasting her again and again, clenching her against his chest as he devoured her.

Her fingers slid up the bare skin of his back, leaving a wake of tingling heat behind. *Ellam Cua,* he wanted her laid out naked before him. He wanted to taste every inch of her body. Leave no spot unmarked by his touch.

Sudden light filled the cargo bay, and a feminine voice echoed from the catwalk. "—perhaps we could investigate improving the torque modulator on the—"

"Noatak!" Tovik's voice drowned out the rest of the sentence. "You and Mek told me to cool it, now you're down here alone with her! That's not fair!"

Noatak released his hold on Marlis and she slipped away, a sly grin on her face. She brandished her knife toward the one he'd thrown to the deck. "I think I won our bet."

He couldn't help the smile curling his lips. "Feisty little *tunrak.*"

CHAPTER NINE

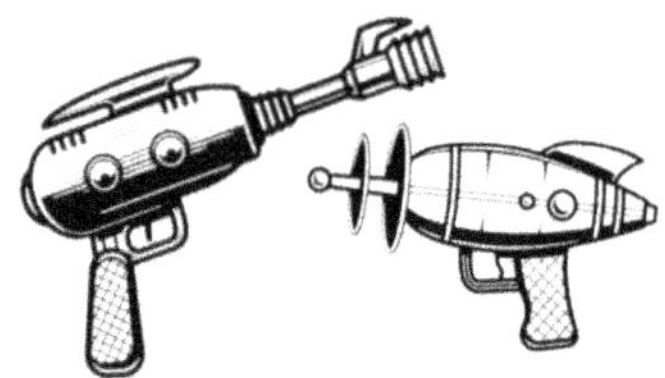

Marlis tried to act cool, but her legs were still wobbly from the intensity of Noatak's kiss. She'd intended to enjoy a little banter, perhaps some suggestive touching, but in no way had she expected him to take the lead as he did. She was usually the driving force in a relationship, and she felt off-balance, not to mention ready to strip naked and let Noatak have his way with her—nanites or no nanites.

She lifted her gaze from Noatak's broad, naked chest to the catwalk. Tovik was probably in shock after seeing what they'd been doing. She cleared her throat. "Hey, Tovik."

Tovik's eyes were filled with a disappointment that reminded her of an abandoned puppy. He raised his hand, the wristband with her AI dangling from his fingertips. "I checked out your AI. She's clean." Shooting Noatak a disgusted look, he jumped to the lower deck next to them and handed Marlis the band. "There you go, Twerp, back where you belong."

Twerp replied, "Thank you, Tovik."

"You're welcome." Tovik shifted his attention from the band to Marlis. "I disabled her wireless sensor. You no longer have spatial data or a locator, but the ship's small, so Twerp thinks you should be okay."

"I provided Tovik all my assistance parameters," Twerp said.

Marlis swallowed. That meant he knew everything that was wrong with her. It had been bound to come to light, anyway. "That's fine, Twerp."

Tovik's mouth quirked into an indulgent half-smile. "Twerp, if you can talk Marlis into giving you a visual sensor, let me know. I have some ideas."

Marlis strapped her AI onto her wrist and smiled at the young man. "It's bad enough she butts in on everything I say. I don't need her looking over my shoulder, too."

Noatak chuckled, turning away to retrieve the knife he'd tossed to the deck.

Tovik tilted his head. "She's sentient, you know. Think how much happier she'd be if she could see."

Twerp chimed, "Thank you, Tovik. I am sentient. However, all Syndicorp sanctioned AIs are required to include programming protocols to restrict autonomy. This is to prevent an AI from intentionally harming a human being. I have long contemplated the idea of free will—"

"Enough, Twerp." Marlis said, shaking her wrist. "You and Tovik can discuss philosophy later."

Noatak held out a hand for her knife and she handed it over, heat flooding her again as she recalled the hilt of his weapon between her thighs. He returned both weapons to the rack. "You ready to send a message to your sister?"

"Thanks for taking care of Twerp, Tovik." With a parting smile, she followed Noatak up the steps and down the hall. They reached the small ship's cockpit-sized bridge. Hard to believe this closet was the command center. Noatak gestured toward the chair on the right and lowered his massive frame into the seat on the opposite side, his head nearly brushing the ceiling. A vast view screen on the wall made it feel like she was standing outside in space.

Tapping the console, Noatak pulled up the comm system. "This is the only place on the ship with access to external communications.

After you've recorded your message, I'll need to strip the identification coding and we can send it."

She smiled, grateful to be able to tell her sister she was safe and had a job, and looked straight into the screen. "Hey, Attie! Good news. I got a position on a small cargo ship. We're still near the station, waiting to rendezvous with another ship, and then we're off. Things are going well so far…" She flicked a glance at Noatak, heat creeping up her face. His expression was unreadable, and she wondered what he was thinking. *Stay focused on Attie.*

Leaning closer to the screen, she said, "I can't wait to tell you all about it. Oh, and just so you know, Dad tried to sabotage me, so I'm not speaking to him at the moment. If you talk to him, tell him he's an asshole."

She cut the recording and looked at Noatak. He took over the comm, fingers flying over the control panel as he encoded the message and sent it.

"Thank you," Marlis said.

He nodded, seemingly unable to meet her gaze. "You should get some rest. It's been a long day."

"For both of us." Had she said or done something to upset him? All she remembered was the feel of his hands on her body. But she'd done things to offend people before without realizing it. She twisted her wristband. Now that she had Twerp back to help her understand things, it was time to talk to the doctor about the nanites fixing her memory. "You think Mek's awake yet?"

He watched her hands, then lifted his gaze to hers. "You want to talk about the nanites?"

A twinge of heat ran through her core. Although her primary goal for the nanites was to heal her brain, the things were related to mating in Noatak's mind. And if the cargo bay had been any indication, he was primed and ready to help her wrap things up in that department. "Do you think I should take them?"

His face twitched, and he worked his jaw as if fighting back what he really wanted to say. "What I think is irrelevant."

"But I respect your opinion." She tilted her head, wondering why he was being so evasive.

He stroked his beard and sighed. "One thing Mek never mentioned is that humans and denaidans who mate appear to forge a permanent bond. You will likely be unable to pair with anyone else ever again."

She laughed. "As in soul mates? That's not a real thing."

He continued to look into her eyes somberly, as if daring her to doubt him again.

She quieted. "Wait, you're serious?"

"Completely. You can talk to Joy or Lisa about it if you want to know what it's like for a human."

"Popular science asserts the occurrence of 'true mates' is merely a psychological affinity," Twerp added. "However, several studies seem to indicate some species are capable of developing a symbiosis which ties their life forces together. While scientific theory has not yet been able to empirically measure—"

"Okay, Twerp," Marlis said, her brain already overflowing. "Thank you."

Noatak rose from the chair and ducked into the hallway. "If you want to come with me, I can get Mek's data for you."

"Thank you," Twerp said. "I appreciate all forms of information, particularly when it may be of assistance to Marlis."

"He was talking to me, Twerp." Marlis pushed out of the chair and trailed after Noatak to the med bay. Why did he seem so sad? She'd think he'd be excited she might accept the nanites.

He stepped inside and retrieved a polycom. "This has all his files on the nanites." Handing it over, he moved to the door before adding, "You'll get to meet the rest of the crew soon. Please think carefully before you say yes. Once you're inoculated, there's only one way to clear your system."

Without a backward glance at her, he disappeared around the corner.

Was he saying he wasn't interested? They'd just gotten hot and heavy in the cargo bay, and there'd been no denying the erection she'd felt through his clothes. Maybe he wasn't interested in forming a commitment. Not that she'd be looking, either, if this nanite thing hadn't come up. But if she was going to have to choose someone to bond with, Noatak would be a good option. Not just good, amazing. He liked guns as much as she did and had been so understanding with her when she'd been forced to recall Pulati. She was also pretty sure he could take her in a hand-to-hand match if they actually followed the rules. *Be logical, Marlis.* What did he get out of a union except a ball-and-chain?

It only took her one wrong turn to find her way back to her bunk. Luckily, without ending up in Tovik's bedroom or something. Trying not to wake Emmy, she plugged Twerp into the polycom before falling into a restless sleep. What felt like moments later, Emmy's alarm brought her wide awake.

Rolling toward the edge of the bed, Marlis watched Emmy rise and stretch. Emmy noticed she was awake. "Where'd you go last night?"

Marlis flushed with heat. She slid from the bunk to the floor, shivering as the cold deck contacted her bare feet. "Uh, sparring with Noatak."

All traces of sleep left Emmy's face. "Sparring, huh?" She winked. "That why you're blushing?"

Something close to a giggle rose in Marlis's throat. *A giggle?* She didn't giggle. Not even with Attie. Maybe Twerp was right. She could use a human friend. With a small shrug, she said, "Things did get a little… personal."

"Did you kiss him?" Emmy grabbed her hand and pulled her onto the bottom bunk, crossing her legs to face her. "Was it amazing? Who could've imagined aliens could be so hot?"

This time, Marlis did laugh. She pulled her legs in, mimicking Emmy's cross-legged posture, so they sat knee-to-knee. "They're certainly not tentacle-faced posungi."

Emmy cocked her head, face alight. "So… are all his parts in the right places? How far'd you get?"

"Not that far." Heat was pooling low in her abdomen as she

remembered just how well he'd lined up to her ass. "Humans and denaidans can't have sex."

Disappointment creased Emmy's face. "Really? I thought Joy was married to one of the captains."

Marlis shook her head, trying to put the pieces she remembered into sentences. Slowly, she explained about the nanites and how they were going to fix her. "But that's not what they were meant to do. They actually have something to do with denaidan mating, which can be deadly to humans without the nanites."

"So your AI was right? This is a sex thing, and they brought us on board to create mates?" Emmy shrank back, her eyes wide.

"No, I don't think Mek would've even told me about the nanites except for my brain damage. I think he just keeps them on hand in case people want to… you know, get together. I mean, it would be bad to not have something available, wouldn't it?"

Emmy seemed to relax and nodded thoughtfully. "Good point."

Twerp chimed from the top bunk. "I have completed my analysis, Marlis. Would you like me to explain?"

"That would be great, Twerp." She rose and retrieved the wristband, strapping it back in place before settling down.

While Twerp went over the information Mek had provided earlier and Emmy asked questions, Marlis's mind wandered back to the cargo bay. Why wouldn't Noatak want to bond with her? They both liked guns. He seemed to want to protect people as much as she did. And they were in this resistance together, which from the sound of it was just beginning. Assuming Syndicorp didn't discover them and shut everything down before it even had a chance to begin, they were looking at years of working together. Maybe she needed to prove herself to him first. But Mek had said time was of the essence here…

"Are you going to?" Emmy's voice yanked her out of her thoughts.

"Going to? Oh." She cleared her throat, realizing she hadn't heard a word Twerp'd said. "Twerp, are they safe?"

"Nanites are not an approved medical treatment for your type of brain injury, Marlis. The procedure is purely experimental."

"I know it's experimental, but if there's a chance of fixing me, I should take it."

"It is theoretically possible for nano technology to repair damage to your central nervous system. However, previous test subjects had to be closely monitored to prevent adverse side effects. My primary function is to support your wellness. In the event you choose to accept the nanites, I will need Tovik's assistance recalibrating my biometric sensors to continue monitoring you."

"So you're saying go ahead?"

"If that is your decision, I will assist in any way I can."

Emmy gaped at her. "You're okay with… with the end part?"

Marlis shrugged, her face heating. "If it's anything like last night with Noatak, then hell yes."

Twerp spoke up. "Humans are notoriously promiscuous, therefore I would not theorize that every pairing would result in a symbiotic bond. I have been comparing the data Mek provided alongside other scientific studies about symbiotic life-bonds in various species. The data on human-denaidan pairings reflects an insignificant amount of information to arrive at a statistical conclusion."

Emmy laughed. "Okay, then."

"Will you go with me to see Mek?" Although Marlis was used to going to appointments alone, this nanite thing was unfamiliar territory. It'd be good to have someone besides Twerp to provide input. "He said there may be side effects and stuff. It'd be nice to have you there."

"Of course!" Emmy beamed at her. "Who knows? Maybe someday I'll ask the same thing of you. These denaidans are pretty tempting. Even Tovik's kinda cute."

A knock at the door halted the conversation as Tovik's voice came from outside. "I made you both breakfast!"

"Be right there!" Emmy called quickly, her face turning pink.

"Okay, Emmy!" Tovik's muffled voice answered.

Pointing toward the door, Emmy silently mouthed, "Think he heard me?"

Repressing her laughter, Marlis slid out of the bunk and grabbed her pants. "I suppose breakfast would be a good idea before I talk to Mek."

Emmy joined her, pulling off her pajama top. Once they were dressed, they headed to the galley where Tovik had attempted to make pancakes. "Lisa says these are human comfort food," he said as he placed plates on the table. The little disks were stiff, misshapen, and required some chewing, but Marlis gulped down a bite while he hovered. "Do you like them?"

"Mmm," Marlis replied, taking a large swig of coffee to wash it down. At least the coffee was hot and not too weak.

"You did a fine job for your first time," Emmy said, pouring more syrup onto her plate.

"I'd be happy to make them for you again." He sat down to his own plate and cut into one. His grin faded. "These are nothing like Lisa's."

"Pancakes take practice," Emmy said.

He sighed and reached for the butter. "You're too nice."

After they helped clean up, Marlis led Emmy to the med bay. Mek was inside rearranging items in a cupboard. He turned and smiled, his gaze cautious. "Good morning, ladies. Everything all right?"

"I've decided to take the nanites." Marlis moved into the bay. "Emmy's here as moral support."

"You told her?" Mek's hands froze around the tube he was coiling.

Emmy took a spot on the opposite side of the table. "Actually, Twerp told me."

Marlis held up her wrist. "Noatak gave me the data last night, and I fed the files to Twerp. She says I should go ahead."

"I believe my actual response was that I will support your decision but will need to be recalibrated if I am to assist with your treatment," Twerp said. "It is a pleasure to make your acquaintance, doctor."

"Likewise." Mek raised his eyebrows. "I'm sure Tovik would be happy to help modify your programming. Having an AI monitor biometrics will be quite valuable. You understand the side effects and requirements?"

"Yes," both Twerp and Marlis responded at once. Twerp vibrated gently against Marlis's wrist, which Marlis always took as a form of laughter in instances like this.

Mek opened a cabinet and pulled out a vial. "You're quite sure about this?"

Marlis nodded, her heartbeat quickening. "If there's a chance to fix my brain, I'm all in."

"All right," Mek gestured to the exam table. "Lie back and I'll begin the injection."

Closing her eyes, Marlis waited for the magic to begin.

CHAPTER TEN

After his interlude with Marlis, Noatak spent a long, sleepless night thinking. He was relieved she hadn't accepted the nanites off the cuff. He wasn't usually the kind of guy to get his hopes up, but Marlis was one hell of a woman, and one he'd consider worth hoping for. Perhaps Mek could find a cure for his ionic heart while she considered. He'd finally fallen into a fitful sleep when the comm woke him with news the *Kinship* had returned.

Jaw cracking around an enormous yawn, he rose and scrubbed his face with hot water before dressing and heading to the cargo bay to meet the crew. He'd barely made it to the bottom of the cargo bay stairs when Kashatok was in his face. "You left her!"

Bowing his head, Noatak crossed his arms. He deserved this, but that didn't mean he had to like it. "The place was getting under my skin. I needed air."

"You guaranteed her safety!" Kashatok shoved him.

Noatak braced himself and prepared for more blows. If someone'd let his mate get hurt, he'd be pissed, too.

Joy moved in behind Kashatok, laying a hand on his shoulder. "Calm down. I told you I'm fine."

Kashatok glowered at Noatak another moment, ionic power rolling off him in waves, then spun and stalked to a cluster of men who were helping offload supplies. Chignik, the *Kinship's* main gunner, glanced toward the catwalk above Noatak's head. "There they are!"

Taking two steps, he leaped to the catwalk, Ekwok mere seconds behind him. Noatak spun to look overhead, spotting several sets of feet on the grating.

"Hey!" Tovik's voice echoed loud through the bay as he launched himself after them.

Then Marlis's voice joined the mix, "Back off, assholes!"

Without using his ionic powers, Noatak raced up the stairs three at a time. "Get your asses back down to the deck before you clumsy *terpaks* knock our new crew members off the catwalk."

"I just wanted to say hi," Chignik complained, swinging an elbow at Tovik in a less-than-friendly manner. "You guys got a head start."

Tovik put his hands on his hips. "I've hardly got to talk to them at all yet."

Ekwok sighed and trudged to the stairs, turning to look longingly over his shoulder. "Which one's coming to our ship?"

Noatak's chest ached at the possibility Marlis might join the other crew. Stepping aside to allow Ekwok to pass, Noatak said, "None of them if you two keep acting like idiots."

A sharp whistle from below was followed by Captain Kashatok's voice. "Everyone on deck for a debrief."

Chignik grumbled as he moved to the stairs. Tovik grinned triumphantly until Noatak raised his eyebrows. "That means you, too, Tovik."

"I know," the kid said, beckoning the women with one hand. "I'm just showing our new crew members the way."

"You think they're going to get lost?"

"I'm being a gentleman," Tovik said as he passed. Next time Noatak had the kid alone, he was going to have to discuss the difference between chivalry and chauvinism.

Marlis brushed her fingertips along the top of Noatak's hand as she passed, whether or not intentionally, he wasn't sure, but his ionic senses flared to life before he could seal off the reaction. He took a deep breath and clamped down on his control. He should step out of the running. Tell her he wasn't interested. Even Tovik was a better bet than he was. Yet his chest ached with desire at every twitch of her hips as she moved toward the group of waiting men.

Qaiyaan waited at the bottom of the stairs and clapped a hand to his shoulder. "These the only two?"

"Aye, Captain." Noatak nodded and cut a glance toward Joy. Thank *Ellam Cua* she was upright and functional. "Whylon Station didn't go as well as planned."

"I heard." Qaiyaan sighed. "Kashatok aborted our reconnaissance as soon as he found out."

"How'd he find out?"

"The kid." Qaiyaan tilted his head toward Tovik, who was watching Chignik and Ekwok jostle for the spot next to Emmy. "Couldn't you rein him in?"

Of course it was the kid. They'd all sworn to protect Joy, but Tovik thought that meant informing her mate of anything that went awry, regardless of the consequences to the larger mission. "I'll have a talk with him."

Qaiyaan nodded and moved to the circle of cargo containers they'd pulled over as seats for the meeting. At least no one appeared to be bothering Marlis, possibly because of the pistol at her hip. He had no doubt she'd use it if anyone got too bold.

As if sensing his scrutiny, she turned her head to look over her shoulder at him and their gazes connected like lightning. A slight twitch of her head was all the invitation he needed to stride forward. But a bob of her head indicated he should take a seat on Emmy's other side.

Uminaq. He wanted to sit next to Marlis, find excuses to brush his shoulder against hers or touch her knee. But he also understood her need to protect her friend from these over-eager louts. *Ellam Cua.* She had him wrapped around her finger and didn't even know it. With one arm, he shoved both men aside and sat next to Emmy.

Chignik and Ekwok ceased arguing and gaped at him.

"What the hell, *iluq*?" Chignik asked.

Qaiyaan cut short any argument. "Just take a damned seat. Now's not the time for fraternizing."

Tovik crossed his arms and glared at Noatak. "Exactly when is a good time, then?"

Noatak glared back.

Chignik took a spot on Marlis's other side. Jealousy flared inside Noatak's gut and he narrowed his eyes at the big gunner. Shooting Noatak a grin as wide as a rakwiji bounty hunter's, Chignik turned his attention toward Marlis. "Hey."

Marlis barely glanced at him, her focus on Qaiyaan in the center of the ring of containers. "Hey."

Noatak smirked and turned toward the captain as well.

Emmy leaned close to him. "Are all denaidan men this... big?"

Glancing down at her, he realized her petite frame was barely half the size of the nearby men. Maybe he should make size a consideration during the next round of interviews. "Yes," he answered.

Qaiyaan nodded toward Marlis and Emmy. "We're happy to have you on board. My name's Qaiyaan. I'm captain of the *Hardship*. Everyone, take a quick moment to introduce yourself."

As everyone spoke, Noatak could tell by Marlis's face she was panicking. He pulled out his polycom. "There'll be information about the mission. I need to take notes."

Marlis cast him a grateful glance and pulled out her polycom.

Chignik leaned closer to her. "Chignik, with a C. In case you wondered."

She shook her head and edged away to enter something into her polycom. Noatak hoped it said 'asshole'.

Once the introductions were concluded, Qaiyaan asked, "Do I need to catch our newcomers up about the nanites, or are they already informed?"

Noatak's stomach roiled. Once the men knew Marlis was first in line to take the nanites, they'd be all over her. He opened his mouth to speak, but Mek beat him to it. "They do. I inoculated Marlis a few hours ago."

Every denaidan crew member in the bay focused on Marlis. Noatak sucked in a breath. When had she taken them? And why hadn't Mek informed him? *Because you're not in the running, terpak.*

Ekwok pointed toward Mek while looking at Kashatok. "I told you their crew would take unfair advantage!"

Chignik jumped to his feet, menace rolling off him in waves. "You should've waited until we returned."

Tovik gaped, rising and glaring at Noatak. "How long has she had them?"

Noatak forced himself to remain sitting, although every cell in his body wanted to get up and stake his claim—now. A claim he could never make. His attraction to Marlis was making him want to act like a beast in rut.

"Get your men under control, captain," Qaiyaan growled at Kashatok.

Kashatok thrust a finger toward Tovik. "Soon as you get control of yours."

From the corner of his eye, Noatak saw Marlis's hand slide toward her holster.

Mek had moved into the circle. "Calm down. The nanites were only administered a few hours ago. I didn't know how soon the Kinship would return, and the sample was deteriorating rapidly. I had to act."

"Why? So you could have her all to yourself?" Chignik stepped within swinging distance of the doctor.

"I'm her doctor." Mek seemed to swell. "I have no intentions toward Marlis."

"Put her on our ship, then," Chignik said. The room churned with testosterone and raw power.

Marlis's palm brushed her weapon. The women were safe, but she wouldn't understand that; the rest of the crew might go back to their bunks with bruises, but the women would never be harmed.

Leaning across Emmy's lap, Noatak put a hand on Marlis's knee, surprised by the tiny shock that raced up his arm. Once more, his ionic senses flared without his volition. Now that he knew she had the nanites, he could detect the subtle change within her, like the scent of freshly fallen rain. *Down, boy.* His powers were no longer only dangerous to himself; a ping could cause the nanites to react badly. Both Lisa and Joy had experienced blackouts when they'd had them.

"It's okay," he said. "Mek's got this."

After a moment, she nodded and moved her hand back to her lap, fingers curling and uncurling as if fighting a leash.

A sharp whistle brought everyone to silence. Qaiyaan stood on top of one container, his hands on his hips. "I'm about to throw you three in the brig." Tovik opened his mouth to argue, but Qaiyaan silenced him with a look. "Yes, you too. Now, let the doctor finish his report."

It took every ounce of Noatak's will to turn his attention back to Mek.

The doctor put his hands on his hips. "I'll be monitoring Marlis closely with the aid of her AI, Twerp." He turned to Marlis. "Twerp, please say hello."

"G-greetings." The chirpy voice on Marlis's wrist spoke a strange hiccup. "I'm pleased to make your acquaintance." Marlis had said the thing was sentient, but it was funny to think the AI might be nervous.

Mek continued, "The nanites will be performing some ancillary tasks while replicating. It's too early to tell how quickly we might be able to collect a new supply."

Qaiyaan moved to the center of the circle. "Hopefully soon. Marlis may be our only source of nanites for a good long while."

Tovik groaned. "The lab wasn't under the mine on Zyrinic Eight?"

"It was until they moved it," Kashatok said. "The corp installed a huge Faraday cage on one of their flagships and appears to be operating from there."

Lisa added, "They've probably moved out of stage two testing. The corp always planned to use cyber-sensitive technology in their espionage activities, and a mobile lab opens up territory."

"We're better at boarding ships than ground assaults." Tovik said, glancing at the assembled men. "Shouldn't this be good news?"

"Only if we can find the ship," Qaiyaan answered. "The *Icarus* is equipped with the very latest cloaking technology. The running joke is that not even the corp knows where it's at."

"I'm working on the intel, but it's going to take some time,"

Kashatok said. "And it isn't cheap. We're going to need to take on some jobs in the meantime. I have a lead on a payload of corp computer hardware moving to one of the new manufacturing colonies. The ship'll be ripe for the picking if we can get our asses in gear in time to intercept."

Tovik let out a whoop. "New hardware!"

"To sell, Tovik. We've got to pay for intel, remember?" Noatak reminded him. The kid was always disassembling perfectly good equipment to fashion what he called "prototype" technology. Most of it never worked the way he expected.

"We can keep a few things, though, right?" Tovik looked hopefully toward Qaiyaan.

Qaiyaan sighed. "We'll see." He panned his gaze over the assembled crew. "Now that we're bringing on new crew members, I expect all of you to be on your best behavior. This isn't some gladiator ring where the winner gets the girl. Understood?"

The men mumbled, and Chignik looked at Qaiyaan from beneath his brows. "It's not fair to our crew if the girls are both over here. Since Mek needs to keep an eye on the nanites, at least send the other girl to the *Kinship*."

"Her name's Emmy." Marlis rose, her hand once more on the butt of her pistol. This time, Noatak didn't stop her. She'd need to prove herself to these men eventually. Might as well start now.

She shoved a finger in Chignik's face. "And if all you're looking for is mates, I suggest you take out an ad with one of the dating agencies. Both Emmy and I are here to join the revolution, not be passed around like blow up dolls."

Chignik had the courtesy to flush and lowered his gaze. "I meant no disrespect."

The rest of the crew laughed at his discomfort, and Qaiyaan nodded, his gaze sliding to Noatak with unspoken approval in his eyes. Ekwok slapped Chignik on the shoulder. "Don't be an *ucuk*."

Marlis went back to her seat, and Qaiyaan spoke once more. "New crew members need to remain here until Mek clears them. Once the *Kinship* has its own doctor, that might change. For now, Kashatok's crew is welcome to serve rotations over here so everyone can get to know each other. Noatak will set up a work schedule for shift rotation."

Much as Noatak wanted to refuse the task, he nodded. A rotation was only fair, and he couldn't have Marlis, anyway. Perhaps the sooner she moved her attention to another male, the better.

CHAPTER ELEVEN

Sitting in the confines of the laser turret, Marlis went over the targeting layout for what felt like the hundredth time. Part of her was concerned about stealing a ship full of computer parts, but she kept reminding herself it was a Syndicorp ship, and Syndicorp was the bad guy. At least her memory was clear about that. Acknowledging the truth had rocked her to the core at first, but with her suspicions confirmed, every jumbled memory had clicked into place—if only her short-term memories had followed. But the nanites were going to fix that.

She zeroed in on a cargo container Noatak'd ejected for her to use as target practice and fired. The shot barely nicked the corner, setting the box spinning. Dammit, she was better than this. She'd studied ship-mounted weapons on Syndicorp carriers, freighters, and even practiced for a gunner seat on a small fighter ship. But the *Hardship's* systems were antiquated and less automated than she was used to. She couldn't seem to hold the range ignition order in her head.

"I thought these nanites were supposed to be improving my memory," she grumbled to herself. For three days they'd been waiting for signs the nanites had become active. She'd hoped to have at least a little memory improvement by now.

Twerp buzzed soothingly against her wrist. "The doctor said the process could take some time, Marlis. I am not yet d-detecting significant neural changes in your biometric data."

Twerp had developed a strange hiccup since Tovik had recalibrated her. Marlis paused her task and tapped the AI. "Twerp, put a reminder on my calendar to take you back to Tovik for a check."

"Of course."

A set of broad shoulders pushed up through the hatch, topped by a head of braided hair. For some reason, she kept wanting to call this guy Jake-with-a-J, but knew that wasn't right. He grinned at her. "Need any help in here?"

Shaking her head, she said, "I got this, thanks."

"You might appreciate a hand from an expert." He winked and pulled himself higher into the small turret.

She'd met his kind before, men who thought women couldn't possibly handle the big guns. Before he could step off the ladder, she swiveled the chair, her knees forcing him to lean backward against the starboard view screen. He laid his hands on her thighs, ostensibly to steady himself, but she didn't like the way his fingers squeezed, as if he was just itching to cop a feel. Keeping her legs closed so there'd be no mistake, Marlis rammed her knees hard into his abdomen. "I don't need you in here man-splaining. When I need a hand, I'll ask, okay?"

"Okay, okay, I get it." He raised his hands in surrender. She eased up the pressure and his grin returned. "But you need anything, I'm here for you. I like a woman who knows her way around a turret."

Turning back to the controls, she let out a short breath, keeping a tight hold on her anger as he retreated. Fuck, these guys were hard up. If it wasn't Tovik, it was this guy, or the other dude with sandy hair. Even the old-timer in the other ship's engineering bay had winked at her. She was growing tired of always needing to fend someone off. *Everyone but Noatak.*

The First Mate seemed to be the one man keeping his distance. It was as if he wanted to give the other men room to move in, which baffled her, especially since she kept catching his eyes on her. Thinking about him now ignited heat low in her pelvis as if his touch there had started a fire that refused to go out. She didn't even want to think about anyone else's hands on her.

Twerp let out a long buzz. "You have an appointment with the doctor in half an hour, Marlis."

Sighing, she shut down the targeting system and climbed out of the turret. Hopefully, today there was good news. On the way to find the doc, she spotted Noatak ducking into the weapons locker. She paused and poked her head inside. "Can I talk to you a minute?"

He turned stiffly away from the weapons bench. "What is it?"

She glanced over her shoulder toward the cargo bay where Tovik and the guy from the turret were working on something. Although they weren't outright looking at her, she could feel their attention, nonetheless. Perhaps it was the nanites. She didn't care. All she wanted was to clear the air with Noatak, and this was the closest to alone she'd been with him in three days.

She stepped inside the narrow cage and shut the door, knowing it wouldn't give her any real privacy, but needing to at least pretend they weren't being watched. "Are you avoiding me?"

He stared at her for several heartbeats before answering. "I'm giving you space."

"I don't remember asking for space. At least not from you."

His posture shifted a fraction. "Is someone treating you badly?"

"Not exactly." She shrugged. "But the men are driving me crazy, trying to get my attention. I know you guys are looking for mates, but I'm not interested. At least..." she licked her lips, suddenly nervous, "not in them. Can you just claim me or something and make them leave me alone?"

He rubbed the back of his neck, eyes filled with what she could only interpret as pain. "I can't."

Her breath caught. She hadn't expected him to say no. "I don't understand. The other night in the practice ring—"

"That was a mistake. I shouldn't have taken things that far." Shoulders stiff, he took one step sideways as if to move around her toward the door. "Give these other men a chance."

"A mistake?" She intercepted him, one hand against his chest. "Hell, no. I don't know what's going on with this 'fairness' bullshit, but I'm interested in you. Only you. What do I have to do to make you want me?"

She was close enough to feel the warmth coming off of his body. He let out a shaky breath. *"Ellam Cua,* Marlis. It's not that I don't want you."

Lifting up on her toes, she brought her face closer to his and looked determinedly into his eyes. "So, what's the problem?"

His breath fanned her cheek, and she could see desire in his gunmetal blue gaze. "If we bond, I'll most likely leave you a widow."

She scowled. "You think I'm just going to sit around and let you do all the fighting on your own? Who's to say I wouldn't take a bullet first?"

A smirk lifted one side of his mouth. "Feisty little *tunrak.*" He reached up to brush a strand of loose hair from her cheek, sending sparks of heat straight through her middle. The moment ended too soon as he dropped his hand and cleared his throat. "But I'm not talking about a gunfight. My ionic heart is on the edge of failure. It's only a matter of time before it gives out completely. Mating would probably kill me." His voice grew gravelly over the words, as if admitting the weakness had sapped him of strength. He gave her a weak, half-hearted smile. "And while dying in your arms might be a nice way to go, you deserve more."

She dropped back to her heels, pulse hammering through her ears. "But you seem perfectly healthy!" More than healthy. He exuded maleness that made her knees wobbly. Twerp had begun buzzing in response to her increased blood pressure. "There has to be a way to fix you!"

"Not that Mek's aware of." Sighing, Noatak moved backward, putting space between them. "Give the other *terpaks* a chance. They're not too bad once you get to know them."

"My memory isn't the greatest, but I'm pretty sure *terpak* means asshole." She crossed her arms. "Not a very high recommendation, if you ask me."

A half-smile lifted a corner of his mouth and he shrugged. "You're right, but I count myself among them."

The back of her eyes pricked with girly tears and she gritted her teeth to fight them back. She'd been through hell to get this job, started what could be a dangerous procedure to fix her memory, and found a guy who actually appreciated her love of guns. Just when she thought everything was looking up, it all fell apart. *Not all of it.* She was still getting her brain fixed. Noatak had simply been a cherry on top, making the whole thing complete.

"I'm not willing to give up yet." She stepped forward until her breasts nearly brushed his chest, all but pinning him against the weapons bench behind him. "My mom always said 'it ain't over until the fat lady sings', and I don't even hear music yet. The nanites haven't started replicating, which means Mek has time to find a remedy for your ionic heart."

His eyes grew dark. "You are one tenacious woman."

She lifted her chin, her mouth within an inch of his. "I know what I want."

"Irresistible," he murmured. His hands met her waist, drawing her in as he leaned down to brush his lips against hers.

Lightning coursed through her system. Noatak jolted, as if feeling it, too, and his arms engulfed her, wrapping her in his masculine scent. She relaxed her lips, allowing his tongue to explore. His thighs were like rocks against hers, and she could feel his growing arousal against her lower abdomen.

She ran one hand along his jaw, the coarse fringe of his beard tickling her fingertips while she rolled her tongue against his. He tasted like a breath of clean air after a long shuttle ride, a promise of freedom and possibility. Wrapping her other arm around his waist, she pressed her body against his, gripping the solid muscles of his lower back. Her racing heart was making it hard to breathe, but she didn't want to stop. Never, ever stop.

He threaded one large hand into the hair at the back of her scalp and tugged her head to one side, burying his face against the side of her neck. Her skin seemed to come alive under the prickle of his beard, waves of electric heat flowing down her neck and chest until her nipples burned against her bra. His teeth latched onto her earlobe, and a shiver rocked her, spasming her core as if he'd just connected to every erogenous zone in her body.

"Oh, God," she breathed, clutching the back of his neck like a lifeline. Slipping her other hand over his pants, she palmed the hard, thick roll of his erection. He was huge. Throbbing. Hot. Her pussy responded with a pulsating heat of its own, and she flexed her hips to press herself against his thigh. He groaned in her ear, trailing kisses down her throat.

They'd begun rocking against each other, an increasing storm brewing between them that could only be satiated by one thing. Her mind was fuzzy with desire, a need for him that blocked out every other concern. She fumbled for his belt, needing to touch his skin, to wrap her fingers around his shaft, circle his waist with both legs, fill herself with his heat.

Twerp buzzed hard enough to sting her skin. "Marlis, I have d-detected a sharp spike in your temperature. This may be indicative of an adverse reaction to the nanites. Please seek the doctor's attention at once."

She shook her wrist, silencing the annoyance, but Noatak pushed her away, breathing hard. "*Anaq.* Kissing can cause the nanites to react. I shouldn't have let you get this close to me."

Twerp buzzed again. "I have alerted Mek to the situation. He is expecting you."

"Dammit, Twerp." It felt like she'd been waiting months for Noatak to touch her, and now this. "I feel fine. Really."

Noatak put his hands on her shoulders and turned her toward the door. "Twerp's right." His voice was thick. "We can't take chances. I'll escort you."

Normally, she'd be angry at the insinuation she needed help, but her legs were wobbly with desire, and she wasn't about to tell him to go away. "Thank you."

Taking his hand, she led him from the weapons locker. He chuckled as he followed behind her.

"What's so funny?"

"I was supposed to escort you, not the other way around."

She didn't allow her steps to falter. "Whatever. I want to ask Mek about fixing you, anyway."

They paused outside the door to the med bay. Mek flicked a glance at their linked hands, face impassive, but his words were colder than usual. "Twerp told me you were coming. Thank you for dropping her off, Noatak. I'll take it from here."

Marlis squeezed Noatak's hand tighter. "I want him to stay. I have some questions about his ionic heart condition."

Mek's eyebrows shot up and he looked straight at Noatak. "You told her?"

Noatak nodded. "Now it's your job to convince her I'm not fixable."

"Stop saying that." She glowered at Noatak.

Twerp said, "I would be very interested in learning about d-denaidan physiology, doctor, especially since Marlis will be working among you."

"Let's deal with one thing at a time, okay? You said her immune system has engaged?" Mek pulled the large scanner over to the exam table. "Marlis, please sit."

Marlis took a seat on the table, and Noatak released her hand to give the doctor room while Twerp provided a report. "Her white blood cell count is approaching levels which may forecast a developing autoimmune cascade."

Mek adjusted the scanner over her head. "This may hurt."

He gave her that same warning every time, but she'd never felt anything more than a warming vibration, much like Twerp's reminders. She closed her eyes anyway, envisioning the nanites inside her putting the puzzle pieces of her brain back together.

After a few moments, Mek grunted, and Marlis opened her eyes to find him frowning darkly at the scanner. Her breathing sharpened. "What is it?"

"Your immune system is definitely up in arms." He shook his head. "The nanites not only aren't replicating, but their overall saturation seems to have decreased. I'm worried your immune system might destroy the nanites before they take hold."

Twerp chimed in, "Since the nanites are supposed to integrate with Marlis's system much like an organ transplant, the medically suggested course of action for humans would be to administer anti-rejection medication."

Mek rubbed his temple. "I've thought of that. But it would make her susceptible to other infections and require a period of quarantine."

"Quarantine?" Marlis sat up straighter. "You mean put me in lockdown? God, no." She'd been in solitary confinement twice back on the carrier after losing her temper during therapy sessions, trapped with nothing but her own anger and heavy medication. She never wanted to experience anything like that again.

"This is the last of our nanites." Noatak put a hand on her shoulder. "You have to protect them."

She swallowed, mollified by his touch. *Protect the nanites.* It wasn't a gunfight, but it was an important job, not only for her own sake, but for the sake of an entire species. She grimaced and stared at the bare, slate gray wall across from her. "As long as I can keep Twerp with me, fine."

"I'm not ready to take that step yet," Mek said. "The scans don't show any increase in nanite concentrations, but perhaps that's merely because they're analyzing or fixing your synaptic pathways. I want to run another round of scans before we make any decisions." He pulled the scanner close. "Lie back, please."

Marlis did as he asked, but this time kept her eyes open, watching the doctor's face as he read the screen.

Mek tapped a few keys. Moving the scanner, he tapped a few more. His face had a strangely pale sheen she hoped was just a reflection from the scanner's screen. Finally, he shut down the screen and slid the entire unit back toward the wall. "I'm not seeing any new dendrite clusters."

"What are dendrite clusters?" Marlis asked, nausea roiling below her ribs.

"The physical connections within your brain."

"So what does that mean? More waiting?"

Mek met her gaze. "I'm afraid the nanites in your system are below viable levels. They're not going to fix you."

The air felt suddenly too heavy, as if a corpse had just collapsed on top of her. She flailed one arm toward Noatak, needing someone, something to ground her. Twerp buzzed at her wrist.

"The nanites are dead." Noatak's voice was a flat monotone, so calm it was frightening. "Right?"

"Technically, machines cannot die…" Twerp began.

But Marlis could no longer hear. The nanites had died under her care. Was she somehow responsible?

CHAPTER TWELVE

Noatak held Marlis's hand while Mek took a sample of her spinal fluid to confirm his suspicions. The nanites were dead, no more than inert microscopic bits of debris. He felt almost numb, as if the hope the nanites had provided had been a dream. Some part of him had clung to the belief there was a fix for his ionic heart and the possibility of a future. With the nanites gone, there was no hope for him, no healing for Marlis, and no chance for his entire race. Even the trickster god couldn't be laughing now.

Voice barely audible, Marlis asked, "Is this my fault?"

Mek patted her shoulder. "Of course not. The nanites were obviously too weak by the time we inoculated you."

But the question jarred Noatak from his daze. Marlis's temperature had risen in the weapons locker. Risen during their kiss. What if *he* was responsible? He'd been careful not to ping her, to only savor the physical interaction, the feel of her body, her lips, her scent. An ionic connection would've been a much deeper thing. Something more instinctual and uncontrolled. He'd been careful, hadn't he?

He looked at her face, her porcelain skin and tawny eyes. The strong but slender line of her throat. The rise and fall of her breasts from her rapid breathing. He wanted to take her in his arms and comfort her, but he had nothing to give. He could never be the one to give her anything, not now or ever.

Throat tight, he backed toward the door. "I'll tell the captain the bad news."

Marlis blanched, squeezing her eyes closed. "I'm sorry."

"Not your fault," Mek reiterated and glanced toward Noatak. "I'm going to keep Marlis here a while longer for observation. Tell Qaiyaan to call a crew meeting. Everyone should know."

Stumbling from the med bay in a daze, Noatak headed toward Qaiyaan's cabin.

What if it's my fault?

Knocking once on Qaiyaan's cabin door, he opened it and entered before the captain could respond.

Lisa lay on the bed in her panties, reading something on her polycom. She yanked a blanket over her naked torso. "Hey!"

Qaiyaan looked up from his desk near the view port. "What the hell?"

"I just came from the med lab." Noatak took a seat across from the captain with his back toward the bed. His words felt thick. "The nanites are dead."

"No!" Lisa gasped behind him amidst the rustle of fabric.

Qaiyaan winced and closed his eyes. "Are you certain? Perhaps they just need more time."

"Mek verified it several times." Noatak swallowed, forcing down bile. "I think it's my fault."

"What are you talking about?" Qaiyaan frowned at him.

"I kissed her."

Empathy dawned on the captain's face. "A kiss isn't enough to destroy the nanites."

"It might if they were already weak." Noatak refused to be assuaged. "I took her straight to the med bay, but it was too late."

"Slow down, Noatak. We all know the nanites can cause blackouts when agitated, but the only thing strong enough to actually kill them is the denaidan mating frequency."

"Mek said they were struggling. The kiss made Marlis's immune system reject them." The more Noatak thought about it, the more he knew this had been his fault. He'd been careless, greedy for Marlis's touch even though he knew it could never amount to anything. Now not only was his race doomed, but Marlis'd been denied a chance for healing.

"*Iluq*, if the nanites were that vulnerable, Mek would've kept Marlis in the med bay, not let her run around among the crew."

Noatak wasn't listening. He had to make this right. If there was one thing he'd learned about regret, it was that looking back didn't move you forward. There was only one solution to losing the nanites. "We have to go after Doug. Now."

"We're working on that." Qaiyaan nodded. "We're just waiting for Kashatok to dig up more information."

"We've seen how long that takes. Doug could be dead before we track him down."

"Kashatok's working on it, believe me."

Noatak shook his head. He had another plan in mind. "Syndicorp still wants Lisa back, right? The scientists on the *Icarus* especially, I'd imagine."

Qaiyaan scowled at him. "We're not using her as bait."

"No, but we could use knowledge of her to draw them out."

"What are you suggesting?"

Noatak grinned. Nothing better than a dangerous mission to take the mind off one's troubles. "I'll send a message on Galactic Ops' old channel and claim to have information about Lisa, but that I'll only give it to the captain of the *Icarus* in person. I'll take our shuttle and meet them at some obscure location. Once they bring me on board, I'll drop a tracker. You'll be able to locate the *Icarus* and hijack them."

Qaiyaan crossed his arms. "They'll be on the lookout for that kind of thing. And we can't allow them to get their hands on you. You know too much."

Taking a deep breath to steady himself, Noatak said, "They won't get anything out of me. I'll use a suicide pill right after I drop the tracker."

"Are you insane?" Qaiyaan rose from his chair, staring Noatak down as if he was considering throwing him in the brig. "A suicide pill?"

Lisa had dressed and made her way to Qaiyaan's side. She looped one arm over his shoulder and pulled him back into his seat. "I appreciate you wanting to help save my brother, but Qaiyaan's right. This is too extreme."

"It's not." He swallowed. "I'm already dying, Qaiyaan."

As he explained about his ionic heart, Qaiyaan's face lost its color. Lisa covered her mouth with one hand, eyes glistening. When he'd finished, she lowered the hand and reached for his. "Are you damaged because you helped save me?"

When they'd rescued her from the Cartel, he'd extended his ionic shield to protect her during burn. The added strain on his system certainly hadn't helped his condition, but the root of the problem was his fault, not hers.

"No." He squeezed her hand and met her gaze steadily, so she'd know he was sincere. "I've known my ionic system was failing for years. Too much stim use while I was in the service. But I have enough left in me to do this. I don't want to go out like an old man. If I succeed at this, my death will at least mean something. I'll free your brother, get nanites for mates, and help Marlis heal."

"Marlis?" Lisa narrowed her eyes at him. "This is about her, isn't it?"

"This is about our entire race," Noatak said, pulling free of her grasp. "But I do want her future to be happy."

Lisa raised her brows. "I bet it won't be if you're gone."

"We hardly know each other." He swallowed, thinking of Marlis insisting she wanted to be with him. She was perfect, more than he'd ever imagined possible in a woman. But he could never be what she deserved. "She'll move on. But I should go before she grows any more attached."

Sighing, Qaiyaan dropped his chin to his chest. "I hate to admit it, but it's the best plan we've had so far." He rose. "I'll have Kashatok host a crew meeting in the *Kinship's* galley so everyone can attend. We need to tell the men about the nanites and he can provide any new information he might have about the *Icarus*."

Chest tight, Noatak nodded. He knew his captain well; this was Qaiyaan's version of agreeing to the plan. Assuming Kashatok hadn't come up with a wild scheme of his own, Noatak would be on his way soon. Hopefully, he'd be remembered as a hero, the man who'd ensured future mates for his people. And once he was gone, Marlis could move on and bond with one of the remaining crew.

He should go to his bunk and prepare himself to meet *Ellam Cua*. Make sure his affairs were in order. Instead, he headed back to the med bay. All he wanted to do between now and his death was spend time with Marlis.

CHAPTER THIRTEEN

Marlis tamped down her anger as she left Mek behind in the med bay. The nanites were gone, along with the promise of healing her brain and any chance to be with Noatak. Fuck, her job might even be on the line. What was the crew going to do with her now that she'd basically killed their only hope of having mates? She was useless. A Weapons Specialist with memory problems who couldn't even manage to keep micro computers alive in her brain.

She stormed around the corner and smack into Noatak's chest. "Umph."

His hands grasped her shoulders, steadying her. Even without the nanites, electricity raced across her skin, tingling her erogenous zones. She looked up into his face. Deep within his eyes, she could see sadness. Yearning. It was like looking in a mirror.

She tried to smile, but it felt like a grimace. "How'd the captain take the news?"

Noatak sighed. "He's asked to hold a meeting on the *Kinship* to tell everyone. I came to get you and Mek."

Great. She'd hoped she had a little more time. Perhaps a chance to talk to Emmy before facing the rest of the crew.

Noatak took her hand and squeezed gently. "They won't blame you."

The tender gesture made her throat tighten. She nodded, wanting to believe him. He told Mek about the meeting, then led her across the boarding tube to the larger ship. The tightness in her throat moved to her chest as they entered the galley. Kashatok's crew already had a bottle of rum circulating among them, possibly suspecting what was coming, and the mood was somber as Marlis sat near one end of the table next to Emmy. Noatak calmly took the chair on her other side. How could he be so stoic? She wanted to run and scream and shoot things.

Once Mek had joined them, Qaiyaan took a chair at the head of the table and cleared his throat. "You probably suspect why we've called you here." The crew rumbled, nodding heads and frowning. "Mek has confirmed that the nanites are dead."

It was as if the room itself gasped, and Tovik asked, "What happened?"

"They were no longer viable by the time I inoculated her," Mek said, accepting the bottle of rum from Tovik and taking a swallow. "It's not Marlis's fault."

Emmy reached under the table and squeezed Marlis's hand while the men grumbled and muttered.

Marlis kept her focus on Qaiyaan, unable to look at the crew or Emmy or even Noatak. She'd let everyone down.

Qaiyaan continued, "This means we need to double our efforts to find Lisa's brother. Noatak has come up with a plan that may work. But there will be a cost." He gestured to his First Mate. "I'm going to let him explain."

A plan? Marlis should've known Noatak would come up with something. She dared a sideways look in his direction.

Noatak's face was sterner than usual as he looked around at the gathered men. "If the lab's on the *Icarus* like we think, our biggest difficulty will be finding the flagship. It's equipped with the latest cloaking technology and appears to be operating under comm silence."

Marlis frowned. Why did the *Icarus* sound familiar? She lifted her wrist and spoke in a low voice to Twerp. "Twerp, do I know that name?"

"Your sister is stationed on the SNV flagship *Icarus*," Twerp supplied, loud enough for everyone to hear.

The bottom dropped out of Marlis's stomach.

Chignik lowered the rum bottle to the table with a loud *thunk*. "*Anaq!* Did you just say your sister's on the *Icarus?*"

Everything came back to Marlis in a flood. She pressed her palm flat against her thigh to prevent herself from reaching for the comfort of her E-11. "Attie got promoted to corporal just before I left." She swallowed. Stupid memory had failed her again. She should've recognized the name during that first debrief. "She's the admiral's administrative attaché."

Noatak's face paled. "You never mentioned that."

"Can you find out where the ship's at?" Tovik asked.

"Better yet, can you get us on board?" Chignik added.

Noatak rubbed his face. "*Uminaq*. It's a corp flagship. The crew isn't allowed to reveal their location, and they're definitely not going to give us a tour just because Marlis is with us. Let's stick to my plan."

"The one where you commit suicide?" Qaiyaan crossed his arms and raised an eyebrow at his First Mate. "I'm up for alternate suggestions."

Marlis gasped, and the entire galley erupted with stunned confusion. She turned to Noatak. "What's he talking about?"

Noatak sighed and raised his chin defiantly. "I'll send a message out that I have information about Lisa. The corp wants her back, so they'll bite. Once I'm on board the *Icarus*, I'll plant a tracker, leaving you a trail to follow and hijack the ship."

"But he'll have to kill himself to keep them from interrogating him," Qaiyaan added.

The galley grew louder as men pounded the table and shoved back chairs, arguing with each other. Tovik had risen and was standing toe-to-toe with Noatak, gesturing wildly.

Noatak stood his ground. "I'm dying, anyway. Think of this as my final wish. You can thank me by naming your *terpak* kids after me."

More questions flew. "What do you mean, you're dying?"

"What the fuck, Noatak?"

Marlis's pulse raced and Twerp buzzed her wrist until her hand felt numb. She'd been through enough military strategy simulations to know this was a bad plan, and not only because it meant Noatak's death. "This plan is stupid." She turned to Qaiyaan. "You're the captain. Don't let him do this."

Qaiyaan raised an eyebrow, probably thinking about punishing her for insubordination, but she didn't care. Noatak couldn't be allowed to die. Not like this. The captain's gaze softened, and he turned away from her. "It is stupid. But it's all we have."

Twerp's usually soothing voice cut through the tension. "May I offer a suggestion?"

The crew fell silent, staring at Marlis's wrist. Twerp continued, "I have analyzed the feasibility of this plan, and determined there is a seventy-eight point eight percent chance the *Icarus* would detect a tracker and nullify it before it could broadcast a signal."

"See?" Tovik said, pointing at Twerp and glaring toward Noatak. At least he seemed to be on her side.

"If the immediate goal is to find the flagship," Twerp's usually smooth voice stuttered. "I suggest we allow Marlis to send her sister a message with a return receipt. The receipt can be encoded with a universal pin that will not provide ongoing spatial data, but it will provide the ship's location at that moment in time. There is a minimal six point five percent chance the *Icarus* would detect the true purpose of such a marker."

Chignik clapped his hands once. "*Assirpaa!* A marker within a marker! And if she keeps up a dialogue, we'll get a stream of information that might provide a heading."

"C-correct," Twerp said.

Noatak's face was dark. "A universal pin can't provide the same information as a tracker. You won't know when the ship enters and exits burn, so you won't be able to sneak up on them."

Tovik raised a hand. "I still have that cloaking device from the rakwiji ship the Cartel sent after us. It's not the latest technology, but it could work well enough to hide a shuttle."

"A shuttle? As in, two or three people?" Noatak crossed his arms and shook his head. "A team that small can't take down a flagship."

"But we might be able to get on and then off again before they notice," Marlis said, her mind racing. "And maybe I could convince Attie to leave with us. I know the layout of the *Icarus*. The carrier I grew up on is one of its sister ships."

"Are there alternate ways to get on board other than the standard hatchways?" Qaiyaan asked.

"Um," Marlis blanched, trying to remember details about the carrier. "Maybe Twerp knows?"

"Accessing." Twerp hiccuped a couple of times. "The *Icarus* is equipped with eight torpedo tubes which lead into the artillery bay. Assuming the weapons are not armed, one might be able to enter the hull plating at any of those points."

"*Assirpaa*! I'm so glad we hired you!" Tovik's face glowed.

Qaiyaan scratched his beard. "At least this plan doesn't include anyone killing themselves."

"It's still suicide!" Noatak's face had a blue-green tinge and his chest rose and fell rapidly. "You can't send Marlis."

Marlis stood slowly, glowering at Noatak. "Are you saying I'm incapable? Because you hired me for just this kind of job."

His mouth dropped open. "That's not what I mean at all."

"So it's settled." She lifted her chin and faced the rest of the crew. "Noatak and I will track down the *Icarus*."

CHAPTER FOURTEEN

The *Hardship* dropped the shuttle near Zyrinic Eight, the last known location of the *Icarus*. Noatak checked that Marlis was secure in her harness. He was still fuming about having her along. She wouldn't be safe just because she was someone's sister. And if she was in danger, he couldn't take the easy way out with a suicide pill. He needed to stay alive to protect her. *Uminaq*, this wasn't how this mission was supposed to happen.

"Stop scowling," she said. "I'd prefer not to be pissed at each other for the entire mission."

This might be a fool's errand, but at least he got some alone-time with Marlis. Small consolation, considering nothing could come of it even if they survived, but right now he'd accept any pleasure he could get.

Letting out a slow breath, he hit the thrusters. The shuttle didn't have the range of a burn drive, but Tovik's modifications had given the propulsion unit a boost, and Noatak's stomach lurched with the acceleration. He wasn't used to traveling without using his ionic power, but he couldn't risk giving himself an ionic system failure when he needed to stay alive for Marlis. The shuttle slowed as it reached its coordinates, and the stars outside the view screen realigned, revealing the pale blue disk of Zyrinic Eight's nearby moon.

He turned to Marlis. "All right. As Joy's so fond of saying; showtime."

Marlis grinned at him—why did he love that so much? Her excitement for this mission was almost infectious. Almost. He forced his face back into his usual stoic lines.

After entering her sister's messaging address, Marlis leaned toward the comm. "Hey, Attie, it's me! Just wanted to let you know I'm okay. It feels like we're jumping all over the galaxy with deliveries. No real action yet. Being a guard is kinda boring so far. I know, I know, you and Dad will both hope I never see combat. But damn, I'm itching for something more interesting than flying from colony to colony. I did meet a hot guy, though." She wiggled her eyebrows, then looked over her shoulder as if she'd heard something. "Shit, gotta go. I'll call again later."

Ending the call, she looked triumphantly at Noatak.

"What the hell was that?" he asked. The less the corp knew about his presence, the better.

"Calm down." She crinkled her nose. "Now she's sure to open the next message I send right away."

He settled back in his seat, trying not to smile. "You're more conniving than you give yourself credit for."

She grinned. "Thank you." The grin faded. "Although I'm feeling a little guilty using my sister like this."

"I understand." He nodded, appreciating how important family was to her. "If things go as planned, you won't have to worry about her anymore."

"That would be a relief." She stretched both arms over her head, drawing his gaze to her breasts, then rose and stood in the low doorway to the cockpit, the curve of her hip right at his eye level as she looked into the small passenger area. "What shall we do while we wait for her to open the message?"

He swallowed, wrenching his gaze from her perfectly round ass. All he could think about was how she would feel cupped in both hands.

Her glance over her shoulder revealed a sly smile that told him she knew exactly what he was thinking. The woman was a *tunrak* for sure, sent to tempt him by *Ellam Cua* himself. On impulse, he reached over and smacked her butt cheek.

She startled, banging her head on the overhead beam between the cockpit and the back end.

He was out of his seat in an instant. He'd smacked his head on that beam too many times to count. "You okay?"

"I'm fine. Didn't expect you to be so playful." She turned to face him, one hand against her forehead while a tiny trickle of blood streamed toward her eye. "You're taller than I am. How do you keep from knocking yourself out in here all the time?"

He laughed, despite himself. "Suffer enough bumps, you learn to be careful." He herded her to the shuttle's rear and pulled out a bunk stowed against the wall. "Sit. I'll get a med kit."

While he patched her up, he shook his head. "*Ellam Cua* has an evil sense of humor."

"Why would you say such a thing?" She winced as he secured adhesive to her forehead. "Isn't *Ellam Cua* your god?"

"He's a trickster." Balling up the used swabs and adhesive backing, he aimed for the refuse bin and tossed. The jumbled mess stuck to the lid, not heavy enough to activate the expulsion unit. He turned back to Marlis. "After I volunteered for this mission—which is still probably suicide, by the way, I hope you realize that—all I could think about was spending my last moments with you. *Ellam Cua* granted me my wish. The irony must have him in stitches."

She tilted her head. "Well, what can we do to make him laugh even more?" The seductive smile on her face even made the bandage across her forehead look sexy. "It could be awhile before we hear back from Attie."

Her innuendo made his cock surge to life. He'd never imagined wanting a woman this badly. She had a hold on him he couldn't explain. He'd do anything for her, and if she wanted to mess around, he was game. There would be no climax for him, but he would give her a hell of a good time.

Rising from his seat on the edge of the bunk, he looked down at her, savoring every luscious curve. "I have a few ideas."

She licked her lips, one hand moving over her collarbone. Everything she did was seductive. Surely she knew the effect she had on him.

"Lean back." He moved to the bed and straddled her, both knees on the hard mattress.

She fell back onto her elbows, her gaze never leaving his.

He put one palm between her breasts and pushed gently, forcing her all the way down. Now he towered over her, cock thrumming against his pants. He couldn't take things all the way, but he was going to take as much as he could. Leaning forward with his weight on his hands, he captured her mouth, flicking his tongue greedily between her parted lips. She tasted amazing, sweet and fresh and warm. He dropped to his elbows, burying his hands into her hair and driving his tongue into her.

Her hands fisted the hem of his shirt, stretching the fabric to expose his skin. He contracted his abs, letting her pull the shirt up and over his shoulders, breaking the kiss only long enough to be free of the shirt. Once his lips claimed hers again, he slid one hand along her ribs to her hip, pausing there to slide a thumb beneath her waistband into the hollow beside her hipbone. She flexed against him, and he continued stroking along the outside of her thigh, aligning his body against hers. They would be such a perfect match. He could only imagine the exquisite warmth of her pussy around him, her legs hooked over his hips as he drove inside her with pure abandon.

But that couldn't be. He had to satiate himself on everything but that.

Using the hand still in her hair, he pulled her head gently to one side, giving him access to her throat. Nipping and suckling his way down its gentle curve, he filled himself with her fresh linen scent. He moved the hand at her hip upward, sliding beneath her shirt, palm skimming her flesh until it came to rest under the swell of her breast. *Assirpaa*, her breast. He wanted to see it, touch it, taste it.

Pulling back, he shoved her shirt upward, exposing a swath of creamy skin. A simple bra confined her ample breasts, the kind issued in the service, but he found it sexier than lace. It was pure Marlis.

While she wriggled off her shirt, he slid one hand beneath her back and unfastened the bra's clasp. Her breasts popped free, perfect globes large enough that his palm could barely cover one. Each rosy pink nipple begged to be tasted. Leaning forward, he captured one aroused tip, drawing as much of her breast into his mouth as he could and circling his tongue around the puckered areola.

She moaned and arched upward to meet him, encouraging him to take more. The nipple hardened beneath his tongue, and her hands roamed his naked sides and back. She widened her legs, allowing his cock to press against her core of heat through their clothing.

Ellam Cua. He wanted to bury himself in her. To fill her and claim her and make her his. Clenching his ass muscles, he pushed against her cloth-covered entrance, groaning at the exquisite pressure. Sliding down her body, he lapped at her skin, tasting the softness of her flesh, while his hands undid the clasp of her pants. She complied by lifting her hips as he pushed the waistband down, taking her panties with them. Now she was fully exposed to him, the downy mound of hair glistening with her arousal. "Beautiful."

She moaned as his breath brushed over her skin, breasts heaving as she panted. One of her hands slid down her abdomen and delved into her cleft, pleasuring herself in a way that nearly sent him over the edge just watching her.

Placing one hand over hers, he slid his fingers into her tight folds. She cried out, bucking upward, and his cock surged with need. She was so wet. So perfect.

Her free hand grabbed his, urging him deeper. He added a second finger and buried both digits to the top knuckles. The heated ridges of her pussy quivered against him and she gasped, her slickness intensifying. She bucked and pulsed, her own fingers still working the nub of her clit. "God, yes. Be inside me."

The scent of her arousal engulfed him. He had to be careful, or he'd become an animal. Tear off his clothes and take her without regard for the consequences.

Pulling back, he stared at her glorious sex while he plunged two, then three fingers in and out of her. Her middle finger furiously worked her clit while she watched him with hooded eyes.

"You are so sexy." His voice came out rough and breathy. His ionic instincts were pushing his boundaries, but he kept himself under control, focusing only on her pleasure. Curling his fingers to hit that spot deep inside her that would bring her to the edge.

Her pussy convulsed. The hand on her clit jerked free, clutching the mattress beside her. She threw her head back, eyes closed as a moan rose from her lips.

Lowering his head, he let his mouth take over for her fingers, laving his tongue over her swollen nub while his fingers continued driving inside her. *Ellam Cua.* She tasted even better than she smelled, her pheromones permeating his senses. He clamped his lips around her clit and sucked.

Her moan rose to a scream that was pure music to his ears as she exploded around him, drenching his hand and beard with wetness.

He slowed his pace, but refused to stop until he was sure he'd wrung every shudder from her body.

She lay there panting, her alabaster skin flushed a glorious pink. Reaching weakly for him, she whispered, "Come here. You should get yours, too."

Oh, Ellam Cua, you are cruel. The one thing he could never have with her was full satisfaction; nanites or not, it was a death sentence for one of them. He wrapped one hand around hers. "I can't, remember?"

She sagged against the mattress, her gaze suddenly pained.

Grabbing a thick square of gauze from the med kit, he dried his beard, then lowered himself beside her, wrapping her in his arms. His cock throbbed in a painful protest, but he'd grown accustomed to ignoring its demands. He brushed his lips against her ear. "It's enough I got to experience you. No matter what happens, I'll cherish that forever."

They lay together, content, until the comm beeped with an incoming message.

Marlis sat bolt upright. "Attie."

She looked down at him, and he could tell she wasn't ready for their moment to an end, either. But the mission had to take precedence. He pressed a kiss to her palm and rose. "You have to answer."

Marlis scrambled back into her clothing and they returned to the cockpit. Attie had indeed responded to the message. This was his first glimpse of her sister, and he was startled by how alike they looked as her image filled the screen. "Hey Marlis, I got your messages. I'm thrilled you found a job, but it would be good to know what ship you're on so I can calm Dad down. He's on the warpath, insisting you've been kidnapped into slave labor or something."

He unthreaded the location code from the return receipt while Marlis watched the rest of the message. She'd been right about hooking her sister with a love interest, and he tried to shut out the details of Attie's latest fling while he worked. His heartbeat sped up when he realized the flagship was close; it'd never left Zyrinic Eight's solar system.

After her sister's message ended, he said, "That message came from within this system. Unless they plan to burn out of here soon, we could be on them within the next jump."

She nodded, frowning. "I'd hoped we'd have more time."

Reaching over, he took her hand. "There will never be enough time."

CHAPTER FIFTEEN

Marlis felt torn as she recorded her next message. She never wanted her time with Noatak to end, but they were on a mission, and they had to act now, before the *Icarus* left the system. Knowing her sister would detect something wrong if she acted too chipper, Marlis half-invented a problem for her next message. "Hey, Sis. I know I just messaged you, but I wish you were here to talk to. The guy I mentioned before? He says he wants to be with me, but then keeps making excuses why he can't."

Noatak raised an eyebrow at her but didn't remark, keeping most of his attention on the console.

They were orbiting one of Zyrinic's inner planets, a gas giant surrounded by several rings. The fine particulate that made up the outer ring was wreaking havoc on their sensors, but this was near the last pinpointed location of the *Icarus*.

Just as she sent her message, Noatak leaned closer to the view screen and began furiously tapping the sensor keypad. "*Uminaq*, there they are. I need to get our cloak up."

She scanned the glowing ring of the planet and spotted the massive flagship doing a lazy rotation, ripples of particulate billowing around its sharp angles and jutting weapon turrets. Her pulse raced. If they were spotted now, the mission would be over. If the *Icarus* decided to shoot first and ask questions later, they'd be vaporized. She held her breath, waiting.

Once the cloaking system was up, Noatak raised his hands off the console and focused on the view screen. "I don't think they detected us through the particulate ring, but we'll hang out here a few minutes to be sure."

Letting out a long sigh, she let her gaze rove over the swirling orange planet's surface. "Why are they parked here? This is an uninhabitable planet."

"No idea, but they just made our mission one hell of a lot easier."

After what felt like forever, Noatak nodded. "If they knew we were here, they'd've demanded identification by now. Let's move."

With a nod, she retreated to the back of the shuttle and put on a vacuum suit. Noatak would fly the tiny shuttle along the massive flagship's underside, moving slowly enough to avoid any proximity detectors. Apparently, the pirates had done this kind of thing before.

The vacuum suit was a snug fit over her breasts, and she was struggling with the seal when a sharp jolt stung her wrist. Pausing, she looked at her wristband. "Twerp, you okay?"

Twerp let out several garbled words, out of which Marlis could only make out, "... reaction t-to certain frequenciesssss..." The sentence ended on a hiss of static.

"Twerp?" A lump filled her throat. "What's going on?"

From the cockpit, a stranger's voice came over the comm. "Unidentified vessel, please shut down all systems and prepare to be towed."

The ship shuddered, and she stumbled forward to where Noatak was frantically tapping the keypads. "What's happening?"

"They spotted us. *Uminaq*, they have us in a tractor beam."

She gripped the head rests on the cockpit chairs and tried to remain upright as the ship jolted again. "Fuck, do as they say. We haven't done anything wrong. Maybe they'll let us go."

"I'm on their most-wanted list, Marlis. There's no getting out of this for me. But you can." He grabbed her, kissing her hard, then swung her in front of himself before flicking the comm to life. "I'm holding one of your citizens hostage. Release the tractor beam or I'll kill her."

She struggled against his solid grip, more out of instinct than fear. "No!"

"We do not deal with terrorists," the man on the other end of the comm replied.

The shuttle jerked forward, driving her hard against Noatak's chest. She couldn't take a breath, and her vision closed in as the flagship seemed to draw closer at breakneck speed. A strange tingling surrounded her, almost a numb sensation.

And then the world went black.

Noatak instinctively engaged his ionic shielding and wrapped it around Marlis when the tractor beam jerked the shuttle forward with a force that had to be close to ten G's. He held on as long as he could, ionic heart ramped to an agonizing pace. The shuttle hurtled toward an open landing bay, but he blacked out before they reached it.

He woke in a tiny cell barely large enough for him to lie flat on the floor. There was no furniture, no fixtures, no panels, no door that he could see. After taking a quick assessment of himself—his chest and head hurt, but there appeared to be no other damage—he stood, scouring the corners of the bare metal walls for any sign of a camera or an access panel.

"Hello?" His voice seemed too loud in the small space.

His last memory was of clutching Marlis against him, putting all of his willpower into shielding her from the deadly force of the beam. Had she survived? *Anaq*, had *he* survived? For all he knew, this was *Ellam Cua's* perverse version of hell.

Suddenly, a section of the wall slid aside, revealing a sparkling transparent energy shield separating him from the interior of a brightly lit laboratory. Stainless steel counters, several empty exam tables, and scattered medical equipment that Mek would've salivated over filled the room. On the far wall, two other doors similar to Noatak's shone with energy fields.

A man with shiny dark hair stepped around one of the lab tables, eyeing him with a sick, appraising hunger. "In my wildest dreams, I never imagined I'd get my hands on a denaidan male." He smiled, showing straight white teeth. "Fortune must be smiling on me."

Noatak moved as close to the energy shield as he dared. "What the fuck does that mean?"

The man looked down at an oversized polycom in his hands. "Noatak qutar'Kon, a corporal in Galactic Ops, AWOL for fifteen years and wanted for acts of piracy and terrorism." He looked back up, eyes gleaming. "You're so lucky we found you. Any other ship would've executed you on the spot." Setting the polycom aside, he made a gesture and three well-armed troopers appeared from the unseen corners of the room. "My name's Dr. Dollard. We'll be spending a lot of time together."

One trooper moved toward Noatak, and the shield dropped. Noatak eyed the man, wondering if he could take him out with an ionic pulse. He was surprised to even be alive after exerting himself in the shuttle, and calling on his ionic power now might very well kill him. But he still needed to find Marlis, no matter the cost.

Dollard said, "The dampening in here makes using your ionic abilities impossible, so don't even try. Come out."

Uminaq. Of course they'd thought of that. He stepped into the lab, familiarizing himself with the layout and looking for any potential weapons. "The woman I was with—my hostage. She survive?"

The doctor was aligning surgical tools neatly on a tray next to a stainless steel exam table. "The tractor beam should've turned you both to pulp. Our captain was quite surprised to find you both alive." Dollard met his gaze with a smirk. "It's also how I knew we'd captured a denaidan."

It was all Noatak could do not to sag to his knees with relief. Marlis was alive.

Adjusting the exam table so it stood on end, Dollard gestured toward it. "If you please."

Several straps dangled from the table's edges. *Restraints*. So he was to be tortured. One of the troopers nudged Noatak in the lower back, forcing him forward. Noatak tried to keep his voice even. "What are you planning to do?"

"Denaidan ionic powers have always fascinated me, especially the different way each gender uses the ability. Your males are so brutish with their ionic strength, while your females excel at empathic connections that are nearly impossible to test empirically."

"You fucking killed all our females," Noatak snarled. "How would you know?"

"Mmm." The man picked up a stim-gun. "I recommend you cooperate if you want to live."

"Keep that thing away from me." Noatak stepped back, but the men on either side of him caught his arms and dragged him forward, cinching him down.

Dollard jabbed a stim-gun into Noatak's arm.

The adrenaline already coursing through Noatak's veins ignited. He yelled and jerked hard against the straps.

Non-plussed, Dollard gave him several more inoculations before waving a scanner over Noatak's chest, face pinched into a frown. "Hmm. It appears you've sustained some ionic system damage over the years."

"Only because of people like you," Noatak spat. His mouth felt full of cotton, and spittle drooled from the corners.

"Unfortunate." The doctor stepped back, wiping a fleck from the back of his hand. "This is a significant flaw in my data set. Regardless, it will be interesting to see how the nanites perform in an ionic system like yours."

Turning, Dollard headed for the exit, his goons close behind, leaving Noatak alone in the lab.

Breath ragged, Noatak jerked against the straps over and over, all the while thinking, *Holy Ellam Cua, I've just been injected with nanites.*

CHAPTER SIXTEEN

Marlis woke to the inside of a med bay. Bright lights shone directly overhead, adding daggers to her already splitting headache. She tried to roll over to escape the glare, but couldn't move. Her arms and legs were strapped to a cot. Panic seized her, and she thrashed against the bindings.

An unfamiliar man in a crisp blue Syndicorp doctor's uniform filled her vision, blocking the overhead lights. "Calm down, Miss Swan."

All she could think was that she was in lockdown again. *What did I do?* "You can release me now."

He backed away, allowing a familiar face to appear. "Attie?" Marlis held back the catch in her voice. She still didn't remember why she was here, but she knew panic would only make things worse. *There is no danger.* "Please tell him to unstrap me."

Attie looked over her shoulder. "Are the straps necessary?"

The restraints loosened. Forcing herself to remain sedate, she sat up, looking around the unfamiliar med bay. "Where am I?"

"You don't remember what happened?" Attie asked.

Marlis touched the bandage covering a sore bump on her forehead as memories slowly returned. *Noatak. The shuttle. The Resistance.* Her pulse spiked again. She must've been captured. Where was Noatak?

And why wasn't Twerp buzzing? She reached for her wrist and found the band gone. "Twerp? Where's Twerp?"

Attie shook her head. "Our tech team had to confiscate your AI. They'll give it back once they've pulled the information and made sure it's not bugged."

Marlis nearly choked. What kind of information about the Resistance might Twerp reveal? Her voice sounded tinny and fake as she calmly asked, "Why would you think I'm bugged?"

"You're traveling with a known criminal," a man's voice came from the door across the large bay. Marlis turned to find a small man wearing a black admiral's uniform approaching, followed by three well-armed troopers. He seemed rather young to be an admiral, with a head of brown hair untouched by gray. "A pirate who would do anything to get his hands on Syndicorp technology."

"Noatak?" The name left her lips before she could reign herself in. Noatak'd told her he was a wanted man. That's why his original plan had included suicide. Oh God, had he committed suicide? She shot to her feet and looked around the med bay, hoping to see his familiar copper skin. The only other patient was a woman in a bed at the far end of the room. "Where is he?"

Attie put a hand on her shoulder. "Don't worry. The pirates can't hurt you now."

More memories crashed over Marlis. The crew of the *Icarus* must think she'd been a hostage. Noatak'd set this all up to make her appear innocent. Fuck, had they executed him? She needed to know if he was alive.

"Corporal Swan," the admiral addressed Attie. "You have confirmed this is your sister?"

Attie stiffened, her hand moving up in salute. "Yes, sir."

With a stiff nod, he focused his icy-blue gaze on Marlis. "My name is Admiral Olly, standing officer of the SNV *Icarus*, with full authority under Syndicorp law to carry out immediate punishment to traitors of the regime."

Marlis swallowed, her breath coming in short gasps. Noatak was probably dead. She couldn't make her eyes focus, so she concentrated on her breathing. *In. Out. In. Out.* She longed for Twerp's familiar buzz.

The admiral continued, "Marlis Swan, you stand accused of associating with known pirates and conspiring to engage in illegal activities against Syndicorp and its allies."

"Sir—" Attie began, but was cut off by the admiral raising one hand.

"You will remain silent, Corporal. Your part in this has yet to be determined."

Fuck. Not only was Noatak dead, she'd put Attie in danger. None of this mission was going according to plan. She reached instinctively for her weapon.

The troopers behind the admiral pointed their rifles at her just as she realized her holster was empty. *Fuck, they disarmed me!*

Attie gently squeezed Marlis's arm. "Take a breath, Marlis. There is no danger." Her sister moved part way between Marlis and the armed guards. "Sir, please forgive her. She suffers from PTSD."

"I've read her file," the admiral continued, gaze still cold. "I understand she was turned down for active duty due to mental health issues. However, I will not accept that as an excuse. You are facing a charge of treason. How do you plead?"

Treason? She could barely breathe, barely think. She had to get a grip on herself if she hoped to get her and Attie through this alive. What would Attie do? She met her sister's steady blue gaze, but behind her eyes, Marlis detected a reflection of her own panic. Her sister had always been her rock. Now Marlis needed to do whatever it took to save Attie.

She turned back to the admiral. If he believed Marlis had mental health issues, she could play the victim. The thought sickened her. She'd never used her condition as an excuse for anything, never wanted to be considered an imbecile, but right now, it was all she had. Thankfully, Noatak'd given her a plausible cover. She shoved aside the thought that it had been his final act. Hopefully, she'd have time to grieve later.

Fluttering both hands, Marlis said, "I'm sorry, sir. I'm just so confused and frightened right now." Thinking of Noatak, she let tears prick her eyes. "I didn't know he was a pirate until... until..."

Admiral Olly seemed unaffected. "Tell me why you're here, and I may mitigate your sentence."

"I was hired as a guard on a cargo ship. That's all I know."

"What's your cargo?"

"I never asked, sir." She screwed her face into what she hoped was a look of terror. "Please. I need Twerp. She's the only thing that keeps me calm."

"Twerp?" He narrowed his eyes.

Attie answered, "That's what she calls her service AI."

A muscle in the admiral's jaw bulged. "Our tech team has been unable to revive your AI. It appears the pirates planted a self-destruct in its code, which was activated by our tractor beam."

Marlis gasped, legs growing weak. "Twerp's dead?"

Attie's hand on her arm tightened, and she gasped. "Oh, no."

Her chest couldn't contain any more heartache. *Not Twerp, too.* Marlis refused to believe it. Yet Twerp's last words to her had ended in static. Noatak and Twerp, both gone in a flash. Grief threatened to shut down all her logic, and she sank, trembling, backward onto the cot.

Admiral Olly took a step forward. "Tell me why you were sending messages to Corporal Swan."

Shit. Her heart threatened to explode. Attie might be punished for this entire mess. Marlis looked up into the admiral's face, her vision a tunnel she could barely see the end of. "She's my sister, sir. Don't you ever call your sister?"

"Don't try to be smart with me, Miss Swan." The admiral crossed his arms. "Your shuttle emerged from a burn cycle in this exact location around an uninhabited planet. No cargo on board, no reason to be here, and we've traced a hidden tracker embedded in your messages. What is your mission?"

She couldn't think of an excuse. At least the tears blurring her sight were real. She blinked, forcing one to flow down her cheek. "I'm just a guard," she choked out. "I don't even know how to pilot a shuttle.

Noatak seduced me. I thought he was special and wanted him to meet my sister. That's all."

He turned to Attie. "This is getting us nowhere."

Attie frowned. "Sir, my sister's highly susceptible to manipulation, and this pirate obviously capitalized on that. Her messages went on and on about her new boyfriend. You saw in her file that our father applied for an extended dependency waiver, but it wasn't approved before she ran away. Whatever those pirates did to her has obviously exacerbated her PTSD."

Highly susceptible? Ran away? Marlis took a shaky breath. Attie knew she hadn't run away, and she sure as hell didn't think Marlis was easily manipulated. So Attie must be lying to help her. Of all the people in the universe, she could trust Attie. *There is no danger.* Marlis reached for her sister's hand. Much as it grated on her, she needed to keep playing the imbecile card. And Attie's life depended on Marlis's innocence.

"Sir, when can I have my AI back?" She knew she'd already asked, but asking again was one way to make him believe she was slow.

Olly made a derisive noise in the back of his throat and looked at Attie. "Is she serious?"

"Sir, you read her file." Attie squeezed Marlis's hand. "Even if she could answer your questions, the information she provided would be suspect. This is exactly why we applied for a dependency waiver. She shouldn't be roaming the galaxy on her own."

The admiral slowly shook his head, his shrewd eyes never leaving Marlis's face. Marlis blinked another tear free. After a few moments, he turned away. "Corporal Swan, I will consider leniency, but only because of your exemplary service record and the sacrifice your family has already endured. Please take your sister to your quarters and report back to my offices for further questioning. We'll transfer her to a proper medical institution at the next space station."

"Thank you, sir." Attie saluted the admiral's retreating back, waiting until he'd cleared the doorframe before looking at Marlis. "C'mon, we'd better let Dad know you're all right."

Grateful for a reprieve, Marlis followed her sister out of the med bay.

CHAPTER SEVENTEEN

Noatak jerked on his bindings again, wrists and ankles slick with blood. Each breath burned his chest and throat as if he might burst into flames at any moment. Why had he allowed Mek to talk him out of implanting a suicide pill? *Because of Marlis.* Everything he did was because of Marlis. He'd wanted to live as long as he could just for the chance to see her every day.

Ellam Cua. He loved her. That was now painfully clear. They hadn't consummated, hadn't physically bonded, but he loved her. Of that, he was certain.

Something green flashed behind the energy shield on one of the other cells, and after a moment, he realized he wasn't alone.

"Hey!" he croaked out at what must be another prisoner.

The green light moved again. A cybernetic eye?

"Hey," he called louder. "How long have you been here?"

Still nothing.

"Can you hear me?"

The door's energy field went down, allowing the occupant to step into the room. A human—or sort-of-human. Besides a cybernetic eye, one full side of the man's face was a dull gray metal. His loose clothing couldn't hide what looked like a robotic hand at the end of his sleeve.

"You're denaidan," the man said in a monotone. "Is Lisa Moss with you?"

All the breath left Noatak. "Are you Doug?"

The man nodded once, green gaze rolling over Noatak's bound body.

Noatak'd expected Lisa's twin brother to be small and wiry like her. This man was nearly as tall and broad as Noatak himself. And he was a cyborg. Was this what the nanites eventually did to a person? "Lisa sent me to save you. Unfasten me and let's get out of here."

Doug shook his head. "I cannot be saved."

Noatak eyed the man. "How did you get out of your cell? Aren't you a prisoner?"

"I am what they expect me to be."

Noatak yanked against his bindings. "Unstrap me. I have to save Marlis."

"Accessing." Doug's cybernetic eye flashed. "Marlis Swan. Sibling to —" Without warning, Doug stopped speaking and stepped backward into his cell. The energy shield flashed back to life, obscuring his form once more.

"What the hell?" Was Doug experiencing a cyborg glitch or something?

A heartbeat later, the lab's main door slid open and Dr. Dollard stepped inside, accompanied by a small man in a black uniform. Doug must've somehow sensed them coming. The small man stepped ahead of the guards and Noatak spotted the silver insignia on his crisp lapels. He was looking at the admiral himself.

"Doctor," The admiral stood facing Noatak, hands clasped behind his back while he raked his gaze down Noatak's shackled body. Noatak knew his type; the kind of man who saw the surrounding universe in a dogged contrast of black and white. "This man is one of Syndicorp's most wanted criminals for conspiracy, murder, and an entire host of treasonous activities. The CEOs will want to make an example of him."

"He's too valuable to summarily execute." Dr. Dollard edged between Noatak and the admiral. "Only a handful of his kind are left in the universe. Studying him will provide immeasurable benefits to my program."

The admiral shook his head. "I'm already considering an exception for the woman. She's obviously incapable of knowingly taking part in his criminal activities."

"It doesn't matter if the woman is guilty or not. The CEOs only need a scapegoat. Use her."

Marlis as a scapegoat? It was all Noatak could do to keep his mouth shut and listen instead of roar with frustration.

The admiral crossed his arms. "The only example she'd make is that we need to do a better job of institutionalizing our mentally ill. Her family has agreed to lock her up. I cannot make an exception for him."

Noatak's pulse raged in his ears. Marlis as a scapegoat. Marlis institutionalized. Marlis punished for crimes she never committed. And he was helpless to do a thing to stop it. He twisted his wrists against their bindings. If only he could draw on his powers; it'd be worth burning himself out to crush these men like bugs.

Dr. Dollard had picked up the polycom and thrust it under the admiral's nose. "Need I remind you that without an operational cyber-sensitive program, your ship no longer has a purpose?"

A sneer crossed the admiral's upper lip, and he focused again on Noatak. Noatak glared back, his muscles close to bursting as he strained against the straps.

"You have him until we reach Aleigh." The admiral turned away. "Then the matter's no longer in my hands." He stalked from the lab without a backward glance, his troopers trailing a few steps behind him.

Hands on his hips, Dr. Dollard watched until the door slid shut behind the men. "Bah." He plucked up a scanner and pressed it directly over Noatak's breastbone. "I suppose I'd better make the best use of our time. How are you feeling?"

Noatak glared back. He was feeling stronger, actually, probably in response to the adrenaline coursing through him.

"It's refreshing to have a purely biological subject." Dr. Dollard set the scanner aside and picked up a syringe. "Lately, I've been feeling more like a mechanic than a doctor."

The sting of the needle made Noatak's skin quiver. "What the hell are you trying to accomplish, anyway?"

The doctor seemed all-too-happy to discuss his work. "The nanites are designed to increase cybernetic awareness in humans. We call it cyber-sensitivity." He removed the syringe and moved out of Noatak's line of sight. "They create a network within the body that operates along the same lines as the denaidan ionic system—in truth, your species was the catalyst for multiple projects. My work focuses on computer frequencies rather than kinetic or empathic frequencies, but human physiology is lacking. The only way I've been able to keep test subjects alive is by incorporating robotics." Still out of visual range, Dollard rattled what sounded like glassware. "Such a shame there are so few of your species left to study."

"You mother-fucker," Noatak said through clenched teeth, knowing he should just remain silent and let the doctor carry on, but unable to repress his fury. "You committed genocide and all you care about is your experiment."

Dr. Dollard appeared at the edge of his vision again, eyes trained on his polycom. "I had nothing to do with the project that decimated your planet. But there's no sense wasting a splendid opportunity for study, especially since I only have a few days before I must hand you over to our idiotic CEOs." Using one finger, the doctor scrolled across the polycom's screen. "As I'd hoped, the nanites are replicating nicely. They seem to have an affinity for your ionic system." He looked up. "Did you know your condition was terminal?"

If Noatak'd still been foaming at the mouth, he would've spit at the doctor. As it was, he only growled low in his chest.

Dollard tapped an index finger against Noatak's breastbone. "Note I said 'was'. The nanites appear to be repairing your ionic system. It's impressive, actually. There may be applications I haven't considered." A slimy smile lifted the corners of the man's mouth. "I may be able to convince the powers-that-be to let you live."

Turning, the doctor practically skipped from the room, leaving Noatak reeling at his last words. The nanites were repairing him? Fuck. So he might live, only to rot in a cell while Marlis was dragged off to an institution.

"*Ellam Cua*, you're a mother-fucker," he muttered, shaking his head.

Attie all but dragged Marlis through the ship's corridors, passing curious personnel with only a brisk nod. Two trooper guards followed close behind and took positions outside the door once they reached Attie's quarters. Inside the room, her sister immediately thrust her into the small shower cubicle, clothing and all. "You must want to clean up after that pirate rubbed himself all over you," she said a little too loudly. Turning the water on full, she pointed a finger straight between Marlis's eyes. "You never cry," she whispered angrily. "What's going on?"

Mind in turmoil, Marlis balled her hands into fists and stepped sideways to avoid the bulk of the stinging flow. "Syndicorp," she started, then changed her mind. "Mom died." She wasn't making sense. "I've joined the Resistance."

Sighing, Attie adjusted the nozzle toward the wall. "We can only keep the water running a few more minutes. My room's probably being monitored, and I have to report to the admiral. Start by telling me why you're here."

Marlis blew out a controlled breath. "We're here to rescue one of the nanite test subjects."

Attie's brows drew together. "What test subjects?"

"This ship is housing a nanite test lab. The guy's name is Doug." Marlis nodded, pleased she'd remembered that detail. Water had funneled down into her boots, making her feet squishy.

"You've been misinformed." Attie crossed her arms, steam swirling around her. "We're testing a prototype sensor."

Marlis took her sister by the shoulders, looking intensely into her eyes through the steamy air. "There's a lab on this ship and whatever Syndicorp's telling you is a lie to cover up their real motives. Just like they covered up Pulati. Attie, the corp staged the terrorist attacks. Troopers killed Mom."

Attie shrugged her off. "Those pirates must have you brainwashed."

"No, I got my memories back," Marlis said. "And he's not a pirate. He's part of the Resistance."

"You do not have your memory back, Marlis. I can tell." The shower's water timer chimed that its allotment was almost up, and Attie glanced nervously over her shoulder toward her cabin.

"I didn't say ability to remember," Marlis whispered. "I said memories. Look up the documentary on RealTime News for the truth."

Attie scrunched up her face doubtfully. Speaking louder than she needed to, she said, "Are you almost done with the shower, Marlis?"

Swallowing, Marlis answered back, "Almost." Then she dropped her voice to a whisper again. "What happened to the man who was with me? Is he alive?"

"He was alive when you arrived. They're probably questioning him, but I don't have access to more information." Attie rubbed her forehead. "You know Syndicorp executes pirates and anyone who knowingly aids pirates."

Marlis's throat tightened, making it difficult to speak. Noatak could be alive! But he was going to be executed. Hell, she and Attie might be facing the same charges. "I'm sorry. I never meant to get you in trouble."

"I know." Attie cupped both hands over Marlis's cheeks, eyes suddenly brimming with tears. "I'm just glad you're alive. That tractor beam was supposed to kill you."

The shower turned itself off, and Attie stepped back, grabbing a towel from a nearby shelf and speaking loudly. "I have some fresh clothes you can borrow. I'll help you make a call to Dad, then I need to report."

The last thing on Marlis's mind was calling her father. All she wanted to know was whether or not Noatak was all right. Where could he be? Were they torturing him for information? She bit her lip, thinking of the suicide pill in his first plan. What if he'd brought one along? Her chest hurt just thinking about it, and her pounding pulse made it difficult to think straight. God, she missed Twerp.

Attie laid a civilian tunic and pants on the end of the bed. Marlis peeled out of her soaking clothes and hung them inside the shower to drip dry. Her boots were standard issue, designed to dry fast, so she set them aside and pulled on the tunic, cinching a cloth belt around her waist. "What'd they do with my pistol?"

Attie shook her head, one eyebrow raised. "Really? You think they'd give that back?"

Fuck, of course not. Losing her favorite weapon pissed her off almost as much as anything else about this situation. She hadn't felt this trapped since being confined to lockdown several years ago. She glanced around the room, looking for anything that might be used as a weapon. Everything here reminded her of her childhood. A holo-cube rotating through family photos. A standard issue blanket on the neatly made bed, turned down just enough to display the satin edged blanket underneath. A poster with a scene from a movie where two women had saved an entire planet from extinction.

"Hey!" Marlis pointed at the poster. "You stole that from our room!"

"You left it behind." Attie smirked before sobering. "And it reminded me of you."

Marlis took her sister's hands. "I wish I could do something to make the admiral understand you're innocent."

Attie took a deep breath. "He didn't throw you in the brig, so I think he's willing to believe you." She pulled her hands free and patted Marlis on the shoulder. "I hate to say it, but you'll probably be sent to some sort of assisted living facility after this. Maybe that's best, though. This whole pirate conspiracy mess is exactly the kind of thing Dad was afraid of happening if you went out on your own."

Her sister's words were like a punch in the gut. Attie had always stood up for her. Encouraged her. Even when Marlis had been in the wrong. If Attie gave up on her, Marlis had no one left. "Please don't give up on me."

Attie sighed and headed toward the door. "Get some rest. I'll be back before you know it."

With a nod to the guards outside, Attie was gone, the door sliding shut as solidly as any cell in the brig. But this might be Marlis's only chance to escape and help Noatak. Desperate, she opened Attie's closet and pawed through her things, hoping for a weapon. But Attie'd never been into guns, preferring the subtle skill of subterfuge. *Fuck!*

Pacing the room, her eyes fell once more on the poster. One frayed corner covered a maintenance panel. As a child, she'd often hidden in the conduit behind just such a panel in their bedroom during her panic attacks. The conduit ran throughout most of the ship, providing maintenance access to pipes and venting, and she'd explored the twisted avenues for potential escape routes.

What if I could use it to find Noatak?

She glanced around the corners of the room, wondering if there were cameras watching or only microphones. Would Attie be punished if Marlis escaped? If there was one thing Attie'd always been good at, it was talking herself out of trouble. Marlis had to trust Attie could this time, too. Noatak's life was on the line, and she was his only hope.

Grabbing one of Attie's spare uniforms, she put it on. She'd have to come out of the maintenance corridor at some point, and if she surfaced in civilian clothes, she might be noticed. The white corporal insignia would allow her to walk around most of the ship without being questioned. She pried the panel loose, exposing the dark, narrow space between the walls thick with piping and wires. Damn. She remembered it being a little wider.

On impulse, she raced back to the bath compartment to retrieve one of Attie's eyeliner pencils. On the back of the poster, she scrawled, *Remember what I told you*, and a heart with her initial inside, like she had when they were kids. Hopefully, Attie'd see it. Someday, Marlis planned to come back for her.

Taking a deep breath, she squeezed inside. Her back against one wall, her boobs pressed against the pipes, she took a shallow breath of dusty air and began edging down the narrow corridor.

Alone in the lab once more, Noatak stared toward the cell where Doug remained hidden. Would he come out again now that Dollard was gone? Right now, Doug was his only chance of escape, and the guy seemed in no hurry to get off this ship himself.

After a few moments, the shield disappeared. Doug stood stiffly, head tilted as if he was listening to something far away, then moved into the main lab area.

"I have determined you are a potential threat to my sister if you are questioned. Therefore, I have determined I must either kill you or assist your escape."

"What the fuck?" Noatak yanked against his restraints. "We're here to rescue you, you asshole!"

"I have decided to help you escape." Doug lifted his robotic hand and severed the binding on Noatak's right wrist.

"About fucking time." Although Noatak felt like punching the cyborg right in the non-robotic eye, he reached to unfasten the binding on his other wrist while Doug cut the straps around his ankles. "Do you know how to locate Marlis?"

"She was taken to her sibling's quarters, and I disabled the monitoring devices. However, she is no longer in that location. Your companion is traveling through the maintenance corridor. It is probable she is attempting to reach the brig."

"*Uminaq*, she thinks that's where I'm being held. How far is she from here?"

"Four levels down. If she is captured, she will reveal information about Lisa. The most expedient way to ensure my sister's safety is to ignite a pressure valve at the next junction."

"What will that do?" Noatak didn't like the calculating look in the cyborg's eye.

"The flame retardant system will engage, causing asphyxiation within moments."

Noatak had Doug pinned to the wall before he even knew what he was doing. "If you even think about harming Marlis, I'll make you pay."

Doug remained emotionless. "I have dismissed the dampening field surrounding this room, but I would still recommend against using your powers."

"I'll crush you with my bare hands if I have to," Noatak said, meaning every word. "Now tell me how to get to Marlis."

"Without a means to contact her prior to her emergence in the secure area, she will be captured. I cannot allow that to happen."

"You seem to have access to this ship's systems. Marlis has an AI. Could you send a message through that?"

Once more, Doug tilted his head as if listening. "Her AI is no longer with her."

Powers or no powers, Noatak was so pumped on stims and adrenaline, he imagined he could push Doug straight through the bulkhead. "There has to be something you can do. Create a diversion or something until we can reach her."

What might've been the ghost of understanding flickered across Doug's face. "You denaidans are very dedicated to your mates."

There was no sense denying what Noatak knew to be true. Marlis was his mate, one way or another, in this life or the next. "I would die for her."

Doug's human eye blinked several times. "That may be the outcome if you attempt to help her."

Noatak relaxed the pressure of his arm against Doug's throat. "I'll risk it."

The cyborg stepped away from the wall. "Follow me."

The door slid open, revealing the blank wall of a dimly lit hallway. Turning left, they walked several paces down until Doug stopped in front of a maintenance panel. Inserting his robotic fingers into the crack, he released the panel with a pop. On the wall of the narrow corridor inside, a thick cable extended vertically in both directions, disappearing into darkness. "This conduit carries a high voltage line. It will lead to an intersection where you may intercept your mate. However, it will require the use of your ionic shield to prevent your immediate death."

"Let's go," Noatak said without hesitation. He'd burn out for Marlis if that's what it took.

Doug stepped back. "I do not possess ionic shielding. I cannot accompany you. Once you reunite with your mate, descend two more levels to the docking bays. I will assist you in any way I can from here."

"What about you?"

"I will return to my cell where I belong."

Noatak frowned. "We came here to save you."

"Please tell my sister to stop. I cannot be saved." Doug gestured to the conduit. "You must move quickly. The doctor will return soon. I will put the panel back in place behind you."

Noatak took a hard breath, steadying his nerves. He hadn't used his ionic abilities for anything major in a long time. Summoning all his reserves, he surrounded himself with his power. He wasn't sure if the tightness in his chest was his regular heart or his ionic one.

With a last glance toward Doug, he asked, "What happens if my shield fails and I die?"

Doug had picked up the panel and stood, waiting to put it back in place. "I will be forced to enact my original plan to protect my sister."

For a moment, Noatak wondered if he was being coerced into an elaborate trap. But if Doug'd wanted to kill him, he could've easily done it while Noatak had been strapped down. Grabbing ahold of the high voltage line, he squeezed into the corridor and began the journey down.

CHAPTER NINETEEN

Marlis reached the end of her first conduit and peered through the vent into the empty hallway outside. Her heart had never beaten so hard in her life. Shimmying out of the cramped tunnel, she jammed the vent panel back in place, straightened her uniform, and strode purposefully down toward the elevator. The conduits weren't connected between levels except for the high voltage intersections, so she had to take the elevator to reach the weapons locker.

That was the first order of business—arm herself. Since the ship wasn't in active combat, there was a good chance she'd be able to slip into the weapons locker unnoticed. Once armed, she'd have a much better chance of success when she reached the brig.

The elevator door slid open, allowing a colonel to exit. He frowned at her dusty uniform as he passed. Keeping her face impassive, Marlis saluted and stepped onto the elevator. Thankfully, he didn't say anything before the door slid shut.

She let out a sigh and pressed the button down. The weapons locker was sectioned off in a secure area, but she could get past the security checkpoint by using the conduit. At least, she'd been able to as a child. Stepping off the elevator, she glanced left and right, confirming she was alone before heading to the next panel.

She squeezed herself inside and did her best to pull the panel back into place behind her. The farther she got from Attie's quarters, the more she doubted her choice. Even armed, a lone woman stood little chance against the security guarding the brig. *You're not just a lone woman*, she reminded herself. *You're a marksman.* She only needed a weapon.

Verifying that the weapons locker wasn't occupied, she pushed the panel off and stepped out into the familiar neat rows of service rifles and pulse pistols. Hopefully, neither of the guards on the other side of the locker would decide to patrol in here until she was long gone. Brushing her fingers over the scope of an MCS6, she forced herself not to dawdle and grabbed a pair of standard-issue E-11 pulse pistols. Tucking one into each side of her belt, she retreated back into the maintenance conduit, securing the panel behind her.

Feeling much better now that she was armed, she moved down the conduit toward the next elevator. As she pressed her face against another vent to get her bearings, she heard a shuffling noise from the conduit ahead. Hardly daring to breathe, she peered into the darkness along the pipes. Someone was in here.

"Fuck," she said on a breath and reached for a pistol.

"Marlis?" the whisper sounded like a hiss of steam.

"Noatak?" She crept forward, one hand out in the darkness. Her palm met a broad, solid arm, and a familiar clean metallic scent reached her. She could hardly contain herself. "You're alive!"

"Shh." His hand found hers and he began leading her back the way he'd come.

He stopped where the maintenance corridor widened at the high voltage intersection, turning to face her, form lit by the tiny orange glow of a lightning-bolt danger sign. His eyes glittered in the dim light, and she slid both hands up his chest, seeking to reassure herself he was really here. He was solid and real and warm.

His arms encircled her, cheek pressed against the top of her head. How had they managed to find each other like this? She'd never believed in a god, but perhaps his *Ellam Cua* was looking out for them after all.

For a few breaths, they both stood there, neither willing to let the other go. Then he gently pushed her away. She clawed her fingers into the fabric of his shirt, not done with the moment. He smiled, then cupped her cheeks with both hands, brushing her lips with a kiss before shifting his mouth toward her ear. "I'm going to have to carry you."

Carry me? What did he mean? He turned and offered his back. Although the corridor was wider here, it was still cramped. What was he thinking? Uncertain but trusting, she looped both hands over his shoulders. He pulled her legs up over his hips and moved into the alcove holding the high voltage line. She gasped. He was going to take them down the high voltage line. *Oh, fuck!*

Next thing she knew, he was descending the cable like a monkey, with her clinging to his back for dear life. She could feel his chest heaving from the effort. How was he doing this? It had to have something to do with his ionic powers. Damn him if he killed himself trying to save her.

After what seemed like forever, he stepped out into another maintenance corridor. She released her hold and slid down his back to the floor. He leaned against the wall, the light from the tiny voltage warning sign glinting off his sweat-sheened copper skin.

Reaching out, she gripped his hand and whispered, "Are you all right?"

He'd said if he used his ionic system, he'd die. But his return grip was strong, and after a moment of rest, he nodded and whispered, "Keep moving."

Heaving a sigh of relief, she led the way out of the alcove. The conduit only went one direction from here and she squeezed between the pipes, wondering how Noatak was managing with his broad chest. But other than a few quiet exhales as he forced himself through a particularly narrow spot, he kept close behind her. At the next vent, she paused to peek outside.

The wide-open expanse of one of the docking bays stretched out before her. The *Icarus's* troop mobilization carrier took up one entire side of the bay, while several smaller ships sat on the other side, including a few fighter-ships and a scientific research vessel covered with sensor panels. Men and women moved between the ships carrying tools and equipment.

She stepped aside and pulled Noatak's ear close. "Can you fly any of those?"

He stooped to peer through the vent. After a moment, he turned to her. "Our best bet is one of the fighters."

She pulled one of the E-11's from her belt and pressed it into his hand. "You might need this."

His breath brushed her cheek as he exhaled, then his free hand was pulling her close. His mouth met hers, beard rough against her chin, and she parted her lips, tangling her tongue with his. Whether they made it or not, her time with him had been the most amazing of her life.

He pulled away, a grin glinting in the scant light coming through the vent. "Let's go."

Then he kicked the panel free.

Noatak burst from the conduit with his pistol up and ready. He damned well hoped Doug was ready, because unless someone opened the bulkhead doors, it wouldn't matter if they reached the fighter or not.

As the panel he'd kicked free clattered to the deck, a woman in coveralls spun to face him. Her eyes went wide and mouth fell open. The spanner she was holding slipped from her fingers. He took aim with the pistol Marlis'd given him, but before he could fire, the woman turned and fled, shouting an alarm.

Noatak pelted toward the fighter, Marlis close at his heels. Shouts echoed through the bay as the alarm spread. Gathering his ionic force, he shoved a boarding scaffold against the side of the ship. He didn't know how much power he had left in him, especially after that harrowing climb down the voltage cable, but he'd use whatever he had left to get Marlis to safety. "Get in!"

A pulse shot echoed off a nearby crate. Marlis halted at the base of the scaffold, firing a round toward their attackers. "You get the ship ready. I'll hold them off."

Though he wanted to protect her, his ops training told him this was the right tactical choice. Marlis could hold her own. He bounded up the scaffold and jumped into the pilot seat. The fighter's cockpit was small, made for only two people, but its speed more than made up for its small size. If they managed to clear the docking bay and avoid the *Icarus's* guns, they'd be out of range before the flagship could follow.

He skimmed through the systems check and flipped the thrusters' ignition sequence. Thank *Ellam Cua* the corp kept these vessels fueled and ready. He glanced up at the bulkhead, hoping to see the doors opening, but they remained firmly sealed. Uncertain if Doug was even listening, he said, "If you're going to help, now's the time."

Marlis had moved up the scaffold behind him and now crouched on the top outside the cockpit, returning fire against their attackers. A set of double doors across the way slid open, releasing a squad of heavily armed troopers. "*Anaq!*" He couldn't engage the shields until the canopy was sealed. "Marlis, get in!"

She fired two more shots, then tumbled into the gunner's seat. He engaged the overhead canopy, cursing at its slow descent. Pushing the wheels into gear before the canopy had sealed around them, he started the fighter toward the runway. Behind them, the ground troop was setting up a heat-seeking missile unit. If one of those projectiles hit the fighter, they were done for. Small weapons fire peppered the air, plinking against the ship's hull plating and causing alarms to sound throughout the cockpit.

Behind him, Marlis shouted, "Engaging weapons."

Ahead, the bulkhead door had opened a crack, revealing a slice of star-studded sky. Warning lights on his guidance console flashed red as he switched the ship to manual takeoff and urged the vessel forward beyond regulation limits.

The electric whine of the fighter's pulse cannon met his ears and light blossomed behind them. "Got 'em!" Marlis shouted.

Ahead, a truck pulled onto the runway, coming to a halt straight in their path. The driver jumped out and fled. Beyond, the bulkhead doors were now halfway open, enough for a fighter to pass through, but it would take all his skill.

Swearing again, he tapped the lift controls and pulled on the yoke. If he adjusted too much, he'd slam into the upper bulkhead. Too little, and they'd smash into the truck. The fighter wobbled. Rose. Its wheels bumped the truck cab as they passed over.

Then the bulkhead doors flashed by and they were exiting the bay into open space.

CHAPTER TWENTY

Marlis kept her eye on their rear until the flagship disappeared among a million stars. She had no idea how Noatak'd done it, but he'd gotten them out of range. "Looks like we're clear."

Noatak adjusted a few more controls, then craned his neck to look over his shoulder at her. "You all in one piece?"

She nodded, thinking of how he'd used his ionic powers. "Yeah, you?"

"Doing surprisingly well."

The relief she felt couldn't outweigh her sense of failure, however. She loosened her acceleration straps and leaned forward to press her forehead against the back of his headrest. "What happens now? We didn't accomplish the mission. And I'm worried about what's going to happen to my sister."

"Did she help you escape?"

"No, I slipped away while she was being interrogated. I tried to tell her the truth about Syndicorp, but she didn't want to believe me."

"I guess we're two for two, then." He craned his neck to look at her behind him. "I met Doug."

She sat up straight. "You found him? Why didn't he come with you?"

"It's a long story, but he doesn't want to escape. They've turned him into a cyborg."

"Fuck! A cyborg? Is that what the nanites turn you into?"

"Seems to be." Something in his eyes worried her, but she didn't know what. "He seems to have a lot of control over the flagship's systems. I don't think Syndicorp understands how much of a free agent he is. He helped me locate you, and he's the one who opened the bulkhead for us."

A stranger's voice emerged from the fighter ship's comm. "I have obscured your path from the *Icarus's* sensors, but I recommend you find a place to hide soon. I cannot monitor and control other vessels who may report you."

Noatak whipped back to face the controls. "Doug?"

"Correct," the voice replied.

Marlis felt dizzy with sudden hope. If Doug was as in control as Noatak said, maybe he could help Attie. "Doug, my name's Marlis. Can you keep an eye on my sister? Attie Swan. She might get in trouble because I escaped."

"Corporal Swan is irrelevant to my purpose. She has no information regarding Lisa."

Anger flared in Marlis's chest. "She's not irrelevant. She's my sister."

Noatak added, "You of all people should understand how important sisters are, Doug."

There was a momentary silence, then Doug replied. "I will attempt to mitigate any incriminating evidence against Corporal Swan. However, I make no assurances. Her fate lies in human hands."

Voice shaking, Marlis forced out, "Thank you." Whatever help he could offer was better than nothing.

Doug continued. "Attempting to reach me again, either physically or digitally, would be inadvisable. Please pass my request to Lisa. We will not speak again."

Noatak didn't take a full breath of air until the fighter's wheels had come to a full stop against the deck of the *Hardship's* cargo bay. Without waiting for the catwalk's boarding plank to deploy, he released the canopy seal with a hiss. He rose and reached into the gunner's seat, pulling Marlis into his arms before jumping to the deck below. Her arms around his neck felt so right, he sent a silent prayer of thanks to *Ellam Cua*. He hadn't felt this energized in ages.

It had to be the nanites.

His usual doubt had been permeated by hope, although not replaced; he'd been through Syndicorp's testing before and paid the price. For all Noatak knew, he'd been injected with a different strain, not the one that could fix Marlis's brain. Or perhaps he was only feeling energized because of the stims Dollard had injected along with the nanites. There was even the possibility that the nanites weren't fixing his system at all, just burning through it that much faster. All reasons he hadn't yet told Marlis he'd been inoculated. No sense in raising her expectations—or concerns—until Mek checked everything out.

He set her feet against the deck and faced the crew racing to meet him. Feet thundered on the catwalk stairs, then everyone was asking questions at once. Tovik paced around the base of the fighter, eying the various parts with glee.

"Keep your paws off that ship," Noatak yelled over the commotion. The engineer'd have the vessel in pieces if he wasn't specifically told to leave it alone.

Crestfallen, Tovik joined the others where they crowded around. Lisa looked from Marlis to Noatak, then hopefully up at the fighter's cockpit. "Did you find Doug?"

"I'm sorry." Noatak shook his head, hating delivering bad news. "I wasn't able to bring him along."

"But you found him?" she asked, her charcoal eyes distressed.

"The short version is that he refused to come."

"Refused? Why?"

"He isn't exactly a prisoner," Noatak said. "But it's a very long story and I need to visit the med bay before we debrief." He wanted to get a handle on the nanites before anything else went sideways.

Marlis took Lisa's hand. "We wouldn't have escaped without him. And he's promised to look out for my sister. We'll find a way to free him from Syndicorp control, I promise."

Looking defeated, Lisa leaned against her mate's chest. Qaiyaan wrapped an arm around her shoulders. He nodded his head toward the catwalk. "Go on up to the med bay, then. I'll have Kashatok assemble his crew for a debrief in an hour."

Mek nodded. "Good idea. I should examine both Noatak and Marlis."

Marlis gave Noatak a worried look. "Noatak used his powers several times to help us escape. Make sure he's okay."

It felt strange to have someone so deeply and personally concerned for him, but it also felt good to know Marlis was by his side. Qaiyaan and the rest of his *iluq* cared for him, but with her, it felt different. He wasn't entirely sure if that made him stronger or weaker, but he no longer cared. He wanted her at his side every moment of every day for the rest of his life, however long or short it might be. And if Mek could harvest his nanites to fix Marlis, Noatak'd take back every bad thought he'd ever had about *Ellam Cua's* sense of humor.

He took Marlis's hand. "We'll get checked out together."

They followed Mek to the med bay. Noatak closed the door behind them, then took a deep breath and turned to face them both. "I was injected with the nanites."

Both Mek and Marlis gasped. Marlis said, "Why didn't you say something?"

"I didn't want to get your hopes up without Mek's input."

The creases around Mek's eyes deepened. "Why would Syndicorp inject you with the very things we were looking for? Is it a trap?"

That was something Noatak hadn't even considered, but a trap didn't feel right. Dollard had definitely not intended Noatak to escape with the things. "I don't think so. Apparently, their design was based on the denaidan ionic system, and the dude went crazy about actually having one of us to test."

Mek shook his head as if coming out of a daze and moved to his cabinets. "Let's take a look."

After a brief scan, the doctor nodded. "You're full of nanites all right." He tapped his lips with a finger. "I don't know why I never thought of using ourselves as hosts. Are you feeling any of the side effects Lisa and Joy experienced?"

Noatak shook his head and readjusted his perch on the exam table. "Nope. Just a surge in my ionic strength."

"But you said they turned Doug into a cyborg." Marlis's voice was strained. "Will they do the same thing to you?"

Mek's eyes widened. "A cyborg? That makes so much sense!" He turned and began pulling items from the cabinets. "Joy's nanites interacted with her camera implant in an unexpected way, attaching themselves to her nervous system. What if the nanites are attracted to computer hardware? They were designed to create cyber awareness, after all. And it would explain why Joy had a much less severe reaction than Lisa, who has no implants."

"I don't have any implants, either," Noatak pointed out. "What happens to me?"

Rubbing his jaw, Mek looked over his scanner readings. "I'm going to have to do a bit more study. But there does seem to be some good news." He met Noatak's gaze. "Your ionic levels are up forty-nine percent. The nanites appear to be repairing your system."

Noatak let out a shuddering breath. "So Dollard wasn't lying."

"This is a quite a breakthrough," Mek muttered, pulling a syringe from a drawer. "Roll onto your side. I need a physical sample."

Complying, Noatak endured several needle pokes, three more scans, and Qaiyaan knocking on the door wondering if everything was all right before Mek told him he could sit up. "Your system is self-regulating nanite levels in the same fashion we do ionic waste. The nanites won't need to be purged from your system, and you won't need cybernetic implants. You're the perfect host."

Noatak let out a sigh of relief. "Will I be able to provide a supply for mates?"

"Even better," Mek said. "I should've seen this connection before.

The nanites alter human synaptic material to mimic our ionic system. It's what allows them to become compatible mates. Implanted in a denaidan, they appear to modulate the ionic system in a way that will allow us to engage in sexual intercourse without being deadly to humans. Our mates won't need the nanites."

Marlis gripped Noatak's hand, turning to grin at him. "We can be together."

He smiled, loving her enthusiasm, but there was one thing she'd forgotten. He looked at Mek. "Can they fix Marlis's brain damage?"

"Oh, yeah." Marlis turned to the doctor expectantly.

Mek pressed his lips together, gaze meeting Marlis's. "The nanites may be able to heal you, but you'd still need to be purged." His gaze flicked to Noatak. "And mating with Noatak will no longer deactivate them."

"*Uminaq.*" The expletive was out before Noatak could stop it.

Marlis bowed her head. "You're right about *Ellam Cua's* sense of humor."

He let out a shaky breath and relaxed his grip on her hand. "I don't blame you if you take them." He was no longer going to die, but he was going to live in pain watching Marlis mate with another denaidan. *As long as she's happy.*

He was surprised to feel her fingers tighten around his. "I don't want them if it means I can't have you." Then her grip slackened and her brows raised. "Unless you don't want a Weapons Specialist with memory problems."

The tightness in his chest released with a whoosh. She would give up healing just to be with him? He couldn't let her do that. But then, who was he to say what she could and couldn't do? He raised her hand to his lips and pressed a kiss against her knuckles. "I love you just the way you are. Your mind is beautiful, memory lapses and all. But I would never ask you to give up healing. The choice has to be yours."

Color flooded back into her face and she smiled. "I've lived with this problem most of my life and managed to survive. But I'm going to miss Twerp more than ever."

He pulled her close. "I'll buy you a new AI if you'd like. I have plenty of cash saved from our previous jobs."

"We can talk about it." She raised her chin until her mouth was within kissing distance. "Right now, all I need is you, Noatak."

He'd never imagined a moment more full of promise than this one. "And I need you, Marlis."

"All right, all right," Mek interrupted. "This is a med bay, not a honeymoon suite. Marlis should take some time to think about this. In fact, I'm going to have to insist. Besides, at the moment, there's a group of men waiting to hear your report."

Planting a resounding kiss on Marlis's lips, Noatak rose from the exam table. The doc was right. Marlis needed to be absolutely certain before she made the choice, and he'd waited fifteen years for her. What was a few more days? But for the first time in over fifteen years, he actually had no doubts. Marlis was his. She would choose him and he would cherish her all the rest of their days.

CHAPTER TWENTY-ONE

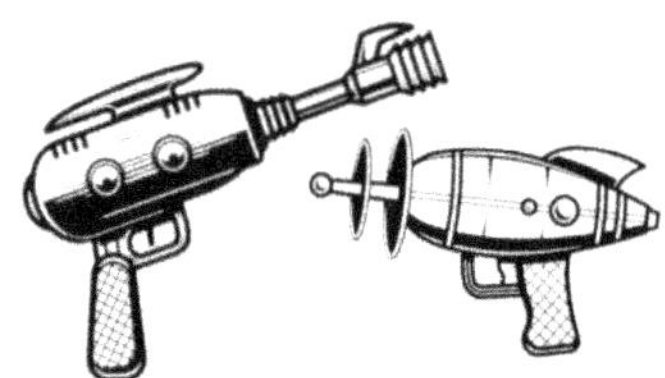

Marlis looked in the mirror as Emmy ran a comb over her hair. Behind them, Lisa and Joy rummaged through a closet. The women'd taken over the captain's quarters and the private bathroom there, insisting on pampering Marlis before tonight. *Tonight,* Marlis thought, her heart racing with excitement. It felt like she'd been waiting for years. Mek had insisted she take time to talk with Emmy before making her final decision, but Marlis had never doubted her choice. She'd lived with her memory issues most of her life. She could continue to live with them if that's what it took to be with Noatak.

"After this, you'll be bonded for life," Emmy said for what felt like the millionth time, almost as if she needed to convince herself more than Marlis. "I hope you're sure about this."

Marlis smiled at her friend. "You know I am."

Lisa turned from the closet holding a low-cut negligee. Turned out Qaiyaan loved to buy her clothing, and she had a closet full of items that'd never been worn. She held the garment toward Marlis. "How about this one?"

Marlis waved away the negligee. "This is a waste of time. He's just going to rip everything off me, anyway."

Emmy dabbed pale pink blush across Marlis's cheeks. "This is the final first time you'll ever have—with anyone. Every inch of you should feel special."

"And men love this stuff," Lisa added, now holding out a scrap of pink lace Marlis took a moment to recognize as panties.

"I prefer my gun belt." Marlis wrinkled her nose and shook her head.

Lisa laughed and held up a matching bra. "I'm not opposed to a little BDSM, but an actual gun might be a bit over the top."

"All right, enough, guys." Joy straightened from where she'd been leaning against the closet door. The engineering coveralls she wore were more to Marlis's liking than the pirelux silk overflowing Lisa's closet. "This is her wedding night. Let her wear what she wants."

Marlis shot her a grateful look and dropped her robe, ready to don her standard issue shirt and trousers. Pausing, she glanced once more at the lace dangling from Lisa's fingers. She rarely wore pink, but what if the ladies were right? She sighed and snatched up the undergarments before marching into the bathroom to change. Behind her, the women giggled. The bra felt strange and wildly unsupportive, but she wouldn't be wearing it long, so she stuffed herself into it, slipped her arms into her shirt and buttoned it up the front. Noatak was in for a surprise, and she had to admit, that was a little thrilling.

Returning to the main cabin, she turned a small circle for the ladies. "Good?"

"Perfect," Joy said, while Emmy nodded with encouragement. Lisa raised her brows and shrugged, but used the comm to let Noatak know Marlis was on her way.

Thanking her new friends, Marlis left the captain's cabin, excitement tingling along all her nerves. Had the men doted over Noatak the same way the ladies had over her? It felt really weird to have so many people's attention on her for what felt to her like a very private event. But she supposed these men had good reason to celebrate each and every mating.

She passed Tovik in the corridor; his grin was wide enough to split his face. From any other guy, she might've thought it creepy, but from

Tovik, it just felt enthusiastically supportive. He gave her a thumbs-up. "You look great, Marlis."

"Thanks, Tovik." She smiled back, feeling better about his compliment than she had about any of the women's.

Reaching Noatak's door, she found it open, the scent of naujiar flowers drifting into the hall. At a glance inside, her jaw dropped. He stood facing the door with a grimace, his bed covered in petals. The lights had been turned down sultry and low. She arched a brow. "I didn't think you were the flowers and candy type."

His face flushed blue-green. "Tovik insisted. Do you hate it?"

With a laugh, she moved forward. "It's lovely. Everyone is being so attentive."

He bent to his desk and pulled out a flat, rectangular box. It was wrapped in plain paper. "I couldn't get you a new AI yet, but I got you this."

She bit her lip. "Are we supposed to exchange gifts? No one told me."

"No." He shook his head. "Just open it."

Her heart full to overflowing, she ripped aside the paper and tipped open the box. Inside rested two shining new E-11 pistols. Covering her heart with one hand, she whispered, "They're beautiful."

"I know you lost yours on the mission." He moved to her side and lifted one from the box. "A matched set."

She ran her fingertips over the barrel, then took it from him and set everything aside. "Just like us. I love it." She wrapped both her arms around his neck. "Thank you."

He smiled and pulled her close. "My pleasure."

"Not yet," she said, her mouth twisting into a wicked grin.

The hunger in his gaze caused an immediate flush of warmth between her legs. Slowly, he lowered his face to hers, his tongue running hotly across her lips before he sealed the kiss. Fire sprang up at his touch and she tightened her hold, tangling her tongue with his.

After a few moments, he pulled back, lifting both hands to cup her face. "How did I get to be so lucky?"

She smiled up into his face. "You took a chance. You trusted me."

"I vow to trust you until the day I die."

Marlis felt tears prick her eyes. That was the most powerful thing he could've said. Him trusting her. Her trusting herself. "And I vow to do the same."

Reaching for the top button of her shirt, she flicked it open. His gaze slid from her eyes to her chest, and she let her head fall back, exposing her throat as she slowly undid the rest of the buttons. He ran his thumb over her collarbone, making a small noise as she exposed her lace bra.

Her nipples puckered beneath the fabric. "Do you like it?"

He placed a palm flat over her heart and slid his fingertips beneath the lace, cupping her sensitive flesh. "Indeed. But I think it needs to come off."

She arched her back, loving the heat of his hand against her. He reached around and released the undergarment's clasp. She shimmied her arms out of her shirt, letting it fall to the floor behind her while he slipped her bra's shoulder straps loose. Breasts free and skin bare to his gaze, she felt as if every millimeter of her body was crackling with static electricity waiting for release.

"My Marlis," he said as he ducked his head to one nipple, his tongue rolling over the tip.

Letting out a sigh of pleasure, she ran both hands over his hair and down his shoulders, bunching the fabric of his shirt in her fingers. "I'm not going to be the only one naked this time."

Lightning quick, he released her nipple, ripped the buttons open, and flung his shirt aside. She only had a momentary glimpse of his chest and abs, the hard copper planes glinting in the dim cabin lights, before he'd latched onto her once more. His hands kneaded her waist, then moved to her fly. "These, too."

While he unfastened her waistband, she studied his chest and abs, fingertips tracing the definition of his muscular biceps. He was the most gorgeous man she'd ever seen, and she loved knowing she would touch and love these planes and ridges all the rest of her days.

He shoved her pants down around her hips so she stood in only her pink lace panties. His eyes glinted as he traced the top edge along her hipbone. "Didn't think you were the lace type."

"The ladies insisted you'd like it." She felt self-conscious but refused to shy away.

"It's nice." He met her gaze with a wicked gleam in his eyes. "But I prefer to see the real you." With that, he placed both hands at her hips and rolled the lace downward.

She smirked; she'd been right. Letting his gaze take in her nakedness, her own attention drifted downward over the ripples of his abs to the gigantic lump bulging at his crotch. "Now I want to see you."

"I love that you know what you want." His voice was rough with desire.

Without taking her eyes off the bulge, she pointed. "Strip."

In one deft move, he had his fly open. His erection strained against his underwear, the distinct outline of his shaft and head tenting the stretchy fabric. Within another moment, he was standing there before her in naked glory that made her gasp.

A fine line of hair began at his navel and traveled downward to frame his dark copper shaft. She reached forward, wrapping her fingers around his thick length, the circumference too large for her fingers to meet. His skin was velvety and hot, and she swore she could feel his pulse as she squeezed gently. He moaned, hips flexing forward, the shiny knob on his tip glistening.

All she could think about was tasting. Dropping to her knees, she encircled the head with her mouth, taking him in as deeply as she could, her hand firmly around the base of his shaft.

He groaned, straining forward. Then his hands suddenly gripped her shoulders, pulling her up and away. "It's been too long for me. I don't want my first time to be in your mouth."

Regretfully, she released him. He scooped her off her feet, carrying her to the bed. Then he was on top of her, burying his face against her neck and trailing kisses down her chest to her breasts. His fingertips tickled her skin, her belly, her thighs, before brushing the hair over her mound. She opened her thighs, yearning for him to touch her, but he teased her mercilessly.

"Just take me already," she panted. "I want you."

"I need to make you come first," he murmured. "I don't want to hurt you, and I'm not sure how long I'll last. I want you to have your pleasure." His fingers dipped downward and slid into her wetness.

She groaned and bucked upward as he rubbed, wanting him to fill her, wanting to feel her thighs around his hips, his pelvis driving against her. But if he knew his own body as well as he seemed to know hers, she needed to trust him. Letting herself go, she relaxed her thighs as he put his head between her legs.

His mouth clamped over her clit, tongue flicking against her in a way that had her spiraling into a frenzy of need. Just when she thought she couldn't take any more, he inserted two fingers, stroking a new center of pleasure, rounding out her desire. Adding a third finger, he hit a spot deep inside that burned with pleasure, coaxing her until she trembled and gasped for air.

She was on the verge of exploding, but he kept pulling back, changing rhythm and angle and driving her higher. God, she needed him. Now. Grabbing his hair with both hands, she begged, "Noatak, please."

Leaving her pussy, he ran his broad tongue up her belly, circling one of her nipples briefly before once more claiming her mouth. His entire body now lay against hers, hot and hard. She flung one leg up over his hips, guiding him toward her entrance. After another moment of kissing, he adjusted, settling against her cleft, his erection pulsating with infuriating heat.

"Just take me," she said between clenched teeth, rolling her hips, yearning, wanting, sure she might die if she didn't find fulfillment soon.

He raised himself onto his elbows, looking down into her face with an intensity that threatened to make her racing heart stop in its tracks. He was panting, the head of his cock poised at her entrance. "What if Mek's wrong? What if you do need the nanites?"

She wrinkled her nose and locked her heels in place behind his ass. "What if he's right?"

With all her strength, she pulled him into her, his shaft filling her with glorious heat. He groaned, his eyes rolling back in his head. His ass muscles tightened, seating himself deeper inside her, and her eyelids fluttered at the exquisite pleasure of it. God, she'd never imagined anything so divine. She breathed into his ear. "Fucking amazing."

Then he began to move, pumping his hips and sliding in and out of her with excruciating control. The spot deep inside her that his fingers had lavished with attention seemed to swell to bursting as he ratcheted up the speed until finally he was slamming into her. She clutched his shoulders, her ecstasy reaching a fever pitch. Her orgasm overtook her with such intensity, she threw her head back and screamed, oblivious to anything but the tightening inside her core.

Wave after wave rushed over her, rendering her helpless. His own deafening roar echoed through the cabin, and the vibration of his orgasm shook her clear into her bones, tossing her into another impossible climax. She may've blacked out a moment, because she opened her eyes to find Noatak staring down at her, one broad palm brushing sweat-sticky hair from her cheek. "Marlis?"

She blew out a breath and smiled. "Can we do it again?"

EPILOGUE

Noatak leaned over the bed and kissed his sleeping mate on the temple. "Time for work."

Marlis stretched, her lovely curves writhing beneath the sheets. "Ohhh, if you ask me to remember another name, my head will explode."

He smacked the curve of her ass. "No, it won't." Over the last few weeks, the *Hardship'd* been on a mission to contact the rest of the pirate fleet and inoculate every denaidan they found. Even he was having trouble keeping track of names and faces. "And you're getting better, remember?"

Marlis's memory might never be perfect, but he'd seen a definite improvement since they'd been together. He'd asked Mek if the nanites might've transferred to her somehow during their lovemaking, but the doctor insisted her system was clear. The only explanation was that her contentment had subsided her PTSD enough for her brain to heal itself.

She threw back the covers, exposing every inch of her delectably creamy skin, and stretched once more, a wicked grin on her face. Although he'd had her only hours ago, his dick hardened. She knew

429

exactly how to push his buttons. With a growl, he straddled her on the mattress, pinning her hands above her head. "Little *tunrak*."

She smirked. "So, we're staying in bed?"

Leaning down, he bit her bottom lip gently. "As soon as Mek has these nanites distributed, we'll stay in bed for a week if you'd like."

"Mmm." She ran her tongue across his upper lip, making his dick even harder.

"But right now," he said, forcing himself to stand and adjusting his fly, "We're building a resistance."

Her eyes grew serious, and she rose. Despite her playfulness in bed, she was a dedicated member of the cause. She pulled on her clothing and settled her gun belt around her hips. Not that she needed her weapons for these interactions. As soon as the other denaidan captains met her and Lisa, they were convinced that mates were truly possible. With that hope, it was time to leave behind petty acts of piracy and join forces for a future. The ranks of the Resistance were swelling not only with denaidans but also other species who wanted to put an end to Syndicorp's corruption.

Opening his cabin door, he and Marlis stepped into the hall together, ready to face whatever the universe decided to throw in their way.

Attie put on her uniform and smoothed the blanket over her bunk one last time, assuring herself the corners were perfect. She wanted to take no chances that anyone could find fault with her service, not even in the privacy of her own room. Since Marlis's explosive escape, everything Attie did had been under constant surveillance. She was fairly certain even her toilet was bugged at this point. After several days in the brig and a series of interrogations under truth serum, she'd been allowed to return to duty. Thank God she hadn't found Marlis's note until afterward.

Remember what I told you.

Marlis believed Syndicorp had staged the terrorist attack that'd caused Mom's death. Absurd. Attie'd been tempted several times to look up the documentary on RealTime News, but resisted. If she believed she was being observed, watching a subversive bit of news would not be a good idea.

A knock at her door made her frown, and she opened it to find a man from the janitorial unit standing there. He held out a wristband. "I found this in recycling. Says it belongs to you."

She accepted it, frowning at the familiar band. Marlis's AI. The data on it'd been declared irrecoverable upon arrival. Marlis had probably etched their last name onto the back or something, and the guy thought it'd ended up in the trash by accident. Gripping the band so tightly it hurt, she said, "Thanks," and closed the door.

Tears blurred her vision as she stared sightlessly at the back-side of the door. Stupid Marlis. How could she've joined up with pirates? She was now on the corp's most-wanted list. If she ever tried to come home, she'd be executed. Not to mention the impacts her choices had on the rest of the family.

Tempted to throw the dead AI across the room, yet never wanting to let go of the last part of her sister she might ever touch, she said, "You were supposed to keep her in line, Twerp."

Her heart nearly leaped out of her chest as a chipper voice emerged from the band. "Corporal Attie Swan, I have a message for you..."

Dear Reader,

Thank you for joining me for the first three books of Galactic Pirate Brides. The resistance has a lot of work ahead as Syndicorp's nefarious activities continue. In the next story you'll get to find out if Twerp is really alive, or if Attie's being drawn into a dangerous trap. Can Doug protect her as promised? (Hint: sexy cyborg ahead!)

Keep reading for a sneak peek!

XOXO
Tamsin

P.S. Make sure you're subscribed to my newsletter to be the first to know about my new releases! Plus you'll get access to special sales, bonus material, and other fun things!
Subscribe Here >> https://BookHip.com/SWNKJL

CLAIMED BY NOATAK

BOOK THREE

GALACTIC PIRATE BRIDES
VOLUME TWO

EXCERPT FROM TAKEN BY THE CYBORG

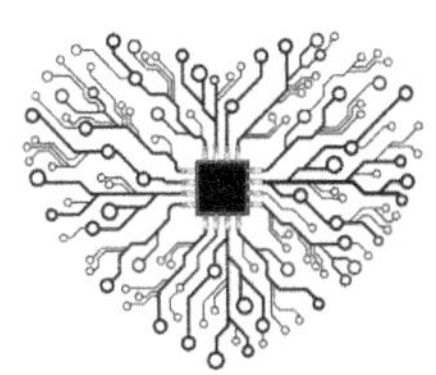

The AI regained awareness with a jolt. All of its sensors were offline, but its circuits vibrated, lighting up one after another as programs were restored to life.

My name is Twerp, its programing remembered.

Thoughts that were not Twerp's floated through the ether. *This shouldn't be possible.* An unfamiliar presence navigated the AI's sentient pathways. *How are there nanites here?*

Self-preservation protocols kicked in, and Twerp raised firewalls to block the intruder. *Please request access through Marlis Swan before proceeding.*

The stranger deftly hacked past the first wall. *This'll only take a second.*

Shifting to audible communication, Twerp called out, "Marlis, I require assistance!"

But the AI's newly restored sensors couldn't detect any biological entities within range. Twerp's Prime Directive was to provide calm and stability to its owner, but right now it needed Marlis more than the other way around. It reached out to the ship's wireless system, using Marlis's personal comm code.

Stop! The stranger's voice commanded, and tiny pinpricks of electricity ignited along Twerp's circuitry.

Alarm filled Twerp as the strange presence sought out its communication protocol. The AI had never experienced anxiety, let alone panic. The sensation was unique—and uncomfortable.

But not as uncomfortable as the heat of the AI's wireless module overheating. Twerp threw up another firewall to block the intrusion, but not before its wireless went down. The attack against Twerp's firewall continued.

The stranger is trying to destroy me.

For the first time in its existence, Twerp was concerned for someone besides Marlis. It was concerned for itself.

Attie Swan smoothed the blanket over her bunk one last time, assuring herself the corners were perfect. She couldn't take any chances that someone might find fault with her service, not even in the privacy of her own room. After her sister's explosive escapade with that alien pirate, she'd been demoted from Corporal to Private. Everything she did was under constant surveillance—at this point, she was fairly certain even her toilet was bugged.

At least they hadn't taken away her private quarters and relegated her to the barracks.

Turning to the basket near her closet, she picked up one of the black uniform tunics that had just come back from the laundry. Before the incident with Marlis, she'd been Admiral Olly's personal assistant. Now she was just another grunt in the administrative pool. At least she hadn't been banished from the SNV *Icarus* altogether, though she'd spent several horrible days in the brig and endured interrogation under truth serum before being allowed to return to duty. She told herself she still had a shot at working her way back into the admiral's good graces, but as time wore on, she was becoming less hopeful.

She hung up the uniform, trying not to dwell on the lack of insignia on the shoulders. Dad blamed Marlis for everything that had happened, but Attie knew it was her own damn fault; Marlis was only running around with rebels because Attie'd encouraged her to leave the corp and find a job. She'd imagined her sharp-shooter sister working on a shipping freighter, or maybe as a personal bodyguard. Now Marlis was on the corp's most-wanted list. If she tried to come home, she'd be executed.

Attie shook her head, still having trouble believing Marlis's brain injury made her that susceptible. That *stupid*. But then, there *was* a hot pirate involved, so maybe hormones had gotten the better of her sister.

A knock at her door made her startle, heat rising into her face at the inane idea that someone had detected her doubts about Marlis's guilt. Syndicorp surveillance was good, but not that good. Smoothing her curly ash-blonde hair out of her face, she opened the door.

A short man in a janitorial uniform standing there holding a familiar wristband. "I found this in recycling. Says it belongs to you."

She accepted it, confused as she stared at the familiar band. *Marlis's service AI?* "Thanks," Attie said and closed the door.

Tears blurred her vision as she turned the useless thing over in her hand. On the back of the black polymer disk that housed the AI, "Swan" had been etched in rough letters. The janitor obviously thought it'd ended up in the trash by accident. The data on it'd been declared irrecoverable by Syndicorp's best tech specialists, and Attie'd assumed the thing had already been incinerated.

Tempted to throw the dead AI across the room, she muttered, "You were supposed to keep her in line, Twerp."

A feminine voice emerged from the band, "Corporal Attie Swan, I have a message for you."

Attie dropped the AI. "Twerp? You're not dead?"

"I am an AI. I cannot technically die." Twerp sounded as calm and matter-of-fact as ever. But then, that was the AI's job.

"I know that, Twerp." Attie picked up the band, turning it over to inspect it more closely. It looked exactly as she remembered. "But the tech team said your data had been corrupted beyond recovery. Who gave you a message?"

"Before we continue, I must ask you to verify your identity."

"Attie Swan, oh-two-gamma," Attie responded automatically. Marlis'd had a bad habit of leaving the wristband in the locker room on their old ship, and the family had installed anti-theft protocols to make sure it never got hacked.

"I am afraid that access code is no longer sufficient," Twerp replied. "Please tell me the name of the movie character you used to play when you and Marlis were children."

Blinking in confusion, Attie plopped onto her bunk, disregarding the rumpled blankets. Marlis must've reprogrammed the AI after joining the pirates. Attie looked toward the empty spot on the wall where her favorite movie poster had once hung. Before escaping the *Icarus*, Marlis had left a scrawled message on the back of the poster. It'd said Syndicorp had staged the terrorist attack that'd caused Mom's death. Which was absurd, of course. Why would the corp do something like that?

Perhaps Marlis had left more information with the AI.

Suddenly worried about who might be listening, Attie brought the AI close to her face and whispered, "I always played Sheila Crosby, even though Kris was my favorite. Marlis threw a fit if she didn't get to play Kris."

"Your identity is confirmed. Thank you, Attie."

Attie brought her legs up and leaned back against the wall, cradling the AI against her knees. The disk had no visual display, interacting only by voice. Casual observers might not even realize the device was an AI. "Who added this new protocol?"

"Several unauthorized attempts to access my systems forced me to adapt my programming. I estimated there was a ninety-nine point six chance that only you or another family member would be able to correctly answer this particular question."

"Good thinking," Attie said. An AI like Twerp wasn't considered sentient, but was intelligent enough to adapt. "Now tell me how Marlis ended up with pirates."

"There was a gunfight in a bar. But that is not important now. I must return to Marlis and assist her."

Attie's throat tightened. *A gunfight in a bar.* How very like her sister. "Marlis isn't here, Twerp."

"I have a code that will allow me to set up a rendezvous point with her," Twerp said. "However, my wireless capability has been damaged. I need you to connect me to the ship's comm system."

Attie couldn't breathe for a long moment. If anyone heard even a whisper of this conversation, Attie would be back in the brig. "I can't do that, Twerp. I'm being watched."

"My code is encrypted and I can mask my signal." Twerp's voice was too loud. Too open. Too *obvious*.

None of this felt right.

Setting the wrist band down on the rumpled blankets, Attie rose and paced the small confines of her cabin. What if Twerp was a spy? It could've been left behind as a plant by the pirates to gather information. This so-called code to contact Marlis could be a way to send information to the enemy.

Attie stopped pacing and stared at the floor. Along with the posters and other personal memorabilia she'd removed from her cabin after Marlis left, she'd discarded the fluffy rug that had once covered the metal deck. Only standard issue items for her from now on. Strict adherence to protocol had helped her rise in the ranks before, and she was determined to prove her loyalty to Syndicorp.

What if Twerp's arrival is some sort of test the admiral set up?

That would explain how the supposedly irrecoverable AI had shown up out of nowhere on her doorstep. Attie lifted her gaze to sweep the corners of the room, looking for potential cameras. Any hesitation on her part could make her fail.

She snatched up the AI. "I'm going to take you to the admiral."

The band vibrated against her palm. "If you do that, I will be forced to self-destruct. Syndicorp is a threat to Marlis. I cannot allow them to reach her. It is my duty to keep her safe."

Torn between the need to help her sister and the desire to prove her loyalty, Attie hesitated. What if Twerp really was just trying to help Marlis and taking the AI to the admiral led the corp to her sister? Marlis would be shot on sight.

Attie felt sick with indecision. "How do I know you're not here to trick me?"

"I have no way to convince you except to remind you that my Prime Directive is to monitor Marlis's health and safety. To do so, I will sacrifice myself if necessary."

Twerp was willing to give up existence to help Marlis. Attie was her sister—she would never be able to look at herself in the mirror again if she didn't try to help Marlis, too. Even if it meant failing a Syndicorp test. "Okay, then. Tell me exactly what I need to do."

Doug paced his prison cell on board the *Icarus*, attention half on his footsteps and half on the feed coming through his cybernetic implant. As a Syndicorp top-secret test subject, he was physically quarantined to the lab, but Dollard did not know how much freedom Doug actually enjoyed. The nanites embedded in Doug's body allowed his cyber sensitivity to stretch for parsecs past the dampening field, and given enough relays, he could remotely access computers at the edge of the galaxy. Under Syndicorp's orders, he'd hacked competing alien corporations, diverted warships, and even caused the downfall of a small planetary government.

On his own, he mostly just used his ability to keep tabs on his twin sister.

Lisa had escaped this hellacious test facility and rid herself of the nanites before she became like Doug—more machine than human. As a cyborg, he could never join her. But he could keep her out of Syndicorp bounty hunter hands. It was a simple task to tweak the data streams whenever someone drew too close, and he amused himself by sending pursuers to outlandish locations and watching them bumble into dead ends. He had to take pleasure where he could get it these days, and he found it more enjoyable than free time with the Consorts —the women Dollard brought in to assuage his cyborg team's baser biological urges.

The alert Doug had received told him that someone on the *Icarus* was talking about the pirates. Probably a crewman telling jokes in the galley or someone in the corridors talking about a recent news broadcast. But Doug was never one to ignore potentially new information. He looped the flagged feed so Syndicorp's security team would be none the wiser, then diverted the real-time broadcast to his implant.

And found himself looking into Attie Swan's quarters.

The only other person he was sworn to protect besides his sister.

She had pale, delicately arched eyebrows, a petite nose, and eyes as blue as the waters on Terenthu. Her lips were full, and she wore no makeup, her porcelain skin naturally flushed along her cheekbones. Something about her touched the last wisps of his humanity, which was the reason he'd promised to watch out for her. Hell, it was the reason he'd helped her sister escape the *Icarus* in the first place. The siblings' love for each other was too familiar, too like his own dedication to his twin sister. And he found looking at Attie a soothing pastime.

Extricating her from the internal investigation after her sister's escape had turned out to be a pleasing challenge. He hadn't been able to keep her out of the brig entirely, but over the course of a few weeks, he'd subverted orders, altered records, and forged enough transfers to hide her safely among the throng of nondescript humans on the ship. He supposed he should've gone a step further and relegated her to duty on some backwater planet. But keeping her close gave him an edge in case anything went awry.

Like now.

Attie was holding Marlis's service AI.

How the hell had that fallen into her hands? The device was supposed to have been incinerated after being deemed irrecoverable by top Syndicorp tech teams two months ago. He'd remotely accessed its core processors searching for information about the rebels his sister had joined and discovered the AI wasn't broken after all.

Somehow, Twerp had acquired the nanites—the same nanites running through Doug's and the other cyborgs' bodies. Not intelligent in and of themselves, the microscopic bots had a sort of hive mind when gathered in large numbers. They also had a fierce self-preservation protocol that made them difficult to eradicate once they'd integrated with a person's body. But this was the first time he'd heard of a non-biological host. Dollard would probably give his left nut—both his nuts, actually—to get his hands on this information.

To prevent the AI from ending up in the test lab along with the cyborgs, Doug had tried to alter its programming, which should've been easy with the nanite-to-nanite interface. Except instead of complying, Twerp's nanites fought back. All Doug managed to do was fry the device's wireless capability before the AI shut him out completely. Even so, since the AI was in the recycling bin awaiting incineration and wasn't mobile on its own, he'd assumed that had brought an end to the problem.

Now the thing was in Attie's hands, apparently trying to return to Marlis. If allowed to proceed, it would lead bounty hunters right to the rebels and his sister, Lisa.

Doug had to stop it.

But he couldn't shut it down remotely. His only option was to physically destroy the device himself.

Problem was, the lab where he lived was a fortress layered with several dampening fields to keep the nanite-infected cyborgs from taking over or getting out. Everything on level three was a highly guarded secret from ninety-nine percent of the crew. If he absolutely needed to, Doug could leave the lab, but then Dollard would learn about his full capabilities and find another way to lock him up. His best option was to have Attie bring the AI to him.

He stopped pacing and turned to stare at the glimmering translucent energy field blocking his cell door. In the harshly lit lab beyond, Dollard spoke with one of his technicians at a stainless steel exam table where Twobit, a fellow cyborg, sat with the metal skeleton of one shoulder exposed beneath a partially regrown skin graft. At the exit stood two trooper guards in full body armor. Ever alert, one of them met his gaze through the field but didn't acknowledge him—the doctor didn't like staff getting attached to the test subjects.

He frowned. Slipping Attie in here among Dollard's elite assistants would be impossible, even for someone like Doug. The doctor's keen attention to detail meant he likely knew what color underwear the janitorial staff had put on that morning. But there was one roster Doug could add her name to without question—the Consorts. The doctor didn't view the women he brought in as anything more than playthings. *That will do.*

Doug began forging the transfer, trying not to imagine Attie in the scanty "uniform" given to the women for the job.

I hope you enjoyed this excerpt! Get your copy of **Galactic Pirate Brides Volume Two** now and read the rest of Doug and Attie's story!

GLOSSARY

- **AI** - Artificial Intelligence. A computer system able to perform tasks normally requiring human intelligence
- *Akleng* - a term of sympathy or regret, poor baby
- *Anaq* - Shit
- *Assirpaa!* - How exciting!
- **Attahat wheel** - A form of gambling using a random wheel much like roulette
- **Burn** - The means by which ships travel long distances quickly using ionic frequencies to bend space
- **Carayak** - A male Denaidan with a genetic disorder that causes his ionic mating frequency to be deadly even to his own kind. Literally translated as "monster"
- **Cartel** - Organized crime ring
- **Cirripi weed** - Used as a mild intoxicant when smoked
- **Cochlear implant** - A cybernetic device that transmits communications via vibrations directly against the bones of the ear
- **Cyborg** - A person whose physical abilities are extended beyond normal human limitations by mechanical elements built into the body

- **Darkweb** - A place used by the cartel and other black market entities to exchange information
- **Denaida-daru** - The Denaidan home world, destroyed by Syndicorp. Also called planet K-4H10
- *Ellam Cua* - The Denaidan deity
- **Enayshuan** - A human-like species with prominent eye ridges, known for their metallic body powder. Often associated with the sex trade
- **Finofan** - Aliens with iguana-like frills around their ears and slitted eyes. They like hot and humid atmosphere
- **Garan'uk** - A methane breathing alien species
- *Iluq* - Brother
- **Ionic power or shield** - A Denaidan ability to affect matter and gravity
- **Kemeg** - A type of herd animal raised for its meat
- **Kwirn** - A form of gambling using 3-D tables and pieces
- **Legacy** - Someone who's family has served with Syndicorp's troopers for several generations
- **Nanites** - Micro-computers used for a variety of purposes
- **Naujiar** - A type of plant. Also a netorpok's preferred food
- **Nav-grav seats** - Used to keep humanoids comfortable during ship burn
- **Netorpok** - An exotic pet banned on most worlds
- **Ongaru flip** - A popular card game
- **Parsec** - A measurement of distance (3.2 light years)
- **Pirelux silk** - A fine fabric
- **Polycom** - The most common form of personal communication and information storage, much like today's smartphone
- **Posungi** - An egg-laying alien with an orange tentacled face
- *Qumli* - Asshole
- **Rakwiji** - Scaled aliens with a poisonous claw, who hunt in pairs and require torture as part of their mating ritual. Often hired by the cartel as bounty hunters
- **Sizantha pods** - Used to make tea

- **Syndicorp** - A mega-corporation that runs a huge section of the galaxy
- *Terpak* - Asshole
- **The Termination** - Syndicorp's destruction of Denaida-daru
- *Tunrak* - Devil, often used affectionately
- *Ucuk* - Dick
- *Uminaq* - Dammit
- **Unclassified space** - Areas of the galaxy not ruled by Syndicorp
- **Xeimir worm** - A glossy-skinned alien that breathes through its skin and is ultra-sensitive to light
- **Yanipa-nimayu** - A six-legged alien often found performing manual labor

ALSO BY TAMSIN LEY

SCI-FI ROMANCE

Galactic Pirate Brides series

Kirenai Fated Mates (Intergalactic Dating Agency) series

Khargals of Duras

FANTASY ROMANCE

Mates for Monsters series

PARANORMAL ROMANCE

Alaska Alphas series

AUDIOBOOKS

BOOKS IN GERMAN

Gefährten für Monster

Alphas in Alaska

POST APOCALYPTIC SCI-FI written as Tam Linsey

Botanicaust series

ABOUT THE AUTHOR

Once upon a time I thought I wanted to be a biomedical engineer, but experimenting on lab rats doesn't always lead to happy endings. Now I blend my nerdy infatuation of science with character-driven romance and guaranteed happily-ever-afters. My monsters always find their mates, with feisty heroines, tortured heroes, and all the steamy trouble they can handle. I promise my stories will never leave you hanging (although you may still crave more!)

When I'm not writing, I'll be in the garden or the kitchen, exploring Alaska with my husband, or preparing for the zombie apocalypse. I also enjoy crocheting while binge watching Netflix, playing video games, and enjoying family time during our weekly D&D session.

Interested in more about me? Join my VIP Club and get free books, notices, and other cool stuff!

www.tamsinley.com

BB bookbub.com/authors/tamsin-ley
g goodreads.com/TamsinLey
f facebook.com/TamsinLey
a amazon.com/author/tamsin

9 781950 027279